EVERYMAN,

I WILL GO WITH THEE,

AND BE THY GUIDE,

IN THY MOST NEED

TO GO BY THY SIDE

EVERYMAN'S POCKET CLASSICS

LONDON
STORIES

EDITED BY JERRY WHITE

EVERYMAN'S POCKET CLASSICS
Alfred A. Knopf New York London Toronto

THIS IS A BORZOI BOOK
PUBLISHED BY ALFRED A. KNOPF

This selection by Jerry White first published in
Everyman's Library, 2014
Copyright © 2014 by Everyman's Library
A list of acknowledgments to copyright owners appears at the back
of this volume.
Third printing (US)

www.randomhouse.com/everymans
www.everymanslibrary.co.uk

ISBN: 978-0-375-71246-3 (US)
978-1-84159-616-7 (UK)

A CIP catalogue reference for this book is available from the
British Library

Library of Congress Cataloging-in-Publication Data
London stories/[edited by] Jerry White.
pages cm.—(Everyman's pocket classics)
"This is a Borzoi book."—Title page verso.
Summary: "An anthology of short fiction and nonfiction about the
city of London from the past four centuries, edited by historian
Jerry White"—Provided by publisher.
ISBN 978–0-375–71246–3 (hardback)
1. London (England)—Fiction. 2. Short stories, English. 3. London
(England)—History. 4. London (England)—Description and travel.
I. White, Jerry, 1949– editor of compilation.
PR1309.L64L595 2014   2013050365
823'.0108358421—dc23

Typography by Peter B. Willberg

Typeset in the UK by AccComputing, Wincanton, Somerset

Printed and bound in Germany by GGP Media GmbH, Pössneck

LONDON
STORIES

CONTENTS

PREFACE

LONDON HAS THE greatest literary tradition of any city in the world. Its roll-call of story-tellers includes cultural giants who changed the way that people thought about writing, like Shakespeare, Defoe and Dickens. But there has also been an innumerable host of writers who have sought to capture the essence of London and what it meant for the people who lived there or were merely passing through. They found a city of boundless wealth and ragged squalor, of moving tragedy and riotous joy; and they faithfully transcribed what they saw and felt in the stories they told of London town.

There have been many previous collections of London short stories, both from a single author and from many hands. This collection is distinctively different in two ways. First, and reflecting the long heritage of London writing, the stories here span four centuries from around 1600 to the present day. Such a long chronological scope gives an insight into the changing preoccupations of Londoners and London writers over that time; and into some of the continuities – trauma both public and private, the never-ending struggle against adversity in the giant city, and the ceaseless stimulation of its delights. Second, I have selected stories that are both fictional and factual. That again reflects the diversity of London writing and the need for the city's writers to live by their pens in a range of media, with short stories, novels and journalism prominent among them.

In exploring this terrain I've constructed a mix of the

familiar and the unusual. Even where authors are expectedly present, notably Dickens, say, or Thackeray, I have presented them in a guise that will be unfamiliar to many – as metropolitan journalists. There will be some, like 'R. Andom' (Alfred Walter Barrett), a witty chronicler of London suburban life, who deserve to be better known and others, like Arthur Conan Doyle, whose names have long been known the whole world over. And there will be others still whose names have been lost to us but whose stories have seized the imagination of subsequent generations, like Sir Frederick Treves who 'rescued' the Elephant Man from a fairground freak-show and recalled the moment with extraordinary vividness many years after.

A similarly contrasting list of writers and stories might have been effortlessly devised to fill many more volumes than this, so rich has London's literary canon grown over the centuries. But while having to make some difficult choices I hope to have devised a collection that will prove as diverse and stimulating as the city that gave these stories their inspiration.

Jerry White

THOMAS DEKKER

LONDON, LYING SICKE OF THE PLAGUE
(1603)

WHAT AN UNMATCHABLE torment were it for a man to be bard up every night in a vast silent Charnell-house? hung (to make it more hideous) with lamps dimly & slowly burning, in hollow and glimmering corners: where all the pavement should in stead of greene rushes, be strewde with blasted Rosemary, withered Hyacinthes, fatall Cipresse and Ewe, thickly mingled with heapes of dead mens bones: the bare ribbes of a father that begat him, lying there: here the Chaples hollow scull of a mother that bore him: round about him a thousand Coarses, some standing bolt upright in their knotted winding sheetes: others halfe mouldred in rotten Coffins, that should suddenly yawne wide open, filling his nosthrils with noysome stench, and his eyes with the sight of nothing but crawling wormes. And to keepe such a poore wretch waking, he should hear no noise but of Toads croaking, Screech-Owles howling, Mandrakes shriking: were not this an infernall prison? would not the strongestharted man (beset with such a ghastly horror) looke wilde? and runne madde? and die? And even such a formidable shape did the diseased Citie appeare in: For he that durst (in the dead houre of gloomy midnight) have bene so valiant, as to have walkte through the stil and melancholy streets, what thinke you should have bene his musicke? Surely the loude grones of raving sicke men: the strugling panges of soules departing: In every house griefe strinking up an Allarum: Servants crying out for maisters: wives for husbands, parents for children, children for their mothers: here he should have met some frantickly running to knock up Sextons; there, others fear-fully sweating with Coffins, to steale forth dead bodies, least the fatall hand-writing of death should seale up their doores. And to make this dismall consort more full, round about him Bells heavily tolling in one place, and ringing out in another: The dreadfulnesse of such an houre, is in-utterable: let us goe further.

If some poore man, suddeinly starting out of a sweet and golden slumber, should behold his house flaming about his eares, all his family destroied in their sleepes by the mercilesse fire; himselfe in the verie midst of it, wofully and like a madde man calling for helpe: would not the misery of such a distressed soule, appeare the greater, if the rich Usurer dwelling next doore to him, should not stirre, (though he felt part of the danger) but suffer him to perish, when the thrusting out of an arme might have saved him! O how many thousandes of wretched people have acted this poore mans part? how often hath the amazed husband waking, found the comfort of his bedde lying breathlesse by his side! his children at the same instant gasping for life! and his servants mortally wounded at the hart by sicknes! the distracted creature, beats at deaths doores, exclaimes at windows, his cries are sharp inough to pierce heaven, but on earth no eare is opend to receive them.

And in this maner do the tedious minutes of the night stretch out the sorrowes of ten thousand: It is now day, let us looke forth and try what Consolation rizes with the Sun: not any, not any: for before the Jewell of the morning be fully set in silver, a hundred hungry graves stand gaping, and every one of them (as at a breakfast) hath swallowed downe ten or eleven liveles carcases: before dinner, in the same gulfe are twice so many more devoured: and before the sun takes his rest, those numbers are doubled: Threescore that not many houres before had every one severall lodgings very delicately furnisht, are now thrust altogether into one close roome: a litle litle noisom roome: not fully ten foote square. Doth not this strike coldly to the hart of a worldly mizer? To some, the very sound of deaths name, is in stead of a passing-bell: what shall become of such a coward, being told that the selfe-same bodie of his, which now is so pampered with superfluous fare, so perfumed and bathed in odoriferous waters, and so gaily apparelled in varietie of fashions, must one day be throwne (like stinking carion) into a rank & rotten grave; where his goodly eies, that did once shoote foorth such amorous glances, must be eaten out of his head: his lockes that hang wantonly dangling, troden in durt under foote: this doubtlesse (like thunder) must needs strike him into the earth. But (wretched man!) when thou shalt see, and be assured (by tokens sent thee from heaven) that to morrow thou must be tumbled into a Mucke-pit, and suffer thy body to be bruisde and prest with threescore dead men, lying slovenly upon thee, and thou to be undermost of all! yea and perhaps halfe of that number were thine enemies! (and see how they may be revenged, for the wormes that breed out of their putrifying carcasses, shall crawle in huge swarmes from them, and quite devoure thee) what agonies wil this straunge newes drive thee into? If thou art in love with thy selfe, this cannot choose but possesse thee with frenzie. But thou art gotten safe (out of the civill citie Calamitie) to thy Parkes and Pallaces in the Country: lading thy Asses and thy Mules with thy gold, (thy god), thy plate, and thy Jewels: and the fruites of thy wombe thriftily growing up but in one onely sonne, (the young Landlord of all thy carefull labours) him also hast thou rescued from the arrowes of infection; Now is thy soule jocund, and thy sences merry. But open thine eyes thou Foole! and behold that darling of thine eye, (thy sonne) turnde suddeinly into a lumpe of clay; the hand of pestilence hath smote him even under thy wing: Now doest thou rent thine haire, blaspheme thy Creator, cursest thy creation, and basely descendest into bruitish & unmanly passions, threatning in despite of death & his Plague, to maintaine the memory of thy childe, in the everlasting brest of Marble: a tombe must now defend him from tempests: And for that purpose, the swetty hinde (that digs the rent he paies thee out of the entrailes of the earth) he is sent for, to convey foorth that burden of thy sorrow: But note how thy pride is disdained: that weather-beaten sun-burnt drudge, that not a month since fawnde upon thy worship like a Spaniell, and like a bond-slave, would have stoopt lower than thy feete, does now stoppe his nose at thy presence, and is readie to set his Mastive as hye as thy throate, to drive thee from his doore: all thy golde and silver cannot hire one of those (whom before thou didst scorne) to carry the dead body to his last home: the Countrey round about thee, shun thee as a Basiliske, and therfore to *London* (from whose armes thou cowardly fledst away) poast upon poast must be galloping, to fetch from thence those that may performe that Funerall office: But there are they so full of grave-matters of their owne, that they have no leisure to attend thine: doth not this cut thy very heart-strings in sunder? If that do not, the shutting up of this Tragicall Act, I am sure will: for thou must be inforced with thine owne handes, to winde up (that blasted flower of youth) in the last linnen, that ever he shall weare: upon thine owne shoulders, must thou beare part of him, thy amazed servant the other: with thine own hands must thou dig his grave, not in the Church, or common place of buriall, (thou hast not favour (for all thy riches) to be so happie,) but in thine Orcharde, or in the proude walkes of thy Garden, wringing thy palsie-shaken hands in stead of belles, (most miserable father) must thou search him out a sepulcher.

My spirit growes faint with rowing in this Stygian Ferry, it can no longer endure the transportation of soules in this dolefull manner: let us therefore shift a point of our Compasse, and (since there is no remedie, but that we must still be tost up and downe in this *Mare mortuum*,) hoist up all our sailes, and on the merry winges of a lustier winde seeke to arrive on some prosperous shoare.

Imagine then that all this while, Death (like a Spanish Leagar, or rather like stalking *Tamberlaine*) hath pitcht his tents, (being nothing but a heape of winding sheetes tackt together) in the sinfully-polluted Suburbes: the Plague is Muster-maister and Marshall of the field: Burning Feavers, Boyles, Blaines, and Carbuncles, the Leaders, Lieutenants, Serjeants, and Corporalls: the maine Army consisting (like *Dunkirke*) of a mingle-mangle, *viz.* dumpish Mourners, merry Sextons, hungry Coffin-sellers, scrubbing Bearers, and nastie Grave-makers: but indeed they are the Pioners of the Campe, that are imployed onely (like Moles) in casting up of earth and digging of trenches; Feare and Trembling (the two Catch-polles of Death) arrest every one: No parley wil be graunted, no composition stood upon, But the Allarum is strucke up, the *Toxin* ringes out for life, and no voice heard but *Tue, Tue, Kill, Kill*; the little Belles onely (like small shot) do yet goe off, and make no great worke for wormes, a hundred or two lost in every skirmish, or so: but alas thats nothing: yet by these desperat sallies, what by open setting upon them by day, and secret Ambuscadoes by night, the skirts of *London* were pittifully pared off, by litle and litle: which they within the gates perceiving, it was no boot to bid them take their heeles, for away they trudge thicke & three-folde, some riding, some on foote, some without bootes, some in their slippers, by water, by land, In shoales swom they west-ward, mary to *Graves-end* none went unlesse they were driven, for whosoever landed there never came back again: Hacknies, watermen & Wagons, were not so terribly imployed many a yeare; so that within a short time, there was not a good horse in Smithfield, nor a Coach to be set eye on. For after the world had once run upon the wheeles of the Pest-cart, neither coach nor caroach durst appeare in his likenesse.

Let us pursue these runnawaies no longer, but leave them in the unmerciful hands of the Country-hard-harted *Hobbi-nolls*, (who are ordaind to be their Tormentors,) and returne backe to the siege of the Citie; for the enemy taking advantage by their flight, planted his ordinance against the walls; here the Canons (like their great Bells) roard: the Plague tooke sore paines for a breach, he laid about him cruelly, ere he could get it, but at length he and his tiranous band entred: his purple colours were presently (with the sound of Bow-bell in stead of a trompet) advanced, and joynd to the Standard of the Citie; he marcht even thorow Cheapside, and the capitall streets of *Troynouant*: the only blot of dishonor that struck upon this Invader, being this, that he plaide the tyrant, not the conqueror, making havock of all, when he had all lying at the foote of his mercy. Men, women & children dropt downe before him: houses were rifled, streetes ransackt, beautifull maydens throwne on their beddes, and ravisht by sicknes, rich-mens Cofers broken open, and shared amongst prodigall heires and unthriftie servants, poore men usde poorely, but not pittifully: he did very much hurt, yet some say he did verie much good. Howsoever he behaved himselfe, this intelligence runs currant, that every house lookte like S. *Barthol-mewes*-Hospitall, and every streete like Bucklersbury, for poore *Mithridatum* and *Dragon-water* (being both of them in all the world, scarce worth three-pence) were boxt in every corner, and yet were both drunke every houre at other mens cost. *Lazarus* laie groning at every mans doore, mary no *Dives* was within to send him a crum, (for all your Gold-finches were fled to the woods) nor a dogge left to licke up his sores, for they (like Curres) were knockt downe like Oxen, and fell thicker than Acornes.

I am amazed to remember what dead Marches were made of three thousand trooping together; husbands, wives & children, being led as ordinarily to one grave, as if they had gone to one bed. And those that could shift for a time, and shrink their heads out of the collar (as many did) yet went they (most bitterly) miching and muffled up & downe with Rue and Wormewood stuft into their eares and nosthrils, looking like so many Bores heads stuck with branches of Rosemary, to be served in for Brawne at Christmas.

This was a rare worlde for the Church, who had wont to complaine for want of living, and now had more living thrust upon her, than she knew how to bestow: to have bene Clarke now to a parish Clarke, was better than to serve some foolish Justice of Peace, or than the yeare before to have had a Benefice. Sextons gave out, if they might (as they hoped) continue these doings but a twelvemoneth longer, they and their posteritie would all ryde upon foote-cloathes to the ende of the worlde. Amongst which worme-eaten genera-tion, the three bald Sextons of limping Saint *Gyles*, *Saint Sepulchres*, and Saint *Olaves*, rulde the roaste more hotly, than ever did the *Triumviri* of *Rome*. *Jehochanan*, *Symeon*, and *Eleazar*, never kept such a plaguy coyle in *Jerusalem* among the hunger-starved Jewes, as these three Sharkers did in their Parishes among naked Christians. Cursed they were I am sure by some to the pitte of hell, for tearing money out of their throates, that had not a crosse in their purses. But alas! they must have it, it is their fee, and therefore give the divel his due: Onely Hearbe-wives and Gardeners (that never prayed before, unlesse it were for raine or faire weather) were now day and nighte uppon their maribones, that God would blesse the labors of these mole-catchers, because they sucke sweetnesse by this; for the price of flowers, hearbes, and garlands, rose wonderfully, in so much that Rosemary which had wont to be solde for 12 pence an armefull, went now for sixe shillings a handfull.

A fourth sharer likewise (of these winding-sheete-weavers) deserves to have my penne give his lippes a Jewes Letter, but because he worships the Bakers good Lord & Maister, charitable S. *Clement* (whereas none of the other three ever had to do with any Saint) he shall scape the better: only let him take heede, that having all this yeare buried his praiers in the bellies of Fat-ones, and plump Capon-eaters, (for no worse meate would downe this Sly-foxes stomach) let him I say take heede, least (his flesh now falling away) his carcas be not plagude with leane-ones, of whom (whilst the bill of *Lord have mercy upon us*, was to be denied in no place) it was death for him to heare.

In this pittifull (or rather pittilesse) perplexitie stood *London*, forsaken like a Lover, forlorne like a widow, and disarmde of all comfort: disarmde I may wel say, for five Rapiers were not stirring all this time, and those that were worne had never bin seene, if any money could have bene lent upon them, so hungry is this Estridge disease, that it will devoure even Iron: let us therefore with bag & baggage march away from this dangerous sore Citie, and visit those that are fled into the Country. But alas! *Decidis in Scyllam*, you are pepperd if you visit them, for they are visited alreadie: the broad Arrow of Death, flies there up & downe, as swiftly as it doth here: they that rode on the lustiest geldings could not out-gallop the Plague, It over-tooke them, and over-turnd them too, horse and foote.

You whom the arrowes of pestilence have reacht at eighteen

and twenty score (tho you stood far enough as you thought from the marke) you that sickning in the hie way, would have bene glad of a bed in an Hospitall, and dying in the open fieldes, have bene buried like dogs, how much better had it bin for you, to have lyen fuller of byles & plague-sores than ever did *Job*, so you might in that extremity have received both bodily & spiritual comfort, which there was denied you? For those misbeleeving Pagans, the plough-drivers, those worse then Infidels, that (like their Swine) never looke up so high as heaven: when Citizens boorded them they wrung their hands, and wisht rather they had falne into the hands of Spaniards: for the sight of a flat-cap was more dreadfull to a Lob, then the discharging of a Caliver: a treble-ruffe (being but once namd the Merchants set) had power to cast a whole houshold into a cold sweate. If one new suite of Sackcloth had bin but knowne to have come out of Burchinlane (being the common Wardrope for all their Clowneships) it had bin enough to make a Market towne give up the ghost. A Crow that had bin seene in a sunne-shine day, standing on the top of Powles would have bin better than a Beacon on fire, to have raizd all the townes within ten miles of *London*, for the keeping her out.

Never let any man aske me what became of our Phisitions in this Massacre, they hid their Synodicall heads as well as the prowdest: and I cannot blame them, for their Phlebotomies, Losinges, and Electuaries, with their Diacatholicons, Diacodions, Amulets, and Antidotes, had not so much strength to hold life and soule together, as a pot of *Pinders* Ale and a Nutmeg: their drugs turned to durt, their simples were simple things: *Galen* could do no more good, than Sir Giles Goosecap: *Hipocrates*, *Avicen*, *Paracelsus*, *Rasis*, *Fernelius*, with all their succeeding rabble of Doctors and Water-casters, were at their wits end, or I thinke rather at the worlds end, for not one of them durst peepe abroad; or if any one did take upon him to play the ventrous Knight, the Plague put him to his *Nonplus*; in such strange, and such changeable shapes did this Cameleon-like sicknes appeare, that they could not (with all the cunning in their budgets) make pursenets to take him napping.

Onely a band of Desper-vewes, some fewe Empiricall madcaps (for they could never be worth velvet caps) turned themselves into Bees (or more properlie into Drones) and went humming up and downe, with hony-brags in their mouthes, sucking the sweetenes of Silver, (and now and then of *Aurum Potabile*) out of the poison of Blaines and Car-buncles: and these jolly Mountibanks clapt up their bils upon every post (like a Fencers Challenge) threatning to canvas the Plague, and to fight with him at all his owne severall weapons: I know not how they sped, but some they sped I am sure, for I have heard them band for the heavens, because they sent those thither, that were wisht to tary longer upon earth.

I could in this place make your cheekes looke pale, and your hearts shake, with telling how some have had 18 sores at one time running upon them, others 10 and 12 many 4 and 5 and how those that have bin foure times wounded by this yeares infection, have dyed of the last wound, whilst others (that were hurt as often) goe up and downe now with sounder limmes, then many that come out of *France*, and the Netherlands. And descending from these, I could draw forth a Catalogue of many poore wretches, that in fields, in ditches, in common Cages, and under stalls (being either thrust by cruell maisters out of doores, or wanting all worldly succor but the common benefit of earth and aire) have most miserablie perished. But to Chronicle these would weary a second *Fabian*.

JOHN EVELYN

THE GREAT FIRE
OF LONDON
(1666)

SEPT. 2ND. This fatal night about ten, began the deplorable fire neere Fish streete in London.

3rd. I had public prayers at home. The fire continuing, after dinner I took coach with my Wife and Sonn and went to the Bank side in Southwark, where we beheld that dismal spectacle, the whole citty in dreadfull flames neare the water side; all the houses from the Bridge, all Thames streete, and upwards towards Cheapeside, downe to the Three Cranes, were now consum'd: and so returned exceeding astonished what would become of the rest.

The fire having continu'd all this night (if I may call that night which was light as day for 10 miles round about, after a dreadfull manner) when conspiring with a fierce eastern wind in a very drie season; I went on foote to the same place, and saw the whole south part of the citty burning from Cheapeside to the Thames, and all along Cornehill (for it likewise kindl'd back against the wind as well as forward), Tower streete, Fen-church streete, Gracious streete, and so along to Bainard's Castle, and was now taking hold of St Paule's church, to which the scaffolds contributed exceedingly. The conflagration was so universal, and the people so astonish'd, that from the beginning, I know not by what despondency or fate, they hardly stirr'd to quench it, so that there was nothing heard or seene but crying out and lamentation, running about like distracted creatures without at all attempting to save even their goods; such a strange consternation there was upon them, so as it burned both in breadth and length, the churches, public halls, Exchange, hospitals, monuments, and ornaments, leaping after a prodigious manner, from house to house and streete to streete, at greate distances one from the other; for the heat with a long set of faire and warm weather had even ignited the aire and prepar'd the materials to conceive the fire, which devour'd after an incredible manner houses, furniture, and every thing. Here we saw the Thames cover'd with goods floating, all the barges and boates laden with what some had time and courage to save, as, on the other, the carts, &c. carrying out to the fields, which for many miles were strew'd with moveables of all sorts, and tents erecting to shelter both people and what goods they could get away. Oh the miserable and calamitous spectacle! such as happly the world had not seene since the foundation of it, nor be outdon till the universal conflagration thereof. All the skie was of a fiery aspect, like the top of a burning oven, and the light seene above 40 miles round about for many nights. God grant mine eyes may never behold the like, who now saw above 10,000 houses all in one flame; the noise and cracking and thunder of the impetuous flames, the shreiking of women and children, the hurry of people, the fall of towers, houses, and churches, was like an hideous storme, and the aire all about so hot and inflam'd that at the last one was not able to approach it, so that they were forc'd to stand still and let the flames burn on, which they did for neere two miles in length and one in breadth. The clowds also of smoke were dismall and reach'd upon computation neer 50 miles in length. Thus I left it this afternoone burning, a resemblance of Sodom, or the last day. It forcibly call'd to my mind that passage – *non enim hic habemus stabilem civitatem*: the ruines resembling the picture of Troy. London was, but is no more! Thus I returned.

Sept. 4th. The burning still rages, and it was now gotten as far as the Inner Temple; all Fleet streete, the Old Bailey, Ludgate hill, Warwick lane, Newgate, Paules chaine, Watling streete, now flaming, and most of it reduc'd to ashes; the stones of Paules flew like granados, the mealting lead running downe the streetes in a streame, and the very pavements glowing with fiery rednesse, so as no horse nor man was able to tread on them, and the demolition had stopp'd all the passages, so that no help could be applied. The eastern wind still more impetuously driving the flames forward. Nothing but the Almighty power of God was able to stop them, for vaine was the help of man.

5th. It crossed towards White-hall; but oh, the confusion there was then at that Court! It pleas'd his Majesty to command me among the rest to looke after the quenching of Fetter lane end, to preserve if possible that part of Holborn, whilst the rest of the gentlemen tooke their several posts, some at one part, some at another (for now they began to bestir themselves, and not till now, who hitherto had stood as men intoxicated, with their hands acrosse) and began to consider that nothing was likely to put a stop but the blowing up of so many houses as might make a wider gap than any had yet been made by the ordinary method of pulling them downe with engines; this some stout seamen propos'd early enough to have sav'd neere the whole citty, but this some tenacious and avaritious men, aldermen, &c. would not permitt, because their houses must have ben of the first. It was therefore now commanded to be practis'd, and my concerne being particularly for the Hospital of St Bartholomew neere Smithfield, where I had many wounded and sick men, made me the more diligent to promote it; nor was my care for the

Savoy lesse. It now pleas'd God by abating the wind, and by the industrie of the people, when almost all was lost, infusing a new spirit into them, that the furie of it began sensibly to abate about noone, so as it came no farther than the Temple westward, nor than the entrance of Smithfield north: but continu'd all this day, and night so impetuous toward Cripplegate and the Tower as made us all despaire; it also brake out againe in the Temple, but the courage of the multitude persisting, and many houses being blown up, such gaps and desolations were soone made, as with the former three days consumption, the back fire did not so vehemently urge upon the rest as formerly. There was yet no standing neere the burning and glowing ruines by neere a furlong's space.

The coale and wood wharfes and magazines of oyle, rosin, &c. did infinite mischeife, so as the invective which a little before I had dedicated to his Majesty and publish'd, giving warning what might probably be the issue of suffering those shops to be in the Citty, was look'd on as a prophecy.

The poore inhabitants were dispers'd about St George's Fields, and Moorefields, as far as Highgate, and severall miles in circle, some under tents, some under miserable hutts and hovells, many without a rag or any necessary utensills, bed or board, who from delicatenesse, riches, and easy accomodations in stately and well furnish'd houses, were now reduc'd to extreamest misery and poverty.

In this calamitous condition I return'd with a sad heart to my house, blessing and adoring the distinguishing mercy of God to me and mine, who in the midst of all this ruine was like Lot, in my little Zoar, safe and sound.

Sept. 6th. Thursday. I represented to his Majesty the case of the French prisoners at war in my custodie, and besought him that there might be still the same care of watching at all places contiguous to unseised houses. It is not indeede imaginable how extraordinary the vigilance and activity of the King and the Duke was, even labouring in person, and being present to command, order, reward, or encourage workmen, by which he shewed his affection to his people and gained theirs. Having then dispos'd of some under cure at the Savoy, I return'd to Whitehall, where I din'd at Mr Offley's, the groome porter, who was my relation.

7th. I went this morning on foote from White-hall as far as London Bridge, thro' the late Fleete-streete, Ludgate hill, by St Paules, Cheapeside, Exchange, Bishopsgate, Aldersgate, and out to Moorefields, thence thro' Cornehill, &c. with extraordinary difficulty, clambering over heaps of yet smoking rubbish, and frequently mistaking where I was. The ground under my feete so hot, that it even burnt the soles of my shoes. In the meantime his Majesty got to the Tower by water, to demolish the houses about the graff, which being built intirely about it, had they taken fire and attack'd the White Tower where the magazine of powder lay, would undoubtedly not only have beaten downe and destroy'd all the bridge, but sunke and torne the vessells in the river, and render'd the demolition beyond all expression for several miles about the countrey.

At my returne I was infinitely concern'd to find that goodly Church St Paules now a sad ruine, and that beautifull portico (for structure comparable to any in Europe, as not long before repair'd by the late King) now rent in pieces, flakes of vast stone split asunder, and nothing remaining intire but the inscription in the architrave, shewing by whom it was built, which had not one letter of it defac'd. It was astonishing to see what immense stones the heate had in a manner calcin'd, so that all the ornaments, columns, freezes, capitals, and projectures of massie Portland stone flew off, even to the very roofe, where a sheet of lead covering a great space (no less than six akers by measure) was totally mealted; the ruines of the vaulted roofe falling broke into St Faith's, which being filled with the magazines of bookes belonging to the Stationers, and carried thither for safety, they were all consum'd, burning for a weeke following. It is also observable that the lead over the altar at the east end was untouch'd, and among the divers monuments, the body of one Bishop remain'd intire. Thus lay in ashes that most venerable church, one of the most antient pieces of early piety in the Christian world, besides neere 100 more. The lead, yron worke, bells, plate, &c. mealted; the exquisitely wrought Mercers Chapell, the sumptuous Exchange, the august fabriq of Christ Church, all the rest of the Companies Halls, splendid buildings, arches, enteries, all in dust; the fountaines dried up and ruin'd, whilst the very waters remain'd boiling; the voragos of subterranean cellars, wells, and dungeons, formerly warehouses, still burning in stench and dark clowds of smoke, so that in five or six miles traversing about, I did not see one loade of timber unconsum'd, nor many stones but what were calcin'd white as snow. The people who now walk'd about the ruines appear'd like men in some dismal desert, or rather in some greate citty laid waste by a cruel enemy; to which was added the stench that came from some poore creatures bodies, beds, and other combustible goods. Sir Tho. Gresham's statue, tho' fallen from its nich in the Royal Exchange, remain'd intire, when all those of the Kings since the Conquest were broken to pieces; also the standard in Cornehill, and Q. Elizabeth's effigies, with some armes on Ludgate, continued with but little detriment, whilst the vast yron chaines of the citty streetes, hinges, barrs and gates of prisons were many of them mealted and reduced to cinders by the vehement heate. Nor was I yet able to pass through any of the narrower streetes, but kept the widest; the ground and air, smoake and fiery vapour, continu'd so intense that my haire was almost sing'd, and my feete unsufferably sur-bated. The bye lanes and narrower streetes were quite fill'd up with rubbish, nor could one have possibly knowne where he was, but by the ruines of some Church or Hall, that had some remarkable tower or pinnacle remaining. I then went toward Islington and Highgate, where one might have seen 200,000 people of all ranks and degrees dispers'd and lying along by their heapes of what they could save from the fire, deploring their losse, and tho' ready to perish for hunger and destitution, yet not asking one penny for reliefe, which to me appear'd a stranger sight than any I had yet beheld. His Majesty and Council indeede tooke all imaginable care for their reliefe by proclamation for the country to come in and refresh them with provisions. In the midst of all this calamity and confusion, there was, I know not how, an alarme begun that the French and Dutch, with whom we were now in hos-tility, were not onely landed, but even entering the Citty. There was in truth some days before great suspicion of those two nations joyning; and now, that they had ben the occa-sion of firing the towne. This report did so terrifie, that on a suddaine there was such an uproare and tumult that they ran from their goods, and taking what weapons they could come at, they could not be stopp'd from falling on some of those nations whom they casualy met, without sense or reason. The clamor and peril grew so excessive that it made the whole Court amaz'd, and they did with infinite paines and great difficulty reduce and appease the people, sending troops of soldiers and guards to cause them to retire into the fields againe, where they were watch'd all this night. I left them pretty quiet, and came home sufficiently weary and broken. Their spirits thus a little calmed, and the affright abated, they now began to repaire into the suburbs about the

Citty, where such as had friends or opportunity got shelter for the present, to which his Majesty's proclamation also invited them.

Still the plague continuing in our parish, I could not without danger adventure to our church.

DANIEL DEFOE

A RAGGED
BOYHOOD
(1722)

SEEING MY LIFE has been such a chequerwork of nature, and that I am able now to look back upon it from a safer distance than is ordinarily the fate of the clan to which I once belonged, I think my history may find a place in the world as well as some whom I see are every day read with pleasure, though they have in them nothing so diverting or instructing as I believe mine will appear to be.

My original may be as high as anybody's, for aught I know, for my mother kept very good company, but that part belongs to her story more than to mine. All I know of it is by oral tradition thus: my nurse told me my mother was a gentlewoman, that my father was a man of quality, and she (my nurse) had a good piece of money given her to take me off his hands, and deliver him and my mother from the importunities that usually attend the misfortune of having a child to keep that should not be seen or heard of.

My father, it seems, gave my nurse something more than was agreed for, at my mother's request, upon her solemn promise that she would use me well and let me be put to school, and charged her that if I lived to come to any bigness, capable to understand the meaning of it, she should always take care to bid me remember that I was a gentleman; and this, he said, was all the education he would desire of her for me, for he did not doubt, he said, but that some time or other the very hint would inspire me with thoughts suitable to my birth, and that I would certainly act like a gentleman if I believed myself to be so.

But my disasters were not directed to end as soon as they began. 'Tis very seldom that the unfortunate are so but for a day; as the great rise by degrees of greatness to the pitch of glory in which they shine, so the miserable sink to the depth of their misery by a continued series of disasters, and are long in the tortures and agonies of their distressed circumstances before a turn of fortune, if ever such a thing happens to them, gives them a prospect of deliverance.

My nurse was as honest to the engagement she had entered into as could be expected from one of her employment, and particularly as honest as her circumstances would give her leave to be; for she bred me up very carefully with her own son, and with another son of shame like me whom she had taken upon the same terms.

My name was John, as she told me, but neither she nor I knew anything of a surname that belonged to me; so I was left to call myself Mr Anything, what I pleased, as fortune and better circumstances should give occasion.

It happened that her own son (for she had a little boy of her own, about one year older than I) was called John too, and about two years after she took another son of shame, as I called it above, to keep as she did me, and his name was John too.

As we were all Johns, we were all Jacks, and soon came to be called so, for at that part of the town where we had our breeding, viz. near Goodman's Fields, the Johns are generally called Jack; but my nurse, who may be allowed to distinguish her own son a little from the rest, would have him called Captain, because forsooth he was the eldest.

I was provoked at having this boy called Captain, and I cried and told my nurse I would be called Captain, for she told me I was a gentleman, and I would be a captain, that I would. The good woman, to keep the peace, told me, ay, ay, I was a gentleman, and therefore I should be above a captain, for I should be a colonel, and that was a great deal better than a captain. 'For, my dear,' says she, 'every tarpaulin, if he gets but to be lieutenant of a press-smack, is called captain, but colonels are soldiers, and none but gentlemen are ever made colonels; besides,' says she, 'I have known colonels come to be lords and generals, though they were b—ds at first, and therefore you shall be called Colonel.'

Well, I was hushed indeed with this for the present, but not thoroughly pleased, till a little while after I heard her tell her own boy that I was a gentleman, and therefore he must call me Colonel, at which her boy fell a-crying, and he would be called Colonel. That part pleased me to the life, that he should cry to be called Colonel, for then I was satisfied that it was above a captain. So universally is ambition seated in the minds of men, that not a beggar-boy but has his share of it.

So here was Colonel Jack and Captain Jack; as for the third boy, he was only plain Jack for some years after, till he came to preferment by the merit of his birth, as you shall hear in its place.

We were hopeful boys all three of us, and promised very early, by many repeated circumstances of our lives, that we would be all rogues, and yet I cannot say, if what I have heard of my nurse's character be true, but the honest woman did what she could to prevent it.

Before I tell you much more of our story, it would be very proper to give you something of our several characters, as I have gathered them up in my memory, as far back as I can recover things, either of myself or my brother Jacks, and they shall be brief and impartial.

Captain Jack was the eldest of us all by a whole year; he was a squat, big, strong-made boy, and promised to be stout when grown up to be a man, but not to be tall. His temper was sly, sullen, reserved, malicious, revengeful; and withal, he was brutish, bloody, and cruel in his disposition. He was as to manners a mere boor, or clown, of a carman-like breed, sharp as a street-bred boy must be, but ignorant and unteachable from a child. He had much the nature of a bulldog, bold and desperate, but not generous at all. All the schoolmistresses we went to could never make him learn, no, not so much as to make him know his letters; and as if he was a born thief, he would steal everything that came near him, even as soon almost as he could speak, and that not from his mother only, but from anybody else, and from us too that were his brethren and companions. He was an original rogue, for he would do the foulest and most villainous things, even by his own inclination. He had no taste or sense of being honest, no, not, I say, to his brother rogues, which is what other thieves make a point of honour of: I mean that of being honest to one another.

The other, that is to say, the youngest of us Johns, was called Major Jack by the accident following. The lady that had deposited him with our nurse had owned to her that it was a Major of the Guards that was the father of the child, but that she was obliged to conceal his name, and that was enough. So he was at first called John the Major, and afterwards the Major, and at last, when we came to rove together, Major Jack, according to the rest, for his name was John, as I have observed already.

Major Jack was a merry, facetious, pleasant boy, had a good share of wit, especially off-hand wit, as they call it, was full of jests and good humour, and, as I often said, had something of a gentleman in him; he had a true manly courage, feared nothing, and could look death in the face without any hesitation; and yet if he had the advantage, was the most generous and most compassionate creature alive. He had native principles of gallantry in him, without anything of the brutal or terrible part that the Captain had; and, in a word, he wanted nothing but honesty to have made him an excellent man. He had learned to read, as I had done, and as he talked very well, so he wrote good sense and very handsome language, as you will see in the process of his story.

As for your humble servant, Colonel Jack, he was a poor, unhappy, tractable dog, willing enough, and capable too, to learn anything if he had had any but the devil for his schoolmaster. He set out into the world so early, that when he began to do evil he understood nothing of the wickedness of it, nor what he had to expect for it. I remember very well that when I was once carried before a Justice, for a theft which indeed I was not guilty of, and defended myself by argument, proving the mistakes of my accusers and how they contradicted themselves, the Justice told me it was a pity I had not been better employed, for I was certainly better taught; in which, however, his worship was mistaken, for I had never been taught anything but to be a thief, except, as I said, to read and write, and that was all, before I was ten years old. But I had a natural talent of talking, and could say as much to the purpose as most people that had been taught no more than I.

I passed among my comrades for a bold, resolute boy, and one that durst fight anything. But I had a different opinion of myself, and therefore shunned fighting as much as I could, though sometimes I ventured too, and came off well, being very strong made and nimble withal. However, I many times brought myself off with my tongue where my hands would not have been sufficient; and this as well after I was a man as while I was a boy.

I was wary and dexterous at my trade, and was not so often caught as my fellow rogues, I mean while I was a boy, and never after I came to be a man, no, not once for twenty-six years, being so old in the trade and still unhanged, as you shall hear.

As for my person, while I was a dirty glass-bottle-house boy, sleeping in the ashes and dealing always in the street dirt, it cannot be expected but that I looked like what I was, and so we did all; that is to say, like a 'Black your shoes, your honour,' a beggar-boy, a blackguard boy, or what you please, despicable and miserable to the last degree; and yet I remember the people would say of me, 'That boy has a good face; if he was washed and well dressed, he would be a good pretty boy; do but look what eyes he has, what a pleasant smiling countenance, 'tis a pity! I wonder what the rogue's father and mother was,' and the like; then they would call me and ask me my name, and I would tell them my name was Jack. 'But what's your surname, sirrah?' says they. 'I don't know,' says I. 'Who is your father and mother?' 'I have none,' said I. 'What! and never had you any?' said they. 'No,' says I, 'not that I know of.' Then they would shake their heads and cry, 'Poor boy!' and ''Tis a pity!' and the like, and so let me go. But I laid up all these things in my heart.

I was almost ten years old, the Captain eleven, and the Major about eight, when the good woman my nurse died. Her husband was a seaman, and had been drowned a little before in the *Gloucester* frigate, one of the King's ships which was cast away going to Scotland with the Duke of York, in the time of King Charles II. And the honest woman dying very poor, the parish was obliged to bury her, when the three young Jacks attended her corpse, and I the Colonel, for we all passed for her own children, was chief mourner, the Captain, who was the eldest son, going back very sick.

The good woman being dead, we, the three Jacks, were turned loose to the world. As to the parish providing for us, we did not trouble ourselves much about that. We rambled about all three together, and the people in Rosemary Lane and Ratcliff and that way knowing us pretty well, we got victuals easily enough and without much begging.

For my particular part, I got some reputation for a mighty civil, honest boy; for if I was sent of an errand, I always did it punctually and carefully, and made haste again; and if I was trusted with anything, I never touched it to diminish it, but made it a point of honour to be punctual to whatever was committed to me, though I was as errant a thief as any of them in all other cases.

In like case, some of the poorer shopkeepers would often leave me at their door, to look after their shops till they went up to dinner, or till they went over the way to an ale-house, and the like, and I always did it freely and cheerfully, and with the utmost honesty.

Captain Jack, on the contrary, a surly, ill-looked, rough boy, had not a word in his mouth that savoured either of good manners or good humour. He would say Yes and No just as he was asked a question, and that was all, but nobody got anything from him that was obliging in the least. If he was sent of an errand, he would forget half of it, and it may be go to play, if he met any boys, and never go at all, or if he went, never come back with an answer; which was such a regardless disobliging way, that nobody had a good word for him, and everybody said he had the very look of a rogue and would come to be hanged. In a word, he got nothing of anybody for goodwill, but was as it were obliged to turn thief for the mere necessity of bread to eat; for if he begged, he did it with so ill a tone, rather like bidding folks give him victuals than entreating them, that one man of whom he had something given, and knew him, told him one day, 'Captain Jack,' says he, 'thou art but an awkward, ugly sort of a beggar now thou art a boy, I doubt thou wilt be fitter to ask a man for his purse than for a penny when thou comest to be a man.'

The Major was a merry, thoughtless fellow, always cheerful, whether he had any victuals or no he never complained, and he recommended himself so well by his good carriage that the neighbours loved him, and he got victuals enough one where or other. Thus we all made a shift, though we were so little to keep from starving, and as for lodging, we lay in the summer-time about the watch-houses, and on bulkheads, and shop-doors, where we were known; as for a bed, we knew nothing what belonged to it for many years after my nurse died, and in winter we got into the ash-holes and nealing-arches in the glass-house, called Dallows's Glasshouse, near Rosemary Lane, or at another glass-house in Ratcliff Highway.

In this manner we lived for some years, and here we failed not to fall among a gang of naked, ragged rogues like ourselves, wicked as the devil could desire to have them be at so early an age, and ripe for all the other parts of mischief that suited them as they advanced in years.

I remember that one cold winter night we were disturbed in our rest with a constable and his watch, crying for one Wry-Neck, who it seems had done some roguery, and required a hue and cry of that kind, and the watch were informed he was to be found among the beggar-boys under the nealing-arches in the glass-house.

The alarm being given, we were awakened in the dead of the night with 'Come out here, ye crew of young devils, come out and show yourselves'. So we were all produced; some came out rubbing their eyes and scratching their heads, and others were dragged out, and I think there was about seventeen of us in all, but Wry-Neck, as they called him, was not among them. It seems this was a good big boy that used to be among the inhabitants of that place, and had been concerned in a robbery the night before, in which his comrade, who was taken, in hopes of escaping punishment, had discovered him and informed where he usually harboured; but he was aware, it seems, and had secured himself, at least for that time. So we were allowed to return to our warm apartment among the coal ashes, where I slept many a cold winter night; nay, I may say, many a winter, as sound and as comfortably as ever I did since, though in better lodging.

In this manner of living we went on a good while, I believe two years, and neither did nor meant any harm. We generally went all three together, for, in short, the Captain for want of address, and for something disagreeable in him, would have starved if we had not kept him with us. As we were always together, we were generally known by the name of the three Jacks; but Colonel Jack had always the preference upon many accounts. The Major, as I have said, was merry and pleasant, but the Colonel always held talk with the better sort; I mean the better sort of those that would converse with a beggar-boy. In this way of talk I was always upon the inquiry, asking questions of things done in public as well as in private; particularly I loved to talk with seamen and soldiers about the war, and about the great sea-fights or battles on shore that any of them had been in; and as I never forgot anything they told me, I could soon, that is to say, in a few years, give almost as good an account of the Dutch War and of the fights at sea, the battles in Flanders, the taking of Maestricht, and the like, as any of those that had been there, and this made those old soldiers and tars love to talk with me too, and to tell me all the stories they could think of, and that not only of the wars then going on, but also of the wars in Oliver's time, the death of King Charles the First, and the like.

By this means, young as I was, I was a kind of an historian, and though I had read no books and never had any books to read, yet I could give a tolerable account of what had been done and of what was then a-doing in the world, especially in those things that our own people were concerned in. I knew the names of every ship in the Navy, and who commanded them too, and all this before I was fourteen years old, or but very soon after.

Captain Jack in this time fell into bad company and went away from us, and it was a good while before we ever heard tale or tidings of him, till about half a year, I think, or thereabouts. I understood he was got among a gang of kidnappers, as they were then called, being a sort of wicked fellows that used to spirit people's children away, that is, snatch them up in the dark and, stopping their mouths, carry them to such houses where they had rogues ready to receive them, and so carry them on board ships bound to Virginia, and sell them.

This was a trade that horrid Jack, for so I called him when we were grown up, was very fit for, especially the violent part; for if a little child got into his clutches, he would stop the breath of it instead of stopping its mouth, and never trouble his head with the child being almost strangled, so he did but keep it from making a noise. There was, it seems, some villainous thing done by this gang about that time, whether a child was murdered among them or a child otherwise abused; but it seems it was a child of an eminent citizen, and the parent somehow or other got a scent of the thing, so that they recovered their child, though in a sad condition and almost killed. I was too young, and it was too long ago for me to remember the whole story, but they were all taken up and sent to Newgate, and Captain Jack among the rest, though he was but young, for he was not then much above thirteen years old.

What punishment was inflicted upon the rogues of that

gang I cannot tell now, but the Captain, being but a lad, was ordered to be three times soundly whipped at Bridewell, my Lord Mayor, or the Recorder, telling him it was done in pity to him, to keep him from the gallows, not forgetting to tell him that he had a hanging look, and bid him have a care on that very account; so remarkable was the Captain's countenance even so young, and which he heard of afterwards on many occasions. When he was in Bridewell I heard of his misfortune, and the Major and I went to see him, for this was the first news we heard of what became of him.

The very day that we went he was called out to be corrected, as they called it, according to his sentence, and as it was ordered to be done soundly, so indeed they were true to the sentence, for the Alderman, who was the President of Bridewell, and who I think they called Sir William Turner, held preaching to him about how young he was, and what a pity it was such a youth should come to be hanged, and a great deal more; how he should take warning by it, and how wicked a thing it was that they should steal away poor innocent children, and the like; and all this while the man with a blue badge on lashed him most unmercifully, for he was not to leave off till Sir William knocked with a little hammer on the table.

The poor Captain stamped and danced and roared out like a mad boy, and I must confess I was frighted almost to death; for though I could not come near enough, being but a poor boy, to see how he was handled, yet I saw him afterwards, with his back all wealed with the lashes and in several places bloody, and thought I should have died with the sight of it; but I grew better acquainted with those things afterwards.

I did what I could to comfort the poor Captain, when I got leave to come to him. But the worst was not over with him, for he was to have two more such whippings before they had done with him; and indeed they scourged him so severely, that they made him sick of the kidnapping trade for a great while, but he fell in among them again, and kept among them as long as that trade lasted, for it ceased in a few years afterwards.

The Major and I, though very young, had sensible impressions made upon us for some time by the severe usage of the Captain, and it might be very well said we were corrected as well as he, though not concerned in the crime. But it was within the year that the Major, a good-conditioned easy boy, was wheedled away by a couple of young rogues that frequented the glass-house apartments, to take a walk with them, as they were pleased to call it. The gentlemen were very well matched, the Major was about twelve years old, and the older of the two that led him out was not above fourteen. The business was to go to Bartholomew Fair, and the end of going to Bartholomew Fair was, in short, to pick pockets.

The Major knew nothing of the trade, and therefore was to do nothing, but they promised him a share with them for all that, as if he had been as expert as themselves; so away they went. The dexterous young rogues managed it so well, that by about eight o'clock at night they came back to our dusty quarters at the glass-house, and, sitting them down in a corner, they began to share their spoil by the light of the glass-house fire. The Major lugged out the goods, for as fast as they made any purchase they unloaded themselves and gave all to him, that if they had been taken, nothing might be found about them.

It was a devilish lucky day to them, the devil certainly assisting them to find their prey, that he might draw in a young gamester, and encourage him to the undertaking, who had been made backward before by the misfortune of the Captain. The list of their purchase the first night was as follows:

1. A white handkerchief from a country wench as she was staring up at a Jack-pudding; there was 3s. 6d. and a row of pins tied up in one end of it.
2. A coloured handkerchief out of a young country-fellow's pocket as he was buying a china orange.
3. A riband purse with 11s. 3d. and a silver thimble in it, out of a young woman's pocket, just as a fellow offered to pick her up.

   N.B. She missed her purse presently, but not seeing the thief, charged the man with it that would have picked her up, and cried out, 'A pickpocket!' and he fell into the hands of the mob, but being known in the street, he got off with great difficulty.
4. A knife and fork that a couple of boys had just bought and were going home with; the young rogue that took it, got it within the minute after the boy had put it in his pocket.
5. A little silver box with seven shillings in it, all in small silver, penny, twopenny, threepenny, and fourpenny pieces.

   N.B. This, it seems, a maid pulled out of her pocket to pay at her going into the booth to see a show, and the little rogue got his hand in and fetched it off just as she put it up again.
6. Another silk handkerchief out of a gentleman's pocket.
7. Another.
8. A jointed baby and a little looking-glass, stolen off a toy-seller's stall in the fair.

All this cargo, to be brought home clear in one afternoon,

or evening rather, and by only two little rogues so young, was, it must be confessed, extraordinary; and the Major was elevated the next day to a strange degree.

He came very early to me, who lay not far from him, and said to me, 'Colonel Jack, I want to speak with you.' 'Well,' said I, 'what do you say?' 'Nay,' said he, 'it is business of consequence, I cannot talk here'; so we walked out. As soon as we were come into a narrow lane by the glass-house, 'Look here,' says he, and pulls out his little hand almost full of money.

I was surprised at the sight, when he puts it up again, and bringing his hand out, 'Here,' says he, 'you shall have some of it,' and gives me a sixpence, and a shillingsworth of the small silver pieces. This was very welcome to me, who, as much as I was of a gentleman and as much as I thought of myself upon that account, never had a shilling of money together before in all my life, not that I could call my own.

I was very earnest then to know how he came by this wealth, for he had for his share 7s. 6d. in money, the silver thimble, and a silk handkerchief, which was, in short, an estate to him that never had, as I said of myself, a shilling together in his life.

'And what will you do with it now, Jack?' said I. 'I do?' says he; 'the first thing I do, I'll go into Rag-fair and buy me a pair of shoes and stockings.' 'That's right,' says I, 'and so will I too.' So away we went together, and we bought each of us a pair of Rag-fair stockings in the first place for 5d., not 5d. a pair, but 5d. together, and good stockings they were too, much above our wear I assure you.

We found it more difficult to fit ourselves with shoes, but at last, having looked a great while before we could find any good enough for us, we found a shop very well stored, and of these we bought two pair for sixteenpence.

We put them on immediately to our great comfort, for we had neither of us had any stockings to our legs that had any feet to them for a long time. I found myself so refreshed with having a pair of warm stockings on and a pair of dry shoes – things, I say, which I had not been acquainted with a great while – that I began to call to mind my being a gentleman, and now I thought it began to come to pass. When we had thus fitted ourselves, I said, 'Hark ye, Major Jack, you and I never had any money in our lives before, and we never had a good dinner in our lives; what if we go somewhere and get some victuals? I am very hungry.'

'So we will, then,' says the Major, 'I am a-hungry too.' So we went to a boiling-cook's in Rosemary Lane, where we treated ourselves nobly and, as I thought with myself, we began to live like gentlemen, for we had three-pennyworth of boiled beef, two-pennyworth of pudding, a penny brick (as they call it, or loaf), and a whole pint of strong beer, which was sevenpence in all.

N.B. We had each of us a good mess of charming beef broth into the bargain; and which cheered my heart wonderfully, all the while we were at dinner, the maid and the boy in the house, every time they passed by the open box where we sat at our dinner, would look in and cry, 'Gentlemen, do ye call?' and 'Do ye call, gentlemen?' I say this was as good to me as all my dinner.

Not the best housekeeper in Stepney parish, not my Lord Mayor of London, no, not the greatest man on earth, could be more happy in their own imagination, and with less mixture of grief or reflection, than I was at this new piece of felicity; though mine was but a small part of it, for Major Jack had an estate compared to me, as I had an estate compared to what I had before. In a word, nothing but an utter ignorance of greater felicity, which was my case, could make anybody think himself so exalted as I did, though I had no share of this booty but eighteenpence.

That night the Major and I triumphed in our new enjoyment, and slept with an undisturbed repose in the usual place, surrounded with the warmth of the glass-house fires above, which was a full amends for all the ashes and cinders which we rolled in below.

Those who know the position of the glass-houses, and the arches where they neal the bottles after they are made, know that those places where the ashes are cast, and where the poor boys lie, are cavities in the brickwork, perfectly close, except at the entrance, and consequently warm as the dressing-room of a bagnio; that it is impossible they can feel any cold there, were it in Greenland or Nova Zembla, and that therefore the boys lie not only safe, but very comfortably, the ashes excepted, which are no grievance at all to them.

The next day the Major and his comrades went abroad again, and were still successful; nor did any disaster attend them for I know not how many months, and by frequent imitation and direction, Major Jack became as dexterous a pickpocket as any of them, and went on through a long variety of fortunes, too long to enter upon now, because I am hastening to my own story, which at present is the main thing I have to set down.

The Major failed not to let me see every day the effects of his new prosperity, and was so bountiful as frequently to throw me a tester, sometimes a shilling; and I might perceive that he began to have clothes on his back, to leave the ash-hole, having gotten a society lodging (of which I may give an explanation by itself on another occasion), and which was more, he took upon him to wear a shirt, which was what neither he nor I had ventured to do for three years before and upwards.

But I observed all this while that though Major Jack was so prosperous and had thriven so well, and notwithstanding he was very kind, and even generous to me, in giving me money upon many occasions, yet he never invited me to enter myself into the society, or to embark with him whereby I might have been made as happy as he, no, nor did he recommend the employment to me at all.

I was not very well pleased with his being thus reserved to me. I had learned from him in general that the business was picking of pockets, and I fancied that though the ingenuity of the trade consisted very much in sleight-of-hand, a good address, and being very nimble, yet that it was not at all difficult to learn; and especially I thought the opportunities were so many, the country-people that came to London, so foolish, so gaping, and engaged in looking about them, that it was a trade with no great hazard annexed to it, and might be easily learned if I did but know in general the manner of it and how they went about it.

The subtle devil, never absent from his business, but ready at all occasions to encourage his servants, removed all these difficulties, and brought me into an intimacy with one of the most exquisite divers, or pickpockets, in the town; and thus our intimacy was of no less a kind than that, as I had an inclination to be as wicked as any of them, he was for taking care that I should not be disappointed.

He was above the little fellows who went about stealing trifles and baubles in Bartholomew Fair and ran the risk of being mobbed for three or four shillings; his aim was at higher things, even at no less than considerable sums of money, and bills for more.

He solicited me earnestly to go and take a walk with him, as above, adding that after he had shown me my trade a little, he would let me be as wicked as I would, that is, as he expressed it, that after he had made me capable I should set up for myself if I pleased, and he would only wish me good luck.

Accordingly as Major Jack went with his gentleman only to see the manner and receive the purchase, and yet come in for a share, so he told me if he had success I should have my share as much as if I had been principal; and this, he assured me, was a custom of the trade, in order to enourage young beginners and bring them into the trade with courage, for that nothing was to be done if a man had not the heart of the lion.

I hesitated at the matter a great while, objecting the hazard, and telling the story of Captain Jack my elder brother, as I might call him. 'Well, Colonel,' says he, 'I find you are faint-hearted, and to be faint-hearted is indeed to be unfit for our trade, for nothing but a bold heart can go through-stitch with this work; but however, as there is nothing for you to do, so there is no risk for you to run in these things the first time, if I am taken,' says he, 'you having nothing to do in it, they will let you go free, for it shall easily be made appear that whatever I have done, you had no hand in it.'

Upon those persuasions I ventured out with him; but I soon found that my new friend was a thief of quality and a pickpocket above the ordinary rank, and that he aimed higher abundantly than my brother Jack. He was a bigger boy than I, a great deal; for though I was now near fifteen years old, I was not big of my age, and as to the nature of the thing, I was perfectly a stranger to it. I knew indeed what at first I did not, for it was a good while before I understood the thing as an offence. I looked on picking pockets as a kind of trade, and thought I was to go apprentice to it. 'Tis true this was when I was young in the society, as well as younger in years, but even now I understood it to be only a thing for which, if we were caught, we ran the risk of being ducked or pumped, which we called soaking, and then all was over; and we made nothing of having our rags wetted a little. But I never understood till a great while after that the crime was capital, and that we might be sent to Newgate for it, till a great fellow, almost a man, one of our society, was hanged for it, and then I was terribly frighted, as you shall hear by and by.

Well, upon the persuasions of this lad I walked out with him, a poor innocent boy, and (as I remember my very thoughts perfectly well) I had had no evil in my intentions. I had never stolen anything in my life, and if a goldsmith had left me in his shop with heaps of money strewed all round me and bade me look after it, I should not have touched it, I was so honest. But the subtle tempter baited his hook for me, as I was a child, in a manner suited to my childishness, for I never took this picking of pockets to be dishonesty, but, as I have said above, I looked on it as a kind of trade that I was to be bred up to, and so I entered upon it, till I became hardened in it beyond the power of retreating. And thus I was made a thief involuntarily, and went on a length that few boys do without coming to the common period of that kind of life, I mean to the transport ship or the gallows.

The first day I went abroad with my new instructor, he carried me directly into the City, and as we went first to the water-side, he led me into the long room at the custom-house. We were but a couple of ragged boys at best, but I was much the worse. My leader had a hat on, a shirt, and a neck-cloth; as for me, I had neither of the three, nor had I spoiled my manners so much as to have a hat on my head since my nurse died, which was now some years. His orders to me were to keep always in sight, and near him, but not close to him, nor to take any notice of him at any time till he came to me;

and if any hurly-burly happened, I should by no means know him or pretend to have anything to do with him.

I observed my orders to a tittle, while he peeped into every corner and had his eye upon everybody. I kept my eye directly upon him, but went always at a distance, and on the other side of the long room, looking as it were for pins and picking them up on the dust as I could find them, and then sticking them on my sleeve, where I had at last gotten forty or fifty good pins; but still my eye was upon my comrade, who, I observed, was very busy among the crowds of people that stood at the board, doing business with the officers who pass the entries and make the cockets, etc.

At length he comes over to me and, stooping as if he would take up a pin close to me, he put something into my hand and said, 'Put that up, and follow me downstairs quickly.' He did not run, but shuffled along apace through the crowd, and went down, not the great stairs which we came in at, but a little narrow staircase at the other end of the long room. I followed, and he found I did, and so went on, stopping below as I expected, nor speaking one word to me, till through innumerable narrow passages, alleys, and dark ways, we were got up into Fenchurch Street, and through Billiter Lane into Leadenhall Street, and from thence into Leadenhall Market.

It was not a meat-market day, so we had room to sit down upon one of the butchers' stalls, and he bade me lug out. What he had given me was a little leather letter-case, with a French almanac stuck in the inside of it and a great many papers in it of several kinds.

We looked them over, and found there was several valuable bills in it, such as bills of exchange, and other notes, things I did not understand; but among the rest was a goldsmith's note, as he called it, of one Sir Stephen Evans for £300 payable to the bearer, and at demand; besides this there was another note for £12 10s., being a goldsmith's bill too, but I forget the name; there was a bill or two also written in French, which neither of us understood, but which it seems were things of value, being called foreign bills accepted.

The rogue my master knew what belonged to the goldsmith's bills well enough, and I observed when he read the bill of Sir Stephen, he said, 'This is too big for me to meddle with,' but when he came to the bill for £12 10s. he said to me, 'This will do; come hither, Jack'; so away he runs to Lombard Street, and I after him, huddling the other papers into the letter-case. As he went along he inquired the name out immediately, and went directly to the shop, put on a good grave countenance, and had the money paid him without any stop or question asked. I stood on the other side of the way looking about the street, as not at all concerned with anybody that way, but observed that when he presented the bill he pulled out the letter-case, as if he had been a merchant's boy acquainted with business, and had other bills about him.

They paid him the money in gold, and he made haste enough in telling it over, and came away, passing by me, and going into Three King Court on the other side of the way; then we crossed back into Clement's Lane, made the best of our way to Cold Harbour at the water-side, and got a sculler for a penny to carry us over the water to St Mary over Stairs, where we landed and were safe enough.

Here he turns to me. 'Colonel Jack,' says he, 'I believe you are a lucky boy; this is a good job, we'll go away to St George's Fields and share our booty.' Away we went to the fields, and sitting down in the grass, far enough out of the path, he pulled out the money. 'Look here, Jack,' says he, 'did you ever see the like before in your life?' 'No, never,' says I; and added very innocently, 'Must we have it all?' 'We have it!'

says he; 'who should have it?' 'Why,' says I, 'must the man have none of it again that lost it?' 'He have it again!' says he; 'what d'ye mean by that?' 'Nay, I don't know,' says I; 'why, you said just now you would let him have the other bill again that you said was too big for you.'

He laughed at me. 'You are but a little boy,' says he, 'that's true, but I thought you had not been such a child neither.' So he mighty gravely explained the thing to me thus: That the bill of Sir Stephen Evans was a great bill for £300; 'And if I,' says he, 'that am but a poor lad should venture to go for the money, they will presently say, how should I come by such a bill, and that I certainly found it or stole it; so they will stop me,' says he, 'and take it away from me, and it may bring me into trouble for it too; so,' says he, 'I did say it was too big for me to meddle with, and that I would let the man have it again if I could tell how. But for the money, Jack, the money that we have got, I warrant you he should have none of that. Besides,' says he, 'whoever he be that has lost this letter-case, to be sure, as soon as he missed it, he would run to a goldsmith and give notice, that if anybody came by the money they should be stopped; but I am too old for him there,' says he.

'Why,' says I, 'and what will you do with the bill; will you throw it away? If you do, somebody else will find it,' says I, 'and they will go and take the money.' 'No, no,' says he, 'then they will be stopped and examined, as I tell you I should be.' I did not know well what all this meant, so I talked no more about that, but we fell to handling the money. As for me, I had never seen so much together in all my life, nor did I know what in the world to do with it, and once or twice I was a-going to bid him keep it for me, which would have been done like a child indeed, for, to be sure, I had never heard a word more of it though nothing had befallen him.

However, as I happened to hold my tongue as to that part, he shared the money very honestly with me, only at the end he told me that though it was true he promised me half, yet as it was the first time and I had done nothing but look on, so he thought it was very well if I took a little less than he did; so he divided the money, which was £12 10s. into two exact parts, viz. £6 5s. in each part, then he took £1 5s. from my part, and told me I should give him that for handsel. 'Well,' says I, 'take it then, for I think you deserve it all'; so, however, I took up the rest. 'And what shall I do with this now,' says I, 'for I have nowhere to put it?' 'Why, have you no pockets?' says he. 'Yes,' says I, 'but they are full of holes.' I have often thought since that, and with some mirth too, how I had really more wealth than I knew what to do with; for lodging I had none, nor any box or drawer to hide my money in, nor had I any pocket but such, as I say, was full of holes. I knew nobody in the world that I could go and desire them to lay it up for me; for, being a poor, naked, ragged boy, they would presently say I had robbed some-body, and perhaps lay hold of me, and my money would be my crime, as they say it often is in foreign countries. And now as I was full of wealth, behold I was full of care, for what to do to secure my money I could not tell, and this held me so long, and was so vexatious to me the next day, that I truly sat down and cried.

Nothing could be more perplexing than this money was to me all that night. I carried it in my hand a good while, for it was in gold all but 14s., and that is to say, it was in four guineas, and that 14s. was more difficult to carry than the four guineas. At last I sat down and pulled off one of my shoes and put the four guineas into that, but after I had gone a while my shoe hurt me so, I could not go, so I was fain to sit down again and take it out of my shoe and carry it in my hand. Then I found a dirty linen rag in the street, and I took that up, and wrapped it all together and carried it in that a good way. I have often since heard people say, when they have been talking of money that they could not get in, 'I wish I had it in a foul clout.' In truth I had mine in a foul clout, for it was foul according to the letter of that saying, but it served me till I came to a convenient place, and then I sat down and washed the cloth in the kennel, and so then put my money in again.

Well, I carried it home with me to my lodging in the glass-house, and when I went to go to sleep I knew not what to do with it. If I had let any of the black crew I was with know of it, I should have been smothered in the ashes for it, or robbed of it, or some trick or other put upon me for it. So I knew not what to do, but lay with it in my hand, and my hand in my bosom, but then sleep went from my eyes. Oh the weight of human care! I, a poor beggar-boy, could not sleep as soon as I had but a little money to keep, who before that could have slept upon a heap of brickbats or stones, cinders or anywhere, as sound as a rich man does on his down bed, and sounder too.

Every now and then dropping asleep, I would dream that my money was lost, and start like one frighted; then, finding it fast in my hand, try to get to sleep again, but could not for a long while; then drop and start again. At last a fancy came into my head that if I fell asleep, I should dream of the money and talk of it in my sleep and tell that I had money, which if I should do, and one of the rogues should hear me, they would pick it out of my bosom, and of my hand too, without waking me, and after that thought I could not sleep a wink more; so that I passed that night over in care and anxiety enough, and this, I may safely say, was the first night's rest that I lost by the cares of this life and the deceitfulness of riches.

JAMES LACKINGTON

LOVE AMONG THE METHODISTS
(1792)

MR R—T, a genteel tradesman with whom I am acquainted, having lost his second wife early in 1790, courted and married one of the holy sisters a few months afterwards. They had lived together about six months, when Mr R—t, one Sunday, being a sober religious man, took down Doddridge's Lectures, and began to read them to his wife and family. But this holy sister found fault with her husband for reading such learned rational discourses, which favoured too much of human reason and vain philosophy, and wished he would read something more spiritual and edifying. He attempted to convince her that Dr Doddridge was not only a good rational divine, but to the full as spiritual as any divine ought to be; and that to be more spiritual he must be less rational, and of course become fanatical and visionary. But these observations of the husband so displeased his spiritual wife, that she retired to bed, and left her husband to read Doddridge's Lectures as long as he chose to his children by a former wife.

The next morning while Mr R—t was out on business, this holy sister, without saying one syllable to any person, packed up all her clothes, crammed them into a hackney coach, and away she went. Mr R—t, poor soul! on coming home discovered his immense loss, and in an almost frantic state, spent the first fortnight in fruitless attempts to discover her retreat.

'Three weeks after her elopement, I was (says Mr R—t)

going down Cheapside one day, and saw a lady something like my wife, but as she was somewhat disguised, and I could not see her face, I was not sure. At last I ventured to look under her bonnet, and found, that, sure enough, it was she. I then walked three times backwards and forwards in Cheapside, endeavouring to persuade her to return with me, or to discover where she lived: but she obstinately refused to return, or to let me see her retreat; and here (says Mr R—t) I begged that she would grant me a kiss; but she would not willingly. However after some bustle in the street, I took a farewel kiss. Poor dear soul! (sigh'd he) she is rather *too spiritual!* for notwithstanding I laid by her side near six months, she never would be prevailed upon to do any thing carnal; and although I did all in my power to get the better of her spiritual scruples, yet she was always so in love with Christ her heavenly spouse, that when she eloped from me, she was, I assure you, as good a virgin as when I married her.'

I must give you one more story of the same nature with the preceding.

A gentleman of London happening to be on a visit at Bristol about three years since, fell in love with a handsome young lady who was one of the holy sisterhood; after a few weeks acquaintance he made her an offer of his person and fortune, and the young lady after proper inquiry had been made into the gentleman's family, fortune, &c. consented to make our lover happy. They were soon after married, and the same day set off in a post-chaise towards London, in order to sleep the first night at an inn, and so save the lady the blushes occasioned by the jokes common on such occasions; this happy couple had been in bed about an hour when the cry of murder alarmed the house, this alarm proceeding from the room that was occupied by the bride and bridegroom, drew the company that way; the innkeeper knocked at the door and demanded admittance, our Benedict appeared at the door, and informed the host that his lady had been taken suddenly ill in a kind of fit he believed, but that she was better; and after the innkeeper's wife had been sent into the room to see the young lady, and had found her well, all retired to bed.

They had, however, not lain more than two hours, when the cry of murder, fire, &c. again alarmed the house, and drew many out of their beds once more.

Our young gentleman then dressed himself, and opening the door, informed the company that he had that morning been married to the young lady in bed, and that being married, he had insisted on being admitted to the privilege of an husband, but that the young lady had talked much about the good of her poor soul, her spiritual husband, &c. and that instead of granting what he conceived to be the right of every husband, she had thought proper to disturb all in the house. He added, that having been thus made very ridiculous, he would take effectual care to prevent a repetition of the same absurd conduct.

He then ordered a post-chaise and set off for London, leaving our young saint in bed to enjoy her spiritual contemplations in their full extent, nor has he ever since paid her any attention.

Some time since being in a large town in the West, she was pointed out to me by a friend, as she was walking in the street . . .

I am informed from good authority that there are now in Mr Wesley's society, in London, some women who ever since they were converted, have refused to sleep with their husbands, and that some of those will not pay the least attention to any temporal concern whatever, being as they term it, wholly wrapped up in divine contemplation, having their souls absorbed in divine love, so as not to be interrupted by the trifling concerns of a husband, family, &c.

* * *

Because some of the holy sisters are in their amours altogether spiritual, you are by no means to understand that they are all totally divested of the carnal propensity.

Some of these good creatures are so far from thinking that their husbands are too carnal in their affections, that they really think that they are not enough so; and instances are not wanting, in which, owing to their having husbands too spiritual, they have been willing to receive assistance from the husbands of other women.

It is but about a year since a certain celebrated preacher used to administer carnal consolation to the wife of his clerk. This holy communication was repeated so often, and so open, that at last it came to the clerk's ears, who watching an opportunity, one day surprized the pious pair at their *devotion*, and so *belaboured* the preacher with his walking-staff, that the public were for near a month deprived of the benefits resulting from his remarkable gift of eloquence.

As I am got into the story-telling way, I cannot resist the temptation of telling another.

A certain holy sister who lately kept a house in a country village, within ten miles of London; and *took in* (as they called it) Mr Wesley's preachers, by taking *in* is only meant, that when they came in their turn to preach in the village she used to supply each with victuals and a bed; (*no doubt* but they slept *alone*.) This lady was so very remarkable for her *spiritual experience* and divine gifts, that she attracted many to her house, besides such as came in the regular course of their duty, and among the former a preacher from London, from whom I learnt the affair. This preacher happening to want a wife, and being very spiritually-minded, actually married her in December 1790, merely for her great gifts and grace, as her fortune was not above the fiftieth part as much as his own; and as to person, she is scarce one degree above ugliness itself; although her husband is well-proportioned, and upon the whole a handsome man. They had not been married a week, when this simple preacher discovered that his gifted gracious saint was an incarnate devil, who had married him only to rob, plunder, and —— him, and in a few months between her and her gallants, they bullied him out of a settlement to the amount of four times the sum she brought him, and the poor pious preacher thinks that he has cheaply got rid of her.

The reason why I interest myself in his behalf is, because I am confident that he really is an honest well-meaning man at the bottom; but withal one that does not possess the greatest share of understanding, and who being formerly but a mean mechanic, never had any education; but although he is a great enthusiast, yet he is one of the good-natured inoffensive sort, who will do no harm to any person, but on the contrary all the good in his power. I am only sorry, as he lately was an honest useful tradesman, that he should have so much spiritual quixotism in him, as at thirty years of age to shut up his shop and turn preacher, without being able to read his primer; which I can assure you is the case. But here, my friend, you see I forgot that these heavenly teachers only speak as the Spirit giveth utterance, and that of course all human learning is entirely superfluous.

A few years fince the methodist-preachers got footing in Wellington (the famous birthplace of your humble servant) and established a society there, soon after which one of their preachers (at Collompton, a neighbouring town) happened to like a young servant girl, who was one of the holy sisters, she having gone through the new birth, better than his wife, because she was an unenlightened, unconverted woman. But this servant girl happening to be with child, the news soon reached Wellington; and a very wealthy gentleman who entertained the preachers there followed the preacher of Collompton's example, and got his own pious maid with child.

After this some of the society in Wellington began to have all things in common, and several more of the holy sisters proved prolific; which so alarmed the parish, that some of the heads of it insisted that the preachers should not be permitted to preach there any longer. 'For, if (said they) the methodist-society continues, we shall have the parish full of bastards.'

A similar affair happened at a country town, ten or twelve miles from Oxford, about two years since, where a very handsome powerful preacher made converts of a great number of women, both married and single, who were wonderfully affected, and great numbers flocked to his standard; but he had not laboured there more than a year, before the churchwardens were made acquainted with his powerful operations on fine young female saints, who all swore bastards to this holy, spiritual labourer in the vineyard; upon which the gentlemen of the town exerted themselves, and prevented the farther propagation of methodism; as

'The ladies by sympathy seem'd to discover
The advantage of having a spiritual lover.
They were sadly afraid that wives, widows, and misses
Would confine to the —— all their favors and kisses.'

The author of a letter to Dr Coke and Mr More, published since the first edition of my Memoirs, informs us, that a gentleman of Chesham had a daughter about seventeen years of age, which he put into the hands of a methodist parson, to have her converted, and was exceedingly kind and liberal to him; and we are informed that this rascal converted her first, and debauched her afterwards.

So you see, my dear friend, by the above examples (were it necessary, I could give you many more) that not all the converted and sanctified females are thereby become so absorbed in the spiritual delights of the mystical union, as to have lost all relish for carnal connections; as we find that many among them are blessed with a mind so capacious, as to be able to participate in the pleasures of both worlds.

SAMUEL WHYTE

A VISIT TO CHARLOTTE CIBBER
(1795)

CIBBER THE ELDER, had a daughter named *Charlotte*, who also took to the stage; her subsequent life was one continued series of misfortune, afflictions and distress, which she sometimes contrived a little to alleviate by the productions of her pen. About the year 1755, she had worked up a novel for the press, which the writer accompanied his friend the bookseller to hear read; she was at this time a widow, having been married to one Charke a musician, long since dead. Her habitation was a wretched thatched hovel, situated on the way to Islington in the purlieus of Clarkenwel Bridewell, not very distant from the new River Head, where at that time it was usual for the scavengers to leave the cleansings of the streets, and the priests of Cloacina to deposit the offerings from the temples of that all-worshipped Power. The night preceding a heavy rain had fallen, which rendered this extraordinary seat of the muses almost inaccessible, so that in our approach we got our white stockings inveloped with mud up to the very calves, which furnished an appearance much in the present fashionable style of half boots. We knocked at the door (not attempting to pull the latch string) which was opened by a tall, meagre, ragged figure, with a blue apron, indicating, what else we might have doubted, the feminine gender. A perfect model for the copper captain's tattered landlady; that deplorable exhibition of the fair sex, in the comedy of Rule-a-Wife. She with a torpid voice and hungry smile desired us to walk in. The first object that presented itself was a dresser, clean, it must be confessed, and furnished with three or four coarse delf plates, two brown platters, and underneath an earthen pipkin and a black pitcher with a snip out of it. To the right we perceived and bowed to the mistress of the mansion sitting on a maimed chair under the mantle piece, by a fire, merely sufficient to put us in mind of starving. On one hob sat a monkey, which by way of welcome chattered at our going in; on the other a tabby cat, of melancholy aspect! and at our author's feet on the flounce of her dingy petticoat reclined a dog, almost a skeleton! he raised his shagged head and eagerly staring with his bleared eyes, saluted us with a snarl. 'Have done, Fidele! these are friends.' The tone of her voice was not harsh; it had something in it humbled and disconsolate; a mingled effort of authority and pleasure – Poor soul! few were her visitors of that description – no wonder the creature barked! – A magpie perched on the top rung of her chair, not an uncomely ornament! and on her lap was placed a mutilated pair of bellows, the pipe was gone, an advantage in their present office, they served as a succedaneum for a writing desk, on which lay displayed her hopes and treasure, the manuscript of her novel. Her inkstand was a broken tea-cup, the pen worn to a stump; she had but one! A rough deal board with three hobbling supporters was brought for our convenience, on which without farther ceremony we contrived to sit down and entered upon business. – The work was read, remarks made, alterations agreed to and thirty guineas demanded for the copy. The squalid handmaiden, who had been an attentive listener, stretched forward her tawny length of neck with an eye of anxious expectation! – The bookseller offered, five! – Our authoress did not appear hurt; disappointments had rendered her mind callous; however some altercation insued. This was the writer's first initiation into the mysteries of bibliopolism and the state of authorcraft. He, seeing both sides pertinacious, at length interposed, and at his instance the wary haberdasher of literature doubled his first proposal with this saving provisoe, that his friend present would pay a moiety and run one half the risk; which was agreed to. Thus matters were accommodated, seemingly to the satisfaction of all parties; the lady's original stipulation of fifty copies for herself being previously acceded to. Such is the story of the once-admired daughter of Colley Cibber, Poet Laureate and patentee of Drury-lane, who was born in affluence and educated with care and tenderness, her servants in livery, and a splendid equipage at her command, with swarms of time-serving sycophants officiously buzzing in her train; yet unmindful of her advantages and improvident in her pursuits, she finished the career of her miserable existence on a dunghill.

The account given of this unfortunate woman is literally correct in every particular, of which, except the circumstance of her death, the writer himself was an eye-witness.

THOMAS DE QUINCEY

ANN OF
OXFORD STREET
(1822)

I LOST NO time in opening the business which had brought me to London. By ten a.m., an hour when all men of business are presumed to be at their posts, personally or by proxy, I presented myself at the money-lender's office. My name was already known there: for I had, by letters from Wales, containing very plain and very accurate statements of my position in life and my pecuniary expectations (some of which statements it afterwards appeared that he had personally investigated and verified), endeavoured to win his favourable attention.

The money-lender, as it turned out, had one fixed rule of action. He never granted a personal interview to any man; no, not to the most beloved of his clients. One and all – myself, therefore, among the crowd – he referred for information, and for the means of prosecuting any kind of negotiation, to an attorney, who called himself, on most days of the week, by the name of Brunell, but occasionally (might it perhaps be on *red-letter* days?) by the more common name of Brown. Mr Brunell-Brown, or Brown-Brunell, had located his hearth (if ever he had possessed one), and his household gods (when they were not in the custody of the sheriff), in Greek Street, Soho. The house was not in itself, supposing that its face had been washed now and then, at all disrespectable. But it wore an unhappy countenance of gloom and unsocial fretfulness, due in reality to the long neglect of painting, cleansing, and in some instances of repairing. There were, however, no fractured panes of glass in the windows; and the deep silence which invested the house, not only from the absence of all visitors, but also of those common household functionaries, bakers, butchers, beer-carriers, sufficiently accounted for the desolation, by suggesting an excuse not strictly true – viz. that it might be tenantless. The house already had tenants through the day, though of a noiseless order, and was destined soon to increase them.

Mr Brown-Brunell, after reconnoitring me through a narrow side-window (such as is often attached to front-doors in London), admitted me cheerfully, and conducted me, as an honoured guest, to his private *officina diplomatum* at the back of the house. From the expression of his face, but much more from the contradictory and self-counteracting play of his features, you gathered in a moment that he was a man who had much to conceal, and much, perhaps, that he would gladly forget. His eye expressed wariness against surprise, and passed in a moment into irrepressible glances of suspicion and alarm. No smile that ever his face naturally assumed but was pulled short up by some freezing counteraction, or was chased by some close-following expression of sadness. One feature there was of relenting goodness and nobleness in Mr Brunell's character, to which it was that subsequently I myself was most profoundly indebted for an asylum that saved my life. He had the deepest, the most liberal, and unaffected love of knowledge, but, above all, of that specific knowledge which we call literature. His own stormy (and no doubt oftentimes disgraceful) career in life, that had entangled him in perpetual feuds with his fellow-men, he ascribed, with bitter imprecations, to the sudden interruption of his studies consequent upon his father's violent death, and to the necessity which threw him, at a boyish age, upon a professional life in the lower branches of law – threw him, therefore, upon daily temptations, by surrounding him with opportunities for taking advantages not strictly honourable, before he had formed any fixed principles at all. From the very first, Mr Brunell had entered zealously into such conversations with myself as either gave openings for reviving his own delightful remembrances of classic authors, or brought up sometimes doubts for solution, sometimes perplexities and cases of intricate construction for illustration and disentanglement.

Hunger-bitten as the house and the household genius seemed, wearing the legend of *Famine* upon every mantel-piece and 'coigne of vantage,' and vehemently protesting as it must have done through all its echoes, against the intro-duction of supernumerary mouths, nevertheless there was (and, I suppose, of necessity) a clerk, who bore the name of Pyment, or Pyemont, then first of all, then last of all, made known to me as a possible surname. Mr Pyment had no *alias* – or not to my knowledge – except, indeed, in the vitupera-tive vocabulary of Mr Brunell; in which most variegated nomenclature he bore many scores of opprobrious names, having no reference whatever to any real habits of the man, good or bad. At two rooms' distance, Mr Brunell always assumed a minute and circumstantial knowledge of what Pyment was doing then, and what he was going to do next. All which Pyment gave himself little trouble to answer, unless it happened (as now and then it did) that he could do so with ludicrous effect. What made the necessity for Pyment was the continual call for 'an appearance' to be put in at some of the subordinate courts in Westminster – courts of conscience, sheriff courts, &c. But it happens often that he who is most indispensable, and gets through most work at one hour, becomes a useless burden at another; as the hardest working reaper seems, in the eyes of an ignoramus, on a wet, wintry day, to be a luxurious idler. Of these ups and downs in Pyment's working life Mr Brunell made a most cynical use; making out that Pyment not only did nothing, but also that he created much work for the afflicted Brunell. However, it happened occasionally that the truth vindicated itself, by making a call upon Pyment's physics – aggressive or defensive – that needed an instant attention. 'Pyment, I say; this way, Pyment – you're wanted, Pyment.' In fact, both were big, hulking men, and had need to be so; for sometimes, whether with good reason or none, clients at the end of a losing suit, or of a suit nominally gained, but unexpectedly laden with heavy expenses, became refractory, showed fight, and gave Pyment reason for saying that at least on this day he had earned his salary by serving an ejectment on a client whom on any other plan it might have been hard to settle with.

But I am anticipating. I go back, therefore, for a few explanatory words, to the day of my arrival in London. How beneficial to me would a little candour have been at that early period! If (which was the simple truth, known to all parties but myself) I had been told that nothing would be brought to a close in less than six months, even assuming the ultimate adoption of my proposals, I should from the first have dismissed all hopes of this nature, as being unsuited to the practicabilities of my situation. It will be seen further on that there was a real and sincere intention of advancing the money wanted. But it was then too late. And universally I believe myself entitled to say that even honourable lawyers will not in a case of this nature move at a faster pace: they will all alike loiter upon varied allegations through six months; and for this reason, – that any shorter period, they fancy, will hardly seem to justify, in the eyes of their client, the sum which they find themselves entitled to charge for their trouble and their preliminary correspondence. How much better for both sides, and more honourable, as more frank and free from disguises, that the client should say, 'Raise this sum' (of, suppose, £400) 'in three weeks, – which can be done, if it can be done in three years; and here is a *bonus* of £100. Delay for two months, and I decline the whole transaction.' Treated with that sort of openness, how much bodily suffering of an extreme order, and how much of the sickness from hope deferred, should I have escaped! Whereas, under the system (pursued with me as with all clients) of continually refreshing my hopes with new delusions, whiling me on with pretended preparation of deeds, and extorting from me, out of every little remittance I received from old family friends casually met in London, as much as possible for the purchase of imaginary stamps, the result was that I myself was brought to the brink of destruction through pure inanition; whilst, on the other hand, those concerned in these deceptions gained nothing that might not have been gained honourably and rightfully under a system of plain dealing.

As it was, subject to these eternal deceptions, I continued for seven or eight weeks to live most parsimoniously in lodgings. These lodgings, though barely decent in my eyes, ran away with at the least two-thirds of my remaining guineas. At length, whilst it was yet possible to reserve a solitary half-guinea towards the more urgent interest of finding daily food, I gave up my rooms, and, stating exactly the circumstances in which I stood, requested permission of Mr Brunell to make use of his large house as a nightly asylum from the open air. Parliament had not then made it a crime, next door to a felony, for a man to sleep out-of-doors (as some twenty years later was done by our benign legislators); as yet *that* was no crime. By the law I came to know sin, and, looking back to the Cambrian hills from distant years, discovered to my surprise what a parliamentary wretch I had been in elder days, when I slept amongst cows on the open hillsides. Lawful as yet this was; but not, therefore, less full of misery. Naturally, then, I was delighted when Mr Brunell not only most readily assented to my request, but begged of me to come that very night, and turn the house to account as fully as I possibly could. The cheerfulness of such a concession brought with it one drawback. I now regretted that I had not, at a much earlier period, applied for this liberty; since I might thus have saved a considerable fund of guineas, applicable, of course, to all urgent necessities, but at this particular moment to one of clamorous urgency – viz. the purchase of blankets. O ancient women, daughters of toil and suffering, amongst all the hardships and bitter inheritances of flesh that ye are called upon to face, not one – not even hunger – seems in my eyes comparable to that of nightly cold. To seek a refuge from cold in bed, and then, from the thin, gauzy texture of the miserable, worn-out blankets, 'not to sleep a wink,' as Wordsworth records of poor old women in Dorsetshire, where coals, from local causes, were at the very dearest – what a terrific enemy was *that* for poor old grandmothers to face in fight! How feelingly I learned at this time, as heretofore I had learned on the wild hillsides in Wales, what an unspeakable blessing is that of warmth! A more killing curse there does not exist for man or woman than the bitter combat between the weariness that prompts sleep and the keen, searching cold that forces you from the first access of sleep to start up horror-stricken, and to seek warmth vainly in renewed exercise, though long since fainting under fatigue. However, even without blankets, it was a fine thing to have an asylum from the open air, and to be assured of this asylum as long as I was likely to want it.

Towards nightfall I went down to Greek Street, and found, on taking possession of my new quarters, that the house already contained one single inmate, – a poor, friendless child, apparently ten years old; but she seemed hunger-bitten; and sufferings of that sort often make children look older than they are. From this forlorn child I learned that she had slept and lived there alone for some time before I came; and great joy the poor creature expressed when she found that I was in future to be her companion through the hours of darkness. The house could hardly be called large – that is, it was not large on each separate storey; but, having four storeys in all, it was large enough to impress vividly the sense of its echoing loneliness; and, from the want of furniture, the noise of the rats made a prodigious uproar on the staircase and hall; so that, amidst the real fleshly ills of cold and hunger, the for-saken child had found leisure to suffer still more from the self-created one of ghosts. Against these enemies I could promise her protection; human companionship was in itself protec-tion; but of other and more needful aid I had, alas! little to offer. We lay upon the floor, with a bundle of law-papers for a pillow, but with no other covering than a large horseman's cloak; afterwards, however, we discovered in a garret an old sofa-cover, a small piece of rug, and some fragments of other articles, which added a little to our comfort. The poor child crept close to me for warmth, and for security against her ghostly enemies. When I was not more than usually ill, I took her into my arms, so that, in general, she was tolerably warm, and often slept when I could not; for, during the last two months of my sufferings, I slept much in the daytime, and was apt to fall into transient dozings at all hours. But my sleep distressed me more than my watching; for, besides the tumul-tuousness of my dreams (which were only not so awful as those which I shall have hereafter to describe as produced by opium), my sleep was never more than what is called *dog-sleep*; so that I could hear myself moaning; and very often

I was awakened suddenly by my own voice. About this time, a hideous sensation began to haunt me as soon as I fell into a slumber, which has since returned upon me, at different periods of my life – viz. a sort of twitching (I knew not where, but apparently about the region of the stomach), which compelled me violently to throw out my feet for the sake of relieving it. This sensation coming on as soon as I began to sleep, and the effort to relieve it constantly awaking me, at length I slept only from exhaustion; and, through increasing weakness (as I said before), I was constantly falling asleep and constantly awaking. Too generally the very attainment of any deep repose seemed as if mechanically linked to some fatal necessity of self-interruption. It was as though a cup were gradually filled by the sleepy overflow of some natural fountain, the fulness of the cup expressing symbolically the completeness of the rest; but then, in the next stage of the process, it seemed as though the rush and torrent-like babbling of the redundant waters, when running over from every part of the cup, interrupted the slumber which in their earlier stage of silent gathering they had so naturally produced. Such and so regular in its swell and its collapse – in its tardy growth and its violent dispersion – did this endless alternation of stealthy sleep and stormy awaking travel through stages as natural as the increments of twilight, or the kindlings of the dawn: no rest that was not a prologue to terror; no sweet tremulous pulses of restoration that did not suddenly explode through rolling clamours of fiery disruption.

Meantime, the master of the house sometimes came in upon us suddenly, and very early; sometimes not till ten o'clock; sometimes not at all. He was in constant fear of arrest. Improving on the plan of Cromwell, every night he slept in a different quarter of London; and I observed that he never failed to examine, through a private window, the appearance of those who knocked at the door, before he would allow it to be opened. He breakfasted alone; indeed, his tea equipage would hardly have admitted of his hazarding an invitation to a second person, any more than the quantity of esculent *material*, which, for the most part, was little more than a roll, or a few biscuits, purchased on his road from the place where he had slept. Or, if he *had* asked a party, as I once learnedly observed to him, the several members of it must have *stood* in the relation to each other (not *sat* in any relation whatever) of succession, and not of co-existence; in the relation of parts of time, and not of the parts of space. During his breakfast, I generally contrived a reason for lounging in; and, with an air of as much indifference as I could assume, took up such fragments as might chance to remain; sometimes, indeed, none at all remained. In doing this, I committed no robbery, except upon Mr Brunell himself, who was thus obliged, now and then, to send out at noon for an extra biscuit; but he, through channels subsequently explained, was repaid a thousand-fold; and, as to the poor child, *she* was never admitted into his study (if I may give that name to his chief depository of parchments, law-writings, &c.); that room was to her the Bluebeard room of the house, being regularly locked on his departure to dinner, about six o'clock, which usually was his final departure for the day. Whether this child were an illegitimate daughter of Mr Brunell, or only a servant, I could not ascertain; she did not herself know; but certainly she was treated altogether as a menial servant. No sooner did Mr Brunell make his appearance than she went below-stairs, brushed his shoes, coat, &c.; and, except when she was summoned to run upon some errand, she never emerged from the dismal Tartarus of the kitchens to the upper air until my welcome knock towards nightfall called up her little trembling footsteps to the front-door.

Of her life during the daytime, however, I knew little but what I gathered from her own account at night; for, as soon as the hours of business commenced, I saw that my absence would be acceptable; and, in general, therefore, I went off and sat in the parks or elsewhere until the approach of twilight.

But who, and what, meantime, was the master of the house himself? Reader, he was one of those anomalous practitioners in lower departments of the law who, on prudential reasons, or from necessity, deny themselves all indulgence in the luxury of too delicate a conscience. In many walks of life a conscience is a more expensive encumbrance than a wife or a carriage; and, as people talk of 'laying down' their carriages, so I suppose my friend Mr Brunell had 'laid down' his conscience for a time; meaning, doubtless, to resume it as soon as he could afford it. He was an advertising attorney, who continually notified to the public, through the morning papers, that he undertook to raise loans for approved parties in what would generally be regarded as desperate cases – viz. where there was nothing better than *personal* security to offer. But, as he took good care to ascertain that there were ample funds in reversion to be counted on, or near connexions that would not suffer the family name to be dishonoured, and as he insured the borrower's life over a sufficient period, the risk was not great; and even of this the whole rested upon the actual money-lender, who stood aloof in the background, and never revealed himself to clients in his proper person, transacting all affairs through his proxies learned in the law, – Mr Brunell or others. The inner economy of such a man's daily life would present a monstrous picture. Even with my limited opportunities for observing what went on, I saw scenes of intrigue and complex chicanery at which I sometimes smile to this day, and at which I smiled then in spite of my misery. My situation, however, at that time, gave me little experience, in my own person, of any qualities in Mr Brunell's character but such as did him honour; and of his whole strange composition I ought to forget everything, but that towards me he was obliging, and, to the extent of his power, generous.

That power was not, indeed, very extensive. However, in common with the rats, I sat rent free; and, as Dr Johnson has recorded that he never but once in his life had as much wall-fruit as he wished, so let me be grateful that, on that single occasion, I had as large a choice of rooms, or even of apart-ments, in a London mansion – viz., as I am now at liberty to add, at the north-west corner of Greek Street, being the house on that side the street nearest to Soho Square – as I could possibly desire. Except the Bluebeard room, which the poor child believed to be permanently haunted, and which, besides, was locked, all others, from the attics to the cellars, were at our service. 'The world was all before us,' and we pitched our tent for the night in any spot we might fancy.

This house I have described as roomy and respectable. It stands in a conspicuous situation, and in a well-known part of London. Many of my readers will have passed it, I doubt not, within a few hours of reading this. For myself, I never fail to visit it when accident draws me to London. About ten o'clock this very night (August 15, 1821, being my birthday), I turned aside from my evening walk along Oxford Street, in order to take a glance at it. It is now in the occupation of some family, apparently respectable. The windows are no longer coated by a paste composed of ancient soot and superannuated rain; and the whole exterior no longer wears an aspect of gloom. By the lights in the front drawing-room, I observed a domestic party, assembled, perhaps, at tea, and apparently cheerful and gay – marvellous contrast, in my eyes, to the darkness, cold, silence, and desolation, of that same house nineteen years ago, when its nightly occupants were one famishing scholar and a poor, neglected child. Her, by the bye, in after years, I vainly endeavoured to trace. Apart from her situation, she was not what would be called an interesting child. She was neither pretty, nor quick in understanding, nor remarkably pleasing in manners. But, thank God! even in those years I needed not the embellishments of elegant accessories to conciliate my affections. Plain human nature, in its humblest and most homely apparel, was enough for me; and I loved the child because she was my partner in wretchedness. If she is now living, she is probably a mother, with children of her own; but, as I have said, I could never trace her.

This I regret; but another person there was, at that time, whom I have since sought to trace with far deeper earnestness, and with far deeper sorrow at my failure. This person was a young woman, and one of that unhappy class who belong to the outcasts and pariahs of our female population. I feel no shame, nor have any reason to feel it, in avowing that I was then on familiar and friendly terms with many women in that unfortunate condition. Smile not, reader too carelessly facile! Frown not, reader too unseasonably austere! Little call was there here either for smiles or frowns. A penniless schoolboy could not be supposed to stand within the range of such temptations; besides that, according to the ancient Latin proverb, '*sine Cerere et Baccho*,' &c. These unhappy women, to me, were simply sisters in calamity; and sisters amongst whom, in as large measure as amongst any other equal number of persons commanding more of the world's respect, were to be found humanity, disinterested generosity, courage that would not falter in defence of the helpless, and fidelity that would have scorned to take bribes for betraying. But the truth is that at no time of my life have

88

I been a person to hold myself polluted by the touch or approach of any creature that wore a human shape. I cannot suppose, I will not believe, that any creatures wearing the form of man or woman are so absolutely rejected and reprobate outcasts that merely to talk with them inflicts pollution. On the contrary, from my very earliest youth, it has been my pride to converse familiarly, *more Socratico*, with all human beings – man, woman, and child – that chance might fling in my way; for a philosopher should not see with the eyes of the poor limitary creature calling himself a man of the world, filled with narrow and self-regarding prejudices of birth and education, but should look upon himself as a catholic creature, and as standing in an equal relation to high and low, to educated and uneducated, to the guilty and the innocent. Being myself, at that time, of necessity a peripatetic, or a walker of the streets, I naturally fell in more frequently with those female peripatetics who are technically called streetwalkers. Some of these women had occasionally taken my part against watchmen who wished to drive me off the steps of houses where I was sitting; others had protected me against more serious aggressions. But one amongst them – the one on whose account I have at all introduced this subject – yet no! let me not class thee, O noble-minded Ann —, with that order of women; let me find, if it be possible, some gentler name to designate the condition of her to whose bounty and compassion – ministering to my necessities when all the world stood aloof from me – I owe it that I am at this time alive. For many weeks I had walked, at nights, with this poor friendless girl up and down Oxford Street, or had rested with her on steps and under the shelter of porticos.

She could not be so old as myself: she told me, indeed, that she had not completed her sixteenth year. By such questions as my interest about her prompted, I had gradually drawn forth her simple history. Hers was a case of ordinary occurrence (as I have since had reason to think), and one in which, if London beneficence had better adapted its arrangements to meet it, the power of the law might oftener be interposed to protect and to avenge. But the stream of London charity flows in a channel which, though deep and mighty, is yet noiseless and underground; – not obvious or readily accessible to poor, houseless wanderers; and it cannot be denied that the outside air and framework of society in London, as in all vast capitals, is unavoidably harsh, cruel, and repulsive. In any case, however, I saw that part of her injuries might have been redressed; and I urged her often and earnestly to lay her complaint before a magistrate. Friendless as she was, I assured her that she would meet with immediate attention; and that English justice, which was no respecter of persons, would speedily and amply avenge her on the brutal ruffian who had plundered her little property. She promised me often that she would; but she delayed taking the steps I pointed out, from time to time; for she was timid and dejected to a degree which showed how deeply sorrow had taken hold of her young heart; and perhaps she thought justly that the most upright judge and the most righteous tribunals could do nothing to repair her heaviest wrongs. Something, however, would perhaps have been done; for it had been settled between us at length (but, unhappily, on the very last time but one that I was ever to see her) that in a day or two I, accompanied by her, should state her case to a magistrate. This little service it was destined, however, that I should never realize. Meantime, that which she rendered to me, and which was greater than I could ever have repaid her, was this: – One night, when we were pacing slowly along Oxford Street, and after a day when I had felt unusually ill and faint, I requested her to turn off with me into Soho

Square. Thither we went; and we sat down on the steps of a house, which to this hour I never pass without a pang of grief, and an inner act of homage to the spirit of that unhappy girl, in memory of the noble act which she there performed. Suddenly, as we sat, I grew much worse. I had been leaning my head against her bosom, and all at once I sank from her arms, and fell backwards on the steps. From the sensations I then had, I felt an inner conviction of the liveliest kind that, without some powerful and reviving stimulus, I should either have died on the spot, or should, at least, have sunk to a point of exhaustion from which all re-ascent, under my friendless circumstances, would soon have become hopeless. Then it was, at this crisis of my fate, that my poor orphan companion, who had herself met with little but injuries in this world, stretched out a saving hand to me. Uttering a cry of terror, but without a moment's delay, she ran off into Oxford Street, and, in less time than could be imagined, returned to me with a glass of port-wine and spices, that acted upon my empty stomach (which at that time would have rejected all solid food) with an instantaneous power of restoration; and for this glass the generous girl, without a murmur, paid out of her own humble purse, at a time, be it remembered, when she had scarcely wherewithal to purchase the bare necessaries of life, and when she could have no reason to expect that I should ever be able to reimburse her. O youthful benefactress! how often in succeeding years, standing in solitary places, and thinking of thee with grief of heart and perfect love – how often have I wished that, as in ancient times the curse of a father was believed to have a supernatural power, and to pursue its object with a fatal necessity of self-fulfilment, even so the benediction of a heart oppressed with gratitude might have a like prerogative; might have power given it from above to chase, to haunt, to waylay, to pursue thee into the central darkness of a London brothel, or (if it were possible) even into the darkness of the grave, there to awaken thee with an authentic message of peace and forgiveness, and of final reconciliation!

Some feelings, though not deeper or more passionate, are more tender than others; and often when I walk, at this time, in Oxford Street by dreary lamp-light, and hear those airs played on a common street-organ which years ago solaced me and my dear youthful companion, I shed tears, and muse with myself at the mysterious dispensation which so suddenly and so critically separated us for ever. How it happened, the reader will understand from what remains of this introductory narration.

Soon after the period of the last incident I have recorded, I met in Albemarle Street a gentleman of his late Majesty's household. This gentleman had received hospitalities, on different occasions, from my family; and he challenged me upon the strength of my family likeness. I did not attempt any disguise, but answered his questions ingenuously; and, on his pledging his word of honour that he would not betray me to my guardians, I gave him my real address in Greek Street. The next day I received from him a ten-pound banknote. The letter enclosing it was delivered, with other letters of business, to the attorney; but, though his look and manner informed me that he suspected its contents, he gave it up to me honourably, and without demur.

This present, from the particular service to which much of it was applied, leads me naturally to speak again of the original purpose which had allured me up to London, and which I had been without intermission prosecuting through Mr Brunell from the first day of my arrival in London.

In so mighty a world as London, it will surprise my readers

that I should not have found some means of staving off the last extremities of penury; and it will strike them that two resources, at least, must have been open to me: viz. either to seek assistance from the friends of my family, or to turn my youthful accomplishments, such as they were, into some channel of pecuniary emolument. As to the first course, I may observe, generally, that what I dreaded beyond all other evils was the chance of being reclaimed by my guardians; not doubting that whatever power the law gave them would have been enforced against me to the utmost; that is, to the extremity of forcibly restoring me to the school which I had quitted, – a restoration which, as it would, in my eyes, have been a dishonour even if submitted to voluntarily, could not fail, when extorted from me in contempt and defiance of my own known wishes and earnest resistance, to have proved a humiliation worse to me than death, and which would, indeed, have terminated in death. I was, therefore, shy enough of applying for assistance even in those quarters where I was sure of receiving it, if at any risk of furnishing my guardians with a clue for tracing me. My father's friends, no doubt, had been many, and were scattered all over the kingdom; but, as to London in particular, though a large section of these friends would certainly be found there, yet (as full ten years had passed since his death) I knew very few of them even by name; and, never having seen London before – except once, in my fifteenth year, for a few hours – I knew not the address of even those few. To this mode of gaining help, therefore, in part the difficulty, but much more the danger which I have mentioned, habitually indisposed me. In regard to the other mode – that of turning any talents or knowledge that I might possess to a lucrative use – I now feel half inclined to join my reader in wondering that I should have overlooked it. As a corrector of Greek proofs (if in no other way), I might surely have gained enough for my slender wants. Such an office as this I could have discharged with an exemplary and punctual accuracy that would soon have gained me the confidence of my employers. And there was this great preliminary advantage in giving such a direction to my efforts, that the intellectual dignity and elegance associated with all ministerial services about the press would have saved my pride and self-respect from mortification. In an extreme case, such as mine had now become, I should not have absolutely disdained the humble station of 'devil.' A subaltern situation in a service inherently honourable is better than a much higher situation in a service pointing to ultimate objects that are mean or ignoble. I am, indeed, not sure that I could adequately have discharged the functions of this office. To the perfection of the diabolic character I fear that patience is one of the indispensable graces; more, perhaps, than I should be found on trial to possess for dancing attendance upon crotchety authors, superstitiously fastidious in matters of punctuation. But why talk of my qualifications? Qualified or not, where could I obtain such an office? For it must not be forgotten that even a diabolic appointment requires interest. Towards *that* I must first of all have an introduction to some respectable publisher; and this I had no means of obtaining. To say the truth, however, it had never once occurred to me to think of literary labours as a source of profit. No mode sufficiently speedy of obtaining money had ever suggested itself but that of borrowing it on the strength of my future claims and expectations. This mode I sought by every avenue to compass; and amongst other persons I applied to a Jew named Dell.

To this Jew, and to other advertising money-lenders, I had introduced myself, with an account of my expectations; which account they had little difficulty in ascertaining to be

correct. The person there mentioned as the second son of —
was found to have all the claims (or more than all) that I had
stated: but one question still remained, which the faces of
the Jews pretty significantly suggested, – was I that person?
This doubt had never occurred to me as a possible one; I had
rather feared, whenever my Jewish friends scrutinized me
keenly, that I might be too well known to be that person,
and that some scheme might be passing in their minds for
entrapping me and selling me to my guardians. It was strange
to me to find my own self, *materialiter* considered (so I
expressed it, for I doated on logical accuracy of distinctions),
suspected of counterfeiting my own self, *formaliter* considered. However, to satisfy their scruples, I took the only course
in my power. Whilst I was in Wales, I had received various
letters from young friends; these I produced, for I carried
them constantly in my pocket. Most of these letters were
from the Earl of Altamont, who was at that time, and had
been for some years back, amongst my confidential friends.
These were dated from Eton. I had also some from the
Marquis of Sligo, his father; who, though absorbed in agri-
cultural pursuits, yet having been an Etonian himself, and
as good a scholar as a nobleman needs to be, still retained
an affection for classical studies and for youthful scholars.
He had, accordingly, from the time that I was fifteen, corre-
sponded with me – sometimes upon the great improvements
which he had made, or was meditating, in the counties of
Mayo and Sligo, since I had been there; sometimes upon the
merits of a Latin poet; at other times, suggesting subjects on
which he fancied that I could write verses myself, or breathe
poetic inspiration into the mind of my once familiar companion, his son.

On reading the letters, one of my Jewish friends agreed
to furnish two or three hundred pounds on my personal

security, provided I could persuade the young earl – who was, by the way, not older than myself – to guarantee the payment on our joint coming of age; the Jew's final object being, as I now suppose, not the trifling profit he could expect to make by me, but the prospect of establishing a connexion with my noble friend, whose great expectations were well known to him. In pursuance of this proposal on the part of the Jew, about eight or nine days after I had received the £10, I prepared to visit Eton. Nearly three guineas of the money I had given to my money-lending friend in the background; or, more accurately, I had given that sum to Mr Brunell, *alias* Brown, as representing Mr Dell, the Jew; and a smaller sum I had given directly to himself, on his own separate account. What he alleged in excuse for thus draining my purse at so critical a moment was that stamps must be bought, in order that the writings might be prepared whilst I was away from London. I thought in my heart that he was lying, but I did not wish to give him any excuse for charging his own delays upon me. About fifteen shillings I had employed in re-establishing (though in a very humble way) my dress. Of the remainder, I gave one-quarter (something more than a guinea) to Ann, meaning, on my return, to have divided with her whatever might remain.

These arrangements made, soon after six o'clock, on a dark winter evening, I set off, accompanied by Ann, towards Piccadilly; for it was my intention to go down as far as the turn to Salt Hill and Slough on the Bath or Bristol mail. Our course lay through a part of the town which has now totally disappeared, so that I can no longer retrace its ancient boundaries – having been replaced by Regent Street and its adjacencies. *Swallow Street* is all that I remember of the names superseded by this large revolutionary usurpation. Having time enough before us, however, we bore away to the left, until we came into Golden Square. There, near the corner of Sherrard Street, we sat down, not wishing to part in the tumult and blaze of Piccadilly. I had told Ann of my plans some time before, and now I assured her again that she should share in my good fortune, if I met with any, and that I would never forsake her, as soon as I had power to protect her. This I fully intended, as much from inclination as from a sense of duty; for, setting aside gratitude (which in any case must have made me her debtor for life), I loved her as affectionately as if she had been my sister; and at this moment with sevenfold tenderness, from pity at witnessing her extreme dejection. I had apparently most reason for dejection, because I was leaving the saviour of my life; yet I, considering the shock my health had received, was cheerful and full of hope. She, on the contrary, who was parting with one who had had little means of serving her, except by kindness and brotherly treatment, was overcome by sorrow, so that when I kissed her at our final farewell, she put her arms about my neck, and wept, without speaking a word. I hoped to return in a week, at furthest, and I agreed with her that, on the fifth night from that, and every night afterwards, she should wait for me, at six o'clock near the bottom of Great Titchfield Street; which had formerly been our customary haven of rendezvous, to prevent our missing each other in the great Mediterranean of Oxford Street. This, and other measures of precaution, I took; one, only, I forgot. She had either never told me, or (as a matter of no great interest) I had forgotten, her surname. It is a general practice, indeed, with girls of humble rank in her unhappy condition, not (as novel-reading women of higher pretensions) to style themselves *Miss Douglas*, *Miss Montague*, &c., but simply by their Christian names, *Mary*, *Jane*, *Frances*, &c. Her surname, as the surest means of tracing her, I ought now to have inquired; but the truth is, having no reason to think that our meeting again could, in consequence of a short interruption, be more difficult or uncertain than it had been for so many weeks, I scarcely for a moment adverted to it as necessary, or placed it amongst my memoranda against this parting interview; and, my final anxieties being spent in comforting her with hopes, and in pressing upon her the necessity of getting some medicine for a violent cough with which she was troubled, I wholly forgot this precaution until it was too late to recall her.

When I reached the Gloucester Coffee-house in Piccadilly, at which, in those days, all the western mails stopped for a few minutes in going out of London, it was already a quarter-of-an-hour past eight o'clock; the Bristol Mail was on the point of going off; and I mounted on the outside. The fine fluent motion of this mail soon laid me asleep. It is somewhat remarkable that the first easy or refreshing sleep which I had enjoyed for some months was on the outside of a mail-coach – a bed which, at this day, I find rather an uneasy one. Connected with this sleep was a little incident which served, as hundreds of others did at that time, to convince me how easily a man who has never been in any great distress may pass through life without knowing in his own person, and experimentally testing, the possible goodness of the human heart, or, as unwillingly I add, its possible churlishness. So thick a curtain of *manners* is drawn over the features and expression of men's natures that, to the ordinary observer, the two extremities, and the infinite field of varieties which lie between them, are all confounded under one neutral disguise. The case was this: – For the first four or five miles out of London, I annoyed my fellow-passenger on the roof by occasionally falling against him when the coach gave a lurch; and, indeed, if the road had been less smooth and level than it was, I should have fallen off from weakness.

Of this annoyance he complained heavily; as, perhaps, in the same circumstances, most people would. He expressed his complaint, however, more morosely than the occasion seemed to warrant; and, if I had parted with him at that moment, I should have thought of him as a surly and almost brutal fellow. Still I was conscious that I had given him some cause for complaint; and therefore I apologized, assuring him that I would do what I could to avoid falling asleep for the future; and, at the same time, in as few words as possible, I explained to him that I was ill, and in a weak state from long suffering, and that I could not afford to take an inside place. The man's manner changed upon hearing this explanation in an instant: and, when I next woke for a minute, from the noise and lights of Hounslow (for, in spite of my efforts, I had again fallen asleep within two minutes), I found that he had put his arm round me to protect me from falling off; and for the rest of my journey he behaved to me with the gentleness of a woman. And this was the more kind, as he could not have known that I was not going the whole way to Bath or Bristol. Unfortunately, indeed, I *did* go further than I intended; for so genial and refreshing was my sleep, being in the open air, that, upon the sudden pulling up of the mail (possibly at a post-office), I found that we had reached some place six or seven miles to the west of Salt Hill. Here I alighted; and, during the half-minute that the mail stopped, I was entreated by my friendly companion (who, from the transient glimpse I had of him under the glaring lights of Piccadilly, might be a respectable upper servant) to go to bed without delay. This, under the feeling that some consideration was due to one who had done me so seasonable a service, I promised, though with no intention of doing so; and, in fact, I immediately moved forward on foot.

It must then have been nearly eleven; but so slowly did I

creep along that I heard a clock in a cottage strike four as I was on the point of turning down the road from Slough to Eton. The air and the sleep had both refreshed me; but I was weary, nevertheless. I remember a thought (obvious enough, and pointedly expressed by a Roman poet) which gave me some consolation, at that moment, under my poverty. There had been, some weeks before, a murder committed on Hounslow Heath, which at that time was really a heath, entirely un-enclosed, and exhibiting a sea-like expanse in all directions, except one. I cannot be mistaken when I say that the name of the murdered person was *Steele*, and that he was the owner of a lavender plantation in that neighbourhood. Every step of my regress (for I now walked with my face towards London) was bringing me nearer to the heath; and it natur-ally occurred to me that I and the accursed murderer, if he were that night abroad, might, at every instant, be uncon-sciously approaching each other through the darkness; in which case, said I, supposing myself – instead of being little better than an outcast,

'Lord of my learning, and no land beside' –

like my friend Lord Altamont, heir, by general repute, to £30,000 per annum, what a panic should I be under at this moment about my throat! Indeed, it was not likely that Lord Altamont should ever be in my situation; but, nevertheless, the spirit of the remark remains true, that vast power and pos-sessions make a man shamefully afraid of dying; and I am convinced that many of the most intrepid adventurers who, being poor, enjoy the full use of their natural energies, would, if at the very instant of going into action news were brought to them that they had unexpectedly succeeded to an estate in England of £50,000 a-year, feel their dislike to bullets furiously sharpened, and their efforts at self-possession proportionately difficult. So true it is, in the language of a wise man, whose own experience had made him acquainted equally with good and evil fortune, that riches are better fitted

> 'To slacken virtue, and abate her edge,
> Than tempt her to do aught may merit praise.'

PARADISE REGAINED

I dally with my subject, because, to myself, the remembrance of these times is profoundly interesting. But my reader shall not have any further cause to complain; for now I hasten to its close. In the road between Slough and Eton I fell asleep; and, just as the morning began to dawn, I was awakened by the voice of a man standing over me, and apparently studying my *physics*, whilst to me – upon so sudden an introduction to him in so suspicious a situation – his *morals* naturally suggested a more interesting subject of inquiry. I know not what he was. He was an ill-looking fellow, but not, therefore, of necessity, an ill-meaning fellow; or, if he were, I suppose he thought that no person sleeping out-of-doors in winter could be worth robbing. In which conclusion, however, as it regarded myself, I have the honour to assure him, supposing him ever to find himself amongst my readers, that he was entirely mistaken. I was not sorry at his disturbance, as it roused me to pass through Eton before people were generally astir. The night had been heavy and misty; but towards the morning it had changed to a slight frost, and the trees were now covered with rime.

I slipped through Eton unobserved; washed myself, and as far as possible adjusted my dress, at a little public-house in Windsor; and, about eight o'clock, went down towards the precincts of the college, near which were congregated the houses of the 'Dames.' On my road I met some junior boys, of whom I made inquiries. An Etonian is always a gentleman;

and, in spite of my shabby habiliments, they answered me civilly. My friend Lord Altamont was gone to Jesus College, Cambridge. 'Ibi omnis effusus labor!' I had, however, other friends at Eton; but it is not to all who wear that name in prosperity that a man is willing to present himself in distress. On recollecting myself, however, I asked for the Earl of Desart, to whom (though my acquaintance with him was not so intimate as with some others) I should not have shrunk from presenting myself under any circumstances. He was still at Eton, though, I believe, on the wing for Cambridge. I called, was received kindly, and asked to breakfast.

Lord Desart placed before me a magnificent breakfast. It was really such; but in my eyes it seemed trebly magnificent from being the first regular meal, the first 'good man's table,' that I had sat down to for months. Strange to say, I could scarcely eat anything. On the day when I first received my ten-pound bank-note, I had gone to a baker's shop and bought a couple of rolls; this very shop I had some weeks before surveyed with an eagerness of desire which it was humiliating to recollect. I remembered the story (which, however, I now believed to be a falsehood) about Otway, and feared that there might be danger in eating too rapidly. But there was no cause for alarm; my appetite was utterly gone, and I nauseated food of every kind. This effect, from eating what approached to a meal, I continued to feel for weeks. On the present occasion, at Lord Desart's table, I found myself not at all better than usual; and, in the midst of luxuries, appetite I had none. I had, however, unfortunately, at all times a craving for wine: I explained my situation, therefore, to Lord Desart, and gave him a short account of my late sufferings; with which he expressed deep sympathy, and called for wine. This gave me instantaneous relief and immoderate pleasure; and on all occasions, when I had an opportunity, I never failed to drink wine. Obvious it is, however, that this indulgence in wine would continue to strengthen my malady, for the tone of my stomach was apparently quite sunk; but, by a better regimen, it might sooner, and, perhaps, effectually, have been restored.

I hope that it was not from this love of wine that I lingered in the neighbourhood of my Eton friends; I persuaded myself *then* that it was from reluctance to ask Lord Desart, on whom I was conscious of having no sufficient claims, the particular service in quest of which I had come to Eton. I was, however, unwilling to lose my journey, and – I asked it. Lord Desart, whose good-nature was unbounded, and which, in regard to myself, had been measured rather by his compassion, perhaps, for my condition, and his knowledge of my intimacy with several of his relatives, than by an over-rigorous inquiry into the extent of my own direct claims, faltered, nevertheless, at this request. He acknowledged that he did not like to have any dealings with money-lenders, and feared lest such a transaction might come to the ears of his connexions. Moreover, he doubted whether *his* signature, whose expectations were so much more bounded than those of his cousin, would avail with my unchristian friends. Still he did not wish, apparently, to mortify me by a refusal peremptory and absolute; for, after a little consideration, he promised, under certain conditions, which he pointed out, to give his security. Lord Desart was at this time not above eighteen years of age; but I have often doubted, on recollecting since the good sense and prudence which on this occasion he mingled with so much urbanity of manner (which in him wore the grace of youthful sincerity), whether any statesman, the oldest and the most accomplished in diplomacy, could have acquitted himself better under the same circumstances.

Re-comforted by this promise, which was not quite equal to the best, but far above the worst that I had anticipated, I returned in a Windsor coach to London three days after I had quitted it. And now I come to the end of my story. The Jews did not approve of Lord Desart's conditions, or so they said. Whether they would in the end have acceded to them, and were only seeking time for making further inquiries, I know not; but many delays were made – time passed on – the small fragment of my bank-note had just melted away, and before any conclusion could have been put to the business I must have relapsed into my former state of wretchedness. Suddenly, at this crisis, an opening was made, almost by accident, for reconciliation with my guardians. I quitted London in haste, and returned to the Priory; after some time, I proceeded to Oxford; and it was not until many months had passed away that I had it in my power again to revisit the ground which had become so interesting to me, and to this day remains so, as the chief scene of my youthful sufferings.

Meantime, what had become of Ann? Where was she? Whither had she gone? According to our agreement, I sought her daily, and waited for her every night, so long as I staid in London, at the corner of Titchfield Street; and during the last days of my stay in London I put into activity every means of tracing her that my knowledge of London suggested, and the limited extent of my power made possible. The street where she had lodged I knew, but not the house; and I remembered, at last, some account which she had given of ill-treatment from her landlord, which made it probable that she had quitted those lodgings before we parted. She had few acquaintance; most people, besides, thought that the earnestness of my inquiries arose from motives which moved their laughter or their slight regard; and others, thinking that I was in chase of a girl who had robbed me of some trifles, were naturally and excusably indisposed to give me any clue to her, if indeed they had any to give. Finally, as my despairing resource, on the day I left London I put into the hands of the only person who (I was sure) must know Ann by sight, from having been in company with us once or twice, an address to the Priory. All was in vain. To this hour I have never heard a syllable about her. This, amongst such troubles as most men meet with in this life, has been my heaviest affliction. If she lived, doubtless we must have been sometimes in search of each other, at the very same moment, through the mighty labyrinths of London; perhaps even within a few feet of each other – a barrier no wider, in a London street, often amounting in the end to a separation for eternity! During some years I hoped that she *did* live; and I suppose that, in the literal and unrhetorical use of the word *myriad*, I must, on my different visits to London, have looked into many myriads of female faces, in the hope of meeting Ann. I should know her again amongst a thousand, and if seen but for a moment. Handsome she was not; but she had a sweet expression of countenance, and a peculiarly graceful carriage of the head. I sought her, I have said, in hope. So it was for years; but now I should fear to see her; and her cough, which grieved me when I parted with her, is now my consolation. Now I wish to see her no longer, but think of her, more gladly, as one long since laid in the grave – in the grave, I would hope, of a Magdalen; taken away before injuries and cruelty had blotted out and transfigured her ingenuous nature, or the brutalities of ruffians had completed the ruin they had begun.

So then, Oxford Street, stony-hearted stepmother, thou that listenest to the sighs of orphans, and drinkest the tears of children, at length I was dismissed from thee! The time was come that I no more should pace in anguish thy never-ending terraces, no more should wake and dream in captivity to the pangs of hunger. Successors too many to myself and Ann have, doubtless, since then trodden in our footsteps, inheritors of our calamities. Other orphans than Ann have sighed; tears have been shed by other children; and thou, Oxford Street, hast since those days echoed to the groans of innumerable hearts. For myself, however, the storm which I had outlived seemed to have been the pledge of a long fair weather; the premature sufferings which I had paid down to have been accepted as a ransom for many years to come, as a price of long immunity from sorrow; and, if again I walked in London, a solitary and contemplative man (as oftentimes I did), I walked for the most part in serenity and peace of mind. And, although it is true that the calamities of my novitiate in London had struck root so deeply in my bodily constitution that afterwards they shot up and flourished afresh, and grew into a noxious umbrage that has over-shadowed and darkened my latter years, yet these second assaults of suffering were met with a fortitude more con-firmed, with the resources of a maturer intellect, and with alleviations, how deep! from sympathizing affection.

WILLIAM MAKEPEACE
THACKERAY

GOING TO SEE
A MAN HANGED
(1840)

July, 1840

x—, WHO HAD voted with Mr Ewart for the abolition of the punishment of death, was anxious to see the effect on the public mind of an execution, and asked me to accompany him to see Courvoisier killed. We had not the advantage of a sheriff's order, like the 'six hundred noblemen and gentle-men' who were admitted within the walls of the prison; but determined to mingle with the crowd at the foot of the scaffold and take up our positions at a very early hour.

As I was to rise at three in the morning, I went to bed at ten, thinking that five hours' sleep would be amply sufficient to brace me against the fatigues of the coming day. But, as might have been expected, the event of the morrow was per-petually before my eyes through the night, and kept them wide open. I heard all the clocks in the neighbourhood chime the hours in succession; a dog from some court hard by kept up a pitiful howling; at one o'clock, a cock set up a feeble, melancholy crowing; shortly after two the daylight came peeping gray through the window-shutters; and by the time that X— arrived, in fulfilment of his promise, I had been asleep about half-an-hour. He, more wise, had not gone to rest at all, but had remained up all night at the Club, along with Dash and two or three more. Dash is one of the most eminent wits in London, and had kept the company merry all night with appropriate jokes about the coming event. It is curious that a murder is a great inspirer of jokes. We all like to laugh and have our fling about it; there is a certain grim pleasure in the circumstance – a perpetual jingling antithesis between life and death, that is sure of its effect.

In mansion or garret, on down or straw, surrounded by weeping friends and solemn oily doctors, or tossing unheeded upon scanty hospital beds, there were many people in this great city to whom that Sunday night was to be the last of any that they should pass on earth here. In the course of half-a-dozen dark, wakeful hours, one had leisure to think of these (and a little, too, of that certain supreme night, that shall come at one time or other, when he who writes shall be stretched upon the last bed, prostrate in the last struggle, taking the last look of dear faces that have cheered us here, and lingering – one moment more – ere we part for the tremendous journey); but, chiefly, I could not help thinking, as each clock sounded, what is *he* doing now? has *he* heard it in his little room in Newgate yonder? Eleven o'clock. He has been writing until now. The gaoler says he is a pleasant man enough to be with; but he can hold out no longer, and is very weary. 'Wake me at four,' says he, 'for I have still much to put down.' From eleven to twelve the gaoler hears how he is grinding his teeth in his sleep. At twelve he is up in his bed, and asks, 'Is it the time?' He has plenty more time yet for sleep; and he sleeps, and the bell goes on tolling. Seven hours more – five hours more. Many a carriage is clattering through the streets, bringing ladies away from evening parties; many bachelors are reeling home after a jolly night; Covent Garden is alive and the light coming through the cell-window turns the gaoler's candle pale. Four hours more! 'Courvoisier,' says the gaoler, shaking him, 'it's four o'clock now, and I've woke you as you told me; but there's no call for you *to get up yet.*' The poor wretch leaves his bed, however, and makes his last toilet; and then falls to writing, to tell the world how he did the crime for which he has suffered. This time he will tell the truth, and the whole truth. They bring him his breakfast 'from the coffee-shop opposite – tea, coffee, and thin bread and butter.' He will take nothing, however, but goes on writing. He has to write to his mother – the pious mother far away in his own country – who reared him and loved him; and even now has sent him her forgiveness and her blessing. He finishes his memorials and letters, and makes his will, disposing of his little miserable property of books and tracts that pious people have furnished him with. '*Ce 6 Juillet, 1840. François Benjamin Courvoisier vous donne ceci, mon ami, pour souvenir.*' He has a token for his dear friend the gaoler; another for his dear friend the under-sheriff. As the day of the convict's death draws nigh, it is painful to see how he fastens upon everybody who approaches him, how pitifully he clings to them and loves them.

While these things are going on within the prison (with which we are made accurately acquainted by the copious chronicles of such events which are published subsequently), X—'s carriage has driven up to the door of my lodgings, and we have partaken of an elegant *déjeûner* that has been prepared for the occasion. A cup of coffee at half-past three in the morning is uncommonly pleasant; and X— enlivens us with the repetition of the jokes that Dash has just been making. Admirable, certainly – they must have had a merry night of it, that's clear; and we stoutly debate whether, when one has to get up so early in the morning, it is best to have an hour or two of sleep, or wait and go to bed afterwards at the end of the day's work. That fowl is extraordinarily tough – the wing, even, is as hard as a board; a slight disappointment, for there is nothing else for breakfast. 'Will any gentleman have some sherry and soda-water before he sets out? It clears the brains famously.' Thus primed, the party sets out. The coachman has dropped asleep on the box, and wakes up wildly as the hall-door opens. It is just four o'clock. About this very time they are waking up poor – pshaw! who is for a cigar? X— does not smoke himself; but vows and protests, in the kindest way in the world, that he does not care in the least for the new drab-silk linings in his carriage. Z— who smokes, mounts, however, the box. 'Drive to Snow Hill,' says the owner of the chariot. The policemen, who are the only people in the street, and are standing by, look knowing – they know what it means well enough.

How cool and clean the streets look, as the carriage startles the echoes that have been asleep in the corners all night. Somebody has been sweeping the pavements clean in the night-time surely; they would not soil a lady's white satin shoes, they are so dry and neat. There is not a cloud or a breath in the air, except Z—'s cigar, which whiffs off, and soars straight upwards in volumes of white, pure smoke. The trees in the squares look bright and green – as bright as leaves in the country in June. We who keep late hours don't know the beauty of London air and verdure; in the early morning they are delightful – the most fresh and lively companions possible. But they cannot bear the crowd and the bustle of mid-day. You don't know them then – they are no longer the same things. We have come to Gray's Inn; there is actually dew upon the grass in the gardens; and the windows of the stout old red houses are all in a flame.

As we enter Holborn the town grows more animated; and there are already twice as many people in the streets as you see at mid-day in a German *Residenz* or an English provincial town. The gin-shop keepers have many of them taken their shutters down, and many persons are issuing from them pipe in hand. Down they go along the broad bright street, their blue shadows marching *after* them; for they are all bound the same way, and are bent like us upon seeing the hanging.

It is twenty minutes past four as we pass St Sepulchre's: by this time many hundred people are in the street, and many more are coming up Snow Hill. Before us lies Newgate Prison; but something a great deal more awful to look at, which seizes the eye at once, and makes the heart beat, is

There it stands black and ready, jutting out from a little door in the prison. As you see it, you feel a kind of dumb electric shock, which causes one to start a little, and give a sort of gasp for breath. The shock is over in a second; and presently you examine the object before you with a certain feeling of complacent curiosity. At least, such was the effect that the gallows produced upon the writer, who is trying to set down all his feelings as they occurred, and not to exaggerate them at all.

After the gallows-shock had subsided, we went down into the crowd, which was very numerous, but not dense as yet. It was evident that the day's *business* had not begun. People sauntered up, and formed groups, and talked; the new comers asking those who seemed *habitués* of the place about former executions; and did the victim hang with his face towards the clock or towards Ludgate Hill? and had he the rope round his neck when he came on the scaffold, or was it put on by Jack Ketch afterwards? and had Lord W— taken a window, and which was he? I may mention the noble Marquis's name, as he was not at the exhibition. A pseudo W— was pointed out in an opposite window, towards whom all the people in our neighbourhood looked eagerly, and with great respect too. The mob seemed to have no sort of ill-will against him, but sympathy and admiration. This noble lord's personal courage and strength have won the plebs over to him. Perhaps his exploits against policemen have occasioned some of this popularity; for the mob hate them, as children the schoolmaster.

Throughout the whole four hours, however, the mob was extraordinarily gentle and good-humoured. At first we had leisure to talk to the people about us; and I recommend X——'s brother senators of both sides of the House to see more of this same people and to appreciate them better. Honourable Members are battling and struggling in the House; shouting, yelling, crowing, hear-hearing, pooh-poohing, making speeches of three columns, and gaining 'great Conservative triumphs,' or 'signal successes of the Reform cause,' as the case may be. Three hundred and ten gentlemen of good fortune, and able for the most part to quote Horace, declare solemnly that unless Sir Robert comes in, the nation is ruined. Three hundred and fifteen on the other side swear by their great gods that the safety of the empire depends upon Lord John; and to this end they quote Horace too. I declare that I have never been in a great London crowd without thinking of what they call the two 'great' parties in England with wonder. For which of the two great leaders do these people care, I pray you? When Lord Stanley withdrew his Irish bill the other night, were they in transports of joy, like worthy persons who read the *Globe* and the *Chronicle*? or when he beat the Ministers, were they wild with delight, like honest gentlemen who read the *Post* and the *Times*? Ask yonder ragged fellow, who has evidently frequented debating-clubs, and speaks with good sense and shrewd good-nature. He cares no more for Lord John than he does for Sir Robert; and, with due respect be it said, would mind very little if both of them were ushered out by Mr Ketch, and took their places under yonder black beam. What are the two great parties to him, and those like him? Sheer wind, hollow humbug, absurd claptraps; a silly mummery of dividing and debating, which does not in the least, however it may turn, affect his condition. It has been so ever since the happy days when Whigs and Tories began; and a pretty pastime no doubt it is for both. August parties, great balances of British freedom: are not the two sides quite as active, and eager, and loud, as at their very birth, and ready to fight for place as stoutly as ever they fought before? But lo! in the meantime, whilst you are jangling and brawling over the accounts, *Populus*, whose estate you have administered while he was an infant, and could not take care of himself – Populus has been growing and growing, till he is every bit as wise as his guardians. Talk to our ragged friend. He is not so polished, perhaps, as a member of the 'Oxford and Cambridge Club'; he has not been to Eton; and never read Horace in his life: but he can think just as soundly as the best of you; he can speak quite as strongly in his own rough way; he has been reading all sorts of books of late years, and gathered together no little information. He is as good a man as the common run of us; and there are ten million more men in the country as good as he, – ten million, for whom we, in our infinite superiority, are acting as guardians, and to whom, in our bounty, we give – exactly nothing. Put yourself in their position, worthy sir. You and a hundred others find yourselves in some lone place, where you set up a government. You take a chief, as is natural; he is the cheapest order-keeper in the world. You establish half-a-dozen worthies, whose families you say shall have the privilege to legislate for you for ever; half-a-dozen more, who shall be appointed by a choice of thirty of the rest: and the other sixty, who shall have no choice, vote, place, or privilege, at all. Honourable sir, suppose that you are one of the last sixty: how will you feel, you who have intelligence, passions, honest pride, as well as your neighbour; how will you feel towards your equals, in whose hands lie all the power and all the property of the community? Would you love and honour them, tamely acquiesce in their superiority, see their privileges, and go yourself disregarded without a pang? you are not a man if you would. I am not talking of right or wrong, or debating questions of government. But ask my friend there, with the ragged elbows and no shirt, what he thinks? You have your party, Conservative or Whig, as it may be. You believe that an aristocracy is an institution necessary, beautiful, and virtuous. You are a gentleman, in other words, and stick by your party.

And our friend with the elbows (the crowd is thickening hugely all this time) sticks by *his*. Talk to him of Whig or Tory, he grins at them: of virtual representation, pish! He is a *democrat*, and will stand by his friends, as you by yours; and they are twenty millions, his friends, of whom a vast minority now, a majority a few years hence, will be as good as you. In the meantime we shall continue electing, and debating, and dividing, and having every day new triumphs for the glorious cause of Conservatism, or the glorious cause of Reform, until—

What is the meaning of this unconscionable republican tirade – *àpropos* of a hanging? Such feelings, I think, must come across any man in a vast multitude like this. What good sense and intelligence have most of the people by whom you are surrounded; how much sound humour does one hear bandied about from one to another! A great number of coarse phrases are used, that would make ladies in drawing-rooms blush; but the morals of the men are good and hearty. A ragamuffin in the crowd (a powdery baker in a white sheep's-wool cap) uses some indecent expression to a woman near: there is an instant cry of shame, which silences the man, and a dozen people are ready to give the woman protection. The crowd has grown very dense by this time, it is about six o'clock, and there is great heaving, and pushing, and swaying to and fro; but round the women the men have formed a circle, and keep them as much as possible out of the rush and trample. In one of the houses near us, a gallery has been formed on the roof. Seats were here let, and a number of persons of various degrees were occupying them. Several tipsy, dissolute-looking young men, of the Dick Swiveller cast, were in this gallery. One was lolling over the sunshiny tiles, with a fierce sodden face, out of which came a pipe, and which was shaded by long matted hair, and a hat cocked very much on one side. This gentleman was one of a party which had evidently not been to bed on Sunday night, but had passed it in some of those delectable night-houses in the neighbourhood of Covent Garden. The debauch was not over yet, and the women of the party were giggling, drinking, and romping, as is the wont of these delicate creatures; sprawling here and there, and falling upon the knees of one or other of the males. Their scarfs were off their shoulders, and you saw the sun shining down upon the bare white flesh, and the shoulder-points glittering like burning-glasses. The people about us were very indignant at some of the proceedings of this debauched crew, and at last raised up such a yell as frightened them into shame, and they were more orderly for the remainder of the day. The windows of the shops opposite began to fill apace, and our before-mentioned friend with ragged elbows pointed out a celebrated fashionable character who occupied one of them; and, to our surprise, knew as much about him as the *Court Journal* or the *Morning Post*. Presently he entertained us with a long and pretty accurate account of the history of Lady —, and indulged in a judicious criticism upon her last work. I have met with many a country gentleman who had not read half as many books as this honest fellow, this shrewd *prolétaire* in a black shirt. The people about him took up and carried on the conversation very knowingly, and were very little behind him in point of information. It was just as good a company as one meets on common occasions. I was in a genteel crowd in one of the galleries at the Queen's coronation; indeed, in point of intelligence, the democrats were quite equal to the aristocrats. How many more such groups were there in this immense multitude of nearly forty thousand, as some say? How many more such throughout the country? I never yet, as I said before, have been in an English mob, without the same feeling for the persons who composed it, and without wonder at the vigorous orderly good sense and intelligence of the people.

The character of the crowd was as yet, however, quite festive. Jokes bandying about here and there, and jolly laughs breaking out. Some men were endeavouring to climb up a leaden pipe on one of the houses. The landlord came out, and endeavoured with might and main to pull them down. Many thousand eyes turned upon this contest immediately. All sorts of voices issued from the crowd, and uttered choice expressions of slang. When one of the men was pulled down by the leg, the waves of this black mob-ocean laughed innumerably; when one fellow slipped away, scrambled up the pipe, and made good his lodgment on the shelf, we were all made happy, and encouraged him by loud shouts of admiration. What is there so particularly delightful in the spectacle of a man clambering up a gas-pipe? Why were we kept for a

quarter of an hour in deep interest gazing upon this remarkable scene? Indeed it is hard to say: a man does not know
what a fool he is until he tries; or, at least, what mean follies
will amuse him. The other day I went to Astley's, and saw
clown come in with a foolscap and pinafore, and six small
boys who represented his school-fellows. To them enters
schoolmaster; horses clown, and flogs him hugely on the
back part of his pinafore. I never read anything in Swift, Boz,
Rabelais, Fielding, Paul de Kock, which delighted me so
much as this sight, and caused me to laugh so profoundly.
And why? What is there so ridiculous in the sight of one
miserably rouged man beating another on the breech? Tell
us where the fun lies in this and the before-mentioned
episode of the gas-pipe? Vast, indeed, are the capacities and
ingenuities of the human soul that can find, in incidents so
wonderfully small, means of contemplation and amusement.

Really the time passed away with extraordinary quickness.
A thousand things of the sort related here came to amuse us.
First the workmen knocking and hammering at the scaffold,
mysterious clattering of blows was heard within it, and a
ladder painted black was carried round, and into the interior
of the edifice by a small side-door. We all looked at this little
ladder and at each other – things began to be very interesting.
Soon came a squad of policemen; stalwart, rosy-looking
men, saying much for City feeding; well-dressed, well-
limbed, and of admirable good-humour. They paced about
the open space between the prison and the barriers which
kept in the crowd from the scaffold. The front line, as far as
I could see, was chiefly occupied by blackguards and boys –
professional persons, no doubt, who saluted the policemen
on their appearance with a volley of jokes and ribaldry.
As far as I could judge from faces, there were more blackguards of sixteen and seventeen than of any maturer age;

stunted, sallow, ill-grown lads, in rugged fustian, scowling about. There were a considerable number of girls, too, of the same age; one that Cruikshank and Boz might have taken as a study for Nancy. The girl was a young thief's mistress evidently; if attacked, ready to reply without a particle of modesty; could give as good ribaldry as she got; made no secret (and there were several inquiries) as to her profession and means of livelihood. But with all this, there was something good about the girl; a sort of devil-may-care candour and simplicity that one could not fail to see. Her answers to some of the coarse questions put to her, were very ready and good-humoured. She had a friend with her of the same age and class, of whom she seemed to be very fond, and who looked up to her for protection. Both of these women had beautiful eyes. Devil-may-care's were extraordinarily bright and blue, an admirably fair complexion, and a large red mouth full of white teeth. *Au reste*, ugly, stunted, thick-limbed, and by no means a beauty. Her friend could not be more than fifteen. They were not in rags, but had greasy cotton shawls, and old, faded, rag-shop bonnets. I was curious to look at them, having, in late fashionable novels, read many accounts of such personages. Bah! what figments these novelists tell us! Boz, who knows life well, knows that his Miss Nancy is the most unreal fantastical personage possible; no more like a thief's mistress than one of Gesner's shepherdesses resembles a real country wench. He dare not tell the truth concerning such young ladies. They have, no doubt, virtues like other human creatures; nay, their position engenders virtues that are not called into exercise among other women. But on these an honest painter of human nature has no right to dwell; not being able to paint the whole portrait, he has no right to present one or two favourable points as characterizing the whole; and therefore, in fact, had better leave the picture alone altogether. The new French literature is essentially false and worthless from this very error – the writers giving us favourable pictures of monsters, and (to say nothing of decency or morality) pictures quite untrue to nature.

But yonder, glittering through the crowd in Newgate Street – see, the Sheriffs' carriages are slowly making their way. We have been here three hours! Is it possible that they can have passed so soon? Close to the barriers where we are, the mob has become so dense that it is with difficulty a man can keep his feet. Each man, however, is very careful in protecting the women, and all are full of jokes and good-humour. The windows of the shops opposite are now pretty nearly filled by the persons who hired them. Many young dandies are there with moustaches and cigars; some quiet, fat, family-parties, of simple, honest tradesmen and their wives, as we fancy, who are looking on with the greatest imaginable calmness, and sipping their tea. Yonder is the sham Lord W—, who is flinging various articles among the crowd; one of his companions, a tall, burly man, with large moustaches, has provided himself with a squirt, and is aspersing the mob with brandy-and-water. Honest gentleman! high-bred aristocrat! genuine lover of humour and wit! I would walk some miles to see thee on the tread-mill, thee and thy Mohawk crew!

We tried to get up a hiss against these ruffians, but only had a trifling success; the crowd did not seem to think their offence very heinous; and our friend, the philosopher in the ragged elbows, who had remained near us all the time, was not inspired with any such savage disgust at the proceedings of certain notorious young gentlemen, as I must confess fills my own particular bosom. He only said, 'So-and-so is a lord, and they'll let him off,' and then discoursed about Lord

Ferrers being hanged. The philosopher knew the history pretty well, and so did most of the little knot of persons about him, and it must be a gratifying thing for young gentlemen to find that their actions are made the subject of this kind of conversation.

Scarcely a word had been said about Courvoisier all this time. We were all, as far as I could judge, in just such a frame of mind as men are in when they are squeezing at the pit-door of a play, or pushing for a review or a Lord Mayor's show. We asked most of the men who were near us, whether they had seen many executions? most of them had, the philosopher especially; whether the sight of them did any good? 'For the matter of that, no; people did not care about them at all; nobody ever thought of it after a bit.' A countryman, who had left his drove in Smithfield, said the same thing; he had seen a man hanged at York, and spoke of the ceremony with perfect good sense, and in a quiet, sagacious way.

J. S—, the famous wit, now dead, had, I recollect, a good story upon the subject of executing, and of the terror which the punishment inspires. After Thistlewood and his companions were hanged, their heads were taken off, according to the sentence, and the executioner, as he severed each, held it up to the crowd, in the proper orthodox way, saying, 'Here is the head of a traitor!' At the sight of the first ghastly head the people were struck with terror, and a general expression of disgust and fear broke from them. The second head was looked at also with much interest, but the excitement regarding the third head diminished. When the executioner had come to the last of the heads, he lifted it up, but, by some clumsiness, allowed it to drop. At this the crowd yelled out, '*Ah, Butter-fingers!*' – the excitement had passed entirely away. The punishment had grown to be a joke –

Butter-fingers was the word – a pretty commentary, indeed, upon the august nature of public executions, and the awful majesty of the law.

It was past seven now; the quarters rang and passed away; the crowd began to grow very eager and more quiet, and we turned back every now and then and looked at St Sepulchre's clock. Half an hour, twenty-five minutes. What is he doing now? He has his irons off by this time. A quarter: he's in the press-room now, no doubt. Now at last we had come to think about the man we were going to see hanged. How slowly the clock crept over the last quarter! Those who were able to turn round and see (for the crowd was now extra-ordinarily dense) chronicled the time, eight minutes, five minutes; at last – ding, dong, dong, dong! – the bell is tolling the chimes of eight.

Between the writing of this line and the last, the pen has been put down, as the reader may suppose, and the person who is addressing him has gone through a pause of no very pleasant thoughts and recollections. The whole of the sickening, ghastly, wicked scene passes before the eyes again; and, indeed, it is an awful one to see, and very hard and painful to describe.

As the clock began to strike, an immense sway and move-ment swept over the whole of that vast dense crowd. They were all uncovered directly, and a great murmur arose, more awful, bizarre, and indescribable than any sound I had ever before heard. Women and children began to shriek horridly. I don't know whether it was the bell I heard; but a dreadful quick, feverish kind of jangling noise mingled with the noise of the people, and lasted for about two minutes. The scaffold stood before us, tenantless and black; the black chain was hanging down ready from the beam. Nobody came. 'He has been respited,' some one said; another said, 'He has killed himself in prison.'

Just then, from under the black prison-door, a pale, quiet head peered out. It was shockingly bright and distinct; it rose up directly, and a man in black appeared on the scaffold, and was silently followed by about four more dark figures. The first was a tall grave man: we all knew who the second man was. '*That's he – that's he!*' you heard the people say, as the devoted man came up.

I have seen a cast of the head since, but, indeed, should never have known it. Courvoisier bore his punishment like a man, and walked very firmly. He was dressed in a new black suit, as it seemed: his shirt was open. His arms were tied in front of him. He opened his hands in a helpless kind of way, and clasped them once or twice together. He turned his head here and there, and looked about him for an instant with a wild, imploring look. His mouth was contracted into a sort of pitiful smile. He went and placed himself at once under the beam, with his face towards St Sepulchre's. The tall, grave man in black twisted him round swiftly in the other direction, and, drawing from his pocket a nightcap, pulled it tight over the patient's head and face. I am not ashamed to say that I could look no more, but shut my eyes as the last dreadful act was going on, which sent this wretched, guilty soul into the presence of God.

If a public execution is beneficial – and beneficial it is, no doubt, or else the wise laws would not encourage forty thousand people to witness it – the next useful thing must be a full description of such a ceremony, and all its *entourages*, and to this end the above pages are offered to the reader. How does an individual man feel under it? In what way does he observe it, – how does he view all the phenomena connected with it, – what induces him, in the first instance, to go and see it, – and how is he moved by it afterwards? The writer has discarded the magazine 'We' altogether, and spoken face to face with the reader, recording every one of the impressions felt by him as honestly as he could.

I must confess, then (for 'I' is the shortest word, and the best in this case), that the sight has left on my mind an extraordinary feeling of terror and shame. It seems to me that I have been abetting an act of frightful wickedness and violence, performed by a set of men against one of their fellows; and I pray God that it may soon be out of the power of any man in England to witness such a hideous and degrading sight. Forty thousand persons (say the Sheriffs), of all ranks and degrees, – mechanics, gentlemen, pickpockets, members of both Houses of Parliament, street-walkers, newspaper-writers, gather together before Newgate at a very early hour; the most part of them give up their natural quiet night's rest, in order to partake of this hideous debauchery, which is more exciting than sleep, or than wine, or the last new ballet, or any other amusement they can have. Pickpocket and Peer each is tickled by the sight alike, and has that hidden lust after blood which influences our race. Government, a Christian government, gives us a feast every now and then: it agrees – that is to say – a majority in the two Houses agrees, that for certain crimes it is necessary that a man should be hanged by the neck. Government commits the criminal's soul to the mercy of God, stating that here on earth he is to look for no mercy; keeps him for a fortnight to prepare, provides him with a clergyman to settle his religious matters (if there be time enough, but Government can't wait); and on a Monday morning, the bell tolling, the clergyman reading out the word of God, 'I am the resurrection and the life,'

'The Lord giveth and the Lord taketh away,' – on a Monday morning, at eight o'clock, this man is placed under a beam, with a rope connecting it and him; a plank disappears from under him, and those who have paid for good places may see the hands of the Government agent, Jack Ketch, coming up from his black hole, and seizing the prisoner's legs, and pulling them, until he is quite dead – strangled.

Many persons, and well-informed newspapers, say that it is mawkish sentiment to talk in this way, morbid humanity, cheap philanthropy, that any man can get up and preach about. There is the *Observer*, for instance, a paper conspicuous for the tremendous sarcasm which distinguishes its articles, and which falls cruelly foul of the *Morning Herald*. 'Courvoisier is dead,' says the *Observer*; 'he died as he had lived – a villain; a lie was in his mouth. Peace be to his ashes. We war not with the dead.' What a magnanimous *Observer*! From this, *Observer* turns to the *Herald*, and says, '*Fiat justitia ruat cœlum.*' So much for the *Herald*.

We quote from memory, and the quotation from the *Observer* possibly is, – *De mortuis nil nisi bonum*; or, *Omne ignotum pro magnifico*; or, *Sero nunquam est ad bonos mores via*; or, *Ingenuas didicisse fideliter artes emollit mores nec sinit esse feros*: all of which pithy Roman apophthegms would apply just as well.

'Peace be to his ashes. He died a villain.' This is both benevolence and reason. Did he die a villain? The *Observer* does not want to destroy him body and soul, evidently, from that pious wish that his ashes should be at peace. Is the next Monday but one after the sentence the time necessary for a villain to repent in? May a man not require more leisure – a week more – six months more – before he has been able to make his repentance sure before Him who died for us all? – for all, be it remembered, – not alone for the judge and jury, or for the sheriffs, or for the executioner who is pulling down the legs of the prisoner, – but for him too, murderer and criminal as he is, whom we are killing for his crime. Do we want to kill him body and soul? Heaven forbid! My lord in the black cap specially prays that heaven may have mercy on him; but he must be ready by Monday morning.

Look at the documents which came from the prison of this unhappy Courvoisier during the few days which passed between his trial and execution. Were ever letters more painful to read? At first, his statements are false, contradictory, lying. He has not repented then. His last declaration seems to be honest, as far as the relation of the crime goes. But read the rest of his statement, the account of his personal history, and the crimes which he committed in his young days, – then 'how the evil thought came to him to put his hand to the work,' – it is evidently the writing of a mad, distracted man. The horrid gallows is perpetually before him; he is wild with dread and remorse. Clergymen are with him ceaselessly; religious tracts are forced into his hands; night and day they ply him with the heinousness of his crime, and exhortations to repentance. Read through that last paper of his; by heaven, it is pitiful to read it. See the Scripture phrases brought in now and anon; the peculiar terms of tract-phraseology (I do not wish to speak of these often meritorious publications with disrespect); one knows too well how such language is learned, – imitated from the priest at the bed-side, eagerly seized and appropriated, and confounded by the poor prisoner.

But murder is such a monstrous crime (this is the great argument), – when a man has killed another it is natural that he should be killed. Away with your foolish sentimentalists who say no – it is *natural*. That is the word, and a fine philosophical opinion it is – philosophical and Christian. Kill a man, and you must be killed in turn; that is the unavoidable *sequitur.* You may talk to a man for a year upon the subject, and he will always reply to you, 'It is natural, and therefore it must be done. Blood demands blood.'

Does it? The system of compensations might be carried on *ad infinitum,* – an eye for an eye, a tooth for a tooth, as by the old Mosaic law. But (putting the fact out of the question, that we have had this statute repealed by the Highest Authority), why, because you lose your eye, is that of your opponent to be extracted likewise? Where is the reason for the practice? And yet it is just as natural as the death dictum, founded precisely upon the same show of sense. Knowing, however, that revenge is not only evil, but useless, we have given it up on all minor points. Only to the last we stick firm, contrary though it be to reason and to Christian law.

There is some talk, too, of the terror which the sight of this spectacle inspires, and of this we have endeavoured to give as good a notion as we can in the above pages. I fully confess that I came away down Snow Hill that morning with a disgust for murder, but it was for *the murder I saw done.* As we made our way through the immense crowd, we came upon two little girls of eleven and twelve years: one of them was crying bitterly, and begged, for heaven's sake, that some one would lead her from that horrid place. This was done, and the children were carried into a place of safety. We asked the elder girl – and a very pretty one – what brought her into such a neighbourhood? The child grinned knowingly, and said, 'We've koom to see the mon hanged!' Tender law, that brings out babes upon such errands, and provides them with such gratifying moral spectacles!

This is the 20th of July, and I may be permitted for my part to declare that, for the last fourteen days, so salutary has the impression of the butchery been upon me, I have had the man's face continually before my eyes; that I can see

Mr Ketch at this moment, with an easy air, taking the rope from his pocket; that I feel myself ashamed and degraded at the brutal curiosity which took me to that brutal sight; and that I pray to Almighty God to cause this disgraceful sin to pass from among us, and to cleanse our land of blood.

HENRY MAYHEW

WATERCRESS GIRL
(1851)

THE LITTLE WATERCRESS girl who gave me the following statement, although only eight years of age, had entirely lost all childish ways, and was, indeed, in thoughts and manner, a woman. There was something cruelly pathetic in hearing this infant, so young that her features had scarcely formed themselves, talking of the bitterest struggles of life, with the calm earnestness of one who had endured them all. I did not know how to talk with her. At first I treated her as a child, speaking on childish subjects; so that I might, by being familiar with her, remove all shyness, and get her to narrate her life freely. I asked her about her toys and her games with her companions; but the look of amazement that answered me soon put an end to any attempt at fun on my part. I then talked to her about the parks, and whether she ever went to them. 'The parks!' she replied in wonder, 'where are they?' I explained to her, telling her that they were large open places with green grass and tall trees, where beautiful carriages drove about, and people walked for pleasure, and children played. Her eyes brightened up a little as I spoke; and she asked, half doubtingly, 'Would they let such as me go there – just to look?' All her knowledge seemed to begin and end with watercresses, and what they fetched. She knew no more of London than that part she had seen on her rounds, and believed that no quarter of the town was handsomer or pleas-anter than it was at Farringdon-market or at Clerkenwell, where she lived. Her little face, pale and thin with privation, was wrinkled where the dimples ought to have been, and she would sigh frequently. When some hot dinner was offered to her, she would not touch it, because, if she eat too much, 'it made her sick,' she said; 'and she wasn't used to meat, only on a Sunday.'

The poor child, although the weather was severe, was dressed in a thin cotton gown, with a threadbare shawl wrapped round her shoulders. She wore no covering to her head, and the long rusty hair stood out in all directions. When she walked she shuffled along, for fear that the large carpet slippers that served her for shoes should slip off her feet.

'I go about the streets with watercreases, crying, "Four bunches a penny, watercreases." I am just eight years old – that's all, and I've a big sister, and a brother and a sister younger than I am. On and off, I've been very near a twelve-month in the streets. Before that, I had to take care of a baby for my aunt. No, it wasn't heavy – it was only two months old; but I minded it for ever such a time – till it could walk. It was a very nice little baby, not a very pretty one; but, if I touched it under the chin, it would laugh. Before I had the baby, I used to help mother, who was in the fur trade; and, if there was any slits in the fur, I'd sew them up. My mother learned me to needle-work and to knit when I was about five. I used to go to school, too; but I wasn't there long. I've forgot all about it now, it's such a time ago; and mother took me away because the master whacked me, though the missus use'n't to never touch me. I didn't like him at all. What do you think? he hit me three times, ever so hard, across the face with his cane, and made me go dancing down stairs; and when mother saw the marks on my cheek, she went to blow him up, but she couldn't see him – he was afraid. That's why I left school.

'The creases is so bad now, that I haven't been out with

'em for three days. They're so cold, people won't buy 'em; for when I goes up to them, they say, "They'll freeze our bellies." Besides, in the market, they won't sell a ha'penny handful now – they're ris to a penny and tuppence. In summer there's lots, and 'most as cheap as dirt; but I have to be down at Farringdon-market between four and five, or else I can't get any creases, because everyone almost – especially the Irish – is selling them, and they're picked up so quick. Some of the saleswomen – we never calls 'em ladies – is very kind to us children, and some of them altogether spiteful. The good one will give you a bunch for nothing, when they're cheap; but the others, cruel ones, if you try to bate them a farden less than they ask you, will say, "Go along with you, you're no good." I used to go down to market along with another girl, as must be about fourteen, 'cos she does her back hair up. When we've bought a lot, we sits down on a door-step, and ties up the bunches. We never goes home to breakfast till we've sold out; but, if it's very late, then I buys a penn'orth of pudden, which is very nice with gravy. I don't know hardly one of the people, as goes to Farringdon, to talk to; they never speaks to me, so I don't speak to them. We children never play down there, 'cos we're thinking of our living. No; people never pities me in the street – excepting one gentle-man, and he says, says he, "What do you do out so soon in the morning?" but he gave me nothink – he only walked away.

'It's very cold before winter comes on reg'lar – specially getting up of a morning. I gets up in the dark by the light of the lamp in the court. When the snow is on the ground, there's no creases. I bears the cold – you must; so I puts my hands under my shawl, though it hurts 'em to take hold of the creases, especially when we takes 'em to the pump to wash 'em. No; I never see any children crying – it's no use.

'Sometimes I make a great deal of money. One day I took 1*s*. 6*d*., and the creases cost 6*d*.; but it isn't often I get such luck as that. I oftener makes 3*d*. or 4*d*. than 1*s*.; and then I'm at work, crying, "Creases, four bunches a penny, creases!" from six in the morning to about ten. What do you mean by mechanics? – I don't know what they are. The shops buys most of me. Some of 'em says, "Oh! I ain't a-goin' to give a penny for these"; and they want 'em at the same price as I buys 'em at.

'I always give mother my money, she's so very good to me. She don't often beat me; but, when she do, she don't play with me. She's very poor, and goes out cleaning rooms some-times, now she don't work at the fur. I ain't got no father, he's a father-in-law. No; mother ain't married again – he's a father-in-law. He grinds scissors, and he's very good to me. No; I don't mean by that that he says kind things to me, for he never hardly speaks. When I gets home, after selling creases, I stops at home. I puts the room to rights: mother don't make me do it, I does it myself. I cleans the chairs, though there's only two to clean. I takes a tub and scrubbing-brush and flannel, and scrubs the floor – that's what I do three or four times a week.

'I don't have no dinner. Mother gives me two slices of bread-and-butter and a cup of tea for breakfast, and then I go till tea, and has the same. We has meat of a Sunday, and, of course, I should like to have it every day. Mother has just the same to eat as we has, but she takes more tea – three cups, sometimes. No; I never has no sweet-stuff; I never buy none – I don't like it. Sometimes we has a game of "honey-pots" with the girls in the court, but not often. Me and Carry H— carries the little 'uns. We plays, too, at "kiss-in-the-ring." I knows a good many games, but I don't play at 'em, 'cos going out with creases tires me. On a Friday night, too,

I goes to a Jew's house till eleven o'clock on Saturday night. All I has to do is to snuff the candles and poke the fire. You see they keep their Sabbath then, and they won't touch anything; so they gives me my wittals and $1\frac{1}{2}d$., and I does it for 'em. I have a reg'lar good lot to eat. Supper of Friday night, and tea after that, and fried fish of a Saturday morning, and meat for dinner, and tea, and supper, and I like it very well.

'Oh, yes; I've got some toys at home. I've a fire-place, and a box of toys, and a knife and fork, and two little chairs. The Jews gave 'em to me where I go to on a Friday, and that's why I said they was very kind to me. I never had no doll; but I misses little sister – she's only two years old. We don't sleep in the same room; for father and mother sleeps with little sister in the one pair, and me and brother and other sister sleeps in the top room. I always goes to bed at seven, 'cos I has to be up so early.

'I am a capital hand at bargaining – but only at buying watercreases. They can't take me in. If the woman tries to give me a small handful of creases, I says, "I ain't a goin' to have that for a ha'porth," and I go to the next basket, and so on, all round. I know the quantities very well. For a penny I ought to have a full market hand, or as much as I could carry in my arms at one time, without spilling. For $3d$. I has a lap full, enough to earn about a shilling; and for $6d$. I gets as many as crams my basket. I can't read or write, but I knows how many pennies goes to a shilling, why, twelve, of course, but I don't know how many ha'pence there is, though there's two to a penny. When I've bought $3d$. of creases, I ties 'em up into as many little bundles as I can. They must look biggish, or the people won't buy them, some puffs them out as much as they'll go. All my money I earns I puts in a club and draws it out to buy clothes with. It's better than spending it in sweet-stuff, for them as has a living to earn. Besides it's like a child to care for sugar-sticks, and not like one who's got a living and vittals to earn. I ain't a child, and I shan't be a woman till I'm twenty, but I'm past eight, I am. I don't know nothing about what I earns during the year, I only know how many pennies goes to a shilling, and two ha'pence goes to a penny, and four fardens goes to a penny. I knows, too, how many fardens goes to tuppence – eight. That's as much as I wants to know for the markets.'

CHARLES DICKENS

DOWN WITH THE TIDE
(1853)

A VERY DARK night it was, and bitter cold; the east wind blowing bleak, and bringing with it stinging particles from marsh, and moor, and fen – from the Great Desert and Old Egypt, may be. Some of the component parts of the sharp-edged vapour that came flying up the Thames at London might be mummy-dust, dry atoms from the Temple at Jerusalem, camels' foot-prints, crocodiles' hatching places, loosened grains of expression from the visages of blunt-nosed sphynxes, waifs and strays from caravans of turbaned merchants, vegetation from jungles, frozen snow from the Himalayas. O! It was very very dark upon the Thames, and it was bitter bitter cold.

'And yet,' said the voice within the great pea-coat at my side, 'you'll have seen a good many rivers too, I dare say?'

'Truly,' said I, 'when I come to think of it, not a few. From the Niagara, downward to the mountain rivers of Italy, which are like the national spirit – very tame, or chafing suddenly and bursting bounds, only to dwindle away again. The Moselle, and the Rhine, and the Rhone; and the Seine, and the Saône; and the St Lawrence, Mississippi, and Ohio; and the Tiber, the Po, and the Arno; and the—'

Peacoat coughing as if he had had enough of that, I said no more. I could have carried the catalogue on to a teasing length, though, if I had been in the cruel mind.

'And after all,' said he, 'this looks so dismal?'

'So awful,' I returned, 'at night. The Seine at Paris is very gloomy too, at such a time, and is probably the scene of far more crime and greater wickedness; but this river looks so broad and vast, so murky and silent, seems such an image of death in the midst of the great city's life, that—'

That Peacoat coughed again. He *could not* stand my holding forth.

We were in a four-oared Thames Police Galley, lying on our oars in the deep shadow of Southwark Bridge – under the corner arch on the Surrey side – having come down with the tide from Vauxhall. We were fain to hold on pretty tight, though close in shore, for the river was swollen and the tide running down very strong. We were watching certain water-rats of human growth, and lay in the deep shade as quiet as mice; our light hidden and our scraps of conversation carried on in whispers. Above us, the massive iron girders of the arch were faintly visible, and below us its ponderous shadow seemed to sink down to the bottom of the stream.

We had been lying here some half an hour. With our backs to the wind, is it true; but the wind being in a determined temper blew straight through us, and would not take the trouble to go round. I would have boarded a fireship to get into action, and mildly suggested as much to my friend Pea.

'No doubt,' says he as patiently as possible; 'but shore-going tactics wouldn't do with us. River thieves can always get rid of stolen property in a moment by dropping it overboard. We want to take them *with* the property, so we lurk about and come out upon 'em sharp. If they see us or hear us, over it goes.'

Pea's wisdom being indisputable, there was nothing for it but to sit there and be blown through, for another half hour. The water-rats thinking it wise to abscond at the end of that time without commission of felony, we shot out, disappointed, with the tide.

'Grim they look, don't they?' said Pea, seeing me glance over my shoulder at the lights upon the bridge, and downward at their long crooked reflections in the river.

'Very,' said I, 'and make one think with a shudder of Suicides. What a night for a dreadful leap from that parapet!'

'Aye, but Waterloo's the favourite bridge for making holes in the water from,' returned Pea. 'By the bye – avast pulling lads! – would you like to speak to Waterloo on the subject?'

My face confessing to a surprised desire to have some friendly conversation with Waterloo Bridge, and my friend Pea being the most obliging of men, we put about, pulled out of the force of the stream, and in place of going at great speed with the tide, began to strive against it, close in shore again. Every colour but black seemed to have departed from the world. The air was black, the water was black, the barges and hulks were black, the piles were black, the buildings were black, the shadows were only a deeper shade of black upon a black ground. Here and there, a coal fire in an iron cresset blazed upon a wharf; but one knew that it too had been black a little while ago, and would be black again soon. Uncomfortable rushes of water suggestive of gurgling and drowning, ghostly rattlings of iron chains, dismal clankings of discordant engines, formed the music that accompanied the dip of our oars and their rattling in the rullocks. Even the noises had a black sound to me – as the trumpet sounded red to the blind man.

Our dexterous boat's crew made nothing of the tide, and pulled us gallantly up to Waterloo Bridge. Here Pea and I disembarked, passed under the black stone archway, and climbed the steep stone steps. Within a few feet of their summit, Pea presented me to Waterloo (or an eminent tolltaker representing that structure), muffled up to the eyes in a thick shawl, and amply great-coated and fur-capped.

Waterloo received us with cordiality, and observed of the night that it was 'a Searcher.' He had been originally called the Strand Bridge, he informed us, but had received his present name at the suggestion of the proprietors, when Parliament had resolved to vote three hundred thousand pound for the erection of a monument in honour of the victory. Parliament took the hint (said Waterloo, with the least flavour of misanthropy), and saved the money. Of course the late Duke of Wellington was the first passenger, and of course he paid his penny, and of course a noble lord preserved it evermore. The treadle and index at the toll-house (a most ingenious contrivance for rendering fraud impossible), were invented by Mr Lethbridge, then property-man at Drury Lane Theatre.

Was it suicide, we wanted to know about? said Waterloo. Ha! Well, he had seen a good deal of that work, he did assure us. He had prevented some. Why, one day a woman, poorish looking, came in between the hatch, slapped down a penny, and wanted to go on without the change! Waterloo suspected this, and says to his mate, 'give an eye to the gate,' and bolted after her. She had got to the third seat between the piers, and was on the parapet just a going over, when he caught her and gave her in charge. At the police office next morning, she said it was along of trouble and a bad husband.

'Likely enough,' observed Waterloo to Pea and myself, as he adjusted his chin in his shawl. 'There's a deal of trouble about, you see – and bad husbands too!'

Another time, a young woman at twelve o'clock in the open day, got through, darted along; and, before Waterloo could come near her, jumped upon the parapet, and shot herself over sideways. Alarm given, watermen put off, lucky escape. – Clothes buoyed her up.

'This is where it is,' said Waterloo. 'If people jump off

straight forards from the middle of the parapet of the bays of the bridge, they are seldom killed by drowning, but are smashed, poor things; that's what *they* are; they dash themselves upon the buttress of the bridge. But, you jump off,' said Waterloo to me, putting his forefinger in a button hole of my great coat; 'you jump off from the side of the bay, and you'll tumble, true, into the stream under the arch. What you have got to do, is to mind how you jump in! There was poor Tom Steele from Dublin. Didn't dive! Bless you, didn't dive at all! Fell down so flat into the water, that he broke his breast-bone, and lived two days!'

I asked Waterloo if there were a favourite side of his bridge for this dreadful purpose? He reflected, and thought yes, there was. He should say the Surrey side.

Three decent looking men went through one day, soberly and quietly, and went on abreast for about a dozen yards; when the middle one, he sung out, all of a sudden, 'Here goes, Jack!' and was over in a minute.

Body found? Well. Waterloo didn't rightly recollect about that. They were compositors, *they* were.

He considered it astonishing how quick people were! Why, there was a cab came up one Boxing-night, with a young woman in it, who looked, according to Waterloo's opinion of her, a little the worse for liquor; very handsome she was too – very handsome. She stopped the cab at the gate, and said she'd pay the cabman then: which she did, though there was a little hankering about the fare, because at first she didn't seem quite to know where she wanted to be drove to. However she paid the man, and the toll too, and looking Waterloo in the face (he thought she knew him, don't you see!) said, 'I'll finish it somehow!' Well, the cab went off, leaving Waterloo a little doubtful in his mind, and while it was going on at full speed the young woman jumped out, never fell, hardly staggered, ran along the bridge pavement a little way passing several people, and jumped over from the second opening. At the inquest it was giv' in evidence that she had been quarrelling at the Hero of Waterloo, and it was brought in jealousy. (One of the results of Waterloo's experience was, that there was a deal of jealousy about.)

'Do we ever get madmen?' said Waterloo in answer to an inquiry of mine. 'Well, we *do* get madmen. Yes, we have had one or two; escaped from 'Sylums, I suppose. One hadn't a halfpenny; and because I wouldn't let him through, he went back a little way, stooped down, took a run, and butted at the hatch like a ram. He smashed his hat rarely, but his head didn't seem no worse – in my opinion on account of his being wrong in it afore. Sometimes people haven't got a halfpenny. If they are really tired and poor we give 'em one and let 'em through. Other people will leave things – pocket handkerchiefs mostly. I *have* taken cravats and gloves, pocket knives, toothpicks, studs, shirt pins, rings (generally from young gents, early in the morning), but handkerchiefs is the general thing.

'Regular customers?' said Waterloo, 'Lord, yes! We have regular customers. One, such a worn out used-up old file as you can scarcely picter, comes from the Surrey side as regular as ten o'clock at night comes; and goes over, *I* think, to some flash house on the Middlesex side. He comes back, he does, as reg'lar as the clock strikes three in the morning, and then can hardly drag one of his old legs after the other. He always turns down the water-stairs, comes up again, and then goes on down the Waterloo Road. He always does the same thing, and never varies a minute. Does it every night – even Sundays.'

I asked Waterloo if he had given his mind to the possibility of this particular customer going down the water-stairs at three o'clock some morning, and never coming up again? He didn't think *that* of him, he replied. In fact, it was Waterloo's opinion, founded on his observation of that file, that he know'd a trick worth two of it.

'There's another queer old customer,' said Waterloo, 'comes over as punctual as the almanack, at eleven o'clock on the sixth of January, at eleven o'clock on the fifth of April, at eleven o'clock on the sixth of July, at eleven o'clock on the tenth of October. Drives a shaggy little, rough poney, in a sort of a rattle-trap arm-chair sort of a thing. White hair he has, and white whiskers, and muffles himself up with all manner of shawls. He comes back again the same afternoon, and we never see more of him for three months. He is a captain in the navy – retired – wery old – wery odd – and served with Lord Nelson. He is particular about drawing his pension at Somerset House afore the clock strikes twelve every quarter. I *have* heerd say that he thinks it wouldn't be according to the Act of Parliament, if he didn't draw it afore twelve.'

Having related these anecdotes in a natural manner, which was the best warranty in the world for their genuine nature, our friend Waterloo was sinking deep into his shawl again, as having exhausted his communicative powers and taken in enough east wind, when my other friend Pea in a moment brought him to the surface by asking whether he had not been occasionally the subject of assault and battery in the execution of his duty? Waterloo recovering his spirits, instantly dashed into a new branch of his subject. We learnt how 'both these teeth' – here he pointed to the places where two front teeth were not – were knocked out by an ugly customer who one night made a dash at him (Waterloo) while his (the ugly customer's) pal and coadjutor made a dash at the toll-taking apron where the money-pockets were; how

Waterloo, letting the teeth go (to Blazes, he observed indefinitely) grappled with the apron-seizer, permitting the ugly one to run away; and how he saved the bank, and captured his man, and consigned him to fine and imprisonment. Also how, on another night, 'a Cove' laid hold of Waterloo, then presiding at the horse gate of his bridge, and threw him unceremoniously over his knee, having first cut his head open with his whip. How Waterloo 'got right,' and started after the Cove all down the Waterloo Road, through Stamford Street, and round to the foot of Blackfriars Bridge, where the Cove 'cut into' a public-house. How Waterloo cut in too; but how an aider and abettor of the Cove's, who happened to be taking a promiscuous drain at the bar, stopped Waterloo; and the Cove cut out again, ran across the road down Holland Street, and where not, and into a beershop. How Waterloo breaking away from his detainer was close upon the Cove's heels, attended by no end of people who, seeing him running with the blood streaming down his face, thought something worse was 'up,' and roared Fire! and Murder! on the hopeful chance of the matter in hand being one or both. How the Cove was ignominiously taken, in a shed where he had run to hide, and how at the Police Court they at first wanted to make a sessions job of it: but eventually Waterloo was allowed to be 'spoke to,' and the Cove made it square with Waterloo by paying his doctor's bill (W. was laid up for a week) and giving him 'Three, ten.' Likewise we learnt what we had faintly suspected before, that your sporting amateur on the Derby day, albeit a captain, can be – 'if he be,' as Captain Bobadil observes, 'so generously minded' – anything but a man of honour and a gentleman; not sufficiently gratifying his nice sense of humour by the witty scattering of flour and rotten eggs on obtuse civilians, but requiring the further excitement of 'bilking the toll,' and 'pitching into' Waterloo, and 'cutting him about the head with his whip'; finally being, when called upon to answer for the assault, what Waterloo described as 'Minus,' or, as I humbly conceived it, not to be found. Likewise did Waterloo inform us, in reply to my inquiries, admiringly and deferentially preferred through my friend Pea, that the takings at the Bridge had more than doubled in amount, since the reduction of the toll one half. And being asked if the aforesaid takings included much bad money, Waterloo responded, with a look far deeper than the deepest part of the river, *he* should think not! – and so retired into his shawl for the rest of the night.

Then did Pea and I once more embark in our four-oared galley, and glide swiftly down the river with the tide. And while the shrewd East rasped and notched us, as with jagged razors, did my friend Pea impart to me confidences of interest relating to the Thames Police; we betweenwhiles finding 'duty boats' hanging in dark corners under banks, like weeds – our own was a 'supervision boat' – and they, as they reported 'all right!' flashing their hidden light on us, and we flashing ours on them. These duty boats had one sitter in each: an Inspector: and were rowed 'Ran-dan,' which for the information of those who never graduated, as I was once proud to do, under a fireman-waterman and winner of Kean's Prize Wherry: who, in the course of his tuition, took hundreds of gallons of rum and egg (at my expense) at the various houses of note above and below bridge; not by any means because he liked it, but to cure a weakness in his liver, for which the faculty had particularly recommended it – may be explained as rowed by three men, two pulling an oar each, and one a pair of sculls.

Thus, floating down our black highway, sullenly frowned upon by the knitted brows of Blackfriars, Southwark, and

London, each in his lowering turn, I was shown by my friend Pea that there are, in the Thames Police Force whose district extends from Battersea to Barking Creek, ninety-eight men, eight duty boats, and two supervision boats; and that these go about so silently, and lie in wait in such dark places, and so seem to be nowhere, and so may be anywhere, that they have gradually become a police of prevention, keeping the river almost clear of any great crimes, even while the increased vigilance on shore has made it much harder than of yore to live by 'thieving' in the streets. And as to the various kinds of water thieves, said my friend Pea, there were the Tier-rangers, who silently dropped alongside the tiers of shipping in the Pool, by night, and who, going to the companion-head, listened for two snores – snore number one, the skipper's; snore number two, the mate's – mates and skippers always snoring great guns, and being dead sure to be hard at it if they had turned in and were asleep. Hearing the double fire, down went the Rangers into the skippers' cabins; groped for the skippers' inexpressibles, which it was the custom of those gentlemen to shake off, watch, money, braces, boots, and all together, on the floor; and therewith made off as silently as might be. Then there were the Lumpers, or labourers employed to unload vessels. They wore loose canvas jackets with a broad hem in the bottom, turned inside, so as to form a large circular pocket in which they could conceal, like clowns in pantomimes, packages of surprising sizes. A great deal of property was stolen in this manner (Pea confided to me) from steamers; first, because steamers carry a larger number of small packages than other ships; next, because of the extreme rapidity with which they are obliged to be unladen for their return voyages. The Lumpers dispose of their booty, easily, to marine store dealers, and the only remedy to be suggested is that marine store shops should be licensed, and thus brought under the eye of the police as rigidly as public-houses. Lumpers also smuggle goods ashore for the crews of vessels. The smuggling of tobacco is so considerable, that it is well worth the while of the sellers of smuggled tobacco to use hydraulic presses, to squeeze a single pound into a package small enough to be contained in an ordinary pocket. Next, said my friend Pea, there were the Truckers – less thieves than smugglers, whose business it was to land more considerable parcels of goods than the Lumpers could manage. They sometimes sold articles of grocery, and so forth, to the crews, in order to cloak their real calling, and get aboard without suspicion. Many of them had boats of their own, and made money. Besides these, there were the Dredgermen, who, under pretence of dredging up coals and such like from the bottom of the river, hung about barges and other undecked craft, and when they saw an opportunity, threw any property they could lay their hands on overboard: in order slyly to dredge it up when the vessel was gone. Sometimes, they dexterously used their dredges to whip away anything that might lie within reach. Some of them were mighty neat at this, and the accomplishment was called dry dredging. Then, there was a vast deal of property, such as copper nails, sheathing, hardwood, &c. habitually brought away by shipwrights and other workmen from their employers' yards, and disposed of to marine store dealers, many of whom escaped detection through hard swearing, and their extraordinary artful ways of accounting for the possession of stolen property. Likewise, there were special-pleading practitioners, for whom barges 'drifted away of their own selves' – they having no hand in it, except first cutting them loose, and afterwards plundering them – innocents, meaning no harm, who had the misfortune to observe those foundlings wandering about the Thames.

We were now going in and out, with little noise and great nicety, among the tiers of shipping whose many hulls, lying close together, rose out of the water like black streets. Here and there, a Scotch, an Irish, or a foreign steamer, getting up her steam as the tide made, looked, with her great chimney and high sides, like a quiet factory among the common buildings. Now, the streets opened into clearer spaces, now contracted into alleys; but the tiers were so like houses, in the dark, that I could almost have believed myself in the narrower bye-ways of Venice. Everything was wonderfully still; for, it wanted full three hours of flood, and nothing seemed awake but a dog here and there.

So we took no Tier-rangers captive, nor any Lumpers, nor Truckers, nor Dredgermen, nor other evil disposed person or persons; but went ashore at Wapping where the old Thames Police office is now a station-house, and where the old Court, with its cabin windows looking on the river, is a quaint charge room: with nothing worse in it usually than a stuffed cat in a glass case, and a portrait, pleasant to behold, of a rare old Thames Police officer, Mr Superintendent Evans, now succeeded by his son. We looked over the charge books, admirably kept, and found the prevention so good, that there were not five hundred entries (including drunken and disorderly) in a whole year. Then, we looked into the store-room; where there was an oakum smell, and a nautical seasoning of dreadnought clothing, rope yarn, boat hooks, sculls and oars, spare stretchers, rudders, pistols, cutlasses, and the like. Then, into the cell, aired high up in the wooden wall through an opening like a kitchen plate-rack: wherein there was a drunken man, not at all warm, and very wishful to know if it were morning yet. Then, into a better sort of watch and ward room, where there was a squadron of stone bottles drawn up, ready to be filled with hot water and applied to any unfortunate creature who might be brought in apparently drowned. Finally we shook hands with our worthy friend Pea, and ran all the way to Tower Hill, under strong Police suspicion occasionally, before we got warm.

C. MAURICE DAVIES

THE WALWORTH JUMPERS
(1876)

SECT-HUNTING, LIKE misery, makes a man acquainted with strange companions, and familiarizes him with strange experiences; but of all the religious phenomena with which I have yet been brought into contact, the latest and certainly the very strangest, have been those connected with the 'Jumpers' at Walworth – the Bible Christians, or Children of God, as they prefer to have themselves called.

Acting on 'information I had received,' I went one Thursday evening, to a certain railway arch in Sutherland Street, Walworth Road, beneath which, in a veritable nineteenth-century church-in-the-catacombs style, I had been given to understand that the Bible Christians gathered thrice a week to listen to the preaching of an inspired woman from Suffolk. There was no difficulty in finding the place, for before half-past six o'clock a mob had gathered round the rough tarred hoarding which formed the entrance of the sanctuary, and had begun hoarsely to clamour for admission. The door-keeper, who evidently knew the material with which he had to deal, admitted the claimants slowly, one by one, after close scrutiny. Young Walworth, in the shape of ragged shock-headed boys and draggle-tailed girls, was rigidly excluded, and a section of New Cut swelldom got in only by dint of considerable manœuvring and no little physical persuasion. On the muddy path between the hoarding and the arch, a slight obstacle intervened in the shafts of a waggon drawn up right across the dark and sloppy roadway, on which a few planks were laid, like the Mahometan sword-bridge, for the feet of the faithful. The building was nothing more than an arch of the London, Chatham, and Dover Railway, roughly boarded in, and lighted with sundry old window-sashes, of which the broken panes too suggestively recalled the missiles of the Walworth Gentiles. A few movable benches and a great many rough planks extemporized into seats, held the place of pews, and the only arrangement approaching the idea of a pulpit, was a carpenter's table at the further end of the edifice, covered with green baize, and furnished with two coffee-cups and a collecting box. A single gaspipe ran longitudinally down the archway, whence descended two burners that shed a dim if not exactly a religious light as I entered. The archway was speedily filled with a congregation consisting of fustian-clad men, women in about the proportion of two to one man, and babies in more than adequate force. Broadcloth was slenderly represented, and one portion of it might have been well away, for it consisted of the New Cut swells, who ensconced themselves in a corner, and began to talk loudly and whistle with their hats on. Those New Cut swells had evidently come in for a 'lark.' In deference, I presume, to something un-Walworth-like in my outer man, I was motioned to a seat near the carpenter's table, among the faithful, who had begun to gather. As they met, the brothers and sisters, or the sisters one among the other, saluted with a kiss of peace; no half-and-half stage salute, but a good whacking kiss that echoed all over the archway, and amused the New Cut swells considerably, for they proceeded at once to imitate the sound, and to remark audibly, 'Ain't it nice?'

A little before seven o'clock the 'minister' entered – a tall thin Suffolk peasant-woman, of middle age, with high cheek-bones and piercing eyes. She was accompanied by a young good-looking girl of twenty, and an inane-visaged man in a broadcloth coat and corduroys – a sort of compromise between the chapel and the world. The woman herself was arrayed, unclerically enough, in a red merino gown and somewhat jaunty black bonnet. She had a large prominent mouth with projecting teeth, and the muscles around the jaw bore that peculiar appearance often observed in habitual speakers, being strongly developed, and giving a sort of animal appearance to the lower portion of the face. In a tone which at first struck me as somewhat affected, she requested all those who could not stay until nine to leave at once, as the door would be closed when service began, and no exit allowed afterwards. This arrangement, she explained, was necessary on account of the outsiders, whose noisy clamours for admittance combined with the frequent passage of trains to mar the tranquillity of the evening. The New Cut gentle-men, too, were troublesome all along, but generally got as good as they gave from the minister, who was quite equal to the occasion, and evidently accustomed to interruption. For instance, when the swelldom in the corner said something particularly rude, she observed, 'I had heard, among my Suffolk people, of the superior wisdom of the Londoners, but if this be London wisdom, commend me to my Suffolk ignorance.' She apologized for the 'ill-convenience' of the archway, and then the service began with a prayer by the young girl, who lifted one hand and prayed with fervour and a certain rough but genuine eloquence for ten minutes. She was followed, but not favourably, by the inane man; then succeeded the minister herself, whose prayer was 'taller' than the young girl's, but on that account not so eloquent. The girl reminded me forcibly of Dinah in 'Adam Bede.' The woman prayed volubly, and used her long arms freely in gesticula-tion. Knowing what was to follow, I at first imagined that she was making mesmeric passes, but in this I was probably mistaken. After the box had been sent round, and a revival hymn sung, the sermon began.

Now it must be premised that the distinguishing doctrine of these Children of God is the assurance that they will never die. Belief not only does away with previous sin, but exempts them from bodily death. The Lord is to come speedily and gather them to Himself, without the previous process of dissolution. From the date of their conversion, in fact, they are immortal. They die at conversion, and die no more. With peculiar delight, therefore, did I find the preacher selecting for her subject the 11th chapter of St John, which contains the account of the resurrection of Lazarus. She spoke on this congenial topic for considerably more than an hour, but, instead of being content to take the narrative in its simple and beautiful form, she allegorized it in a way that would have astonished Origen himself. Lazarus, for instance, who had been four days dead, typified the people who died before the Mosaic dispensation 4000 years previously. Martha signified the Law, and Mary the Gospel. Speaking of the actual resuscitation, she kept asking 'Why did Lazarus come back?' and the New Cut section, who would persist in thinking that every question was addressed personally to them, and demanded an audible reply, suggested that he 'had got a return ticket.' 'No; he never was dead. He had died before,' etc. I am free to confess, however, that I should scarcely have gathered the peculiar doctrines of the sect from the sermon, had I not come prepared with some previous knowledge, – so wrapped up was it in far fetched imagery and aimless 'tall' talk. The sermon was fluent, and at times eloquent, but scarcely exciting. There was certainly nothing in it to make one 'jump.' The preacher went so far as to assert that the brethren had never 'given the undertaker a job yet, and didn't mean to.' I subsequently inquired the age and numbers of the sect, and found that it had been in existence seven years, and numbered some two hundred in London. It would be curious to calculate the effect of its wider extension on the present bills of mortality.

During the discourse I had noticed more than one lady subside into an apparently comatose condition, which I could easily have mistaken for natural sleep – for the sermon was long and unexciting – had I not noticed a peculiar twitching of the limbs, and an expression of face like that which I have observed on the features of the mesmerized; in fact, what mesmerizers call 'the superior condition.' The New Cut gentry were immensely interested when these ladies began to drop off, and were proportionately disappointed when they woke up at the conclusion of the sermon, as though nothing had happened. I confess to feeling disappointed myself when, after a queer, jumpy, John-Brown-Glory-Hallelujah kind of hymn, the meeting was dismissed, without any Terpsichorean performance having taken place. However, we were not to be altogether unrewarded for our two hours' sojourn in that damp vault, reeking with the odours of a too nearly adjoining stable. When some of the congregation had left – I think the New Cut swells among the number – two little girls got up and began to dance, much in the same way as they might do if a grinding-organ had struck up an appropriate air in a quiet street. They were followed by a youth of eighteen or nineteen, who hopped very much like Mr Stead in the 'Perfect Cure.' But all three wore that strange vacant countenance so suggestive of animal magnetism, and so difficult – especially for children – to assume. A proud and happy father, dressed like a respectable tradesman, stepped into the centre of the throng gathered round the children, and said, 'There, fellow Christians!

There's a sight to make you reflect. That is the power of the Holy Ghost.' It was, I agreed, a sight to make one reflect; but I could not quite follow the assertion as to its source. I spoke to a respectable woman next me, and learnt from her that every member of this sect, upon conversion, undergoes *death* – an actual process analogous to physical death, and exactly corresponding with it in external signs, only that it is not permanent. 'Some die very hard, in great agony,' she said; 'others quite peacefully.' They never 'jump' until after they have 'died'; that is, as I understand it, they are not liable to these magnetic affections in public, until they have been under the influence. Once under the influence, it may recur at any moment. I acquit the woman of having made mesmeric passes. I told her so, for she anticipated such an explanation, and disclaimed it. I am also well aware that to explain 'jumping' by animal magnetism is very like explaining *obscurum per obscurius*; but I feel convinced that, whatever be the origin of the so-called mesmeric condition, the same is the cause of 'jumping.' The magnetic 'sleep-waking' may be produced without contact or passes – at least, so say its professors – and religious excitement is certainly an adequate cause to produce such an effect. 'Once dead, not only will they die no more, but they suffer no pain, they feel no sorrow,' said my informant. During the whole of this time, the little girls and the hobbledehoy had gone on dancing; and now a female who had up to this time been sitting still, grimacing and gesticulating in a slightly idiotic manner, jumped up and joined the dance. Her demeanour, however, was anything but happy; she prayed as in an unknown tongue, and called out 'The devil! the devil!' I mentioned this fact to the person with whom I was conversing, and she said, 'Yes, there is something wrong' – so even the immortals go wrong sometimes – adding, 'You see when they are in that state they have the gift of prophecy and clear vision. She can see the state of those around.' I felt myself instinctively looking towards the corner the New Cut swells had vacated. Probably – as the spiritists would say – their presence had 'disturbed the conditions.' When deprecating to me any use of mesmerism or chloroform, the minister said, 'I wish I had been able to use the one or the other once or twice tonight,' alluding to those incorrigible gentlemen from Lambeth.

I was of course obliged to personate an 'anxious inquirer' to the good lady who was my informant. She will see my little *ruse* now, and – I hope – pardon me. I was an 'anxious inquirer,' though not precisely in her sense of the words. She begged me to come some evening 'if the Lord tarried,' to an address I will not name, because she gave it to me in confidence; but it is there they have their more private meetings, and where 'deaths' are of more frequent occurrence, though they may happen anywhere. The 'Children of God,' I found, had the Walworth 'world' up in arms against them. 'Some of the men wait for our brothers,' said a decent matron to me, 'and almost kill them.' Perhaps this is accounted for by the kissing, or, it may be, by the slender accommodation of the railway arch, which necessitates the exclusion of so many. It took two policemen to get us quietly out, and I kept on the *qui vive*, lest some honest Walworthian should mistake me for a 'brother.'

The 'Jumpers' are as old as history – older, as Niebuhr tells us – in the persons of the Salii, or dancing priests of Mars; and *convulsionnaires* have been common in many ages, and under widely different religious systems. Those beneath the railway arch at Walworth are only the latest, and certainly not the most picturesque or interesting, edition of phenomena rather curious than uncommon.

ELIZA LYNN LINTON

MY FIRST SOIRÉE
(1891)

I AM A YOUNG housekeeper of large ideas, married to a quiet man of small means. I have extensive notions of how things ought to be done, and I endeavour to carry them out with refinement and economy combined. But it is rather difficult to keep to that happy ideal when dragged first to one side and then to the other – now by my husband's limited balance, and now by my own unlimited aspirations. Struggling always between these two opposite poles, my life has a certain uncomfortable misfit about it – a want of harmony between desires and attainments that strikes one as disagreeably as a velvet dress trimmed with imitation lace, or a homely carmelite bedecked with gold and silver tags.

I have been married now about two years. This is not a comfortable period. It is just long enough to see the lover break to pieces on the sandbar of marriage, but not long enough for the building up of the friend out of the wreck. I have begun to reason on my husband's character – never a wise thing for a wife to do – to weigh his imperfections, to criticize his good qualities, to penetrate the meaning of his actions – in a word, to understand him; and I do not think that husbands gain by being understood. But then perhaps I am prejudiced in favour of romance, and am more fretful and exacting than I ought to be. Jonathan – Jonathan is my husband – says I am.

Married two years, as I have said, and we had never yet given a party! – when one day, three weeks since, my husband proposed to me, quite of his own accord, that we should invite a few friends to tea – just a few, and without ceremony – as we had been out a good deal lately and had given no kind of return.

'How many do you think of, Jonathan?' I asked, taking out my tablets, which I always carried in my pocket. Jonathan gave them to me before we married; and my naughty baby *would* play with them the other day, and broke one of the leaves. Jonathan was so angry about it!

'Oh, just one or two, Totty! The A—s; and the B—s; old C—, perhaps; and the D—s too, if you like.'

'And the E—s,' I said. 'We went to them, if you remember, last Christmas; – we must have them in return.'

'Very well, as you wish it; and I should like to show the F—s a little attention as well. But, remember, Totty, I want only a very few, and no fuss or ostentation.'

It was all very well for Jonathan to say this; but I should like to know where we were to draw the line? and whom we were to leave out? and if we asked all that we ought to ask, and so made a large party of it as we ought to do, how could we possibly give only beef and bread? as he said, in his slow, stupid way. But men are so stupid! They never see things in a rational light! However, Jonathan had done it himself, and had only himself to blame when he came home that night, and I showed him my list of a hundred and forty – each of whom it was absolutely imperative on us to invite, either as an acknowledgement of kindness shown to ourselves; or because of the wisdom of conciliating influential friends for dear baby's sake; or from the principle of mere ornamentation, and the advantage of good names and smart toilettes in a drawing-room of no pretensions. Whatever the reason, there was the necessity; one hundred and forty to be invited, not one of whom could possibly be knocked off the list.

Jonathan was very savage when I read the names over to him. 'What could I mean by such absurdity?' he said. 'Did I want to ruin him outright? A hundred and forty people, indeed! How could all, or half of them, cram into our small rooms? and what were they to do when they had crammed in? That was always the way! If ever he proposed anything quiet and rational and inexpensive I must break it up with my absurd notions of gentility and cost, and either make the whole thing impossible, or to be attained at too great a sacrifice.'

And so he went on scolding for half an hour – I saying nothing, but drawing spider-legs from every name, till the tablets looked tattooed. At last, when he had finished – for even a husband's lecture must come to an end some time – I said, very quietly: 'Well, now that you have done, will you kindly look over this list with me, and tell me who are to be left out?'

He did not like being spoken to so coolly, but he could not find fault with me because I kept my temper when he lost his; so he took the tablets from my hand, and began checking off the names, one by one, as he spelt them out. Of course we had a little quarrelling over some of them; for all that he particularly disliked I particularly desired should be asked, and all that he cared most for I thought of least importance. This is generally the way with husbands and wives – is it not? I do not mention it as anything extra-ordinary. After we had fought about fifty battles in this manner, ending always by retaining the name in question as indispensable, Jonathan's patience gave way; I knew it would; besides, his smoking time had come.

'There, do as you like!' he cried, ungraciously flinging the tablets into my lap. 'I wash my hands of the whole affair, and will take neither interest nor responsibility in it. I am very sorry that I said a word about it. I meant a quiet little friendly evening of one or two only, and you have swelled it up into a monstrous party, as you always do. So now you may manage it for yourself. It is your own affair, not mine!'

And then he stalked away to the door and I began to cry. But, as he did not look back – and, indeed, he would not have cared for my tears if he had; he was far too cross – after a little time I thought it wiser to leave off and begin my calculations for supper; for *now* I was determined on my party, and determined, too, to have it my own way.

The next day I really set to work. First there were the printed invitations to get, with envelopes to match; and this was the beginning of my troubles, for I could not find any in our whole neighbourhood of the pattern I wanted. I remembered a certain form which Lady Twoshoes always used, and I was determined I would have this, or none. I cannot describe to you half the difficulties I encountered. I think I must have walked between twenty and thirty miles looking for this form, which at last I found in an obscure printer's in the City – the only house in London where it was to be had, and which was, in point of fact, the source of supply to my Lady Twoshoes' own stationer's. I was not a little proud of this triumph of energy, as you may suppose, and ordered my four quires with the feelings of a successful general; but when they came home – which they did by post – they were not quite what I expected. They were very dirty – all the outside leaves unusable by reason of grimy thumb-marks; and the string, which had been tied too tightly round them, had cut into some and marked all. Besides, they were a shilling a quire more than the ordinary forms; the man making that addition as his commentary on my violent exclamation of pleasure when I found them, and the frankness with which I told him I had searched all over London for them in vain, and would have given anything in the world for that one special form of invitation, which no one but my Lady Twoshoes ever used. I had lost a great deal of time in this search – so much that, instead of giving a three weeks' invitation, as I had intended, I was obliged to cut it down to a fortnight and two days, which was a bad augury to start with; for, as we were going to give a party, I wanted it thoroughly well done, and without flaw or blemish anywhere. However, I was obliged to put up with this small mortification, and issued my hundred and forty invitations with a proud heart if a beating one.

I expected all the answers in twenty-four hours at the very least; but by the end of three days I had received only five – five of the least important; and then came three, conditional and doubtful; and then one refusal; and then another acceptance. So slowly they all came in, that it was not till the very morning of the day that I received the last. Fancy my feelings, being kept in suspense for a fortnight and two days as to the number of guests to come, and consequently to provide for, both in seats and supper! I do think that people should reply to invitations more promptly. I am sure I always do, for mamma taught me that it was a point of good-breeding to do so; but people are so odd and uncouth nowadays! And all this time Jonathan was so sulky there was hardly any living with him, and he would neither talk of the evening nor help me in the least. I had never seen him so cross since I married; and he has a temper, too, and not always under control.

Well! I had at first resolved that the evening should not cost above five pounds. I had made the most minute calculations with my cook Betsy, and we both came to the conclusion that five pounds would see us safely and handsomely through the undertaking. She was to cook the supper; we were to have the greengrocer's boy to help the housemaid, and a little girl to wash up; and then the greengrocer himself, in a nice new suit, would come and open the door and hand the refreshments; for I was not going to do the thing shabbily, and have only my stupid women to wait; and altogether I thought we should get through famously. But at the eleventh hour – I mean the day before – Betsy lost her nerve, and threw up her place and the supper in a breath. My friend the greengrocer, I found out afterwards, had frightened her. He had a sister, a cook out of place, whom he wanted engaged for the job, which I was obliged to do, giving her ten shillings for the day's work.

The greengrocer's sister was a woman of as large ideas as my own – larger, indeed, for she scouted my programme as utterly inadequate, and silenced me with a word when I attempted to interpose a faint caution as to the need of economy. 'She knew her business,' she said loftily; 'and as she was responsible for the supper she must be allowed to do it in her own way.'

I had nothing for it, then, but to submit, privately beseeching Betsy to be as careful of matters as possible; but Betsy was a weak-minded girl who always gave in to everybody; so that I was quite convinced I had no background in her, and that the greengrocer's sister might ruin us if she liked. But in the ruin surely the supper would be perfect!

The evening came, and the rooms really looked very pretty. I had spent a good deal of the allotted five pounds on flowers; but then flowers are as indispensable to the success of an evening as lights and cakes; and it was the supper, not the adjuncts, that I had limited to that small sum, which now I began to think ridiculous and impossible; – the greengrocer's sister told me I might be thankful if I did it under twenty. I had a pretty new dress for the occasion, blue and white, and really I believe that I looked very well; but Jonathan, who was awfully cross, told me I looked worse than I had ever done before, and that my dress – especially my head, of which I was immensely proud – was a perfect ridicule – pronounced in the French manner, which I thought more ridiculous than my bright-blue pompon. So that did not raise my spirits to begin with; neither did the successive arrival of the families of my two grandest lions, without the lions, help to their exaltation. Still, I bore up against the feeling – terribly increasing both in depth and intensity – that the thing was destined to be a failure, and resolved to do my best to make it yet a success. But something stronger than my will fought against me that night; and my poor party was doomed.

We had asked everyone we knew, so the consequence was that all sorts of wrong people jostled each other. People who had publicly insulted each other met, hot and flurried, at the doorway; people who had cut each other stood face to face, not a couple of inches apart; people with a life-feud between them stretched out their hands at the same moment to the same common friend. One lady, whom I wished to conciliate most of all who came, was 'talked at' by a gentleman in a loud voice – loud enough for all the room to hear; another was ridiculed to her face, poor thing! (Well! her head-dress was very odd, certainly – a Madame de Pompadour kind of thing, with a tower of pearls and horsehair behind). A gentleman to whom I was under life-long obligations – one of my dearest friends, indeed – stood at my back for five minutes, while I was using my best energies to fascinate a man I had never seen before, and by whose intrigues and unaccountable enmity my friend had been turned out of a lucrative post somewhere. And I, who did not know one hundredth part of the secret histories enacting before me, made matters ten times worse by the way in which I blundered into all manner of difficulties, and brought in contact all sorts of explosive materials; so that, from the very beginning of the evening, there was discord and disunion. And how could one silly little woman set all these grave disasters straight? Then there were the quiet and untalkative people who would not 'circulate,' but who sat in corners, and on the benches by the doors, expecting others to find them out, and who were particularly ill-used when they were left alone for five minutes, looking reproachfully at me. As if I was to blame for all the stupid isolation they gave themselves! And there were the people of forward manners and very rusty 'small change,' who talked to everyone and said nothing worth hearing, thrusting themselves into every animated group and dividing couples less animated, but perhaps more inter-ested – interfering without adding and only irritating, not amusing. And there were the deaf people, who had to be screamed at; and the low-voiced people, who could scarcely speak above a whisper – and these two always came together. So that what with mental unfitness and personal disharmony I had a troublesome time of it to put things into even the semblance of working order.

Jonathan was worse than unhelpful in these straits. He had attended to nothing all throughout, having, as I have said, lost his temper from the beginning, only finding the most fault where I had taken extra pains to put things nice; but now he made everything worse by his strange conduct. Of course, if we had committed the blunder of asking incon-gruities together, we must make the best of it, and not show that we knew or suspected anything, and certainly not take sides. The merest good-breeding and sacredness of hospi-tality demanded *that*. But my husband did not think so, and from the first ranged himself as a partisan, paying all manner of attention to some people while entirely neglecting the rest. Consequently I had the sole care of the obnoxious ones, which forced me also to assume the attitude of a partisan. This I told him when they had all gone; but he only said I talked nonsense, and used too fine phrases. He is so rude when he is in a bad humour!

But nothing of this was eternal; and there would soon be the supper to cheer us all up, and rearrange the spirits of the company. Our rooms were far too small to enable us to do anything all this time; we had a little music, certainly, but only one or two waltzes and polkas by young ladies, dreadfully shy, so that this part of the programme counted for nothing. It was getting near to supper-time now – eleven o'clock, so I thought I would just quietly vanish down stairs, and see how my greengrocer's sister was progressing. I had seen enough to be aware that something was not quite right with that individual before tea-time even, but I was far from suspecting the truth. I went down, then, expecting to find all done, save, perhaps, the last little ornaments, which belong to the mistress; but this is what I found instead; and when you have read it, picture my feelings as the commentary. The exhibition vase of flowers, which I had taken a world of pains with, wreathing the long slender stem with maidenhair, just like those on the stand in the International, was smashed to pieces; and such of the flowers as were saved had been thrust pell-mell into a celery-glass which Jonathan had in his bachelor days. And we all know that the arrangement of flowers is everything, making them either graceful adornments or vulgar encumbrances. Then there was the trifle-bowl, hired for the occasion – cost price two pounds sixteen – broken right across, and tied with string, with the wine oozing steadily through the crack and dripping in heavy drops on the cloth below. Jellies were shaking themselves to pieces on the table – some, indeed, were wandering over the sides of the dishes and quivering, like transparent dice, on the cloth. A few – very few – shapes of cream and blanc-mange, flattened and broken, were returning to their original liquidity – not one of them retaining any completeness or beauty. Just one plateful of sandwiches had been cut, with all the potted meat and ham left out. The lobster-salad was mixed and messed as if it had been already rifled and the best parts picked out. There were no forks, spoons, glasses, nor plates at hand – a trayful had just been let fall, and I picked up the fragments of no fewer than three plates – hired – on the dining-room floor. The lemonade, which was to have been superb and iced, according to a new recipe, was sour, full of pips, and as warm as boiling water could make it. The claret-cup – my great point of pride – was ruined in the pre-paration, and the borage had been stuck in with its heels in the air. The lamp was smoking – it was a camphine lamp, so I need say no more; while Betsy was standing, limp and help-less by the door, in tears; the greengrocer was speaking very thick; and the greengrocer's sister was lying incapable across the kitchen dresser, with the fragments of my ruined supper about her. There was no help for it now: – the thing was a failure – a confessed, irrevocable, unconcealed failure!

I went upstairs in undisguised tears, and whispered the news to a few intimate friends, who good-naturedly enough made the best of it, but who could not give me back my supper; nor prevent those who were not my friends from laughing at me; nor make less than a quarter of what would have been a well-conditioned table do for a party of a hun-dred and ten; nor yet pay the terrible bills which poured in on us the next week. Bills – oh, such bills! bills for cream and eggs and butter enough to have fed a garrison, all swamped into a few liquefying creams and a battered old blanc-mange! – bills for broken glass and china enough to have re-furnished my china closet – bills for flowers, bills for wines, for lemons and oranges, for lobsters and groceries – bills for every conceivable thing and every inconceivable – bills that straitened us for weeks and months after; and all for what? – a gigantic failure! But Jonathan said: 'it was all my fault, and it served me right; what business had I to attempt more than I could do or had means for? That the thing was a failure was plain enough to the meanest understanding; and though he felt for me a little, yet he was glad of it, for the useful lesson he hoped it would be to me in the future. When I could accept the fact that a poor man's wife might still be a gentlewoman, though she entertained her friends without ostentation, and gave a quiet little tea-drinking instead of a monstrous, ill-done parade like this, I should be a better and a happier woman; but while I was vulgar enough to attempt things beyond my means I should never succeed as a hostess, and would always expose myself to mortification and defeat.'

I wonder if Jonathan is right? Perhaps he is, after all! Perhaps simplicity and true hospitality are the best tests of refinement, and these grand attempts with hungry purses in the background are follies and vulgarities too; and inevitable failures with all who make them. I think I shall kiss Jonathan when he comes home tonight, and tell him that I have been a sad little goose, and that I am very sorry I did not take his advice from the first. Poor Jonathan! he is very good on the whole; and, who knows? he may be a better judge than I about some things in life! But what would dear mamma say if she heard me?

CHARLOTTE BRIGGS,

née MANDEVILLE MONTGOMERY.

ARTHUR CONAN DOYLE

THE ADVENTURE OF THE BLUE CARBUNCLE
(1892)

I HAD CALLED upon my friend Sherlock Holmes upon the second morning after Christmas, with the intention of wishing him the compliments of the season. He was lounging upon the sofa in a purple dressing gown, a pipe rack within his reach upon the right, and a pile of crumpled morning papers, evidently newly studied, near at hand. Beside the couch was a wooden chair, and on the angle of the back hung a very seedy and disreputable hard felt hat, much the worse for wear, and cracked in several places. A lens and a forceps lying upon the seat of the chair suggested that the hat had been suspended in this manner for the purpose of examination.

'You are engaged,' said I; 'perhaps I interrupt you.'

'Not at all. I am glad to have a friend with whom I can discuss my results. The matter is a perfectly trivial one' – he jerked his thumb in the direction of the old hat – 'but there are points in connection with it which are not entirely devoid of interest and even of instruction.'

I seated myself in his armchair and warmed my hands before his crackling fire, for a sharp frost had set in, and the windows were thick with the ice crystals. 'I suppose,' I remarked, 'that, homely as it looks, this thing has some deadly story linked on to it – that it is the clue which will guide you in the solution of some mystery and the punishment of some crime.'

'No, no. No crime,' said Sherlock Holmes, laughing.

'Only one of those whimsical little incidents which will happen when you have four million human beings all jostling each other within the space of a few square miles. Amid the action and reaction of so dense a swarm of humanity, every possible combination of events may be expected to take place, and many a little problem will be presented which may be striking and bizarre without being criminal. We have already had experience of such.'

'So much so,' I remarked, 'that of the last six cases which I have added to my notes, three have been entirely free of any legal crime.'

'Precisely. You allude to my attempt to recover the Irene Adler papers, to the singular case of Miss Mary Sutherland, and to the adventure of the man with the twisted lip. Well, I have no doubt that this small matter will fall into the same innocent category. You know Peterson, the commissionaire?'

'Yes.'

'It is to him that this trophy belongs.'

'It is his hat.'

'No, no; he found it. Its owner is unknown. I beg that you will look upon it not as a battered billycock but as an intellectual problem. And, first, as to how it came here. It arrived upon Christmas morning, in company with a good fat goose, which is, I have no doubt, roasting at this moment in front of Peterson's fire. The facts are these: about four o'clock on Christmas morning, Peterson, who, as you know, is a very honest fellow, was returning from some small jollification and was making his way homeward down Tottenham Court Road. In front of him he saw, in the gaslight, a tallish man, walking with a slight stagger, and carrying a white goose slung over his shoulder. As he reached the corner of Goodge Street, a row broke out between the stranger and a little knot of roughs. One of the latter knocked off the man's hat, on which he raised his stick to defend himself and, swinging it over his head, smashed the shop window behind him. Peterson had rushed forward to protect the stranger from his assailants; but the man, shocked at having broken the window, and seeing an official-looking person in uniform rushing towards him, dropped his goose, took to his heels, and vanished amid the labyrinth of small streets which lie at the back of Tottenham Court Road. The roughs had also fled at the appearance of Peterson, so that he was left in possession of the field of battle, and also of the spoils of victory in the shape of the battered hat and a most unimpeachable Christmas goose.'

'Which surely he restored to their owner?'

'My dear fellow, there lies the problem. It is true that "For Mrs Henry Baker" was printed upon a small card which was tied to the bird's left leg, and it is also true that the initials "H.B." are legible upon the lining of this hat; but as there are some thousands of Bakers, and some hundreds of Henry Bakers in this city of ours, it is not easy to restore lost property to any one of them.'

'What, then, did Peterson do?'

'He brought round both hat and goose to me on Christmas morning, knowing that even the smallest problems are of interest to me. The goose we retained until this morning, when there were signs that, in spite of the slight frost, it would be well that it should be eaten without unnecessary delay. Its finder has carried it off, therefore, to fulfil the ultimate destiny of a goose, while I continue to retain the hat of the unknown gentleman who lost his Christmas dinner.'

'Did he not advertise?'

'No.'

'Then, what clue could you have as to his identity?'

'Only as much as we can deduce.'

'From his hat?'

'Precisely.'

'But you are joking. What can you gather from this old battered felt?'

'Here is my lens. You know my methods. What can you gather yourself as to the individuality of the man who has worn this article?'

I took the tattered object in my hands and turned it over rather ruefully. It was a very ordinary black hat of the usual round shape, hard and much the worse for wear. The lining had been of red silk, but was a good deal discoloured. There was no maker's name; but, as Holmes had remarked, the initials 'H.B.' were scrawled upon one side. It was pierced in the brim for a hat-securer, but the elastic was missing. For the rest, it was cracked, exceedingly dusty, and spotted in several places, although there seemed to have been some attempt to hide the discoloured patches by smearing them with ink.

'I can see nothing,' said I, handing it back to my friend.

'On the contrary, Watson, you can see everything. You fail, however, to reason from what you see. You are too timid in drawing your inferences.'

'Then, pray tell me what it is that you can infer from this hat?'

He picked it up and gazed at it in the peculiar introspective fashion which was characteristic of him. 'It is perhaps less suggestive than it might have been,' he remarked, 'and yet there are a few inferences which are very distinct, and a few others which represent at least a strong balance of probability. That the man was highly intellectual is of course obvious upon the face of it, and also that he was fairly well-to-do within the last three years, although he has now fallen upon evil days. He had foresight, but has less now than formerly, pointing to a moral retrogression, which, when taken with the decline of his fortunes, seems to indicate some evil influence, probably drink, at work upon him. This may account also for the obvious fact that his wife has ceased to love him.'

'My dear Holmes!'

'He has, however, retained some degree of self-respect,' he continued, disregarding my remonstrance. 'He is a man who leads a sedentary life, goes out little, is out of training entirely, is middle-aged, has grizzled hair which he has had cut within the last few days, and which he anoints with lime cream. These are the more patent facts which are to be deduced from his hat. Also, by the way, that it is extremely improbable that he has gas laid on in his house.'

'You are certainly joking, Holmes.'

'Not in the least. Is it possible that even now, when I give you these results, you are unable to see how they are attained?'

'I have no doubt that I am very stupid, but I must confess that I am unable to follow you. For example, how did you deduce that this man was intellectual?'

For answer Holmes clapped the hat upon his head. It came right over the forehead and settled upon the bridge of his nose. 'It is a question of cubic capacity,' said he; 'a man with so large a brain must have something in it.'

'The decline of his fortunes, then?'

'This hat is three years old. These flat brims curled at the edge came in then. It is a hat of the very best quality. Look at the band of ribbed silk and the excellent lining. If this man could afford to buy so expensive a hat three years ago, and has had no hat since, then he has assuredly gone down in the world.'

'Well, that is clear enough, certainly. But how about the foresight and the moral retrogression?'

Sherlock Holmes laughed. 'Here is the foresight,' said he, putting his finger upon the little disc and loop of the hat-securer. 'They are never sold upon hats. If this man ordered one, it is a sign of a certain amount of foresight, since he went out of his way to take this precaution against the wind. But since we see that he has broken the elastic and has not troubled to replace it, it is obvious that he has less foresight now than formerly, which is a distinct proof of a weakening nature. On the other hand, he has endeavoured to conceal some of these stains upon the felt by daubing them with ink, which is a sign that he has not entirely lost his self-respect.'

'Your reasoning is certainly plausible.'

'The further points, that he is middle-aged, that his hair is grizzled, that it has been recently cut, and that he uses lime cream, are all to be gathered from a close examination of the lower part of the lining. The lens discloses a large number of hair ends, clean cut by the scissors of the barber. They all appear to be adhesive, and there is a distinct odour of lime cream. This dust, you will observe, is not the gritty, grey dust of the street but the fluffy brown dust of the house, showing that it has been hung up indoors most of the time; while the marks of moisture upon the inside are proof positive that the wearer perspired very freely, and could therefore, hardly be in the best of training.'

'But his wife – you said that she had ceased to love him.'

'This hat has not been brushed for weeks. When I see you, my dear Watson, with a week's accumulation of dust upon your hat, and when your wife allows you to go out in such a state, I shall fear that you also have been unfortunate enough to lose your wife's affection.'

'But he might be a bachelor.'

'Nay, he was bringing home the goose as a peace offering to his wife. Remember the card upon the bird's leg.'

'You have an answer to everything. But how on earth do you deduce that the gas is not laid on in his house?'

'One tallow stain, or even two, might come by chance; but when I see no less than five, I think that there can be little doubt that the individual must be brought into frequent contact with burning tallow – walks upstairs at night probably with his hat in one hand and a guttering candle in the other. Anyhow, he never got tallow stains from a gas jet. Are you satisfied?'

'Well, it is very ingenious,' said I, laughing; 'but since, as you said just now, there has been no crime committed, and no harm done save the loss of a goose, all this seems to be rather a waste of energy.'

Sherlock Holmes had opened his mouth to reply, when the door flew open, and Peterson, the commissionaire, rushed into the apartment with flushed cheeks and the face of a man who is dazed with astonishment.

'The goose, Mr Holmes! The goose, sir!' he gasped.

'Eh? What of it, then? Has it returned to life and flapped off through the kitchen window?' Holmes twisted himself round upon the sofa to get a fairer view of the man's excited face.

'See here, sir! See what my wife found in its crop!' He held out his hand and displayed upon the centre of the palm a brilliantly scintillating blue stone, rather smaller than a bean in size, but of such purity and radiance that it twinkled like an electric point in the dark hollow of his hand.

Sherlock Holmes sat up with a whistle. 'By Jove, Peterson!' said he, 'this is treasure trove indeed. I suppose you know what you have got?'

'A diamond, sir? A precious stone. It cuts into glass as though it were putty.'

'It's more than a precious stone. It is *the* precious stone.'

'Not the Countess of Morcar's blue carbuncle!' I ejaculated.

'Precisely so. I ought to know its size and shape, seeing that I have read the advertisement about it in *The Times* every day lately. It is absolutely unique, and its value can only be conjectured, but the reward offered of £1000 is certainly not within a twentieth part of the market price.'

'A thousand pounds! Great Lord of mercy!' The commissionaire plumped down into a chair and stared from one to the other of us.

'That is the reward, and I have reason to know that there are sentimental considerations in the background which would induce the Countess to part with half her fortune if she could but recover the gem.'

'It was lost, if I remember aright, at the Hotel Cosmopolitan,' I remarked.

'Precisely so, on December 22nd, just five days ago. John Horner, a plumber, was accused of having abstracted it from the lady's jewel case. The evidence against him was so strong that the case has been referred to the Assizes. I have some account of the matter here, I believe.' He rummaged amid his newspapers, glancing over the dates, until at last he smoothed one out, doubled it over, and read the following paragraph:

'Hotel Cosmopolitan Jewel Robbery. John Horner, 26, plumber, was brought up upon the charge of having upon the 22nd inst., abstracted from the jewel case of the Countess of Morcar the valuable gem known as the blue carbuncle. James Ryder, upper-attendant at the hotel, gave his evidence to the effect that he had shown Horner up to the dressing room of the Countess of Morcar upon the day of the robbery in order that he might solder the second bar of the grate, which was loose. He had remained with Horner some little time, but had finally been called away. On returning, he found that Horner had disappeared, that the bureau had been forced open, and that the small morocco casket in which, as it afterwards transpired, the Countess was accustomed to keep her jewel, was lying empty upon the dressing table. Ryder instantly gave the alarm, and Horner was arrested the same evening; but the stone could not be found either upon his person or in his rooms. Catherine Cusack, maid to the Countess, deposed to having heard Ryder's cry of dismay on discovering the robbery, and to having rushed into the room, where she found matters as described by the last witness. Inspector Bradstreet, B division, gave evidence as to the arrest of Horner, who struggled frantically, and protested his innocence in the strongest terms. Evidence of a previous conviction for robbery having been given against the prisoner, the magistrate refused to deal summarily with the offence, but referred it to the Assizes. Horner, who had shown signs of intense emotion during the proceedings, fainted away at the conclusion and was carried out of court.

'Hum! So much for the police court,' said Holmes thoughtfully, tossing aside the paper. 'The question for us now to solve is the sequence of events leading from a rifled jewel case at one end to the crop of a goose in Tottenham Court Road at the other. You see, Watson, our little deductions have suddenly assumed a much more important and less innocent aspect. Here is the stone; the stone came from the goose, and the goose came from Mr Henry Baker, the gentleman with the bad hat and all the other characteristics with which I have bored you. So now we must set ourselves very seriously to finding this gentleman and ascertaining what part he has played in this little mystery. To do this, we must try the simplest means first, and these lie undoubtedly in an advertisement in all the evening papers. If this fail, I shall have recourse to other methods.'

'What will you say?'

'Give me a pencil and that slip of paper. Now, then:

'Found at the corner of Goodge Street, a goose and a black felt hat. Mr Henry Baker can have the same by applying at 6.30 this evening at 221B, Baker Street. That is clear and concise.'

'Very. But will he see it?'

'Well, he is sure to keep an eye on the papers, since, to a poor man, the loss was a heavy one. He was clearly so scared by his mischance in breaking the window and by the approach of Peterson that he thought of nothing but flight, but since then he must have bitterly regretted the impulse which caused him to drop his bird. Then, again, the introduction of his name will cause him to see it, for everyone who knows him will direct his attention to it. Here you are, Peterson, run down to the advertising agency and have this put in the evening papers.'

'In which, sir?'

'Oh, in the *Globe*, *Star*, *Pall Mall*, *St James's*, *Evening News Standard*, *Echo*, and any others that occur to you.'

'Very well, sir. And this stone?'

'Ah, yes, I shall keep the stone. Thank you. And, I say, Peterson, just buy a goose on your way back and leave it here with me, for we must have one to give to this gentleman in place of the one which your family is now devouring.'

When the commissionaire had gone, Holmes took up the stone and held it against the light. 'It's a bonny thing,' he said. 'Just see how it glints and sparkles. Of course it is a nucleus and focus of crime. Every good stone is. They are the devil's pet baits. In the larger and older jewels every facet may stand for a bloody deed. This stone is not yet twenty years old. It was found in the banks of the Amoy River in southern China and is remarkable in having every characteristic of the carbuncle, save that it is blue in shade instead of ruby red. In spite of its youth, it has already a sinister history. There have been two murders, a vitriol-throwing, a suicide, and several robberies brought about for the sake of this fortygrain weight of crystallized charcoal. Who would think that so pretty a toy would be a purveyor to the gallows and the prison? I'll lock it up in my strongbox now and drop a line to the Countess to say that we have it.'

'Do you think that this man Horner is innocent?'

'I cannot tell.'

'Well, then, do you imagine that this other one, Henry Baker, had anything to do with the matter?'

'It is, I think, much more likely that Henry Baker is an absolutely innocent man, who had no idea that the bird which he was carrying was of considerably more value than if it were made of solid gold. That, however, I shall determine by a very simple test if we have an answer to our advertisement.'

'And you can do nothing until then?'

'Nothing.'

'In that case I shall continue my professional round. But I shall come back in the evening at the hour you have mentioned, for I should like to see the solution of so tangled a business.'

'Very glad to see you. I dine at seven. There is a woodcock I believe. By the way, in view of recent occurrences, perhaps I ought to ask Mrs Hudson to examine its crop.'

I had been delayed at a case, and it was a little after halfpast six when I found myself in Baker Street once more.

As I approached the house I saw a tall man in a Scotch bonnet with a coat which was buttoned up to his chin waiting outside in the bright semicircle which was thrown from the fanlight. Just as I arrived the door was opened, and we were shown up together to Holmes's room.

'Mr Henry Baker, I believe,' said he, rising from his armchair and greeting his visitor with the easy air of geniality which he could so readily assume. 'Pray take this chair by the fire, Mr Baker. It is a cold night, and I observe that your circulation is more adapted for summer than for winter. Ah, Watson, you have just come at the right time. Is that your hat, Mr Baker?'

'Yes, sir, that is undoubtedly my hat.'

He was a large man with rounded shoulders, a massive head, and a broad, intelligent face, sloping down to a pointed beard of grizzled brown. A touch of red in nose and cheeks, with a slight tremor of his extended hand, recalled Holmes's surmise as to his habits. His rusty black frock coat was buttoned right up in front, with the collar turned up, and his lank wrists protruded from his sleeves without a sign of cuff or shirt. He spoke in a slow staccato fashion, choosing his words with care, and gave the impression generally of a man of learning and letters who had had ill-usage at the hands of fortune.

'We have retained these things for some days,' said Holmes, 'because we expected to see an advertisement from you giving your address. I am at a loss to know now why you did not advertise.'

Our visitor gave a rather shamefaced laugh. 'Shillings have not been so plentiful with me as they once were,' he remarked. 'I had no doubt that the gang of roughs who assaulted me had carried off both my hat and the bird. I did not care to spend more money in a hopeless attempt at recovering them.'

'Very naturally. By the way, about the bird, we were compelled to eat it.'

'To eat it!' Our visitor half rose from his chair in his excitement.

'Yes, it would have been of no use to anyone had we not done so. But I presume that this other goose upon the sideboard, which is about the same weight and perfectly fresh, will answer your purpose equally well?'

'Oh, certainly, certainly,' answered Mr Baker with a sigh of relief.

'Of course, we still have the feathers, legs, crop, and so on of your own bird, so if you wish—'

The man burst into a hearty laugh. 'They might be useful to me as relics of my adventure,' said he, 'but beyond that I can hardly see what use the *disjecta membra* of my late acquaintance are going to be to me. No, sir, I think that, with your permission, I will confine my attentions to the excellent bird which I perceive upon the sideboard.'

Sherlock Holmes glanced sharply across at me with a slight shrug of his shoulders.

'There is your hat, then, and there your bird,' said he. 'By the way, would it bore you to tell me where you got the other one from? I am somewhat of a fowl fancier, and I have seldom seen a better grown goose.'

'Certainly, sir,' said Baker, who had risen and tucked his newly gained property under his arm. 'There are a few of us who frequent the Alpha Inn, near the Museum – we are to be found in the Museum itself during the day, you understand. This year our good host, Windigate by name, instituted a goose club, by which, on consideration of some few pence every week, we were each to receive a bird at Christmas. My pence were duly paid, and the rest is familiar to you. I am much indebted to you, sir, for a Scotch bonnet is fitted neither to my years nor my gravity.' With a comical pomposity of manner he bowed solemnly to both of us and strode off upon his way.

'So much for Mr Henry Baker,' said Holmes when he had closed the door behind him. 'It is quite certain that he knows nothing whatever about the matter. Are you hungry, Watson?'

'Not particularly.'

'Then I suggest that we turn our dinner into a supper and follow up this clue while it is still hot.'

'By all means.'

It was a bitter night, so we drew on our ulsters and wrapped cravats about our throats. Outside, the stars were shining coldly in a cloudless sky, and the breath of the passers-by blew out into smoke like so many pistol shots. Our footfalls rang out crisply and loudly as we swung through the doctors' quarter, Wimpole Street, Harley Street, and so through Wigmore Street into Oxford Street. In a quarter of an hour we were in Bloomsbury at the Alpha Inn, which is a small public house at the corner of one of the streets which runs down into Holborn. Holmes pushed open the door of the private bar and ordered two glasses of beer from the ruddy-faced, white-aproned landlord.

'Your beer should be excellent if it is as good as your geese,' said he.

'My geese!' The man seemed surprised.

'Yes. I was speaking only half an hour ago to Mr Henry Baker, who was a member of your goose club.'

'Ah! yes, I see. But you see, sir, them's not *our* geese.'

'Indeed? Whose, then?'

'Well, I got the two dozen from a salesman in Covent Garden.'

'Indeed? I know some of them. Which was it?'

'Breckinridge is his name.'

'Ah! I don't know him. Well, here's your good health, land-lord, and prosperity to your house. Good night.

'Now for Mr Breckinridge,' he continued, buttoning up his coat as we came out into the frosty air. 'Remember, Watson, that though we have so homely a thing as a goose at one end of this chain, we have at the other a man who will certainly get seven years' penal servitude unless we can establish his innocence. It is possible that our inquiry may but confirm his guilt; but, in any case, we have a line of investigation which has been missed by the police, and which a singular chance has placed in our hands. Let us follow it out to the bitter end. Faces to the south, then, and quick march!'

We passed across Holborn, down Endell Street, and so through a zigzag of slums to Covent Garden Market. One of the largest stalls bore the name of Breckinridge upon it, and the proprietor, a horsy-looking man, with a sharp face and trim side whiskers, was helping a boy to put up the shutters.

'Good evening. It's a cold night,' said Holmes.

The salesman nodded and shot a questioning glance at my companion.

'Sold out of geese, I see,' continued Holmes, pointing at the bare slabs of marble.

'Let you have five hundred tomorrow morning.'

'That's no good.'

'Well, there are some on the stall with the gas flare.'

'Ah, but I was recommended to you.'

'Who by?'

'The landlord of the Alpha.'

'Oh, yes; I sent him a couple of dozen.'

'Fine birds they were, too. Now where did you get them from?'

To my surprise the question provoked a burst of anger from the salesman.

'Now, then, mister,' said he, with his head cocked and his arms akimbo, 'what are you driving at? Let's have it straight now.'

'It is straight enough. I should like to know who sold you the geese which you supplied to the Alpha.'

'Well, then, I shan't tell you. So now!'

'Oh, it is a matter of no importance; but I don't know why you should be so warm over such a trifle.'

'Warm! You'd be as warm, maybe, if you were as pestered as I am. When I pay good money for a good article there should be an end of the business; but it's "Where are the geese?" and "Who did you sell the geese to?" and "What will you take for the geese?" One would think they were the only geese in the world, to hear the fuss that is made over them.'

'Well, I have no connection with any other people who have been making inquiries,' said Holmes carelessly. 'If you won't tell us the bet is off, that is all. But I'm always ready to back my opinion on a matter of fowls, and I have a fiver on it that the bird I ate is country bred.'

'Well, then, you've lost your fiver, for it's town bred,' snapped the salesman.

'It's nothing of the kind.'

'I say it is.'

'I don't believe it.'

'D'you think you know more about fowls than I, who have handled them ever since I was a nipper? I tell you, all those birds that went to the Alpha were town bred.'

'You'll never persuade me to believe that.'

'Will you bet, then?'

'It's merely taking your money, for I know that I am right.

But I'll have a sovereign on with you, just to teach you not to be obstinate.'

The salesman chuckled grimly. 'Bring me the books, Bill,' said he.

The small boy brought round a small thin volume and a great greasy-backed one, laying them out together beneath the hanging lamp.

'Now then, Mr Cocksure,' said the salesman, 'I thought that I was out of geese, but before I finish you'll find that there is still one left in my shop. You see this little book?'

'Well?'

'That's the list of folk from whom I buy. D'you see? Well, then, here on this page are the country folk, and the numbers after their names are where their accounts are in the big ledger. Now, then! You see this other page in red ink? Well, that is a list of my town suppliers. Now, look at that third name. Just read it out to me.'

'Mrs Oakshott, 117, Brixton Road – 249,' read Holmes.

'Quite so. Now turn that up in the ledger.'

Holmes turned to the page indicated. 'Here you are, "Mrs Oakshott, 117, Brixton Road, egg and poultry supplier".'

'Now, then, what's the last entry?'

' "December 22nd. Twenty-four geese at 7s. 6d." '

'Quite so. There you are. And underneath?'

' "Sold to Mr Windigate of the Alpha at 12s." '

'What have you to say now?'

Sherlock Holmes looked deeply chagrined. He drew a sovereign from his pocket and threw it down upon the slab, turning away with the air of a man whose disgust is too deep for words. A few yards off he stopped under a lamppost and laughed in the hearty, noiseless fashion which was peculiar to him.

'When you see a man with whiskers of that cut and the "Pink 'un" protruding out of his pocket, you can always draw him by a bet,' said he. 'I daresay that if I put £100 down in front of him, that man would not have given me such complete information as was drawn from him by the idea that he was doing me on a wager. Well, Watson, we are, I fancy, nearing the end of our quest, and the only point which remains to be determined is whether we should go to this Mrs Oakshott tonight, or whether we should reserve it for tomorrow. It is clear from what that surly fellow said that there are others besides ourselves who are anxious about the matter, and I should—'

His remarks were suddenly cut short by a loud hubbub which broke out from the stall which we had just left. Turning round we saw a little rat-faced fellow standing in the centre of the circle of yellow light which was thrown by the swinging lamp, while Breckinridge, the salesman, framed in the door of his stall, was shaking his fists fiercely at the cringing figure.

'I've had enough of you and your geese,' he shouted. 'I wish you were all at the devil together. If you come pestering me any more with your silly talk I'll set the dog at you. You bring Mrs Oakshott here and I'll answer her, but what have you to do with it? Did I buy the geese off you?'

'No; but one of them was mine all the same,' whined the little man.

'Well, then, ask Mrs Oakshott for it.'

'She told me to ask you.'

'Well, you can ask the King of Proosia, for all I care. I've had enough of it. Get out of this!' He rushed fiercely forward, and the inquirer flitted away into the darkness.

'Ha! this may save us a visit to Brixton Road,' whispered Holmes. 'Come with me, and we will see what is to be made of this fellow.' Striding through the scattered knots of people who lounged round the flaring stalls, my companion speedily overtook the little man and touched him upon the shoulder. He sprang round, and I could see in the gaslight that every vestige of colour had been driven from his face.

'Who are you, then? What do you want?' he asked in a quavering voice.

'You will excuse me,' said Holmes blandly, 'but I could not help overhearing the questions which you put to the salesman just now. I think that I could be of assistance to you.'

'You? Who are you? How could you know anything of the matter?'

'My name is Sherlock Holmes. It is my business to know what other people don't know.'

'But you can know nothing of this?'

'Excuse me, I know everything of it. You are endeavouring to trace some geese which were sold by Mrs Oakshott, of Brixton Road, to a salesman named Breckinridge, by him in turn to Mr Windigate, of the Alpha, and by him to his club, of which Mr Henry Baker is a member.'

'Oh, sir, you are the very man whom I have longed to meet,' cried the little fellow with outstretched hands and quivering fingers. 'I can hardly explain to you how interested I am in this matter.'

Sherlock Holmes hailed a four-wheeler which was passing. 'In that case we had better discuss it in a cosy room rather than in this windswept marketplace,' said he. 'But pray tell me, before we go farther, who is it that I have the pleasure of assisting.'

The man hesitated for an instant. 'My name is John Robinson,' he answered with a sidelong glance.

'No, no; the real name,' said Holmes sweetly. 'It is always awkward doing business with an alias.'

A flush sprang to the white cheeks of the stranger. 'Well, then,' said he, 'my real name is James Ryder.'

'Precisely so. Head attendant at the Hotel Cosmopolitan. Pray step into the cab, and I shall soon be able to tell you everything which you would wish to know.'

The little man stood glancing from one to the other of us with half-frightened, half-hopeful eyes, as one who is not sure whether he is on the verge of a windfall or of a catastrophe. Then he stepped into the cab, and in half an hour we were back in the sitting room at Baker Street. Nothing had been said during our drive, but the high, thin breathing of our new companion, and the claspings and unclaspings of his hands, spoke of the nervous tension within him.

'Here we are!' said Holmes cheerily as we filed into the room. 'The fire looks very seasonable in this weather. You look cold, Mr Ryder. Pray take the basket chair. I will just put on my slippers before we settle this little matter of yours. Now, then! You want to know what became of those geese?'

'Yes, sir.'

'Or rather, I fancy, of that goose. It was one bird, I imagine, in which you were interested – white, with a black bar across the tail.'

Ryder quivered with emotion. 'Oh, sir,' he cried, 'can you tell me where it went to?'

'It came here.'

'Here?'

'Yes, and a most remarkable bird it proved. I don't wonder that you should take an interest in it. It laid an egg after it was dead – the bonniest, brightest little blue egg that ever was seen. I have it here in my museum.'

Our visitor staggered to his feet and clutched the mantelpiece with his right hand. Holmes unlocked his strongbox and held up the blue carbuncle, which shone out like a star, with a cold, brilliant, many-pointed radiance. Ryder stood glaring with a drawn face, uncertain whether to claim or to disown it.

'The game's up, Ryder,' said Holmes quietly. 'Hold up, man, or you'll be into the fire! Give him an arm back into his chair, Watson. He's not got blood enough to go in for felony with impunity. Give him a dash of brandy. So! Now he looks a little more human. What a shrimp it is, to be sure!'

For a moment he had staggered and nearly fallen, but the brandy brought a tinge of colour into his cheeks, and he sat staring with frightened eyes at his accuser.

'I have almost every link in my hands, and all the proofs which I could possibly need, so there is little which you need tell me. Still, that little may as well be cleared up to make the case complete. You had heard, Ryder, of this blue stone of the Countess of Morcar's?'

'It was Catherine Cusack who told me of it,' said he in a crackling voice.

'I see – her ladyship's waiting maid. Well, the temptation of sudden wealth so easily acquired was too much for you, as it has been for better men before you; but you were not very scrupulous in the means you used. It seems to me, Ryder, that there is the making of a very pretty villain in you. You knew that this man Horner, the plumber, had been concerned in some such matter before, and that suspicion would rest the more readily upon him. What did you do, then? You made some small job in my lady's room – you and your confederate Cusack – and you managed that he should be the man sent for. Then, when he had left, you rifled the jewel case, raised the alarm, and had this unfortunate man arrested. You then—'

Ryder threw himself down suddenly upon the rug and clutched at my companion's knees. 'For God's sake, have mercy!' he shrieked. 'Think of my father! of my mother! It would break their hearts. I never went wrong before! I never will again. I swear it. I'll swear it on a Bible. Oh, don't bring it into court! For Christ's sake, don't!'

'Get back into your chair!' said Holmes sternly. 'It is very well to cringe and crawl now, but you thought little enough of this poor Horner in the dock for a crime of which he knew nothing.'

'I will fly, Mr Holmes. I will leave the country, sir. Then the charge against him will break down.'

'Hum! We will talk about that. And now let us hear a true account of the next act. How came the stone into the goose, and how came the goose into the open market? Tell us the truth, for there lies your only hope of safety.'

Ryder passed his tongue over his parched lips. 'I will tell you it just as it happened, sir,' said he. 'When Horner had been arrested, it seemed to me that it would be best for me to get away with the stone at once, for I did not know at what moment the police might not take it into their heads to search me and my room. There was no place about the hotel where it would be safe. I went out, as if on some commission, and I made for my sister's house. She had married a man named Oakshott, and lived in Brixton Road, where she fattened fowls for the market. All the way there every man I met seemed to me to be a policeman or a detective; and, for all that it was a cold night, the sweat was pouring down my face before I came to the Brixton Road. My sister asked me what was the matter and why I was so pale; but I told her that I had been upset by the jewel robbery at the hotel. Then I went into the back yard and smoked a pipe, and wondered what it would be best to do.

'I had a friend once called Maudsley, who went to the bad, and has just been serving his time in Pentonville. One day he had met me, and fell into talk about the ways of thieves, and how they could get rid of what they stole. I knew that he would be true to me, for I knew one or two things about him; so I made up my mind to go right on to Kilburn, where he lived, and take him into my confidence. He would show me how to turn the stone into money. But how to get to him in safety? I thought of the agonies I had gone through in coming from the hotel. I might at any moment be seized and searched, and there would be the stone in my waistcoat pocket. I was leaning against the wall at the time and looking at the geese which were waddling about round my feet, and suddenly an idea came into my head which showed me how I could beat the best detective that ever lived.

'My sister had told me some weeks before that I might have the pick of her geese for a Christmas present, and I knew that she was always as good as her word. I would take my goose now, and in it I would carry my stone to Kilburn. There was a little shed in the yard, and behind this I drove one of the birds – a fine big one, white, with a barred tail. I caught it, and, prying its bill open, I thrust the stone down its throat as far as my finger could reach. The bird gave a gulp, and I felt the stone pass along its gullet and down into its crop. But the creature flapped and struggled, and out came my sister to know what was the matter. As I turned to speak to her the brute broke loose and fluttered off among the others.

' "Whatever were you doing with that bird, Jem?" says she.

' "Well", said I, "you said you'd give me one for Christmas, and I was feeling which was the fattest."

' "Oh," says she, "we've set yours aside for you – Jem's bird, we call it. It's the big white one over yonder. There's twenty-six of them, which makes one for you, and one for us, and two dozen for the market."

' "Thank you, Maggie," says I; "but if it is all the same to you, I'd rather have that one I was handling just now."

' "The other is a good three pound heavier," said she, "and we fattened it expressly for you."

' "Never mind. I'll have the other, and I'll take it now," said I.

' "Oh, just as you like," said she, a little huffed. "Which is it you want, then?"

' "That white one with the barred tail, right in the middle of the flock."

' "Oh, very well. Kill it and take it with you."

'Well, I did what she said, Mr Holmes, and I carried the bird all the way to Kilburn. I told my pal what I had done, for he was a man that it was easy to tell a thing like that to. He laughed until he choked, and we got a knife and opened the goose. My heart turned to water, for there was no sign of the stone, and I knew that some terrible mistake had occurred. I left the bird, rushed back to my sister's, and hurried into the back yard. There was not a bird to be seen there.

' "Where are they all, Maggie?" I cried.

' "Gone to the dealer's, Jem."

' "Which dealer's?"

' "Breckinridge, of Covent Garden."

' "But was there another with a barred tail?" I asked, "the same as the one I chose?"

' "Yes, Jem; there were two barred-tailed ones, and I could never tell them apart."

'Well, then, of course, I saw it all, and I ran off as hard as my feet would carry me to this man Breckinridge; but he had sold the lot at once, and not one word would he tell me as to where they had gone. You heard him yourselves tonight. Well, he has always answered me like that. My sister thinks I am going mad. Sometimes I think that I am myself. And now – and now I am myself a branded thief, without ever having touched the wealth for which I sold my character. God help me! God help me!' He burst into convulsive sobbing, with his face buried in his hands.

There was a long silence, broken only by his heavy breathing, and by the measured tapping of Sherlock Holmes's fingertips upon the edge of the table. Then my friend rose and threw open the door.

'Get out!' said he.

'What, sir! Oh, Heaven bless you!'

'No more words. Get out!'

And no more words were needed. There was a rush, a clatter upon the stairs, the bang of a door, and the crisp rattle of running footfalls from the street.

'After all, Watson,' said Holmes, reaching up his hand for his clay pipe, 'I am not retained by the police to supply their deficiencies. If Horner were in danger it would be another thing; but this fellow will not appear against him, and the case must collapse. I suppose that I am commuting a felony, but it is just possible that I am saving a soul. This fellow will not go wrong again; he is too terribly frightened. Send him to jail now, and you make him a jailbird for life. Besides, it is the season of forgiveness. Chance has put in our way a most singular and whimsical problem, and its solution is its own reward. If you will have the goodness to touch the bell, Doctor, we will begin another investigation, in which, also a bird will be the chief feature.'

GEORGE GISSING

CHRISTOPHERSON
(1906)

IT WAS TWENTY years ago, and on an evening in May. All day long there had been sunshine. Owing, doubtless, to the incident I am about to relate, the light and warmth of that long-vanished day live with me still; I can see the great white clouds that moved across the strip of sky before my window, and feel again the spring languor which troubled my solitary work in the heart of London.

Only at sunset did I leave the house. There was an unwonted sweetness in the air; the long vistas of newly lit lamps made a golden glow under the dusking flush of the sky. With no purpose but to rest and breathe, I wandered for half an hour, and found myself at length where Great Portland Street opens into Marylebone Road. Over the way, in the shadow of Trinity Church, was an old bookshop, well known to me: the gas-jet shining upon the stall with its rows of volumes drew me across. I began turning over pages, and – invariable consequence – fingering what money I had in my pocket. A certain book overcame me; I stepped into the little shop to pay for it.

While standing at the stall, I had been vaguely aware of some one beside me, a man who also was looking over the books; as I came out again with my purchase, this stranger gazed at me intently, with a half-smile of peculiar interest. He seemed about to say something. I walked slowly away; the man moved in the same direction. Just in front of the church he made a quick movement to my side, and spoke.

'Pray excuse me, sir – don't misunderstand me – I only wished to ask whether you have noticed the name written on the flyleaf of the book you have just bought?'

The respectful nervousness of his voice naturally made me suppose at first that the man was going to beg; but he seemed no ordinary mendicant. I judged him to be about sixty years of age; his long, thin hair and straggling beard were grizzled, and a somewhat rheumy eye looked out from his bloodless, hollowed countenance; he was very shabbily clad, yet as a fallen gentleman, and indeed his accent made it clear to what class he originally belonged. The expression with which he regarded me had so much intelligence, so much good-nature, and at the same time such a pathetic diffidence, that I could not but answer him in the friendliest way. I had not seen the name on the flyleaf, but at once I opened the book, and by the light of a gas-lamp read, inscribed in a very fine hand, 'W. R. Christopherson, 1849.'

'It is my name,' said the stranger, in a subdued and uncertain voice.

'Indeed? The book used to belong to you?'

'It belonged to me.' He laughed oddly, a tremulous little crow of a laugh, at the same time stroking his head, as if to deprecate disbelief. 'You never heard of the sale of the Christopherson library? To be sure, you were too young; it was in 1860. I have often come across books with my name in them on the stalls – often. I had happened to notice this just before you came up, and when I saw you look at it, I was curious to see whether you would buy it. Pray excuse the freedom I am taking. Lovers of books – don't you think—?'

The broken question was completed by his look, and when I said that I quite understood and agreed with him he crowed his little laugh.

'Have you a large library?' he inquired, eyeing me wistfully.

'Oh dear, no. Only a few hundred volumes. Too many for one who has no house of his own.'

He smiled good-naturedly, bent his head, and murmured just audibly:

'My catalogue numbered 24,718.'

I was growing curious and interested. Venturing no more direct questions, I asked whether, at the time he spoke of, he lived in London.

'If you have five minutes to spare,' was the timid reply, 'I will show you my house. I mean' – again the little crowing laugh – 'the house which *was* mine.'

Willingly I walked on with him. He led me a short distance up the road skirting Regent's Park, and paused at length before a house in an imposing terrace.

'There,' he whispered, 'I used to live. The window to the right of the door – that was my library. Ah!'

And he heaved a deep sigh.

'A misfortune befell you,' I said, also in a subdued voice.

'The result of my own folly. I had enough for my needs, but thought I needed more. I let myself be drawn into business – I, who knew nothing of such things – and there came the black day – the black day.'

We turned to retrace our steps, and walking slowly, with heads bent, came in silence again to the church.

'I wonder whether you have bought any other of my books?' asked Christopherson, with his gentle smile, when we had paused as if for leave-taking.

I replied that I did not remember to have come across his name before; then, on an impulse, asked whether he would care to have the book I carried in my hand; if so, with pleasure I would give it him. No sooner were the words spoken than I saw the delight they caused the hearer. He hesitated, murmured reluctance, but soon gratefully accepted my offer, and flushed with joy as he took the volume.

'I still have a few books,' he said, under his breath, as if he spoke of something he was ashamed to make known. 'But it is very rarely indeed that I can add to them. I feel I have not thanked you half enough.'

We shook hands and parted.

My lodging at that time was in Camden Town. One afternoon, perhaps a fortnight later, I had walked for an hour or two, and on my way back I stopped at a bookstall in the High Street. Some one came up to my side; I looked, and recognized Christopherson. Our greeting was like that of old friends.

'I have seen you several times lately,' said the broken gentleman, who looked shabbier than before in the broad daylight, 'but I – I didn't like to speak. I live not far from here.'

'Why, so do I,' and I added, without much thinking what I said, 'do you live alone?'

'Alone? oh no. With my wife.'

There was a curious embarrassment in his tone. His eyes were cast down and his head moved uneasily.

We began to talk of the books on the stall, and turning away together continued our conversation. Christopherson was not only a well-bred but a very intelligent and even learned man. On his giving some proof of erudition (with the excessive modesty which characterized him), I asked whether he wrote. No, he had never written anything – never; he was only a bookworm, he said. Thereupon he crowed faintly and took his leave.

It was not long before we again met by chance. We came face to face at a street corner in my neighbourhood, and I was struck by a change in him. He looked older; a profound melancholy darkened his countenance; the hand he gave me was limp, and his pleasure at our meeting found only a faint expression.

'I am going away,' he said in reply to my inquiring look. 'I am leaving London.'

'For good?'

'I fear so, and yet' – he made an obvious effort – 'I am glad of it. My wife's health has not been very good lately. She has need of country air. Yes, I am glad we have decided to go away – very glad – very glad indeed!'

He spoke with an automatic sort of emphasis, his eyes wandering, and his hands twitching nervously. I was on the point of asking what part of the country he had chosen for his retreat, when he abruptly added:

'I live just over there. Will you let me show you my books?'

Of course I gladly accepted the invitation, and a couple of minutes' walk brought us to a house in a decent street where most of the ground-floor windows showed a card announcing lodgings. As we paused at the door, my companion seemed to hesitate, to regret having invited me.

'I'm really afraid it isn't worth your while,' he said timidly. 'The fact is, I haven't space to show my books properly.'

I put aside the objection, and we entered. With anxious courtesy Christopherson led me up the narrow staircase to the second-floor landing, and threw open a door. On the threshold I stood astonished. The room was a small one, and would in any case have only just sufficed for homely comfort, used as it evidently was for all daytime purposes; but certainly a third of the entire space was occupied by a solid mass of books, volumes stacked several rows deep against two of the walls and almost up to the ceiling. A round table and two or three chairs were the only furniture – there was no room, indeed, for more. The window being shut, and the sunshine glowing upon it, an intolerable stuffiness oppressed the air. Never had I been made so uncomfortable by the odour of printed paper and bindings.

'But,' I exclaimed, 'you said you had only a *few* books! There must be five times as many here as I have.'

'I forget the exact number,' murmured Christopherson, in great agitation. 'You see, I can't arrange them properly. I have a few more in – in the other room.'

He led me across the landing, opened another door, and showed me a little bedroom. Here the encumberment was less remarkable, but one wall had completely disappeared behind volumes, and the bookishness of the air made it a disgusting thought that two persons occupied this chamber every night.

We returned to the sitting-room, Christopherson began picking out books from the solid mass to show me. Talking nervously, brokenly, with now and then a deep sigh or a crow of laughter, he gave me a little light on his history. I learnt that he had occupied these lodgings for the last eight years; that he had been twice married; that the only child he had had, a daughter by his first wife, had died long ago in childhood; and lastly – this came in a burst of confidence, with a very pleasant smile – that his second wife had been his daughter's governess. I listened with keen interest, and hoped to learn still more of the circumstances of this singular household.

'In the country,' I remarked, 'you will no doubt have shelf room?'

At once his countenance fell; he turned upon me a woe-begone eye. Just as I was about to speak again sounds from within the house caught my attention; there was a heavy foot on the stairs, and a loud voice, which seemed familiar to me.

'Ah!' exclaimed Christopherson with a start, 'here comes

some one who is going to help me in the removal of the books. Come in, Mr Pomfret, come in!'

The door opened, and there appeared a tall, wiry fellow, whose sandy hair, light blue eyes, jutting jaw-bones, and large mouth made a picture suggestive of small refinement but of vigorous and wholesome manhood. No wonder I had seemed to recognize his voice. Though we only saw each other by chance at long intervals, Pomfret and I were old acquaintances.

'Hallo!' he roared out, 'I didn't know you knew Mr Christopherson.'

'I'm just as much surprised to find that *you* know him!' was my reply.

The old book-lover gazed at us in nervous astonishment, then shook hands with the newcomer, who greeted him bluffly, yet respectfully. Pomfret spoke with a strong Yorkshire accent, and had all the angularity of demeanour which marks the typical Yorkshireman. He came to announce that everything had been settled for the packing and transporting of Mr Christopherson's library; it remained only to decide the day.

'There's no hurry,' exclaimed Christopherson. 'There's really no hurry. I'm greatly obliged to you, Mr Pomfret, for all the trouble you are taking. We'll settle the date in a day or two – a day or two.'

With a good-humoured nod Pomfret moved to take his leave. Our eyes met; we left the house together. Out in the street again I took a deep breath of the summer air, which seemed sweet as in a meadow after that stifling room. My companion evidently had a like sensation, for he looked up to the sky and broadened out his shoulders.

'Eh, but it's a grand day! I'd give something for a walk on Ilkley Moors.'

As the best substitute within our reach we agreed to walk across Regent's Park together. Pomfret's business took him in that direction, and I was glad of a talk about Christopherson. I learnt that the old book-lover's landlady was Pomfret's aunt. Christopherson's story of affluence and ruin was quite true. Ruin complete, for at the age of forty he had been obliged to earn his living as a clerk or something of the kind. About five years later came his second marriage.

'You know Mrs Christopherson?' asked Pomfret.

'No! I wish I did. Why?'

'Because she's the sort of woman it does you good to know, that's all. She's a lady – *my* idea of a lady. Christopherson's a gentleman too, there's no denying it; if he wasn't, I think I should have punched his head before now. Oh, I know 'em well! why, I lived in the house there with 'em for several years. She's a lady to the end of her little finger, and how her husband can 'a borne to see her living the life she has, it's more than I can understand. By—! I'd have turned burglar, if I could 'a found no other way of keeping her in comfort.'

'She works for her living, then?'

'Ay, and for his too. No, not teaching; she's in a shop in Tottenham Court Road; has what they call a good place, and earns thirty shillings a week. It's all they have, but Christopherson buys books out of it.'

'But has he never done anything since their marriage?'

'He did for the first few years, I believe, but he had an illness, and that was the end of it. Since then he's only loafed. He goes to all the book-sales, and spends the rest of his time sniffing about the second-hand shops. She? Oh, she'd never say a word! Wait till you've seen her.'

'Well, but,' I asked, 'what has happened? How is it they're leaving London?'

'Ay, I'll tell you; I was coming to that. Mrs Christopherson has relatives well off – a fat and selfish lot, as far as I can make out – never lifted a finger to help her until now. One of them's a Mrs Keeting, the widow of some City porpoise, I'm told. Well, this woman has a home down in Norfolk. She never lives there, but a son of hers goes there to fish and shoot now and then. Well, this is what Mrs Christopherson tells my aunt, Mrs Keeting has offered to let her and her husband live down yonder, rent free, and their food provided. She's to be housekeeper, in fact, and keep the place ready for any one who goes down.'

'Christopherson, *I* can see, would rather stay where he is.'

'Why, of course, he doesn't know how he'll live without the bookshops. But he's glad for all that, on his wife's account. And it's none too soon, I can tell you. The poor woman couldn't go on much longer; my aunt says she's just about ready to drop, and sometimes, I know, she looks terribly bad. Of course, she won't own it, not she; she isn't one of the complaining sort. But she talks now and then about the country – the places where she used to live. I've heard her, and it gives me a notion of what she's gone through all these years. I saw her a week ago, just when she had Mrs Keeting's offer, and I tell you I scarcely knew who it was! You never saw such a change in any one in your life! Her face was like that of a girl of seventeen. And her laugh – you should have heard her laugh!'

'Is she much younger than her husband?' I asked.

'Twenty years at least. She's about forty, I think.'

I mused for a few moments.

'After all, it isn't an unhappy marriage?'

'Unhappy?' cried Pomfret. 'Why, there's never been a disagreeable word between them, that I'll warrant. Once Christopherson gets over the change, they'll have nothing more in the world to ask for. He'll potter over his books—'

'You mean to tell me,' I interrupted, 'that those books have all been bought out of his wife's thirty shillings a week?'

'No, no. To begin with, he kept a few out of his old library. Then, when he was earning his own living, he bought a great many. He told me once that he's often lived on sixpence a day to have money for books. A rum old owl; but for all that he's a gentleman, and you can't help liking him. I shall be sorry when he's out of reach.'

For my own part, I wished nothing better than to hear of Christopherson's departure. The story I had heard made me uncomfortable. It was good to think of that poor woman rescued at last from her life of toil, and in these days of midsummer free to enjoy the country she loved. A touch of envy mingled, I confess, with my thought of Christopherson, who henceforth had not a care in the world, and without reproach might delight in his hoarded volumes. One could not imagine that he would suffer seriously by the removal of his old haunts. I promised myself to call on him in a day or two. By choosing Sunday, I might perhaps be lucky enough to see his wife.

And on Sunday afternoon I was on the point of setting forth to pay this visit, when in came Pomfret. He wore a surly look, and kicked clumsily against the furniture as he crossed the room. His appearance was a surprise, for, though I had given him my address, I did not in the least expect that he would come to see me; a certain pride, I suppose, characteristic of his rugged strain, having always made him shy of such intimacy.

'Did you ever hear the like of *that*!' he shouted, half angrily. 'It's all over. They're not going! And all because of those blamed books!'

And spluttering and growling, he made known what he had just learnt at his aunt's home. On the previous afternoon the Christophersons had been surprised by a visit from their relatives and would-be benefactress, Mrs Keeting. Never before had that lady called upon them; she came, no doubt (this could only be conjectured), to speak with them of their approaching removal. The close of the conversation (a very brief one) was overheard by the landlady, for Mrs Keeting spoke loudly as she descended the stairs. 'Impossible! Quite impossible! I couldn't think of it! How could you dream for a moment that I would let you fill my house with musty old books? Most unhealthy! I never knew anything so extra-ordinary in my life, never!' And so she went out to her carriage, and was driven away. And the landlady, presently having occasion to go upstairs, was aware of a dead silence in the room where the Christophersons were sitting. She knocked – prepared with some excuse – and found the couple side by side, smiling sadly. At once they told her the truth. Mrs Keeting had come because of a letter in which Mrs Christopherson had mentioned the fact that her husband had a good many books, and hoped he might be permitted to remove them to the house in Norfolk. She came to see the library – with the result already heard. They had the choice between sacrificing the books and losing what their relative offered.

'Christopherson refused?' I let fall.

'I suppose his wife saw that it was too much for him. At all events, they'd agreed to keep the books and lose the house. And there's an end of it. I haven't been so riled about any-thing for a long time!'

Meantime I had been reflecting. It was easy for me to understand Christopherson's state of mind, and without knowing Mrs Keeting, I saw that she must be a person whose benefactions would be a good deal of a burden. After all, was Mrs Christopherson so very unhappy? Was she not the kind of woman who lived by sacrifice – one who had far rather lead a life disagreeable to herself than change it at the cost of discomfort to her husband? This view of the matter irritated Pomfret, and he broke into objurgations, directed partly against Mrs Keeting, partly against Christopherson. It was an 'infernal shame,' that was all he could say. And after all, I rather inclined to his opinion.

When two or three days had passed, curiosity drew me towards the Christophersons' dwelling. Walking along the opposite side of the street, I looked up at their window, and there was the face of the old bibliophile. Evidently he was standing at the window in idleness, perhaps in trouble. At once he beckoned to me; but before I could knock at the house-door he had descended, and came out.

'May I walk a little way with you?' he asked.

There was worry on his features. For some moments we went on in silence.

'So you have changed your mind about leaving London?' I said, as if carelessly.

'You have heard from Mr Pomfret? Well – yes, yes – I think we shall stay where we are – for the present.'

Never have I seen a man more painfully embarrassed. He walked with head bent, shoulders stooping; and shuffled, indeed, rather than walked. Even so might a man bear himself who felt guilty of some peculiar meanness.

Presently words broke from him.

'To tell you the truth, there's a difficulty about the books.' He glanced furtively at me, and I saw he was trembling in all his nerves. 'As you see, my circumstances are not brilliant.' He half-choked himself with a crow. 'The fact is we were offered a house in the country, on certain conditions, by a relative of Mrs Christopherson; and, unfortunately, it turned out that my library is regarded as an objection – a fatal objection. We have quite reconciled ourselves to staying where we are.'

I could not help asking, without emphasis, whether Mrs Christopherson would have cared for life in the country. But no sooner were the words out of my mouth than I regretted them, so evidently did they hit my companion in a tender place.

'I think she would have liked it,' he answered, with a strangely pathetic look at me, as if he entreated my forbearance.

'But,' I suggested, 'couldn't you make some arrangements about the books? Couldn't you take a room for them in another house, for instance?'

Christopherson's face was sufficient answer; it reminded me of his pennilessness. 'We think no more about it,' he said. 'The matter is settled – quite settled.'

There was no pursuing the subject. At the next parting of the ways we took leave of each other.

I think it was not more than a week later when I received a postcard from Pomfret. He wrote: 'Just as I expected. Mrs C. seriously ill.' That was all.

Mrs C. could, of course, only mean Mrs Christopherson. I mused over the message – it took hold of my imagination, wrought upon my feelings; and that afternoon I again walked along the interesting street.

There was no face at the window. After a little hesitation I decided to call at the house and speak with Pomfret's aunt. It was she who opened the door to me.

We had never seen each other, but when I mentioned my name and said I was anxious to have news of Mrs Christopherson, she led me into a sitting-room, and began to talk confidentially.

She was a good-natured Yorkshirewoman, very unlike the

common London landlady. 'Yes, Mrs Christopherson had been taken ill two days ago. It began with a long fainting fit. She had a feverish, sleepless night; the doctor was sent for; and he had her removed out of the stuffy, book-cumbered bedroom into another chamber, which luckily happened to be vacant. There she lay utterly weak and worn, all but voiceless, able only to smile at her husband, who never moved from the bedside day or night. He, too,' said the land-lady, 'would soon break down: he looked like a ghost, and seemed "half-crazed."'

'What,' I asked, 'could be the cause of this illness?'

The good woman gave me an odd look, shook her head, and murmured that the reason was not far to seek.

'Did she think,' I asked, 'that disappointment might have something to do with it?'

Why, of course she did. For a long time the poor lady had been all but at the end of her strength, and *this* came as a blow beneath which she sank.

'Your nephew and I have talked about it,' I said. 'He thinks that Mr Christopherson didn't understand what a sacrifice he asked his wife to make.'

'I think so too,' was the reply. 'But he begins to see it now, I can tell you. He says nothing but—'

There was a tap at the door, and a hurried tremulous voice begged the landlady to go upstairs.

'What is it, sir?' she asked.

'I'm afraid she's worse,' said Christopherson, turning his haggard face to me with startled recognition. 'Do come up at once, please.'

Without a word to me he disappeared with the landlady. I could not go away; for some ten minutes I fidgeted about the little room, listening to every sound in the house. Then came a footfall on the stairs, and the landlady rejoined me.

'It's nothing,' she said. 'I almost think she might drop off to sleep, if she's left quiet. He worries her, poor man, sitting there and asking her every two minutes how she feels. I've persuaded him to go to his room, and I think it might do him good if you went and had a bit o' talk with him.'

I mounted at once to the second-floor sitting-room, and found Christopherson sunk upon a chair, his head falling forwards, the image of despairing misery. As I approached he staggered to his feet. He took my hand in a shrinking, shamefaced way, and could not raise his eyes. I uttered a few words of encouragement, but they had the opposite effect to that designed.

'Don't tell me that,' he moaned, half resentfully. 'She's dying – she's dying – say what they will, I know it.'

'Have you a good doctor?'

'I think so – but it's too late – it's too late.'

As he dropped to his chair again I sat down by him. The silence of a minute or two was broken by a thunderous rat-tat at the house-door. Christopherson leapt to his feet, rushed from the room; I, half fearing that he had gone mad, followed to the head of the stairs.

In a moment he came up again, limp and wretched as before.

'It was the postman,' he muttered. 'I am expecting a letter.'

Conversation seeming impossible, I shaped a phrase preliminary to withdrawal; but Christopherson would not let me go.

'I should like to tell you,' he began, looking at me like a dog under punishment, 'that I have done all I could. As soon as my wife fell ill, and when I saw – I had only begun to think of it in that way – how she felt the disappointment, I went at once to Mrs Keeting's house to tell her that I would sell the books. But she was out of town. I wrote to her – I said

I regretted my folly – I entreated her to forgive me and to renew her kind offer. There has been plenty of time for a reply, but she doesn't answer.'

He had in his hand what I saw was a bookseller's catalogue, just delivered by the postman. Mechanically he tore off the wrapper and even glanced over the first page. Then, as if conscience stabbed him, he flung the thing violently away.

'The chance has gone!' he exclaimed, taking a hurried step or two along the little strip of floor left free by the mountain of books. 'Of course she said she would rather stay in London! Of course she said what she knew would please me! When – when did she ever say anything else! And I was cruel enough – base enough – to let her make the sacrifice!' He waved his arms frantically. 'Didn't I know what it cost her? Couldn't I see in her face how her heart leapt at the hope of going to live in the country! I knew what she was suffering; I *knew* it, I tell you! And, like a selfish coward, I let her suffer – I let her drop down and die – die!'

'Any hour,' I said, 'may bring you the reply from Mrs Keeting. Of course it will be favourable, and the good news—'

'Too late, I have killed her! That woman won't write. She's one of the vulgar rich, and we offended her pride; and such as she never forgive.'

He sat down for a moment, but started up again in an agony of mental suffering.

'She is dying – and there, there, that's what has killed her!' He gesticulated wildly towards the books. 'I have sold her life for those. Oh! – oh!'

With this cry he seized half a dozen volumes, and, before I could understand what he was about, he had flung up the window-sash, and cast the books into the street. Another batch followed; I heard the thud upon the pavement. Then

I caught him by the arm, held him fast, begged him to control himself.

'They shall all go!' he cried. 'I loathe the sight of them. They have killed my dear wife!'

He said it sobbing, and at the last words tears streamed from his eyes. I had no difficulty now in restraining him. He met my look with a gaze of infinite pathos, and talked on while he wept.

'If you knew what she has been to me! When she married me I was a ruined man twenty years older. I have given her nothing but toil and care. You shall know everything – for years and years I have lived on the earnings of her labour. Worse than that, I have starved and stinted her to buy books. Oh, the shame of it! The wickedness of it! It was my vice – the vice that enslaved me just as if it had been drinking or gambling. I couldn't resist the temptation – though every day I cried shame upon myself and swore to overcome it. She never blamed me; never a word – nay, not a look – of a reproach. I lived in idleness. I never tried to save her that daily toil at the shop. Do you know that she worked in a shop? – She, with her knowledge and her refinement leading such a life as that! Think that I have passed the shop a thousand times, coming home with a book in my hands! I had the heart to pass, and to think of her there! Oh! Oh!'

Some one was knocking at the door. I went to open, and saw the landlady, her face set in astonishment, and her arms full of books.

'It's all right,' I whispered. 'Put them down on the floor there; don't bring them in. An accident.'

Christopherson stood behind me; his look asked what he durst not speak. I said it was nothing, and by degrees brought him into a calmer state. Luckily, the doctor came before I went away, and he was able to report a slight improvement.

The patient had slept a little and seemed likely to sleep again. Christopherson asked me to come again before long – there was no one else, he said, who cared anything about him – and I promised to call the next day.

I did so, early in the afternoon. Christopherson must have watched for my coming: before I could raise the knocker the door flew open, and his face gleamed such a greeting as astonished me. He grasped my hand in both his.

'The letter has come! We are to have the house.'

'And how is Mrs Christopherson?'

'Better, much better, Heaven be thanked! She slept almost from the time when you left yesterday afternoon till early this morning. The letter came by the first post, and I told her – not the whole truth,' he added, under his breath. 'She thinks I am to be allowed to take the books with me; and if you could have seen her smile of contentment. But they will all be sold and carried away before she knows about it; and when she sees that I don't care a snap of the fingers—!'

He had turned into the sitting-room on the ground floor. Walking about excitedly, Christopherson gloried in the sacrifice he had made. Already a letter was despatched to a bookseller, who would buy the whole library as it stood. But would he not keep a few volumes? I asked. Surely there could be no objection to a few shelves of books; and how would he live without them? At first he declared vehemently that not a volume should be kept – he never wished to see a book again as long as he lived. But Mrs Christopherson? I urged. Would she not be glad of something to read now and then? At this he grew pensive. We discussed the matter, and it was arranged that a box should be packed with select volumes and taken down into Norfolk together with the rest of their luggage. Not even Mrs Keeting could object to this, and I strongly advised him to take her permission for granted.

And so it was done. By discreet management the piled volumes were stowed in bags, carried downstairs, emptied into a cart, and conveyed away, so quietly that the sick woman was aware of nothing. In telling me about it, Christopherson crowed as I had never heard him; but methought his eye avoided that part of the floor which had formerly been hidden, and in the course of our conversation he now and then became absent, with head bowed. Of the joy he felt in his wife's recovery there could, however, be no doubt. The crisis through which he had passed had made him, in appearance, a yet older man; when he declared his happiness tears came into his eyes, and his head shook with a senile tremor.

Before they left London, I saw Mrs Christopherson – a pale, thin, slightly made woman, who had never been what is called good-looking, but her face, if ever face did so, declared a brave and loyal spirit. She was not joyous, she was not sad; but in her eyes, as I looked at them again and again, I read the profound thankfulness of one to whom fate has granted her soul's desire.

R. ANDOM

THE FETCHING
OF SUSAN
(1912)

MERRIDEW IS MY next-door neighbour on the right. He is what I call a dangerous optimist, but because I am easy-going and good-natured, and he is generally genial, we got on so well together from the first that, when he found himself up against a natural history puzzle, and lacking an encyclopædia, he came to me with it.

'I say,' he remarked casually across the fence, 'what sort of thing is an emu?'

I thought a bit and told him, more or less correctly, it was a sort of an ostrich with a bald head and a vicious eye. Then he said I should have a founder's share in his and come and help him fetch it home.

'Uncle Jack is sending us one from Australia,' he explained. 'He knows we are fond of a bit of poultry, and these roosters are gay old chicks, I understand. They lay eggs thirteen inches across and holding a couple of gallons.'

'That's good enough for an omelette,' said I. 'It seems to me you are mixing yourself up with the roc, which did that sort of thing with impunity; but whether or no, you'll find a pet emu a bit costly, won't you?'

Merridew thought not. He had a vague sort of impression that a few pennyworths of meal, supplemented by all the bird of promise could glean for itself about his garden and waste places adjoining, would fill the bill – and its bill.

I protested that I had not given him information concerning emus for the hope of reward, and I tried to convince Merridew that I had an engagement which would prevent me accompanying him to fetch his uncle's singular present. I added that I regretted the fact; there are occasions when it is permissible to lie.

'If it had been today, I could have managed it,' said I. 'As a matter of fact, I am finishing up early today, and don't quite know what to do with the time.'

Merridew – artful beast! – said not a word, but at four o'clock he presented himself at my office.

'Come along, old man,' he shouted, in high glee. 'The *Babylon* got in at midday, and we'll go and fetch Susan at once. Fortunate, isn't it, and you being disengaged, too?'

'Very,' said I dismally.

I didn't know as much about emus then as I do now; but I had a sort of presentiment that I was embarking on a sea of troubles, and I would have sprung five shillings gladly if the boy had come down just then and told me that my presence would be needed until midnight. But that sort of thing never happens when you really want it to. Had I been going to a dance or a theatre I might have relied upon some such obstacle intervening; but when it was a question of fetching emus I could have got away at any time I wished.

I was up against it, and, short of offending Merridew and displaying a whole bunch of white feathers, I could not get out. So I plunged in with both feet, recklessly, all the while hoping fervently that the beastly bird had died on the voyage, or got lost or something.

'How do you propose to get it home?' I queried, when we were in the train at Fenchurch Street on our way to the docks.

Merridew hadn't thought of that. He is the sort of man who never does think of anything useful. Anyway, he said he supposed it would be crated, in which case it would go on the top of a 'growler.' If not it could come inside.

'My dear chap,' I protested, 'don't you know that a healthy

232

emu is about eight feet high? It would require a small pan-technicon to accommodate it in a crate. Without one I don't precisely know what conveyance would serve; but this I do know – the cab that holds Susan shall never hold me. If you think I am going to ride ten miles with an emu squatting on my knee with several yards of neck overflowing through the window you are under a wrong impression. Apart from the discomfort, there is my dignity to be thought of, and to be concerned in such a fool show as that would annihilate the dignity of an archbishop.'

Merridew laughed good-temperedly.

'Let's see the mountain before we devise methods of cross-ing it,' he said. 'Whatever the job is we ought to be able to tackle it. Lend me your aid and don't be cantankerous, and you shall have half-a-gallon of Susan's first egg for your reward – or a wing feather for your next season's Sunday straw.'

'Thanks,' said I. 'I'll have three of brandy before we so much as look at the job, and another three before we tackle it. I have a superstition that this is an undertaking that calls for stimulants.'

Merridew asked me if I was afraid of it, and if so, why so? I hadn't the heart to tell him that I had once seen a bird of the emu breed kick a hole in a two-course wall and then start in to eat up the broken brickwork it had created. It might have made him nervous, and then he would have got trying to shunt the job on me while he directed opera-tions from a safe distance. I was intending to save the post of overseer for myself.

We found Susan on deck in charge of one of the sailors who had had the care of her during the voyage. When we first caught sight of her she was diving into the man's pockets after some broken ship's biscuits, and at the sight the nervous depression under which I had been labouring left me.

She was big and muscular, but there was nothing, as far as I could see, to cause apprehension.

It was a friendly deal between Merridew's uncle and the captain of the ship, and, as far as we could learn, Susan had travelled with the full liberty of the ship, and had won golden opinions by her docility and affection. The sailors had made quite a pet of her, and the one who had had chiefly to do with her mentioned the fact with sufficient emphasis to draw another golden opinion from Merridew.

Despite this – the first of many turn-outs – my neighbour was in good feather, and as the sailor walked Susan off the ship on to the dock, with his arm affectionately around her neck, he rallied me gaily on my dismal forebodings.

'Hasn't she got lovely ways?' he concluded gleefully.

'She has a lovely club of a foot,' said I more soberly. 'Get the man to come with us as far as the station, anyhow. If we can only get her in the train we can manage to walk her the rest of the way without bothering about a conveyance.'

Merridew was sharp enough to see the wisdom of my suggestion, because even a friendly and good-natured emu is not the handiest thing to travel about with. He put the proposition to the sailor, who consented readily enough when he understood that free drinks went with the outfit, and he led the way while Merridew and I brought up the rear and tried to look as though we did not belong to the procession.

It was a good step from the docks to the station, and the neighbourhood I judged was not the nicest that could be found for taking a walk in.

'Hallo, Bill, I'll tell your missus!' was the first greeting, and it caught on and set the fashion immediately. We heard it from all sides and every quarter as we progressed, and a crowd of dirty little urchins picked it and us up and came along in steadily growing numbers to see the thing out.

At the outset the sailorman smiled, but by-and-by he began to redden and grow short in his replies to those of the jokers with whom he was acquainted, and no wonder.

'Say, Bill, how much for your canary?' 'Hi, 'Arry, come and 'ave a look at Bill's new donah!' 'Cheero, Bill, who's your gal?'

I got hot in sympathy, but Merridew, who has a vein of coarseness in his make-up, rather enjoyed it until a lady of William's acquaintance snatched off a friend's hat and placed it jauntily on the head of the emu. Susan didn't take kindly to Merry Widows, or else she had a well-bred repugnance to wearing other ladies' hats. She stopped suddenly, and then her near leg shot out and Bill sat down in the muddy road and groaned and swore alternately.

The lady who had caused the commotion laughed heartlessly, but her friend assisted William to swear. It was able assistance, too. If I had been making a book and free of other food for reflection I should have backed the lady. Susan was half way through the hat before its owner realized that this was tragedy, not comedy. In fact, she was laughing too when she became aware of the fact, and after telling her friend what she thought of her, in two concise and pithy words, she appealed to Merridew.

''Ere, mister, your chicking is eating up my 'at,' she sobbed. ''Arriet, you cat, I'll maul you for this!'

The hat had disappeared before Merridew could do anything to save it, even if he had been fool enough to try, and the fight that followed between the two erstwhile bosom friends was the finest display I have ever seen outside the National Sporting Club. Even Susan stayed to watch it, when she might so easily have saved us all further trouble by walking off and taking the next boat back to Australia.

The combatants started at scratch, and they were still scratching when a policeman strolled up and requested enlightenment on 'these here goings on.' We would have got out if we could, Susan or no Susan, but there was a solid crowd of four or five hundred pinning us in, and we had perforce to stay. The policeman pluckily pushed between the viragoes, and, seeing their sport in danger of being stopped, the crowd swayed and brought the three immediately concerned down on top of the emu. The bobby was nearest, and when that terrible leg shot out for the second time he caught it low down and full square. He travelled rapidly on his ear and nose for a few yards, and came to anchor in the crowd, fetching down one of the belligerents and a couple of disinterested spectators on top of him.

He was plucky, I will say that for him. The next moment he was on his feet, whistle in hand and minus his helmet.

'Who did that?' he shouted.

Someone in the crowd wittily suggested 'Lloyd George,' but the policeman wasn't liberal enough to appreciate the joke, and by this time Merridew, rendered plucky by desperation, had collared Susan by the neck, and hauled her out of the crowd; the whistle was blown, more police arrived, and a fair-sized riot was in progress, which ended in twelve arrests and no end of damage to windows in the vicinity.

We lost the sailor in the crowd, which saved Merridew something on his drink bill and lost him a good deal in other ways. It took us over an hour to get to the station. Fair walking, it was about a quarter of a mile; but Susan had an inquiring mind, and when she saw a side street which looked cut-throaty she persisted in going down it to see life. She didn't insist on us coming. In justice I must admit that; but we went – Merridew to safeguard Susan, and I because I hadn't the moral courage to back out and go home.

We got to the station eventually, and there a fresh obstacle presented itself. The booking clerk didn't refuse us a ticket outright, but he lodged an objection. He didn't think they would carry Susan – alive, anyhow, he said. We appealed to the stationmaster, and he was about to give his decision in our favour, I believe, when Susan playfully kicked a milk churn through the booking-office door on to the line. That did it. The stationmaster not only refused to carry us, but he ordered us off the station on pains and penalties duly set forth in the company's rules and regulations, over a dozen of which we had infringed, or were infringing, to the tune of four hundred and eighty shillings apiece, not to mention Susan's share. Fortunately, the churn was an empty, or Merridew's milk bill for that quarter would have been distressful to a man of limited means; but he didn't seem to be as grateful for these small mercies as resentful of the growing difficulty and foolishness of his position.

'Hang it all, man!' he complained, 'set your wits to work and suggest some way of getting us out of this. At least, don't stand grinning there like a corner-man at a festival of fools! We are ten miles from home, and it is getting late, I may remind you.'

Thus implored, I studied the matter from a practical and helpful point of view.

'Is it absolutely essential to get her home alive?' I queried. 'If it were not, the job would be simplified amazingly, and there is a licensed knacker's along the road I noticed when—'

Merridew stayed me with a gesture of indignation. He said he liked his emus alive. They might be quieter and easier to handle the other way, but they were not so interesting.

There was something in this contention, and I suggested bribery.

'You wait here while I run round and get a cabbage,' said I. 'I have got an old horse along for miles that way, and it ought to answer with an emu.'

Merridew refused to be left with his bird, so we coaxed it off the station premises and along the road a bit until we came to a shop where they sold cabbages and other things for profit combined with pleasure.

We all went into the shop together. I hadn't intended that, but Susan had ideas of her own, and trotted in after me to see that I picked out one with plenty of heart to it. The shop-keeper was elderly and dim of sight, and he didn't perceive Susan, who kept discreetly behind me, at first. But when he turned to me again with the finest sample his shop contained, three feet of neck shot over my shoulder towards him.

'Luvus!' he groaned, 'this is a new sort.' And he dropped the cabbage, bolted into the shop-parlour, and locked the door.

We couldn't get him to come out again and take his money, knock and call as we would, so we left twopence in the scales for honesty and went out, Merridew leading the way with the cabbage and I bringing up the rear.

When we got outside Susan took the cabbage away from us and ate it. It didn't seem to me that my plan was going to work. Though but a bird of the wilderness, Susan was too shrewd and prompt for us to handle effectively, and I asked Merridew whether he didn't think it time to give her best and put the job into the hands of a furniture remover, or Pickford, or somebody with appliances and experience in these things.

'It is past nine now,' I urged, 'and, as far as I can see, the job hasn't more than begun yet.'

'Well, what can we do?' said Merridew miserably. 'You don't suppose I am enjoying this, do you?'

'I didn't know,' I retorted innocently. 'Some people have such queer tastes. Anyway, I hope you recognize it's your funeral and not mine. If the responsibility rested on me I should purchase a few yards of clothes-line and a stout strap; then I should charter a cab and pay the man handsomely to drive me and tow the canary.'

'Urgh!' said Merridew casually. 'You are not such a fool as you look. Why the thunder couldn't you have suggested that before, and not go wasting time and cash on silly cabbage bait? Mind Susan and I'll go and fix it up.'

Merridew trotted off with renewed hope and eagerness, and I sat down on the kerb and filled my pipe while Susan banqueted on the cabbage and felt that civilization had prospects which offered a very good compensation for the loss of home and kindred.

The cabby Merridew secured and brought back with him was a cheerful optimist, and not even the sight of his tow served to daunt his noble spirit.

'Give us a quid, guv'nor, and I'll get you and your dicky-bird 'ome for you,' he said.

Merridew accepted the offer under protest. He thought it was steep, and so did I; but the cabby stood out for his price and got it. He earned it too.

We got the strap adjusted and the tow-line attached with the man's assistance, and hitched Susan securely to the supports of the driving seat. Then the cabby climbed up to his box, Merridew and I filed in, and the procession started.

At the outset it was orderly and dignified, and it remained so for about three minutes, when Susan suddenly lodged a protest and proceeded to rearrange things more to her liking. We had calculated on her jibbing and hanging back, and on the compelling influence of the collar and line to check the tendency or choke Susan.

Unfortunately Susan was not of a mind to be either checked or choked, and as soon as she caught the drift of our reasoning she spread her wings and stretched her neck and pounded after us to tell us exactly what she thought of the business.

Turning to see how his tow was coming along, the cabby caught sight of the advancing fury, and, reading the signs aright, he whipped up his horse and fled before the storm. The cab lurched and bounded, and, afraid for himself and his bird, Merridew pushed up the trap and advised more care.

'Steady on,' he said; 'you'll pull the neck off her!'

'Pull!' screamed the cabby, lashing away frantically in reckless disregard of legal and humane ordinances. 'It ain't pulling she's at, but pushing. She's jabbed a hole in the blooming dicky and about broke my arm. I don't know if this is a joke, mister, but it's going to cost you a bit.'

The next moment there was a jar which pitched us both off the seat and nearly brought the horse to her knees as the cab tried to climb over her and dodge out of the way of Susan's foot. The cabby yelled and swore – oh, how he did swear! – but, as Merridew told him, swearing was no use. What he had to do was to run for it, and run he did, with Susan prodding him viciously wherever she could reach him with her clubby beak, and every now and again picking up a foot, and throwing it bodily at the cab.

It was a filthy night – pitch dark, drizzling slightly, and blowing hard – and once we got away from the docks we were committed to a series of dreary, desolate and muddy lanes, which had a nasty way of running off into deep ditches. Fortunately a London-trained cab-horse is about the cleverest thing running, and, screw though she was, the one that had our lives and fortunes in her control knew her business, and did it despite the inconsiderate and jumpy action of the driver, who must have seemed to her limited intelligence to be more drunk than usual, and quite unnecessarily vicious with his whip.

We were not able to quite understand what was going on behind us; but we could read the signs of a cab driven madly and a driver hoarse with fear, and in our way we were as panicky as he. The only one who was really enjoying the drive was Susan, and, so far from tiring, she freshened to the fun to such an extent that the exasperated driver, turning with his whip to stave off another playful jab in a place already rendered sore by a score of playful jabs, got jerked off his perch. By the time he had gathered himself out of the mud we were far ahead. He made a plucky effort to recapture his property, and pursued us for a hundred yards or so, waving his whip and swearing to his horse to linger for him to come up and kill that blankety bird and break our blankety necks, and do other things of a violent nature.

At that time, of course, we didn't know that the cabby had deserted us. It was miles beyond the point at which he had stepped down that, growing alarmed at the reckless driving as much as at the fact that we seemed to be going more into the country than our proper route should have led us, Merridew once more essayed to open up communication with the quarter-deck. I propped him up firmly from below, and he shoved open the trap and made the ghastly discovery that we were skipperless.

'Why, he's gone!' said Merridew, dropping back on me for comfort.

'Who's gone? ' I queried.

'The cabby,' said Merridew.

'In that case,' said I, 'we shall very soon be gone too, unless we can grab the reins and pull up. Have a try, I'll hold you.'

Merridew tried to get me to do the trying while he supported me from behind, but I wasn't having any of that, and I declined so firmly that he had perforce to take the post of peril himself. I had better have accepted his suggestion. The first grab shot him on to the tail end of the horse, and put another five miles an hour on to our pace; at the next he got the reins in his possession. He tightened them incautiously, and the next moment there was a sickening shock; the cab went down on the near side, and we piled out into a ditch waiting handy to receive us. Susan brought up in such a hurry that she stubbed her nose on the driver's box, which was the only bit of consolation we had.

We must have looked a party of fools as we stood out there on that deserted road and scraped ourselves and cussed. I had a nasty gash on the leg and had lost my hat. Merridew's coat was torn across the shoulder, and he told me that his arm was broken. It wasn't really, but he is the sort of man who likes to make the worst of things and have himself as chief martyr.

It didn't seem much use waiting for the cabby or any other assistance, and at my suggestion we undressed the horse and got her up and on to the road. While we were back trying to get the cab out to hitch her up again she bolted. We gave chase, of course, but it was a useless waste of breath and energy, and we required all we could command for the rest of our silly adventure.

One of the shafts was broken, and except for firewood purposes the rest of the cab didn't seem worth removing; but it was not my property, and Merridew decreed that we salved it. So we got it on to the road, put the broken shaft inside, and set out to lose our fortunes. We hadn't a ghost of an idea where we were, and for nearly a mile I hauled the cab through the mud while Merridew hauled Susan, and then we came to a finger-post.

I swarmed up and read the inscription by the aid of a match.

'Come on,' said I blithely. 'It's only nine miles, and a lovely bit of walking.'

'Get out,' said Merridew incredulously. 'It was only ten when we started, and we have come that far.'

'Yes – in the wrong direction, chiefly,' said I. 'I know where we are, and you can take it from me that you have nine miles to go to sleep in tonight. If you want my advice you'll abandon the cab. We shall travel lighter without it; at least I shall, and I can give you a hand with the bird. Jolly expensive you're going to find her.'

Merridew writhed.

'I sha'n't pay anything,' he said stubbornly. 'It's contributory negligence, anyhow, and I bargained to be driven home – not to walk. Now you mention it, leave the confounded thing where it is.'

'I don't suppose it will cost you any more,' said I. I pulled the remnants on to the grass, and we filled our pipes and walked away from the evidence of our crime and folly – or limped rather. And we kept limping until nearly two, owing to missing our road several times and the vagaries of Susan, who wanted us to get another cab and continue the sport which she enjoyed.

It was over a week before the cabby got his stock-in-trade together again, and the case of the cabman v. Merridew, at which I am the chief witness on Merridew's behalf, is down for hearing. The claim is only for fourteen pounds seventeen and sixpence, and costs, and I rather hope the cabby will win.

FREDERICK TREVES

THE
ELEPHANT MAN
(1923)

IN THE MILE END Road, opposite to the London Hospital, there was (and possibly still is) a line of small shops. Among them was a vacant greengrocer's which was to let. The whole of the front of the shop, with the exception of the door, was hidden by a hanging sheet of canvas on which was the announcement that the Elephant Man was to be seen within and that the price of admission was twopence. Painted on the canvas in primitive colours was a life-size portrait of the Elephant Man. This very crude production depicted a frightful creature that could only have been possible in a nightmare. It was the figure of a man with the characteristics of an elephant. The transfiguration was not far advanced. There was still more of the man than of the beast. This fact – that it was still human – was the most repellent attribute of the creature. There was nothing about it of the pitiableness of the misshapened or the deformed, nothing of the gro-tesqueness of the freak, but merely the loathsome insinua-tion of a man being changed into an animal. Some palm trees in the background of the picture suggested a jungle and might have led the imaginative to assume that it was in this wild that the perverted object had roamed.

When I first became aware of this phenomenon the exhibition was closed, but a well-informed boy sought the proprietor in a public house and I was granted a private view on payment of a shilling. The shop was empty and grey with dust. Some old tins and a few shrivelled potatoes occupied a shelf and some vague vegetable refuse the window. The light in the place was dim, being obscured by the painted placard outside. The far end of the shop – where I expect the late proprietor sat at a desk – was cut off by a curtain or rather by a red tablecloth suspended from a cord by a few rings. The room was cold and dank, for it was the month of November. The year, I might say, was 1884.

The showman pulled back the curtain and revealed a bent figure crouching on a stool and covered by a brown blanket. In front of it, on a tripod, was a large brick heated by a Bunsen burner. Over this the creature was huddled to warm itself. It never moved when the curtain was drawn back. Locked up in an empty shop and lit by the faint blue light of the gas jet, this hunched-up figure was the embodiment of loneliness. It might have been a captive in a cavern or a wizard watching for unholy manifestations in the ghostly flame. Outside the sun was shining and one could hear the footsteps of the passers-by, a tune whistled by a boy and the companionable hum of traffic in the road.

The showman – speaking as if to a dog – called out harshly: 'Stand up!' The thing arose slowly and let the blanket that covered its head and back fall to the ground. There stood revealed the most disgusting specimen of humanity that I have ever seen. In the course of my profession I had come upon lamentable deformities of the face due to injury or disease, as well as mutilations and contortions of the body depending upon like causes; but at no time had I met with such a degraded or perverted version of a human being as this lone figure displayed. He was naked to the waist, his feet were bare, he wore a pair of threadbare trousers that had once belonged to some fat gentleman's dress suit.

From the intensified painting in the street I had imagined the Elephant Man to be of gigantic size. This, however, was a little man below the average height and made to look shorter by the bowing of his back. The most striking feature about him was his enormous and misshapened head. From the brow there projected a huge bony mass like a loaf, while from the back of the head hung a bag of spongy, fungous-looking skin, the surface of which was comparable to brown cauliflower. On the top of the skull were a few long lank hairs. The osseous growth on the forehead almost occluded one eye. The circumference of the head was no less than that of the man's waist. From the upper jaw there projected another mass of bone. It protruded from the mouth like a pink stump, turning the upper lip inside out and making of the mouth a mere slobbering aperture. This growth from the jaw had been so exaggerated in the painting as to appear to be a rudimentary trunk or tusk. The nose was merely a lump of flesh, only recognizable as a nose from its position. The face was no more capable of expression than a block of gnarled wood. The back was horrible, because from it hung, as far down as the middle of the thigh, huge, sack-like masses of flesh covered by the same loathsome cauliflower skin.

The right arm was of enormous size and shapeless. It suggested the limb of the subject of elephantiasis. It was overgrown also with pendent masses of the same cauliflower-like skin. The hand was large and clumsy – a fin or paddle rather than a hand. There was no distinction between the palm and the back. The thumb had the appearance of a radish, while the fingers might have been thick, tuberous roots. As a limb it was almost useless. The other arm was remarkable by contrast. It was not only normal but was, moreover, a delicately shaped limb covered with fine skin and provided with a beautiful hand which any woman might have envied. From the chest hung a bag of the same repulsive flesh. It was like a dewlap suspended from the neck of a lizard. The lower limbs had the characters of the deformed arm. They were unwieldy, dropsical looking and grossly misshapened.

To add a further burden to his trouble the wretched man, when a boy, developed hip disease, which had left him permanently lame, so that he could only walk with a stick. He was thus denied all means of escape from his tormentors. As he told me later, he could never run away. One other feature must be mentioned to emphasize his isolation from his kind. Although he was already repellent enough, there arose from the fungous skin-growth with which he was almost covered a very sickening stench which was hard to tolerate. From the showman I learnt nothing about the Elephant Man, except that he was English, that his name was John Merrick and that he was twenty-one years of age.

As at the time of my discovery of the Elephant Man I was the Lecturer on Anatomy at the Medical College opposite, I was anxious to examine him in detail and to prepare an account of his abnormalities. I therefore arranged with the showman that I should interview his strange exhibit in my room at the college. I became at once conscious of a difficulty. The Elephant Man could not show himself in the streets. He would have been mobbed by the crowd and seized by the police. He was, in fact, as secluded from the world as the Man with the Iron Mask. He had, however, a disguise, although it was almost as startling as he was himself. It consisted of a long black cloak which reached to the ground. Whence the cloak had been obtained I cannot imagine. I had only seen such a garment on the stage wrapped about the figure of a Venetian bravo. The recluse was provided with a pair of bag-like slippers in which to hide his deformed feet. On his head was a cap of a kind that never before was seen. It was black like the cloak, had a wide peak, and the general outline of a yachting cap. As the circumference of Merrick's head was that of a man's waist, the size of this headgear may be imagined. From the attachment of the peak a grey flannel curtain hung in front of the face. In this mask was cut a wide horizontal slit through which the wearer could look out. This costume, worn by a bent man hobbling along with a stick, is probably the most remarkable and the most uncanny that has as yet been designed. I arranged that Merrick should cross the road in a cab, and to insure his immediate admission to the college I gave him my card. This card was destined to play a critical part in Merrick's life.

I made a careful examination of my visitor the result of which I embodied in a paper. I made little of the man himself. He was shy, confused, not a little frightened and evidently much cowed. Moreover, his speech was almost unintelligible. The great bony mass that projected from his mouth blurred his utterance and made the articulation of certain words impossible. He returned in a cab to the place of exhibition, and I assumed that I had seen the last of him, especially as I found next day that the show had been forbidden by the police and that the shop was empty.

I supposed that Merrick was imbecile and had been imbecile from birth. The fact that his face was incapable of expression, that his speech was a mere spluttering and his attitude that of one whose mind was void of all emotions and concerns gave grounds for this belief. The conviction was no doubt encouraged by the hope that his intellect was the blank I imagined it to be. That he could appreciate his position was unthinkable. Here was a man in the heyday of youth who was so vilely deformed that everyone he met confronted him with a look of horror and disgust. He was taken about the country to be exhibited as a monstrosity and an object of loathing. He was shunned like a leper, housed like a wild beast, and got his only view of the world from a peep-hole in a showman's cart. He was, moreover, lame, had but one available arm, and could hardly make his utterances understood. It was not until I came to know that Merrick was highly intelligent, that he possessed an acute sensibility and – worse than all – a romantic imagination that I realized the overwhelming tragedy of his life.

The episode of the Elephant Man was, I imagined, closed; but I was fated to meet him again – two years later – under more dramatic conditions. In England the showman and Merrick had been moved on from place to place by the police, who considered the exhibition degrading and among the things that could not be allowed. It was hoped that in the uncritical retreats of Mile End a more abiding peace would be found. But it was not to be. The official mind there, as elsewhere, very properly decreed that the public exposure of Merrick and his deformities transgressed the limits of decency. The show must close.

The showman, in despair, fled with his charge to the Continent. Whither he roamed at first I do not know; but he came finally to Brussels. His reception was discouraging. Brussels was firm; the exhibition was banned; it was brutal, indecent and immoral, and could not be permitted within the confines of Belgium. Merrick was thus no longer of value. He was no longer a source of profitable entertainment. He was a burden. He must be got rid of. The elimination of Merrick was a simple matter. He could offer no resistance. He was as docile as a sick sheep. The impresario, having robbed Merrick of his paltry savings, gave him a ticket to London, saw him into the train and no doubt in parting condemned him to perdition.

His destination was Liverpool Street. The journey may be imagined. Merrick was in his alarming outdoor garb. He would be harried by an eager mob as he hobbled along the quay. They would run ahead to get a look at him. They would lift the hem of his cloak to peep at his body. He would try to hide in the train or in some dark corner of the boat, but never could he be free from that ring of curious eyes or from those whispers of fright and aversion. He had but a few shillings in his pocket and nothing either to eat or drink on the way. A panic-dazed dog with a label on his collar would have received some sympathy and possibly some kindness. Merrick received none.

What was he to do when he reached London? He had not a friend in the world. He knew no more of London than he knew of Pekin. How could he find a lodging, or what lodging-house keeper would dream of taking him in? All he wanted was to hide. What most he dreaded were the open street and the gaze of his fellow-men. If even he crept into a cellar the horrid eyes and the still more dreaded whispers would follow him to its depths. Was there ever such a home-coming!

At Liverpool Street he was rescued from the crowd by the police and taken into the third-class waiting-room. Here he sank on the floor in the darkest corner. The police were at a loss what to do with him. They had dealt with strange and mouldy tramps, but never with such an object as this. He could not explain himself. His speech was so maimed that he might as well have spoken in Arabic. He had, however, something with him which he produced with a ray of hope. It was my card.

The card simplified matters. It made it evident that this curious creature had an acquaintance and that the individual must be sent for. A messenger,was dispatched to the London Hospital which is comparatively near at hand. Fortunately I was in the building and returned at once with the messenger to the station. In the waiting-room I had some difficulty in making a way through the crowd, but there, on the floor in the corner, was Merrick. He looked a mere heap. It seemed as if he had been thrown there like a bundle. He was so huddled up and so helpless looking that he might have had both his arms and his legs broken. He seemed pleased to see me, but he was nearly done. The journey and want of food had reduced him to the last stage of exhaustion. The police kindly helped him into a cab, and I drove him at once to the hospital. He appeared to be content, for he fell asleep almost as soon as he was seated and slept to the journey's end. He never said a word, but seemed to be satisfied that all was well.

In the attics of the hospital was an isolation ward with a single bed. It was used for emergency purposes – for a case of delirium tremens, for a man who had become suddenly insane or for a patient with an undetermined fever. Here the Elephant Man was deposited on a bed, was made comfortable and was supplied with food. I had been guilty of an irregularity in admitting such a case, for the hospital was neither a refuge nor a home for incurables. Chronic cases were not accepted, but only those requiring active treatment, and Merrick was not in need of such treatment. I applied to the sympathetic chairman of the committee, Mr Carr Gomm, who not only was good enough to approve my action but who agreed with me that Merrick must not again be turned out into the world.

Mr Carr Gomm wrote a letter to the *Times* detailing the circumstances of the refugee and asking for money for his support. So generous is the English public that in a few days – I think in a week – enough money was forthcoming to maintain Merrick for life without any charge upon the hospital funds. There chanced to be two empty rooms at the back of the hospital which were little used. They were on the ground floor, were out of the way, and opened upon a large courtyard called Bedstead Square, because here the iron beds were marshalled for cleaning and painting. The front room was converted into a bed-sitting room and the smaller chamber into a bathroom. The condition of Merrick's skin rendered a bath at least once a day a necessity, and I might here mention that with the use of the bath the unpleasant odour to which I have referred ceased to be noticeable. Merrick took up his abode in the hospital in December, 1886.

Merrick had now something he had never dreamed of, never supposed to be possible – a home of his own for life. I at once began to make myself acquainted with him and to endeavour to understand his mentality. It was a study of much interest. I very soon learnt his speech so that I could talk freely with him. This afforded him great satisfaction, for, curiously enough, he had a passion for conversation, yet all his life had had no one to talk to. I – having then much leisure – saw him almost every day, and made a point of spending some two hours with him every Sunday morning when he would chatter almost without ceasing. It was unreasonable to expect one nurse to attend to him continuously, but there was no lack of temporary volunteers. As they did not all acquire his speech it came about that I had occasionally to act as an interpreter.

I found Merrick, as I have said, remarkably intelligent. He had learnt to read and had become a most voracious reader. I think he had been taught when he was in hospital with his diseased hip. His range of books was limited. The Bible and Prayer Book he knew intimately, but he had subsisted for the most part upon newspapers, or rather upon such fragments of old journals as he had chanced to pick up. He had read a few stories and some elementary lesson books, but the delight of his life was a romance, especially a love romance. These tales were very real to him, as real as any narrative in the

Bible, so that he would tell them to me as incidents in the lives of people who had lived. In his outlook upon the world he was a child, yet a child with some of the tempestuous feelings of a man. He was an elemental being, so primitive that he might have spent the twenty-three years of his life immured in a cave.

Of his early days I could learn but little. He was very loath to talk about the past. It was a nightmare, the shudder of which was still upon him. He was born, he believed, in or about Leicester. Of his father he knew absolutely nothing. Of his mother he had some memory. It was very faint and had, I think, been elaborated in his mind into something definite. Mothers figured in the tales he had read, and he wanted his mother to be one of those comfortable lullaby-singing persons who are so lovable. In his subconscious mind there was apparently a germ of recollection in which some-one figured who had been kind to him. He clung to this conception and made it more real by invention, for since the day when he could toddle no one had been kind to him. As an infant he must have been repellent, although his deformities did not become gross until he had attained his full stature.

It was a favourite belief of his that his mother was beautiful. The fiction was, I am aware, one of his own making, but it was a great joy to him. His mother, lovely as she may have been, basely deserted him when he was very small, so small that his earliest clear memories were of the workhouse to which he had been taken. Worthless and inhuman as this mother was, he spoke of her with pride and even with reverence. Once, when referring to his own appearance, he said: 'It *is* very strange, for, you see, mother was so beautiful.'

The rest of Merrick's life up to the time that I met him at Liverpool Street Station was one dull record of degradation and squalor. He was dragged from town to town and from fair to fair as if he were a strange beast in a cage. A dozen times a day he would have to expose his nakedness and his piteous deformities before a gaping crowd who greeted him with such mutterings as 'Oh! what a horror! What a beast!' He had had no childhood. He had had no boyhood. He had never experienced pleasure. He knew nothing of the joy of living nor of the fun of things. His sole idea of happiness was to creep into the dark and hide. Shut up alone in a booth, awaiting the next exhibition, how mocking must have sounded the laughter and merriment of the boys and girls outside who were enjoying the 'fun of the fair'! He had no past to look back upon and no future to look forward to. At the age of twenty he was a creature without hope. There was nothing in front of him but a vista of caravans creeping along a road, of rows of glaring show tents and of circles of staring eyes with, at the end, the spectacle of a broken man in a poor law infirmary.

Those who are interested in the evolution of character might speculate as to the effect of this brutish life upon a sensitive and intelligent man. It would be reasonable to surmise that he would become a spiteful and malignant misanthrope, swollen with venom and filled with hatred of his fellow-men, or, on the other hand, that he would degenerate into a despairing melancholic on the verge of idiocy. Merrick, however, was no such being. He had passed through the fire and had come out unscathed. His troubles had ennobled him. He showed himself to be a gentle, affectionate and lovable creature, as amiable as a happy woman, free from any trace of cynicism or resentment, without a grievance and without an unkind word for anyone. I have never heard him complain. I have never heard him deplore his ruined life or resent the treatment he had received at the

257

hands of callous keepers. His journey through life had been indeed along a *via dolorosa*, the road had been uphill all the way, and now, when the night was at its blackest and the way most steep, he had suddenly found himself, as it were, in a friendly inn, bright with light and warm with welcome. His gratitude to those about him was pathetic in its sincerity and eloquent in the childlike simplicity with which it was expressed.

As I learnt more of this primitive creature I found that there were two anxieties which were prominent in his mind and which he revealed to me with diffidence. He was in the occupation of the rooms assigned to him and had been assured that he would be cared for to the end of his days. This, however, he found hard to realize, for he often asked me timidly to what place he would next be moved. To understand his attitude it is necessary to remember that he had been moving on and moving on all his life. He knew no other state of existence. To him it was normal. He had passed from the workhouse to the hospital, from the hospital back to the workhouse, then from this town to that town or from one showman's caravan to another. He had never known a home nor any semblance of one. He had no possessions. His sole belongings, besides his clothes and some books, were the monstrous cap and the cloak. He was a wanderer, a pariah and an outcast. That his quarters at the hospital were his for life he could not understand. He could not rid his mind of the anxiety which had pursued him for so many years – where am I to be taken next?

Another trouble was his dread of his fellow-men, his fear of people's eyes, the dread of being always stared at, the lash of the cruel mutterings of the crowd. In his home in Bedstead Square he was secluded; but now and then a thoughtless porter or a wardmaid would open his door to let curious friends have a peep at the Elephant Man. It therefore seemed to him as if the gaze of the world followed him still.

Influenced by these two obsessions he became, during his first few weeks at the hospital, curiously uneasy. At last, with much hesitation, he said to me one day: 'When I am next moved can I go to a blind asylum or to a lighthouse?' He had read about blind asylums in the newspapers and was attracted by the thought of being among people who could not see. The lighthouse had another charm. It meant seclusion from the curious. There at least no one could open a door and peep in at him. There he would forget that he had once been the Elephant Man. There he would escape the vampire showman. He had never seen a lighthouse, but he had come upon a picture of the Eddystone, and it appeared to him that this lonely column of stone in the waste of the sea was such a home as he had longed for.

I had no great difficulty in ridding Merrick's mind of these ideas. I wanted him to get accustomed to his fellow-men, to become a human being himself and to be admitted to the communion of his kind. He appeared day by day less frightened, less haunted looking, less anxious to hide, less alarmed when he saw his door being opened. He got to know most of the people about the place, to be accustomed to their comings and goings, and to realize that they took no more than a friendly notice of him. He could only go out after dark, and on fine nights ventured to take a walk in Bedstead Square clad in his black cloak and his cap. His greatest adventure was on one moonless evening when he walked alone as far as the hospital garden and back again.

To secure Merrick's recovery and to bring him, as it were, to life once more, it was necessary that he should make the acquaintance of men and women who would treat him as a normal and intelligent young man and not as a monster of deformity. Women I felt to be more important than men in bringing about his transformation. Women were the more frightened of him, the more disgusted at his appearance and the more apt to give way to irrepressible expressions of aversion when they came into his presence. Moreover, Merrick had an admiration of women of such a kind that it attained almost to adoration. This was not the outcome of his personal experience. They were not real women but the products of his imagination. Among them was the beautiful mother surrounded, at a respectful distance, by heroines from the many romances he had read.

His first entry to the hospital was attended by a regrettable incident. He had been placed on the bed in the little attic, and a nurse had been instructed to bring him some food. Unfortunately she had not been fully informed of Merrick's unusual appearance. As she entered the room she saw on the bed, propped up by white pillows, a monstrous figure as hideous as an Indian idol. She at once dropped the tray she was carrying and fled, with a shriek, through the door. Merrick was too weak to notice much, but the experience, I am afraid, was not new to him.

He was looked after by volunteer nurses whose ministrations were somewhat formal and constrained. Merrick, no doubt, was conscious that their service was purely official, that they were merely doing what they were told to do and that they were acting rather as automata than as women. They did not help him to feel that he was of their kind. On the contrary they, without knowing it, made him aware that the gulf of separation was immeasurable.

Feeling this, I asked a friend of mine, a young and pretty widow, if she thought she could enter Merrick's room with a smile, wish him good morning and shake him by the hand. She said she could and she did. The effect upon poor

Merrick was not quite what I had expected. As he let go her hand he bent his head on his knees and sobbed until I thought he would never cease. The interview was over. He told me afterwards that this was the first woman who had ever smiled at him, and the first woman, in the whole of his life, who had shaken hands with him. From this day the transformation of Merrick commenced and he began to change, little by little, from a hunted thing into a man. It was a wonderful change to witness and one that never ceased to fascinate me.

Merrick's case attracted much attention in the papers, with the result that he had a constant succession of visitors. Everybody wanted to see him. He must have been visited by almost every lady of note in the social world. They were all good enough to welcome him with a smile and to shake hands with him. The Merrick whom I had found shivering behind a rag of a curtain in an empty shop was now conversant with duchesses and countesses and other ladies of high degree. They brought him presents, made his room bright with ornaments and pictures, and, what pleased him more than all, supplied him with books. He soon had a large library and most of his day was spent in reading. He was not the least spoiled; not the least puffed up; he never asked for anything; never presumed upon the kindness meted out to him, and was always humbly and profoundly grateful. Above all he lost his shyness. He liked to see his door pushed open and people to look in. He became acquainted with most of the frequenters of Bedstead Square, would chat with them at his window and show them some of his choicest presents. He improved in his speech, although to the end his utterances were not easy for strangers to understand. He was beginning, moreover, to be less conscious of his unsightliness, a little disposed to think it was, after all, not so very extreme. Possibly this was aided by the circumstance that I would not allow a mirror of any kind in his room.

The height of his social development was reached on an eventful day when Queen Alexandra – then Princess of Wales – came to the hospital to pay him a special visit. With that kindness which has marked every act of her life, the Queen entered Merrick's room smiling and shook him warmly by the hand. Merrick was transported with delight. This was beyond even his most extravagant dream. The Queen has made many people happy, but I think no gracious act of hers has ever caused such happiness as she brought into Merrick's room when she sat by his chair and talked to him as to a person she was glad to see.

Merrick, I may say, was now one of the most contented creatures I have chanced to meet. More than once he said to me: 'I am happy every hour of the day.' This was good to think upon when I recalled the half-dead heap of miserable humanity I had seen in the corner of the waiting-room at Liverpool Street. Most men of Merrick's age would have expressed their joy and sense of contentment by singing or whistling when they were alone. Unfortunately poor Merrick's mouth was so deformed that he could neither whistle nor sing. He was satisfied to express himself by beating time upon the pillow to some tune that was ringing in his head. I have many times found him so occupied when I have entered his room unexpectedly. One thing that always struck me as sad about Merrick was the fact that he could not smile. Whatever his delight might be, his face remained expressionless. He could weep but he could not smile.

The Queen paid Merrick many visits and sent him every year a Christmas card with a message in her own handwriting. On one occasion she sent him a signed photograph of herself. Merrick, quite overcome, regarded it as a sacred object and would hardly allow me to touch it. He cried over it, and after it was framed had it put up in his room as a kind of ikon. I told him that he must write to Her Royal Highness to thank her for her goodness. This he was pleased to do, as he was very fond of writing letters, never before in his life having had anyone to write to. I allowed the letter to be dispatched unedited. It began 'My dear Princess' and ended 'Yours very sincerely.' Unorthodox as it was it was expressed in terms any courtier would have envied.

Other ladies followed the Queen's gracious example and sent their photographs to this delighted creature who had been all his life despised and rejected of men. His mantelpiece and table became so covered with photographs of handsome ladies, with dainty knicknacks and pretty trifles that they may almost have befitted the apartment of an Adonis-like actor or of a famous tenor.

Through all these bewildering incidents and through the glamour of this great change Merrick still remained in many ways a mere child. He had all the invention of an imaginative boy or girl, the same love of 'make-believe,' the same instinct of 'dressing up' and of personating heroic and impressive characters. This attitude of mind was illustrated by the following incident. Benevolent visitors had given me, from time to time, sums of money to be expended for the comfort of the *ci-devant* Elephant Man. When one Christmas was approaching I asked Merrick what he would like me to purchase as a Christmas present. He rather startled me by saying shyly that he would like a dressing-bag with silver fittings. He had seen a picture of such an article in an advertisement which he had furtively preserved.

The association of a silver-fitted dressing-bag with the poor wretch wrapped up in a dirty blanket in an empty shop was hard to comprehend. I fathomed the mystery in time, for Merrick made little secret of the fancies that haunted his boyish brain. Just as a small girl with a tinsel coronet and a window curtain for a train will realize the conception of a countess on her way to court, so Merrick loved to imagine himself a dandy and a young man about town. Mentally, no doubt, he had frequently 'dressed up' for the part. He could 'make-believe' with great effect, but he wanted something to render his fancied character more realistic. Hence the jaunty bag which was to assume the function of the toy coronet and the window curtain that could transform a mite with a pigtail into a countess.

As a theatrical 'property' the dressing-bag was ingenious, since there was little else to give substance to the transformation. Merrick could not wear the silk hat of the dandy nor, indeed, any kind of hat. He could not adapt his body to the trimly cut coat. His deformity was such that he could wear neither collar nor tie, while in association with his bulbous feet the young blood's patent leather shoe was unthinkable. What was there left to make up the character? A lady had given him a ring to wear on his undeformed hand, and a noble lord had presented him with a very stylish walking-stick. But these things, helpful as they were, were hardly sufficing.

The dressing-bag, however, was distinctive, was explanatory and entirely characteristic. So the bag was obtained and Merrick the Elephant Man became, in the seclusion of his chamber, the Piccadilly exquisite, the young spark, the gallant, the 'nut.' When I purchased the article I realized that as Merrick could never travel he could hardly want a dressing-bag. He could not use the silver-backed brushes and the comb because he had no hair to brush. The ivory-handled razors were useless because he could not shave. The deformity of his mouth rendered an ordinary toothbrush of no avail, and as his monstrous lips could not hold a cigarette the cigarette-case was a mockery. The silver shoe-horn would be of no service in the putting on of his ungainly slippers, while the hat-brush was quite unsuited to the peaked cap with its visor.

Still the bag was an emblem of the real swell and of the knockabout Don Juan of whom he had read. So every day Merrick laid out upon his table, with proud precision, the silver brushes, the razors, the shoe-horn and the silver cigarette-case which I had taken care to fill with cigarettes. The contemplation of these gave him great pleasure, and such is the power of self-deception that they convinced him he was the 'real thing.'

I think there was just one shadow in Merrick's life. As I have already said, he had a lively imagination; he was romantic; he cherished an emotional regard for women and his favourite pursuit was the reading of love stories. He fell in love – in a humble and devotional way – with, I think, every attractive lady he saw. He, no doubt, pictured himself the hero of many a passionate incident. His bodily deformity had left unmarred the instincts and feelings of his years. He was amorous. He would like to have been a lover, to have walked with the beloved object in the languorous shades of some beautiful garden and to have poured into her ear all the glowing utterances that he had rehearsed in his heart. And yet – the pity of it! – imagine the feelings of such a youth when he saw nothing but a look of horror creep over the face of every girl whose eyes met his. I fancy when he talked of life among the blind there was a half-formed idea in his mind that he might be able to win the affection of a woman if only she were without eyes to see.

As Merrick developed he began to display certain modest ambitions in the direction of improving his mind and enlarging his knowledge of the world. He was as curious as a child and as eager to learn. There were so many things he wanted to know and to see. In the first place he was anxious to view the interior of what he called 'a real house,' such a house as figured in many of the tales he knew, a house with a hall, a drawing-room where guests were received and a dining-room with plate on the sideboard and with easy chairs into which the hero could 'fling himself.' The workhouse, the common lodging-house and a variety of mean garrets were all the residences he knew. To satisfy this wish I drove him up to my small house in Wimpole Street. He was absurdly interested, and examined everything in detail and with untiring curiosity. I could not show him the pampered menials and the powdered footmen of whom he had read, nor could I produce the white marble staircase of the mansion of romance nor the gilded mirrors and the brocaded divans which belong to that style of residence. I explained that the house was a modest dwelling of the Jane Austen type, and as he had read 'Emma' he was content.

A more burning ambition of his was to go to the theatre. It was a project very difficult to satisfy. A popular pantomime was then in progress at Drury Lane Theatre, but the problem was how so conspicuous a being as the Elephant Man could be got there, and how he was to see the performance without attracting the notice of the audience and causing a panic or, at least, an unpleasant diversion. The whole matter was most ingeniously carried through by that kindest of women and most able of actresses – Mrs Kendal. She made the necessary arrangements with the lessee of the theatre. A box was obtained. Merrick was brought up in a carriage with drawn blinds and was allowed to make use of the royal entrance so as to reach the box by a private stair. I had begged three of the hospital sisters to don evening dress and to sit in the front row in order to 'dress' the box, on the one hand, and to form a screen for Merrick on the other. Merrick and I occupied the back of the box which was kept in shadow. All went well, and no one saw a figure, more monstrous than any on the stage, mount the staircase or cross the corridor.

One has often witnessed the unconstrained delight of a child at its first pantomime, but Merrick's rapture was much more intense as well as much more solemn. Here was a being with the brain of a man, the fancies of a youth and the imagination of a child. His attitude was not so much that of delight as of wonder and amazement. He was awed. He was enthralled. The spectacle left him speechless, so that if he were spoken to he took no heed. He often seemed to be panting for breath. I could not help comparing him with a man of his own age in the stalls. This satiated individual was bored to distraction, would look wearily at the stage from time to time and then yawn as if he had not slept for nights; while at the same time Merrick was thrilled by a vision that was almost beyond his comprehension. Merrick talked of this pantomime for weeks and weeks. To him, as to a child with the faculty of make-believe, everything was real; the palace was the home of kings, the princess was of royal blood, the fairies were as undoubted as the children in the street, while the dishes at the banquet were of unquestionable gold. He did not like to discuss it as a play but rather as a vision of some actual world. When this mood possessed him he would say: 'I wonder what the prince did after we left,' or 'Do you think that poor man is still in the dungeon?' and so on and so on.

The splendour and display impressed him, but, I think, the ladies of the ballet took a still greater hold upon his fancy. He did not like the ogres and the giants, while the funny men impressed him as irreverent. Having no experience as a boy of romping and ragging, of practical jokes or of 'larks,' he had little sympathy with the doings of the clown, but, I think (moved by some mischievous instinct in his sub-conscious mind), he was pleased when the policeman was smacked in the face, knocked down and generally rendered undignified.

Later on another longing stirred the depths of Merrick's mind. It was a desire to see the country, a desire to live in some green secluded spot and there learn something about flowers and the ways of animals and birds. The country as viewed from a wagon on a dusty high road was all the country he knew. He had never wandered among the fields nor followed the windings of a wood. He had never climbed to the brow of a breezy down. He had never gathered flowers in a meadow. Since so much of his reading dealt with coun-try life he was possessed by the wish to see the wonders of that life himself.

This involved a difficulty greater than that presented by a visit to the theatre. The project was, however, made possible on this occasion also by the kindness and generosity of a lady – Lady Knightley – who offered Merrick a holiday home in a cottage on her estate. Merrick was conveyed to the railway station in the usual way, but as he could hardly venture to appear on the platform the railway authorities were good enough to run a second-class carriage into a distant siding. To this point Merrick was driven and was placed in the carriage unobserved. The carriage, with the curtains drawn, was then attached to the mainline train.

He duly arrived at the cottage, but the housewife (like the nurse at the hospital) had not been made clearly aware of the unfortunate man's appearance. Thus it happened that when Merrick presented himself his hostess, throwing her apron over her head, fled, gasping, to the fields. She affirmed that such a guest was beyond her powers of endurance, for, when she saw him, she was 'that took' as to be in danger of being permanently 'all of a tremble.'

Merrick was then conveyed to a gamekeeper's cottage which was hidden from view and was close to the margin of a wood. The man and his wife were able to tolerate his presence. They treated him with the greatest kindness, and with them he spent the one supreme holiday of his life. He could roam where he pleased. He met no one on his wanderings, for the wood was preserved and denied to all but the gamekeeper and the forester.

There is no doubt that Merrick passed in this retreat the happiest time he had as yet experienced. He was alone in a land of wonders. The breath of the country passed over him like a healing wind. Into the silence of the wood the fearsome voice of the showman could never penetrate. No cruel eyes could peep at him through the friendly undergrowth. It seemed as if in this place of peace all stain had been wiped away from his sullied past. The Merrick who had once crouched terrified in the filthy shadows of a Mile End shop was now sitting in the sun, in a clearing among the trees, arranging a bunch of violets he had gathered.

His letters to me were the letters of a delighted and enthusiastic child. He gave an account of his trivial adventures, of the amazing things he had seen, and of the beautiful sounds he had heard. He had met with strange birds, had startled a hare from her form, had made friends with a fierce dog, and had watched the trout darting in a stream. He sent me some of the wild flowers he had picked. They were of the commonest and most familiar kind, but they were evidently regarded by him as rare and precious specimens.

He came back to London, to his quarters in Bedstead Square, much improved in health, pleased to be 'home' again and to be once more among his books, his treasures and his many friends.

Some six months after Merrick's return from the country he was found dead in bed. This was in April, 1890. He was lying on his back as if asleep, and had evidently died suddenly and without a struggle, since not even the coverlet of the bed was disturbed. The method of his death was peculiar. So large and so heavy was his head that he could not sleep lying down. When he assumed the recumbent position the massive skull was inclined to drop backwards, with the result that he experienced no little distress. The attitude he was compelled to assume when he slept was very strange. He sat up in bed with his back supported by pillows, his knees were drawn up, and his arms clasped round his legs, while his head rested on the points of his bent knees.

He often said to me that he wished he could lie down to sleep 'like other people.' I think on this last night he must, with some determination, have made the experiment. The pillow was soft, and the head, when placed on it, must have fallen backwards and caused a dislocation of the neck. Thus it came about that his death was due to the desire that had dominated his life – the pathetic but hopeless desire to be 'like other people.'

As a specimen of humanity, Merrick was ignoble and repulsive; but the spirit of Merrick, if it could be seen in the form of the living, would assume the figure of an upstanding and heroic man, smooth browed and clean of limb, and with eyes that flashed undaunted courage.

His tortured journey had come to an end. All the way he, like another, had borne on his back a burden almost too grievous to bear. He had been plunged into the Slough of Despond, but with manly steps had gained the farther shore.

He had been made 'a spectacle to all men' in the heartless streets of Vanity Fair. He had been ill-treated and reviled and bespattered with the mud of Disdain. He had escaped the clutches of the Giant Despair, and at last had reached the 'Place of Deliverance,' where 'his burden loosed from off his shoulders and fell from off his back, so that he saw it no more.'

JOHN GALSWORTHY

A FORSYTE ENCOUNTERS THE PEOPLE, 1917
(1930)

IN OCTOBER 1917, when the air raids on London were acutely monotonous, there was a marked tendency on the part of Eustace Forsyte to take Turkish baths. The most fastidious of his family, who had carried imperturbability of demeanour to the pitch of defiance, he had perceived in the Turkish bath a gesture, as of a finger to a nose, in the face of a boring peril. As soon then as the maroons of alarm went off, he would issue from his rooms or club and head straight for Northumberland Avenue. With his springy and slightly arched walk, as of a man spurning a pavement, he would move deliberately among the hurrying throng; and, undressing without haste, would lay his form, remarkably trim and slim for a man well over fifty, on a couch in the hottest room at about the moment when less self-contained citizens were merely sweating in their shoes. Confirmed in the tastes of a widower of somewhat self-centred character, he gave but few damns to what happened to anything – he it was who used to set his study on fire at school in order to practise being cool in moments of danger, and at college, on being dared, had jumped through a first-floor window and been picked up sensible. On his back, with his pale clean-shaven face composed to a slight superciliousness and his dark grey eyes, below the banding towel, fixed on those golden stars that tick the domed ceilings of any room with aspirations to be oriental, he would think of Maidenhead, or of Chelsea china, and now and then glance at his skin to see if it was glistening. Not a good mixer, as the saying was, he seldom spoke to his bathing fellows, and they mostly fat. Thus would he pass the hours of menace, and when the 'all clear' had sounded, return to his club or to his rooms with the slight smile of one who has perspired well. There he would partake of a repast feeling that he had cheated the Boche.

On a certain occasion, however, towards the end of that invasive period, events did not run true to type. The alarm had sounded, and Eustace had pursued his usual course, but the raid had not matured. Cool and hungry, he emerged from the Baths about eight o'clock and set his face towards the Strand. He had arrived opposite Charing Cross when a number of explosions attracted his attention; people began to run past him and a special constable cried loudly: 'Take cover, take cover!' Eustace frowned. A second Turkish bath was out of the question, and he stood still wondering what he should do, the only person in the street not in somewhat violent motion. Before he could make up his mind whether to walk back to his club or on to the restaurant where he had meant to dine, a large and burly 'special' had seized him by the shoulders and pushed him into the entrance of the Tube Station.

'Take cover, can't you!' he said, rudely.

Eustace freed his sleeve. 'I don't wish to.'

'Then you — well will,' replied the 'special.'

Perceiving that he could only proceed over the considerable body of this intrusive being, Eustace shrugged his shoulders and endeavoured to stand still again, but an inflowing tide of his fellow-beings forced him down the slope into the hallway and on towards the stairs. Here he made a resolute effort to squeeze his way back towards the air. It was totally unavailing, and he was swept on till he was standing about halfway down the stairs among a solid mass of men, women and children of types that seemed to him in no way attractive. He had frequently noticed that mankind in the bulk is unpleasing to the eye, the ear, and the nose; but this deduction had, as it were, been formed by his brain. It was now reinforced by his senses in a manner, to one purified by a Turkish bath, intensely vivid and unpleasing. The air in this rat-run, normally distasteful to Eustace, who never took the Tube, was rapidly becoming fetid, and he at once decided that he would rather brave all the shrapnel of all the anti-aircraft guns defending him than stay where he was. Unfortunately the decision was rendered nugatory by the close pressure of a stout woman with splotches on her face, who kept saying: 'We're all right in 'ere, 'Enry'; by 'Enry, a white-faced mechanician with a rat-gnawed moustache; by their spindle-legged child, who muttered at intervals: 'I'll kill that Kaiser'; and by two Jewish-looking youths, on whom Eustace had at once passed the verdict 'better dead'! His back, moreover, was wedged partly against the front of a young woman smelling of stale powder who panted in one of his ears, and partly against the bow window of her partner, who, judging from the breeze that came from him, was a whisky-taster. On the slopes to right and left, and further to the front were dozens and dozens of other beings, none of whom had for Eustace any fascination. It was as if Fate had designed at one stroke to remove every vestige of the hedge which had hitherto divided him from 'the general.'

Placing his handkerchief, well tinctured by eau-de-Cologne, to his nose, he tried to calculate: It would probably be a couple of hours before the 'all clear' sounded. Could he not squeeze his way very gradually to the entrance? His neighbours seemed to think that by being where they were they had 'struck it lucky' and scored off the by-our-lady Huns. Since they evidently had no intention of departing, it seemed to Eustace that they would prefer his room to his company. He was startled, therefore, when his attempt to escape was greeted by growling admonitions not to 'go shovin',' 'to keep still, couldn't he,' and other displeased comments. It was his first lesson in mob psychology: what was good enough for them was good enough for him. If he persisted, he would be considered a traitor to the body politic, and would meet with strenuous resistance! So he abandoned his design and endeavoured to make himself slimmer, that the bodies round him might be in contact with his shell rather than with his essence. Behind his fast evaporating eau-de-Cologne he developed a kind of preservative disdain of people who clearly preferred this stinking ant-heap to the shrapnel and bombs of the open. Had they no sense of smell; were they totally indifferent to heat, had they no pride that they let the Huns inflict on them this exquisite discomfort? Did none of them feel, with him, that the only becoming way to treat danger was to look down your nose at it?

On the contrary, all these people seemed to think that by taking refuge in the bowels of the earth they had triumphed over the enemy. Their mental pictures of being blown into little bits, or stunned by the shrapnel, must be more vivid than anything he could conjure up. And Eustace had a stab of vision. Good form discouraged the imagination till it had lost the power of painting. Like the French aristocrats who went unruffled to the guillotine, he felt that he would rather be blown up, or shot down, than share this 'rat-run' triumph of his neighbours. The more he looked at them, the more his nose twitched. Even the cheeriness with which they were accepting their rancid situation annoyed him. The sentiment of the spindly child: 'I'll kill that Kaiser,' awakened in him, for the first time since the war began, a fellow-feeling for the German Emperor; the simplification of responsibility

278

adopted by his countrymen stood out so grotesquely in the saying of this Cockney infant.

'He ought to be 'ung,' said a voice to his right.

'My! Ain't it hot here!' said a voice to his left. 'I shall faint if it goes on much longer.'

'It'll stop her panting,' thought Eustace, rubbing his ear.

'Am I standing on your foot, Sir?' asked the stout and splotchy woman.

'Thanks, not particularly.'

'Shift a bit, 'Enry.'

'Shift a bit?' repeated the white-faced mechanician cheerfully: 'That's good, ain't it? There's not too much room, is there, Sir?'

The word 'Sir' thus repeated, or perhaps the first stirrings of a common humanity, moved Eustace to reply:

'The black hole of Calcutta's not in it.'

'I'll kill that Kaiser.'

'She don't like these air-raids, and that's a fact,' said the stout woman: 'Do yer, Milly? But don't you worry, dearie, we're all right down 'ere.'

'Oh! You think so?' said Eustace.

'Ow! Yes! Everyone says the Tubes are safe.'

'What a comfort!'

As if with each opening of his lips some gas of rancour had escaped, Eustace felt almost well disposed to the little family which oppressed his front.

'Wish I 'ad my girl 'ere,' said one of the Jewish youths, suddenly; 'this is your cuddlin' done for you, this is.'

'Strike me!' said the other.

'Better dead!' thought Eustace, even more emphatically.

''Ow long d'you give it, Sir?' said the mechanician, turning his white face a little.

'Another hour and a half, I suppose.'

'I'll kill that Kaiser.'

'Stow it, Milly, you've said that before. One can 'ave too much of a good thing, can't one, Sir?'

'I was beginning to think so,' murmured Eustace.

'Well, she's young to be knocked about like this. It gets on their nerves, ye know. I'll be glad to get 'er and the missis 'ome, and that's a fact.'

Something in the paper whiteness of his face, something in the tone of his hollow-chested voice, and the simple altruism of his remark, affected Eustace. He smelled of sweat and sawdust, but he was jolly decent!

And time went by, the heat and odour thickening; there was almost silence now. A voice said: 'They're a — long time abaht it!' and was greeted with a sighing clamour of acquiescence. All that crowded mass of beings had become preoccupied with the shifting of their limbs, the straining of their lungs towards any faint draught of air. Eustace had given up all speculation, his mind was concentrated blankly on the words: 'Stand straight – stand straight!' The spindly child, discouraged by the fleeting nature of success, had fallen into a sort of coma against his knee; he wondered whether she had ringworm; he wondered why everybody didn't faint. The white-faced mechanician had encircled his wife's waist. His face, ghostly patient, was the one thing Eustace noticed from time to time; it emerged as if supported by no body. Suddenly with a whispering sigh the young woman, behind, fell against his shoulder, and by a sort of miracle found space to crumple down. The mechanician's white face came round:

'Poor lidy, she's gone off!'

'Ah!' boomed the whisky-taster, 'and no wonder, with this 'eat.' He waggled his bowler hat above her head.

'Shove 'er 'ead between her knees,' said the mechanician. Eustace pushed the head downwards, the whisky-taster applied a bunch of keys to her back. She came to with a loud sigh.

'Better for her dahn there,' said the mechanician, 'the 'ot air rises.'

And again time went on, with a ground bass of oaths and cheerios. Then the lights went out to a sound as if souls in an underworld had expressed their feelings. Eustace felt a shuddering upheaval pass through the huddled mass. A Cockney voice cried: 'Are we dahn-'earted?' And the movement subsided in a sort of dreadful calm.

Down below a woman shrieked; another and another took it up.

''Igh-strikes,' muttered the mechanician; 'cover 'er ears, Polly.' The child against Eustace's knee had begun to whimper. 'Milly, where was Moses when the light went out?'

Eustace greeted the sublime fatuity with a wry and wasted smile. He could feel the Jewish youths trying to elbow themselves out. 'Stand still,' he said, sharply.

'That's right, Sir,' said the mechanician; 'no good makin' 'eavy weather of it.'

'Sing, you blighters – sing!' cried a voice: ' "When the fields were white wiv disies." ' And all around they howled a song which Eustace did not know; and then, abruptly as it had gone out, the light went up again. The song died in a prolonged 'Aoh!' Eustace gazed around him. Tears were running down the splotchy woman's cheeks. A smile of relief was twitching at the mechanician's mouth. 'The all clear's gone! The all clear's gone! . . . 'Ip, 'ip, 'ooraay!' The cheering swelled past Eustace, and a swinging movement half lifted him from his feet.

'Catch hold of the child,' he said to the mechanician, 'I've got her other hand.' Step by step they lifted her, under incredible pressure, with maddening slowness, into the hall.

Eustace took a great breath, expanding his lungs while the crowd debouched into the street like an exploding shell. The white-faced mechanician had begun to cough, in a strangled manner alarming to hear. He stopped at last and said:

'That's cleared the pipes. I'm greatly obliged to you, Sir; I dunno 'ow we'd 'a got Milly up. She looks queer, that child.'

The child's face, indeed, was whiter than her father's, and her eyes were vacant.

'Do you live far?'

'Nao, just rahnd the corner, Sir.'

'Come on, then.'

They swung the child, whose legs continued to move mechanically, into the open. The street was buzzing with people emerging from shelter and making their way home. Eustace saw a clock's face. Ten o'clock!

'Damn these people,' he thought. 'The restaurants will be closed.'

The splotchy woman spoke as if answering his thought.

'We oughtn't to keep the gentleman, 'Enry, 'e must be properly tired. I can ketch 'old of Milly. Don't you bother with us, Sir, and thank you kindly.'

'Not a bit,' said Eustace: 'it's nothing.'

''Ere we are, Sir,' said the mechanician, stopping at the side door of some business premises; 'we live in the basement. If it's not presuming, would you take a cup o' tea with us?' And at this moment the child's legs ceased to function altogether.

''Ere, Milly, 'old up, dearie, we're just 'ome.'

But the child's head sagged.

'She's gone off – paw little thing!'

'Lift her!' said Eustace.

'Open the door, Mother, the key's in my pocket; you go on and light the gas.'

282

They supported the spindly child, who now seemed to weigh a ton, down stone stairs into a basement, and laid her on a small bed in a room where all three evidently slept. The mechanician pressed her head down towards her feet.

'She's comin' to. Why, Milly, you're in your bed, see! And now you'll 'ave a nice 'ot cup o' tea! There!'

'I'll kill that Kaiser,' murmured the spindly child, her china-blue eyes fixed wonderingly on Eustace, her face waxy in the gaslight.

'Stir yer stumps, Mother, and get this gentleman a cup. A cup'll do you good, Sir, you must be famished. Will you come in the kitchen and have a smoke, while she's gettin' it?'

A strange fellow-feeling pattered within Eustace looking at that white-faced altruist. He stretched out his cigarette case, shining, curved, and filled with gold-tipped cigarettes. The mechanician took one, held it for a second politely as who should imply: 'Hardly my smoke, but since you are so kind.'

'Thank'ee, Sir. A smoke'll do us both a bit o' good, after that Tube. It was close in there.'

Eustace greeted the miracle of understatement with a smile.

'Not exactly fresh.'

'I'd 'a come and 'ad the raid comfortable at 'ome, but the child was scared and the Tube just opposite. Well, it's all in the day's work, I suppose; but it comes 'ard on children and elderly people, to say nothing of the women. 'Ope you're feelin' better, Sir. You looked very white when you come out.'

'Thanks,' said Eustace, thinking: 'Not so white as you, my friend!'

'The tea won't be a minute. We got the gas 'ere, it boils a kettle a treat. You sit down, old girl, I'll get it for yer.'

Eustace went to the window. The kitchen was hermetically sealed.

'Do you mind if I open the window,' he said, 'I'm still half suffocated from that Tube.'

On the window-sill, in company with potted geraniums, he breathed the dark damp air of a London basement, and his eyes roved listlessly over walls decorated with coloured cuts from Christmas supplements, and china ornaments perched wherever was a spare flat inch. These presents from seaside municipalities aroused in him a sort of fearful sympathy.

'I see you collect china,' he said, at last.

'Ah! The missis likes a bit of china,' said the mechanician, turning his white face illumined by the gas ring; 'reminds 'er of 'olidays. It's a cheerful thing, I think meself, though it takes a bit o' dustin'.'

'You're right there,' said Eustace, his soul fluttering suddenly with a feather brush above his own precious Ming. Ming and the present from Margate! The mechanician was stirring the teapot.

'Weak for me, if you don't mind,' said Eustace, hastily.

The mechanician poured into three cups, one of which he brought to Eustace with a jug of milk and a basin of damp white sugar. The tea looked thick and dark and Indian, and Eustace, who partook habitually of thin pale China tea flavoured with lemon, received the cup solemnly. It was better than he hoped, however, and he drank it gratefully.

'She's drunk her tea a treat,' said the splotchy woman, returning from the bedroom.

''Ere's yours, Mother.'

''Aven't you 'ad a cup yerself, 'Enry?'

'Just goin' to,' said the white-faced mechanician, pouring

284

into a fourth cup and pausing to add: 'Will you 'ave another, Sir? There's plenty in the pot.'

Eustace shook his head: 'No, thanks very much. I must be getting on directly.' But he continued to sit on the window-sill, as a man on a mountain lingers in the whiffling wind before beginning his descent to earth. The mechanician was drinking his tea at last. 'Sure you won't 'ave another cup, Sir?' and he poured again into his wife's cup and his own. The two seemed to expand visibly as the dark liquid passed into them.

'I always say there's nothin' like tea,' said the woman.

'That's right; we could 'a done with a cup dahn there, couldn't we, Sir?'

Eustace stood up.

'I hope your little girl will be all right,' he said: 'and thank you very much for the tea. Here's my card. I've enjoyed meeting you.'

The mechanician took the card, looking up at Eustace rather like a dog.

'I'm sure it's been a pleasure to us, and it's you we got to thank, Sir. I shall remember what you did for the child.'

Eustace shook his head: 'No, really. Good-night, Mrs – er –'

'Thompson, the nyme is, Sir.'

He shook her hand, subduing the slight shudder which her face still imposed on him.

'Good-night, Mr Thompson.'

The hand of the white-faced mechanician, polished on his trousers, grasped Eustace's hand with astonishing force.

'Good-night, Sir.'

'I hope we shall meet again,' said Eustace.

Out in the open it was a starry night, and he paused for a

285

minute in the hooded street with his eyes fixed on those specks of far-off silver, so remarkably unlike the golden asterisks which decorated the firmament of his Turkish bath. And there came to him, so standing, a singular sensation almost as if he had enjoyed his evening, as a man will enjoy that which he has never seen before and wonders if he will ever see again.

GRAHAM GREENE

A LITTLE PLACE OFF THE EDGWARE ROAD
(1939)

CRAVEN CAME UP past the Achilles statue in the thin summer rain. It was only just after lighting-up time, but already the cars were lined up all the way to the Marble Arch, and the sharp acquisitive faces peered out ready for a good time with anything possible which came along. Craven went bitterly by with the collar of his mackintosh tight round his throat: it was one of his bad days.

All the way up the park he was reminded of passion, but you needed money for love. All that a poor man could get was lust. Love needed a good suit, a car, a flat somewhere, or a good hotel. It needed to be wrapped in cellophane. He was aware all the time of the stringy tie beneath the mackintosh, and the frayed sleeves: he carried his body about with him like something he hated. (There were moments of happiness in the British Museum reading-room, but the body called him back.) He bore, as his only sentiment, the memory of ugly deeds committed on park chairs. People talked as if the body died too soon – that wasn't the trouble, to Craven, at all. The body kept alive – and through the glittering tinselly rain, on his way to a rostrum, he passed a little man in a black suit carrying a banner, 'The Body shall rise again.' He remembered a dream from which three times he had woken trembling: he had been alone in the huge dark cavernous burying ground of all the world. Every grave was connected to another under the ground: the globe was honeycombed for the sake of the dead, and on each occasion of dreaming he had discovered anew the horrifying fact that the body doesn't decay. There are no worms and dissolution. Under the ground the world was littered with masses of dead flesh ready to rise again with their warts and boils and eruptions. He had lain in bed and remembered – as 'tidings of great joy' – that the body after all was corrupt.

He came up into the Edgware Road walking fast – the Guardsmen were out in couples, great languid elongated beasts – the bodies like worms in their tight trousers. He hated them, and hated his hatred because he knew what it was, envy. He was aware that every one of them had a better body than himself: indigestion creased his stomach: he felt sure that his breath was foul – but who could he ask? Sometimes he secretly touched himself here and there with scent: it was one of his ugliest secrets. Why should he be asked to believe in the resurrection of this body he wanted to forget? Sometimes he prayed at night (a hint of religious belief was lodged in his breast like a worm in a nut) that *his* body at any rate should never rise again.

He knew all the side streets round the Edgware Road only too well: when a mood was on, he simply walked until he tired, squinting at his own image in the windows of Salmon & Gluckstein and the ABCs. So he noticed at once the posters outside the disused theatre in Culpar Road. They were not unusual, for sometimes Barclays Bank Dramatic Society would hire the place for an evening – or an obscure film would be trade-shown there. The theatre had been built in 1920 by an optimist who thought the cheapness of the site would more than counter-balance its disadvantage of lying a mile outside the conventional theatre zone. But no play had ever succeeded, and it was soon left to gather rat-holes and spider-webs. The covering of the seats was never renewed, and all that ever happened to the place was the temporary false life of an amateur play or a trade show.

Craven stopped and read – there were still optimists it appeared, even in 1939, for nobody but the blindest optimist could hope to make money out of the place as 'The Home of the Silent Film'. The first season of 'primitives' was announced (a high-brow phrase): there would never be a second. Well, the seats were cheap, and it was perhaps worth a shilling to him, now that he was tired, to get in somewhere out of the rain. Craven bought a ticket and went in to the darkness of the stalls.

In the dead darkness a piano tinkled something monotonous recalling Mendelssohn: he sat down in a gangway seat, and could immediately feel the emptiness all round him. No, there would never be another season. On the screen a large woman in a kind of toga wrung her hands, then wobbled with curious jerky movements towards a couch. There she sat and stared out like a sheep-dog distractedly through her loose and black and stringy hair. Sometimes she seemed to dissolve altogether into dots and flashes and wiggly lines. A sub-title said, 'Pompilia betrayed by her beloved Augustus seeks an end to her troubles.'

Craven began at last to see – a dim waste of stalls. There were not twenty people in the place – a few couples whispering with their heads touching, and a number of lonely men like himself, wearing the same uniform of the cheap mackintosh. They lay about at intervals like corpses – and again Craven's obsession returned: the tooth-ache of horror. He thought miserably – I am going mad: other people don't feel like this. Even a disused theatre reminded him of those interminable caverns where the bodies were waiting for resurrection.

'A slave to his passion Augustus calls for yet more wine.'

A gross middle-aged Teutonic actor lay on an elbow with his arm round a large woman in a shift. The Spring Song tinkled ineptly on, and the screen flickered like indigestion. Somebody felt his way through the darkness, scrabbling past Craven's knees – a small man: Craven experienced the unpleasant feeling of a large beard brushing his mouth. Then there was a long sigh as the newcomer found the next chair, and on the screen events had moved with such rapidity that Pompilia had already stabbed herself – or so Craven supposed – and lay still and buxom among her weeping slaves.

A low breathless voice sighed out close to Craven's ear, 'What's happened? Is she asleep?'

'No. Dead.'

'Murdered?' the voice asked with a keen interest.

'I don't think so. Stabbed herself.'

Nobody said 'Hush': nobody was enough interested to object to a voice. They drooped among the empty chairs in attitudes of weary inattention.

The film wasn't nearly over yet: there were children somehow to be considered: was it all going on to a second generation? But the small bearded man in the next seat seemed to be interested only in Pompilia's death. The fact that he had come in at that moment apparently fascinated him. Craven heard the word 'coincidence' twice, and he went on talking to himself about it in low out-of-breath tones. 'Absurd when you come to think of it,' and then 'no blood at all'. Craven didn't listen; he sat with his hands clasped between his knees, facing the fact as he had faced it so often before, that he was in danger of going mad. He had to pull himself up, take a holiday, see a doctor (God knew what infection moved in his veins). He became aware that his bearded neighbour had addressed him directly. 'What?' he asked impatiently, 'what did you say?'

'There would be more blood than you can imagine.'

'What are you talking about?'

When the man spoke to him, he sprayed him with damp breath. There was a little bubble in his speech like an impediment. He said, 'When you murder a man . . .'

'This was a woman,' Craven said impatiently.

'That wouldn't make any difference.'

'And it's got nothing to do with murder anyway.'

'That doesn't signify.' They seemed to have got into an absurd and meaningless wrangle in the dark.

'I know, you see,' the little bearded man said in a tone of enormous conceit.

'Know what?'

'About such things,' he said with guarded ambiguity.

Craven turned and tried to see him clearly. Was he mad? Was this a warning of what he might become – babbling incomprehensibly to strangers in cinemas? He thought, By God, no, trying to see: I'll be sane yet. I *will* be sane. He could make out nothing but a small black hump of body. The man was talking to himself again. He said, 'Talk. Such talk. They'll say it was all for fifty pounds. But that's a lie. Reasons and reasons. They always take the first reason. Never look behind. Thirty years of reasons. Such simpletons,' he added again in that tone of breathlessness and unbounded conceit. So this was madness. So long as he could realize that, he must be sane himself – relatively speaking. Not so sane perhaps as the seekers in the park or the Guardsmen in the Edgware Road, but saner than this. It was like a message of encouragement as the piano tinkled on.

Then again the little man turned and sprayed him. 'Killed

herself, you say? But who's to know that? It's not a mere question of what hand holds the knife.' He laid a hand suddenly and confidingly on Craven's: it was damp and sticky: Craven said with horror as a possible meaning came to him, 'What are you talking about?'

'I know,' the little man said. 'A man in my position gets to know almost everything.'

'What is your position?' Craven asked, feeling the sticky hand on his, trying to make up his mind whether he was being hysterical or not – after all, there were a dozen explanations – it might be treacle.

'A pretty desperate one *you'd* say.' Sometimes the voice almost died in the throat altogether. Something incomprehensible had happened on the screen – take your eyes from these early pictures for a moment and the plot had proceeded on at such a pace ... Only the actors moved slowly and jerkily. A young woman in a night-dress seemed to be weeping in the arms of a Roman centurion: Craven hadn't seen either of them before. '*I am not afraid of death, Lucius – in your arms.*'

The little man began to titter – knowingly. He was talking to himself again. It would have been easy to ignore him altogether if it had not been for those sticky hands which he now removed: he seemed to be fumbling at the seat in front of him. His head had a habit of lolling sideways – like an idiot child's. He said distinctly and irrelevantly: 'Bayswater Tragedy.'

'What was that?' Craven said. He had seen those words on a poster before he entered the park.

'What?'

'About the tragedy.'

'To think they call Cullen Mews Bayswater.' Suddenly the little man began to cough – turning his face towards Craven and coughing right at him: it was like vindictiveness. The voice said, 'Let me see. My umbrella.' He was getting up.

'You didn't have an umbrella.'

'My umbrella,' he repeated. 'My—' and seemed to lose the word altogether. He went scrabbling out past Craven's knees.

Craven let him go, but before he had reached the billowy dusty curtains of the Exit the screen went blank and bright – the film had broken, and somebody immediately turned up one dirt-choked chandelier above the circle. It shone down just enough for Craven to see the smear on his hands. This wasn't hysteria: this was a fact. He wasn't mad: he had sat next to a madman who in some mews – what was the name, Colon, Collin . . . Craven jumped up and made his own way out: the black curtain flapped in his mouth. But he was too late: the man had gone and there were three turnings to choose from. He chose instead a telephone-box and dialled with a sense odd for him of sanity and decision 999.

It didn't take two minutes to get the right department. They were interested and very kind. Yes, there had been a murder in a mews – Cullen Mews. A man's neck had been cut from ear to ear with a bread knife – a horrid crime. He began to tell them how he had sat next the murderer in a cinema: it couldn't be anyone else: there was blood on his hands – and he remembered with repulsion as he spoke the damp beard. There must have been a terrible lot of blood. But the voice from the Yard interrupted him. 'Oh no,' it was saying, 'we have the murderer – no doubt of it at all. It's the body that's disappeared.'

Craven put down the receiver. He said to himself aloud, 'Why should this happen to *me*? Why to *me*?' He was back in the horror of his dream – the squalid darkening street outside was only one of the innumerable tunnels connecting grave to grave where the imperishable bodies lay. He said,

'It was a dream, a dream,' and leaning forward he saw in the mirror above the telephone his own face sprinkled by tiny drops of blood like dew from a scent-spray. He began to scream, 'I won't go mad. I won't go mad. I'm sane. I won't go mad.' Presently a little crowd began to collect, and soon a policeman came.

MOLLIE PANTER-DOWNES

GOOD EVENING, MRS CRAVEN
(1942)

FOR YEARS NOW they had been going to Porter's, in one of the little side streets off the Strand. They had their own particular table in the far corner of the upstairs room, cosily near the fire in winter, cooled in summer by a window at their backs, through which drifted soot and the remote bumble of traffic. Everything contemporary seemed remote at Porter's. The whole place looked as though it had been soaked in Madeira – the rich brown walls crowded with signed photographs of Irving and Bancroft and Forbes-Robertson, the plush seats, the fly-spotted marble Muses forever turning their classic noses hopefully towards the door, as though expecting to see Ellen Terry come in. The waiters were all very old. They carried enormous napkins over their arms and produced the menu with a special flourish from the tails of their old-fashioned coats. The waiter who attended to the corner table looked as though he could have walked on as a senator in a Lyceum production of *Julius Caesar*. Leaning protectively over them, he would say in a hoarse, fruity voice, into which Madeira seemed to have seeped too, 'The steak-and-kidney pudding is just as you like it today, Mr Craven.'

Every Thursday evening, wet or fine, they would be dining in their corner under the bust of Mrs Siddons, talking quietly, sometimes holding hands under the tablecloth. It was the evening when he was supposed to have a standing engagement to play bridge at his club. Sometimes he called for her at her flat; more often they arrived separately. Out of all their Thursdays she loved the foggy winter evenings best, when the taxi-driver growled, 'Wot a night!' as she fumbled in her purse for change, when she ran coughing up the stairs into the plushy warmth and light and their waiter greeted her with a 'Good evening, Mrs Craven. Mr Craven's waiting at your table. I'll bring along your sherries right away.'

She would go over to their table, sit down, and slide her hand palm upwards along the sofa seat until his hand closed round it.

'Good evening, Mrs Craven,' he would say, and they would both laugh.

They always enjoyed the joke that the waiter supposed they were married. It went with the respectability of Porter's that any nice couple who dined together continuously over a long period of time should be thought of as husband and wife. 'We're one in the sight of God and Mrs Siddons,' he said, but although she laughed, it wasn't a joke with her. She liked being called Mrs Craven. It gave her a warm feeling round the heart, because she could pretend for a moment that things were different and that he had no wife and three fine children who would be broken in bits by a divorce. He had long ago made her see the sense of this, and now she was careful never to make scenes or to sound the demanding note which he hated. Her value for him was to be always there, calm and understanding. 'You smooth me out,' he said sometimes. 'You give me more peace than anyone in the world.' She was a wonderful listener. She would sit watching him with a little smile while he told her all the details of his week. He often talked about the children. At her flat, standing in front of the mirror tying his tie, he would tell her proudly how clever eight-year-old Jennifer was, or how well Pete was coming on at school. On these occasions the little smile sometimes grew a trifle rigid on her lips.

They never went anywhere but Porter's. In a queer sort

of way, although he was known by name, he seemed to feel safe and anonymous there. 'None of the people one knows comes here,' he said, by which he meant none of the people his wife knew. More men than women ate at Porter's. Very occasionally he was greeted by a business acquaintance, who would nod and call across the room, 'How are you?' Then he would call back heartily, 'Fine! How are *you*?' but he would be a little uncomfortable all through the meal. If she slid her hand towards his knee, he would pretend not to notice, and he would talk in a brisk, cheerful way which, at a distance, might look like the kind of manner one would use when dining with a female cousin up from the country or a secretary one had kept working late and taken along for some food out of sheer good nature.

Sometimes she felt that she would like to put on a low-cut gown and go somewhere where there were lights and dancing, where she could walk in proudly, with him following her without taking a swift, surreptitious look round the room first to see who was there. But she knew how worried he would look if she suggested it, how he would say, 'Darling, I wish we could, but you know it's impossible. Someone would be sure to spot us. We've got to be careful – haven't we?' By now she had learned exactly how to dress for their Thursday evenings. The clothes had to make her look beautiful for him, but they must be on the unadventurous side so that no one would cast an interested remembering glance from an opposite table. She often wore brown, and sometimes she had a funny feeling that she was invisible against the brown wall and the faded prints of the Prince of Denmark and the noblest Roman of them all.

When the war came, he got a commission in a mechanized regiment. Their Thursday evenings were interrupted, and when he got home on leave things were often difficult. There was a family dinner party, or the children were back from school. 'You know how it is, darling,' he would say ruefully on the telephone. But every now and then he sent her a telegram and came dashing up to London for a few hours. Porter's still looked the same except that most of the men were in uniform, and the old waiter always saw to it that they got their usual table. 'Good evening, Mrs Craven,' he would say shambling forward when he saw her. 'You're expecting Mr Craven? . . . Ah, that's fine. The pigeon casserole is just how he likes it today.'

They dined together just before he went to Libya. There were two men drinking port at the next table, one with white hair and beautiful, long hands who looked like a Galsworthy family lawyer, the other round and red.

'Don't think I'm being stupid and morbid,' she said, 'but supposing anything happens. I've been worrying about that. You might be wounded or ill and I wouldn't know.' She tried to laugh. 'The War Office doesn't have a service for sending telegrams to mistresses, does it?'

He frowned, because this sounded hysterical, and glanced sharply at the old men at the next table, who went right on drinking port and talking in their tired old voices.

'Darling,' he said, 'don't start getting ideas like that into your head. If anything did happen – but it won't – I'd get someone to let you know right away.'

She had a wild impulse to ask him how this would be possible when he would be lying broken and bloody, alone in the sand. With an effort, she remembered that he loved her because she was calm, because she was not the kind of woman to make scenes or let the tears run down her face in public.

'I know you would,' she said. 'Don't worry about me.

Remember, dearest, you don't have to worry about me one little bit.'

'Good night, Mrs Craven. Good night, Mr Craven,' said the old waiter, hurrying after them as they went out.

A long time after he left, his letters began to arrive. They were not very satisfactory. He wrote in the same hearty style that he put on at Porter's for the business acquaintances' benefit, and she had the feeling he was worried the censor might turn out to be his wife's second cousin. She worked hard at a war job and lost a lot of weight. The girl who washed her hair said, 'My goodness, aren't you getting grey!' and she longed foolishly to be able to tell her about it and get her sympathy. There was no one to confide in; all these years she had been so careful that she had hardly mentioned his name to anyone else. She went out with other people, but she imagined that she wasn't so amusing or attractive as she used to be and that they noticed it. She began to stay home most evenings, reading in bed or writing him long letters. Before he left, they had settled on various little code words which would give her an idea of where he was, so she was able to tell when he was up in the front lines or when he had gone back to Cairo for leave.

After a while his letters stopped, but she wasn't seriously worried at first. She knew that the mails were often bad; there had been long gaps before. But this time hard fighting was going on in Libya, and she had a terrible premonition that something had happened. She found that she could hardly sleep at all, and when she came home in the evenings, her hand shook as she put the key in the door. She made herself take the letters out of the box and look through them very slowly. Afterwards she would go into the living-room, sit down, and stare blankly out of the window at the barrage balloons glittering in the late sunlight.

One evening she came in after a hard day's work, and as she stood getting the key out of her purse, she knew that there would be a letter or a cable waiting for her. She was so positive of it that she was tremulous with relief as she got the door open and stooped to the mailbox. There was nothing except a bill for a repair to the radio set. She stood, feeling cold and stupid, then she went swiftly to the living-room telephone and looked up a number in the book. As she dialled it and then listened to the bell buzzing, it seemed odd to her to think how many times he must have heard it ring through that unknown house.

When a child's voice, high, and carefully a little overloud, answered, she was slightly taken aback. She said, 'Is this Mrs Craven's house?' The child's voice said, 'Yes. This is Jennifer. Do you want Mummy? . . . I'll get her.'

After a pause she heard footsteps on a hardwood floor, and then a new voice said, 'Hello? Yes?'

She had thought out what to say, and she made her voice crisp and friendly.

'Good evening, Mrs Craven,' she said. 'I do want to apologize for troubling you like this. You won't know my name, but I'm an old friend of Mr Craven's, and I've only just heard that he's in Libya. I thought I'd like to ring up and see if you've had good news of him.'

'Why, that's nice of you,' Mrs Craven said pleasantly. 'To tell you the truth, I've heard nothing very recently, but I try not to worry. He'll cable me when he has a minute. Judging by the papers, I shouldn't think any of them have a minute.'

'No, I don't suppose they have,' she said. She could hear the little girl calling out, as if to a dog. She knew that there were two dogs, and that there was French Empire furniture

304

in the room, and on the mantelpiece stood a little Chinese figure in white porcelain with a scroll in its hand. She had helped choose it one Christmas. Mrs Craven sounded calm and unfussed. She could picture her standing at the telephone, smiling slightly, secure in the middle of her own familiar things, maybe watching the child abstractedly out of the corner of her eye while she dealt courteously with this well-meaning stranger.

The pleasant voice said, 'Luckily, I'm tremendously busy myself. That helps to keep one's mind off things, doesn't it? I'm so sorry, I don't think I quite caught the name.'

She mumbled a name that might have been anything and added lightly, 'Just someone Mr Craven used to know a long while ago. Goodbye, Mrs Craven, and thanks so much. I hope you hear good news very soon.'

She hung up the receiver and sat for a long time without moving. Then she began to weep bitterly. The tears poured down her face, and she rocked her body backward and forward. 'I can't go on,' she sobbed, as though he were there in the room with her. 'I can't, can't go on. You'll have to break them up – I don't care. I just can't go on this way any longer.' She thought of his wife sitting in their home on the other side of town, and the contrast seemed too bitter to bear. All those years of Thursday evenings seemed like a pathetic game of make-believe – two children playing at housekeeping in a playhouse with three walls. After a while she grew quieter. She sat thinking of him, wondering whether, wherever he was, he would have had a sense of something breaking sharply in two, coming apart with a hum, like a snapped wire. Already she could feel the relaxed tension, as though whatever had been holding her taut all these years had suddenly gone limp.

Tomorrow she would write and tell him, but not now. She couldn't remember when she had felt so tired. She went into the bathroom to bathe her face, and then came back and began taking off her dress. There was a brooch pinned at the neck, and she undid it and stood looking at it for a moment. It was a discreetly beautiful thing of dark, old garnets – diamonds, he had pointed out, were too likely to cause comment, and didn't suit her, either. She put down the brooch and finished undressing. Maybe, she thought, she would wait until after tomorrow to write to him, for she had a feeling that tomorrow there would be a letter from him. She was sure of it. She could see it lying in the mailbox, addressed in that small, neat, familiar hand. If it wasn't there tomorrow, it would be there the next day. She would go to Porter's for dinner, sit at their table, and read it over and over. 'Good news from Mr Craven, Mrs Craven?' the old waiter would say as he leaned protectively over her. 'Ah, that's fine, that's fine.'

She began to smile, but suddenly she closed her eyes for a minute. She had had a queer sensation of falling, of the room slipping away and of herself falling, falling, as one does in a dream, without being able to stop and without wondering or caring what lies at the bottom.

WILLIAM SANSOM

THE WALL
(1944)

IT WAS OUR third job that night.

Until this thing happened, work had been without incident. There had been shrapnel, a few enquiring bombs, and some huge fires; but these were unremarkable and have since merged without identity into the neutral maze of fire and noise and water and night, without date and without hour, with neither time nor form, that lowers mistily at the back of my mind as a picture of the air-raid season.

I suppose we were worn down and shivering. Three a.m. is a meanspirited hour. I suppose we were drenched, with the cold hose water trickling in at our collars and settling down at the tails of our shirts. Without doubt the heavy brass couplings felt moulded from metal-ice. Probably the open roar of the pumps drowned the petulant buzz of the raiders above, and certainly the ubiquitous fire-glow made an orange stage-set of the streets. Black water would have puddled the City alleys and I suppose our hands and our faces were black as the water. Black with hacking about among the burnt up rafters. These things were an every-night nonentity. They happened and they were not forgotten because they were never even remembered.

But I do remember it was our third job. And there we were – Len, Lofty, Verno and myself, playing a fifty foot jet up the face of a tall city warehouse and thinking of nothing at all. You don't think of anything after the first few hours. You just watch the white pole of water lose itself in the fire and you think of nothing. Sometimes you move the jet over to another window. Sometimes the orange dims to black – but you only ease your grip on the ice-cold nozzle and continue pouring careless gallons through the window. You know the fire will fester for hours yet. However, that night the blank, indefinite hours of waiting were sharply interrupted – by an unusual sound. Very suddenly a long rattling crack of bursting brick and mortar perforated the moment. And then the upper half of that five-storey building heaved over towards us. It hung there, poised for a timeless second before rumbling down at us. I was thinking of nothing at all and then I was thinking of everything in the world.

In that simple second my brain digested every detail of the scene. New eyes opened at the sides of my head so that, from within, I photographed a hemispherical panorama bounded by the huge length of the building in front of me and the narrow lane on either side.

Blocking us on the left was the squat trailer pump, roaring and quivering with effort. Water throbbed from its overflow valves and from leakages in the hose and couplings. A ceaseless stream spewed down its grey sides into the gutter. But nevertheless a fat iron exhaust pipe glowed red-hot in the middle of the wet engine. I had to look past Lofty's face. Lofty was staring at the controls, hands tucked into his armpits for warmth. Lofty was thinking of nothing. He had a black diamond of soot over one eye, like the White-eyed Kaffir in negative.

To the other side of me was a free run up the alley. Overhead swung a sign – 'Catto and Henley.' I wondered what in hell they sold. Old stamps? The alley was quite free. A couple of lengths of dead, deflated hose wound over the darkly glistening pavement. Charred flotsam dammed up one of the gutters. A needle of water fountained from a hole in a live hose-length. Beneath a blue shelter light lay a shattered coping stone. The next shop along was a tobacconist's, windowless, with fake display cartons torn open for anybody to see. The alley was quite free.

Behind me, Len and Verno shared the weight of the hose. They heaved up against the strong backward drag of water-pressure. All I had to do was yell 'Drop it' – and then run. We could risk the live hose snaking up at us. We could run to the right down the free alley – Len, Verno and me. But I never moved. I never said 'Drop it' or anything else. That long second held me hypnotized, rubber boots cemented to the pavement. Ton upon ton of red-hot brick hovering in the air above us numbed all initiative. I could only think. I couldn't move.

Six yards in front stood the blazing building. A minute before I would never have distinguished it from any other drab Victorian atrocity happily on fire. Now I was immediately certain of every minute detail. The building was five storeys high. The top four storeys were fiercely alight. The rooms inside were alive with red fire. The black outside walls remained untouched. And thus, like the lighted carriages of a night express, there appeared alternating rectangles of black and red that emphasized vividly the extreme symmetry of the window spacing: each oblong window shape posed as a vermilion panel set in perfect order upon the dark face of the wall. There were ten windows to each floor, making forty windows in all. In rigid rows of ten, one row placed precisely above the other, with strong contrasts of black and red, the blazing windows stood to attention in strict formation. The oblong building, the oblong windows, the oblong spacing. Orange-red colour seemed to *bulge* from the black framework, assumed tactile values, like boiling jelly that expanded inside a thick black squared grill.

Three of the storeys, thirty blazing windows and their huge frame of black brick, a hundred solid tons of hard, deep Victorian wall, pivoted over towards us and hung flatly over the alley. Whether the descending wall actually paused in its fall I can never know. Probably it never did. Probably it only seemed to hang there. Probably my eyes digested its action at an early period of momentum, so that I saw it 'off true' but before it had gathered speed.

The night grew darker as the great mass hung over us. Through smoke-fogged fireglow the moonlight had hitherto penetrated to the pit of our alley through declivities in the skyline. Now some of the moonlight was being shut out as the wall hung ever further over us. The wall shaded the moonlight like an inverted awning. Now the pathway of light above had been squeezed to a thin line. That was the only silver lining I ever believed in. It shone out – a ray of hope. But it was a declining hope, for although at this time the entire hemispherical scene appeared static, an imminence of movement could be sensed throughout – presumably because the scene was actually moving. Even the speed of the shutter which closed the photograph on my mind was powerless to exclude this motion from a deeper consciousness. The picture appeared static to the limited surface senses, the eyes and the material brain, but beyond that there was hidden movement.

The second was timeless. I had leisure to remark many things. For instance, that an iron derrick, slightly to the left, would not hit me. This derrick stuck out from the building and I could feel its sharpness and hardness as clearly as if I had run my body intimately over its contour. I had time to notice that it carried a foot-long hook, a chain with three-inch rings, two girder supports and a wheel more than twice as large as my head.

A wall will fall in many ways. It may sway over to the one side or the other. It may crumble at the very beginning of its fall. It may remain intact and fall flat. This wall fell as flat as a pancake. It clung to its shape through ninety degrees to the horizontal. Then it detached itself from the pivot and slammed down on top of us.

The last resistance of bricks and mortar at the pivot point cracked off like automatic gun fire. The violent sound both deafened us and brought us to our senses. We dropped the hose and crouched. Afterwards Verno said that I knelt slowly on one knee with bowed head, like a man about to be knighted. Well, I got my knighting. There was an incredible noise – a thunderclap condensed into the space of an eardrum – and then the bricks and the mortar came tearing and burning into the flesh of my face.

Lofty, away by the pump, was killed. Len, Verno and myself they dug out. There was very little brick on top of us. We had been lucky. We had been framed by one of those symmetrical, oblong window spaces.

ELIZABETH BOWEN

MYSTERIOUS KÔR
(1945)

FULL MOONLIGHT DRENCHED the city and searched it; there was not a niche left to stand in. The effect was remorseless: London looked like the moon's capital – shallow, cratered, extinct. It was late, but not yet midnight; now the buses had stopped the polished roads and streets in this region sent for minutes together a ghostly unbroken reflection up. The soaring new flats and the crouching old shops and houses looked equally brittle under the moon, which blazed in windows that looked its way. The futility of the black-out became laughable: from the sky, presumably, you could see every slate in the roofs, every whited kerb, every contour of the naked winter flowerbeds in the park; and the lake, with its shining twists and tree-darkened islands would be a landmark for miles, yes, miles, overhead.

However, the sky, in whose glassiness floated no clouds but only opaque balloons, remained glassy-silent. The Germans no longer came by the full moon. Something more immaterial seemed to threaten, and to be keeping people at home. This day between days, this extra tax, was perhaps more than senses and nerves could bear. People stayed indoors with a fervour that could be felt: the buildings strained with battened-down human life, but not a beam, not a voice, not a note from a radio escaped. Now and then under streets and buildings the earth rumbled: the Underground sounded loudest at this time.

Outside the now gateless gates of the park, the road

coming downhill from the north-west turned south and became a street, down whose perspective the traffic lights went through their unmeaning performance of changing colour. From the promontory of pavement outside the gates you saw at once up the road and down the street: from behind where you stood, between the gateposts, appeared the lesser strangeness of grass and water and trees. At this point, at this moment, three French soldiers, directed to a hostel they could not find, stopped singing to listen derisively to the waterbirds wakened up by the moon. Next, two wardens coming off duty emerged from their post and crossed the road diagonally, each with an elbow cupped inside a slung-on tin hat. The wardens turned their faces, mauve in the moonlight, towards the Frenchmen with no expression at all. The two sets of steps died in opposite directions, and, the birds subsiding, nothing was heard or seen until, a little way down the street, a trickle of people came out of the Underground, around the anti-panic brick wall. These all disappeared quickly, in an abashed way, or as though dissolved in the street by some white acid, but for a girl and a soldier who, by their way of walking, seemed to have no destination but each other and to be not quite certain even of that. Blotted into one shadow he tall, she little, these two proceeded towards the park. They looked in, but did not go in; they stood there debating without speaking. Then, as though a command from the street behind them had been received by their synchronized bodies, they faced round to look back the way they had come.

His look up the height of a building made his head drop back, and she saw his eyeballs glitter. She slid her hand from his sleeve, stepped to the edge of the pavement and said: 'Mysterious Kôr.'

'What is?' he said, not quite collecting himself.

'This is –

> "*Mysterious Kôr thy walls forsaken stand,*
> *Thy lonely towers beneath a lonely moon –*"
>> *– this is Kôr.*'

'Why,' he said, 'it's years since I've thought of that.'
She said: 'I think of it all the time –

> "*Not in the waste beyond the swamps and sand,*
> *The fever-haunted forest and lagoon,*
> *Mysterious Kôr thy walls—*"

– a completely forsaken city, as high as cliffs and as white as bones, with no history—'

'But something must once have happened: why had it been forsaken?'

'How could anyone tell you when there's nobody there?'

'Nobody there since how long?'

'Thousands of years.'

'In that case, it would have fallen down.'

'No, not Kôr,' she said with immediate authority. 'Kôr's altogether different; it's very strong; there is not a crack in it anywhere for a weed to grow in; the corners of stones and the monuments might have been cut yesterday, and the stairs and arches are built to support themselves.'

'You know all about it,' he said, looking at her.

'I know, I know all about it.'

'What, since you read that book?'

'Oh, I didn't get much from that; I just got the name. I knew that must be the right name; it's like a cry.'

'Most like the cry of a crow to me.' He reflected, then said: 'But the poem begins with "Not" – "*Not in the waste beyond the swamps and sand—*" And it goes on, as I remember, to prove Kôr's not really anywhere. When even a poem says there's no such place—'

'What it tries to say doesn't matter: I see what it makes me see. Anyhow, that was written some time ago, at that time when they thought they had got everything taped, because the whole world had been explored, even the middle of Africa. Every thing and place had been found and marked on some map; so what wasn't marked on any map couldn't be there at all. So *they* thought: that was why he wrote the poem. "*The world is disenchanted,*" it goes on. That was what set me off hating civilization.'

'Well, cheer up,' he said; 'there isn't much of it left.'

'Oh, yes, I cheered up some time ago. This war shows we've by no means come to the end. If you can blow whole places out of existence, you can blow whole places into it. I don't see why not. They say we can't say what's come out since the bombing started. By the time we've come to the end, Kôr may be the one city left: the abiding city. I should laugh.'

'No, you wouldn't,' he said sharply. '*You* wouldn't – at least, I hope not. I hope you don't know what you're saying – does the moon make you funny?'

'Don't be cross about Kôr; please don't, Arthur,' she said. 'I thought girls thought about people.'

'What, these days?' she said. 'Think about people? How can anyone think about people if they've got any heart? I don't know how other girls manage: I always think about Kôr.'

'Not about me?' he said. When she did not at once answer, he turned her hand over, in anguish, inside his grasp. 'Because I'm not there when you want me – is that my fault?'

'But to think about Kôr *is* to think about you and me.'

'In that dead place?'

'No, ours – we'd be alone here.'

Tightening his thumb on her palm while he thought this

over, he looked behind them, around them, above them – even up at the sky. He said finally: 'But we're alone here.'

'That was why I said "Mysterious Kôr".'

'What, you mean we're there now, that here's there, that now's then? . . . *I* don't mind,' he added, letting out as a laugh the sigh he had been holding in for some time. 'You ought to know the place, and for all I could tell you we might be anywhere: I often do have it, this funny feeling, the first minute or two when I've come up out of the Underground. Well, well: join the Army and see the world.' He nodded towards the perspective of traffic lights and said, a shade craftily: 'What are those, then?'

Having caught the quickest possible breath, she replied: 'Inexhaustible gases; they bored through to them and lit them as they came up; by changing colour they show the changing of minutes; in Kôr there is no sort of other time.'

'You've got the moon, though: that can't help making months.'

'Oh, and the sun, of course; but those two could do what they liked; we should not have to calculate when they'd come or go.'

'We might not have to,' he said, 'but I bet I should.'

'I should not mind what you did, so long as you never said, "What next?"'

'I don't know about "next", but I do know what we'd do first.'

'What, Arthur?'

'Populate Kôr.'

She said: 'I suppose it would be all right if our children were to marry each other?'

But her voice faded out; she had been reminded that they were homeless on this his first night of leave. They were, that was to say, in London without any hope of any place of their

321

own. Pepita shared a two-roomed flatlet with a girl friend, in a by-street off the Regent's Park Road, and towards this they must make their half-hearted way. Arthur was to have the sitting-room divan, usually occupied by Pepita, while she herself had half of her girl friend's bed. There was really no room for a third, and least of all for a man, in those small rooms packed with furniture and the two girls' belongings: Pepita tried to be grateful for her friend Callie's forbearance – but how could she be, when it had not occurred to Callie that she would do better to be away tonight? She was more slow-witted than narrow-minded – but Pepita felt she owed a kind of ruin to her. Callie, not yet known to be home later than ten, would be now waiting up, in her house-coat, to welcome Arthur. That would mean three-sided chat, drinking cocoa, then turning in: that would be that, and that would be all. That was London, this war – they were lucky to have a roof – London, full enough before the Americans came. Not a place: they would even grudge you sharing a grave – that was what even married couples complained. Whereas in Kôr . . .

In Kôr . . . Like glass, the illusion shattered: a car hummed like a hornet towards them, veered, showed its scarlet tail-light, streaked away up the road. A woman edged round a front door and along the area railings timidly called her cat; meanwhile a clock near, then another set further back in the dazzling distance, set about striking midnight. Pepita, feeling Arthur release her arm with an abruptness that was the inverse of passion, shivered; whereat he asked brusquely: 'Cold? Well, which way? – we'd better be getting on.'

Callie was no longer waiting up. Hours ago she had set out the three cups and saucers, the tins of cocoa and household milk and, on the gas-ring, brought the kettle to just short of the boil. She had turned open Arthur's bed, the living-room divan, in the neat inviting way she had learnt at home – then, with a modest impulse, replaced the cover. She had, as Pepita foresaw, been wearing her cretonne house-coat, the nearest thing to a hostess gown that she had; she had already brushed her hair for the night, rebraided it, bound the braids in a coronet round her head. Both lights and the wireless had been on, to make the room both look and sound gay: all alone, she had come to that peak moment at which company should arrive – but so seldom does. From then on she felt welcome beginning to wither in her, a flower of the heart that had bloomed too early. There she had sat like an image, facing the three cold cups, on the edge of the bed to be occupied by an unknown man.

Callie's innocence and her still unsought-out state had brought her to take a proprietary pride in Arthur; this was all the stronger, perhaps, because they had not yet met. Sharing the flat with Pepita, this last year, she had been content with reflecting the heat of love. It was not, surprisingly, that Pepita seemed very happy – there were times when she was palpably on the rack, and this was not what Callie could understand. 'Surely you owe it to Arthur,' she would then say, 'to keep cheerful? So long as you love each other—' Callie's calm brow glowed – one might say that it glowed in place of her friend's; she became the guardian of that ideality which for Pepita was constantly lost to view. It was true, with the sudden prospect of Arthur's leave, things had come nearer to earth: he became a proposition, and she would have been as glad if he could have slept somewhere else. Physically shy, a brotherless virgin, Callie shrank from sharing this flat with a young man. In this flat you could hear everything: what was once a three-windowed Victorian drawing-room had been partitioned, by very thin walls, into kitchenette, living-room, Callie's bedroom. The living-room was in the centre; the two others open off it. What was once the conservatory, half a flight down, was now converted into a draughty bathroom, shared with somebody else on the girls' floor. The flat, for these days, was cheap – even so, it was Callie, earning more than Pepita, who paid the greater part of the rent: it thus became up to her, more or less, to express good will as to Arthur's making a third. 'Why, it will be lovely to have him here,' Callie said. Pepita accepted the good will without much grace – but then, had she ever much grace to spare? – she was as restlessly secretive, as self-centred, as a little half-grown black cat. Next came a puzzling moment: Pepita seemed to be hinting that Callie should fix herself up somewhere else. 'But where would I go?' Callie marvelled when this was at last borne in on her. 'You know what London's like now. And, anyway' – here she laughed, but hers was a forehead that coloured as easily as it glowed – 'it wouldn't be proper, would it, me going off and leaving just you and Arthur; I don't know what your mother would say to me. No, we may be a little squashed, but we'll make things ever so homey. I shall not mind playing gooseberry, really, dear.'

But the hominess by now was evaporating, as Pepita and Arthur still and still did not come. At half-past ten, in obedience to the rule of the house, Callie was obliged to turn off the wireless, whereupon silence out of the stepless street began seeping into the slighted room. Callie recollected the fuel target and turned off her dear little table lamp, gaily painted with spots to make it look like a toadstool, thereby leaving only the hanging light. She laid her hand on the kettle, to find it gone cold again and sigh for the wasted gas if not for her wasted thought. Where are they? Cold crept up her out of the kettle; she went to bed.

Callie's bed lay along the wall under the window: she did

not like sleeping so close up under glass, but the clearance that must be left for the opening of door and cupboards made this the only possible place. Now she got in and lay rigidly on the bed's inner side, under the hanging hems of the window curtains, training her limbs not to stray to what would be Pepita's half. This sharing of her bed with another body would not be the least of her sacrifice to the lovers' love; tonight would be the first night – or at least, since she was an infant – that Callie had slept with anyone. Child of a sheltered middle-class household, she had kept physical distances all her life. Already repugnance and shyness ran through her limbs; she was preyed upon by some more obscure trouble than the expectation that she might not sleep. As to *that*, Pepita was restless; her tossings on the divan, her broken-off exclamations and blurred pleas had been to be heard, most nights, through the dividing wall.

Callie knew, as though from a vision, that Arthur would sleep soundly, with assurance and majesty. Did they not all say, too, that a soldier sleeps like a log? With awe she pictured, asleep, the face that she had not yet, awake, seen – Arthur's man's eyelids, cheekbones and set mouth turned up to the darkened ceiling. Wanting to savour darkness herself, Callie reached out and put off her bedside lamp.

At once she knew that something was happening – outdoors, in the street, the whole of London, the world. An advance, an extraordinary movement was silently taking place; blue-white beams overflowed from it, silting, dropping round the edges of the muffling black-out curtains. When, starting up, she knocked a fold of the curtain, a beam like a mouse ran across her bed. A searchlight, the most powerful of all time, might have been turned full and steady upon her defended window; finding flaws in the black-out stuff, it made veins and stars. Once gained by this idea of pressure she could not lie down again; she sat tautly, drawn-up knees touching her breasts, and asked herself if there were anything she should do. She parted the curtains, opened them slowly wider, looked out – and was face to face with the moon.

Below the moon, the houses opposite her window blazed back in transparent shadow; and something – was it a coin or a ring? – glittered half-way across the chalk-white street. Light marched in past her face, and she turned to see where it went: out stood the curves and garlands of the great white marble Victorian mantelpiece of that lost drawing-room; out stood, in the photographs turned her way, the thoughts with which her parents had faced the camera, and the humble puzzlement of her two dogs at home. Of silver brocade, just faintly purpled with roses, became her house-coat hanging over the chair. And the moon did more: it exonerated and beautified the lateness of the lovers' return. No wonder, she said to herself, no wonder – if this was the world they walked in, if this was whom they were with. Having drunk in the white explanation, Callie lay down again. Her half of the bed was in shadow, but she allowed one hand to lie, blanched, in what would be Pepita's place. She lay and looked at the hand until it was no longer her own.

Callie woke to the sound of Pepita's key in the latch. But no voices? What had happened? Then she heard Arthur's step. She heard his unslung equipment dropped with a weary, dull sound, and the plonk of his tin hat on a wooden chair. 'Sssh-sssh!' Pepita exclaimed, 'she *might* be asleep!'

Then at last Arthur's voice: 'But I thought you said—'

'I'm not asleep; I'm just coming!' Callie called out with rapture, leaping out from her form in shadow into the moon-light, zipping on her enchanted house-coat over her night-dress, kicking her shoes on, and pinning in place, with a trembling firmness, her plaits in their coronet round her head. Between these movements of hers she heard not another sound. Had she only dreamed they were there? Her heart beat: she stepped through the living-room, shutting her door behind her.

Pepita and Arthur stood the other side of the table; they gave the impression of being lined up. Their faces, at different levels – for Pepita's rough, dark head came only an inch above Arthur's khaki shoulder – were alike in abstention from any kind of expression; as though, spiritually, they both still refused to be here. Their features looked faint, weathered – was this the work of the moon? Pepita said at once: 'I suppose we are very late?'

'I don't wonder,' Callie said, 'on this lovely night.'

Arthur had not raised his eyes; he was looking at the three cups. Pepita now suddenly jogged his elbow, saying, 'Arthur, wake up; say something; this is Callie – well, Callie, this is Arthur, of course.'

'Why, yes of course this is Arthur,' returned Callie, whose candid eyes since she entered had not left Arthur's face. Perceiving that Arthur did not know what to do, she advanced round the table to shake hands with him. He looked up, she looked down, for the first time: she rather beheld than felt his red-brown grip on what still seemed her glove of moonlight. 'Welcome, Arthur,' she said. 'I'm so glad to meet you at last. I hope you will be comfortable in the flat.'

'It's been kind of you,' he said after consideration.

'Please do not feel that,' said Callie. 'This is Pepita's home, too, and we both hope – don't we, Pepita? – that you'll regard it as yours. Please feel free to do just as you like. I am sorry it is so small.'

'Oh, I don't know,' Arthur said, as though hypnotized; 'it seems a nice little place.'

Pepita, meanwhile, glowered and turned away.

Arthur continued to wonder, though he had once been told, how these two unalike girls had come to set up together – Pepita so small, except for her too-big head, compact of childish brusqueness and of unchildish passion, and Callie, so sedate, waxy and tall – an unlit candle. Yes, she was like one of those candles on sale outside a church; there could be something votive even in her demeanour. She was unconscious that her good manners, those of an old fashioned country doctor's daughter, were putting the other two at a disadvantage. He found himself touched by the grave good faith with which Callie was wearing that tartish house-coat, above which her face kept the glaze of sleep; and, as she knelt to relight the gas-ring under the kettle, he marked the strong, delicate arch of one bare foot, disappearing into the arty green shoe. Pepita was now too near him ever again to be seen as he now saw Callie – in a sense, he never *had* seen Pepita for the first time: she had not been, and still sometimes was not, his type. No, he had not thought of her twice; he had not remembered her until he began to remember her with passion. You might say he had not seen Pepita coming: their love had been a collision in the dark.

Callie, determined to get this over, knelt back and said: 'Would Arthur like to wash his hands?' When they had heard him stumble down the half-flight of stairs, she said to Pepita: 'Yes, I was so glad you had the moon.'

'Why?' said Pepita. She added: 'There was too much of it.'

'You're tired. Arthur looks tired, too.'

'How would you know? He's used to marching about. But it's all this having no place to go.'

'But, Pepita, you—'

But at this point Arthur came back: from the door he

noticed the wireless, and went direct to it. 'Nothing much on now, I suppose?' he doubtfully said.

'No; you see it's past midnight; we're off the air. And, anyway, in this house they don't like the wireless late. By the same token,' went on Callie, friendly smiling, 'I'm afraid I must ask you, Arthur, to take your boots off, unless, of course, you mean to stay sitting down. The people below us—'

Pepita flung off, saying something under her breath, but Arthur, remarking, 'No, I don't mind,' both sat down and began to take off his boots. Pausing, glancing to left and right at the divan's fresh cotton spread, he said: 'It's all right is it, for me to sit on this?'

'That's my bed,' said Pepita. 'You are to sleep in it.'

Callie then made the cocoa, after which they turned in. Preliminary trips to the bathroom having been worked out, Callie was first to retire, shutting the door behind her so that Pepita and Arthur might kiss each other good night. When Pepita joined her, it was without knocking: Pepita stood still in the moon and began to tug off her clothes. Glancing with hate at the bed, she asked: 'Which side?'

'I expected you'd like the outside.'

'What are you standing about for?'

'I don't really know: as I'm inside I'd better get in first.'

'Then why not get in?'

When they had settled rigidly, side by side, Callie asked: 'Do you think Arthur's got all he wants?'

Pepita jerked her head up. 'We can't sleep in all this moon.'

'Why, you don't believe the moon does things, actually?'

'Well, it couldn't hope to make some of us *much* more screwy.'

Callie closed the curtains, then said: 'What do you mean? And – didn't you hear? – I asked if Arthur's got all he wants.'

'That's what I meant – have you got a screw loose, really?'

'Pepita, I won't stay here if you're going to be like this.'

'In that case, you had better go in with Arthur.'

'What about me?' Arthur loudly said through the wall. 'I can hear practically all you girls are saying.'

They were both startled – rather that than abashed. Arthur, alone in there, had thrown off the ligatures of his social manner: his voice held the whole authority of his sex – he was impatient, sleepy, and he belonged to no one.

'Sorry,' the girls said in unison. Then Pepita laughed soundlessly, making their bed shake, till to stop herself she bit the back of her hand, and this movement made her elbow strike Callie's cheek. 'Sorry,' she had to whisper. No answer: Pepita fingered her elbow and found, yes, it was quite true, it was wet. 'Look, shut up crying, Callie: what have I done?'

Callie rolled right round, in order to press her forehead closely under the window, into the curtains, against the wall. Her weeping continued to be soundless: now and then, unable to reach her handkerchief, she staunched her eyes with a curtain, disturbing slivers of moon. Pepita gave up marvelling, and soon slept: at least there is something in being dog-tired.

A clock struck four as Callie woke up again – but something else had made her open her swollen eyelids. Arthur, stumbling about on his padded feet, could be heard next door attempting to make no noise. Inevitably, he bumped the edge of the table. Callie sat up: by her side Pepita lay like a mummy rolled half over, in forbidding, tenacious sleep. Arthur groaned. Callie caught a breath, climbed lightly over Pepita, felt for her torch on the mantelpiece, stopped to listen again. Arthur groaned again: Callie, with movements soundless as they were certain, opened the door and slipped through to the living-room. 'What's the matter?' she whispered. 'Are you ill?'

'No; I just got a cigarette. Did I wake you up?'

'But you groaned.'

'I'm sorry; I'd no idea.'

'But do you often?'

'I've no idea, really, I tell you,' Arthur repeated. The air of the room was dense with his presence, overhung by tobacco. He must be sitting on the edge of his bed, wrapped up in his overcoat – she could smell the coat, and each time he pulled on the cigarette his features appeared down there, in the fleeting, dull reddish glow. 'Where are you?' he said. 'Show a light.'

Her nervous touch on her torch, like a reflex to what he said, made it flicker up for a second. 'I am just by the door; Pepita's asleep; I'd better go back to bed.'

'Listen. Do you two get on each other's nerves?'

'Not till tonight,' said Callie, watching the uncertain swoops of the cigarette as he reached across to the ashtray on the edge of the table. Shifting her bare feet patiently, she added: 'You don't see us as we usually are.'

'She's a girl who shows things in funny ways – I expect she feels bad at our putting you out like this – I know I do. But then we'd got no choice, had we?'

'It is really I who am putting you out,' said Callie.

'Well, that can't be helped either, can it? You had the right to stay in your own place. If there'd been more time, we might have gone to the country, though I still don't see where we'd have gone there. It's one harder when you're not married, unless you've got the money. Smoke?'

'No, thank you. Well, if you're all right, I'll go back to bed.'

'I'm glad she's asleep – funny the way she sleeps, isn't it? You can't help wondering where she is. You haven't got a boy, have you, just at present?'

'No. I've never had one.'

'I'm not sure in one way that you're not better off. I can see there's not so much in it for a girl these days. It makes me feel cruel the way I unsettle her: I don't know how much it's me myself or how much it's something the matter that I can't help. How are any of us to know how things could have been? They forget war's not just only war; it's years out of people's lives that they've never had before and won't have again. Do you think she's fanciful?'

'Who, Pepita?'

'It's enough to make her – tonight was the pay-off. We couldn't get near any movie or any place for sitting; you had to fight into the bars, and she hates the staring in bars, and with all that milling about, every street we went, they kept on knocking her even off my arm. So then we took the tube to that park down there, but the place was as bad as daylight, let alone it was cold. We hadn't the nerve – well, that's nothing to do with you.'

'I don't mind.'

'Or else you don't understand. So we began to play – we were off in Kôr.'

'Core of what?'

'Mysterious Kôr – ghost city.'

'Where?'

'You may ask. But I could have sworn she saw it, and from the way she saw it I saw it, too. A game's a game, but what's a hallucination? You begin by laughing, then it gets in you and you can't laugh it off. I tell you, I woke up just now not knowing where I'd been; and I had to get up and feel round this table before I even knew where I was. It wasn't till then that I thought of a cigarette. Now I see why she sleeps like that, if that's where she goes.'

'But she is just as often restless; I often hear her.'

'Then she doesn't always make it. Perhaps it takes me, in

some way— Well, I can't see any harm: when two people have got no place, why not want Kôr, as a start? There are no restrictions on wanting, at any rate.'

'But, oh, Arthur, can't wanting want what's human?'

He yawned. 'To be human's to be at a dead loss.' Stopping yawning, he ground out his cigarette: the china tray skidded at the edge of the table. 'Bring that light here a moment – that is, will you? I think I've messed ash all over these sheets of hers.'

Callie advanced with the torch alight, but at arm's length: now and then her thumb made the beam wobble. She watched the lit-up inside of Arthur's hand as he brushed the sheet; and once he looked up to see her white-nightgowned figure curving above and away from him, behind the arc of light. 'What's that swinging?'

'One of my plaits of hair. Shall I open the window wider?'

'What, to let the smoke out? Go on. And how's your moon?'

'Mine?' Marvelling over this, as the first sign that Arthur remembered that she was Callie, she uncovered the window, pushed up the sash, then after a minute said: 'Not so strong.'

Indeed, the moon's power over London and the imagination had now declined. The siege of light had relaxed; the search was over; the street had a look of survival and no more. Whatever had glittered there, coin or ring, was now invisible or had gone. To Callie it seemed likely that there would never be such a moon again; and on the whole she felt this was for the best. Feeling air reach in like a tired arm round her body, she dropped the curtains against it and returned to her own room.

Back by her bed, she listened: Pepita's breathing still had the regular sound of sleep. At the other side of the wall the divan creaked as Arthur stretched himself out again. Having felt ahead of her lightly, to make sure her half was empty, Callie climbed over Pepita and got in. A certain amount of warmth had travelled between the sheets from Pepita's flank, and in this Callie extended her sword-cold body: she tried to compose her limbs; even they quivered after Arthur's words in the dark, words *to* the dark. The loss of her own mysterious expectation, of her love for love, was a small thing beside the war's total of unlived lives. Suddenly Pepita flung out one hand: its back knocked Callie lightly across the face.

Pepita had now turned over and lay with her face up. The hand that had struck Callie must have lain over the other, which grasped the pyjama collar. Her eyes, in the dark, might have been either shut or open, but nothing made her frown more or less steadily: it became certain, after another moment, that Pepita's act of justice had been unconscious. She still lay, as she had lain, in an avid dream, of which Arthur had been the source, of which Arthur was not the end. With him she looked this way, that way, down the wide, void, pure streets, between statues, pillars and shadows, through archways and colonnades. With him she went up the stairs down which nothing but moon came; with him trod the ermine dust of the endless halls, stood on terraces, mounted the extreme tower, looked down on the statued squares, the wide, void, pure streets. He was the password, but not the answer: it was to Kôr's finality that she turned.

J. B. PRIESTLEY

COMING TO
LONDON
(1957)

IT WAS IN the early autumn of 1922 that I arrived in London, to live and work there. I had taken my degree at Cambridge the year before, and had also got married; but as my ex-officer's grant still had a year to run, I returned to Cambridge, to do some coaching in English and to write essays and reviews. Even by the May Term of 1922 I was still uncertain what I wanted to do – that is, to earn a living, for I meant to go on writing whatever else I might do. I refused the chances of several remote professorships, in places like Dorpat, partly because I could never discover what the salaries were worth in sterling, for no country whose currency was quoted in *The Times* wanted my services. I qualified, if that is the term, as a University Extension lecturer, by delivering a sample lecture to ten depressed working men and a large bored cleric in a Cambridgeshire village institute; and finally was told I had been appointed for the autumn session to the North Devon region. (A summary of a proposed Extension course, given to me as a model to copy, was the work of an older Cambridge man – one Forster, E. M.) Then dear old 'Q', whom I parodied in the *Cambridge Review*, suggested I should stay on to give some lectures in Eng. Lit., but I think I pleased him, and certainly annoyed the University Extension people, by suddenly deciding I would freelance in London. So there I went, with a young wife, no regular job, and a total capital of less than fifty pounds.

We found a seven-roomed flat on the ground floor of King Edward's Mansions, Walham Green, which perhaps I ought to explain is a seedy district between Chelsea and Fulham, their rather raffish poor relation. The rent was about seventy-five pounds a year – and ours was probably the roomiest flat in the building. But for the first few months we shared the flat with our Cambridge friend, Edward Davison the poet, who had edited the *Cambridge Review* and now came to London to edit a Liberal Church weekly called *The Challenge*. We shopped sketchily for odd bits of furniture along the Fulham Road, our one solid piece being a Broadwood grand on hire purchase; we did our own decorating, half poisoning ourselves with white lead; we settled in. Many of our neighbours there were music-hall performers, who were on tour most of the year and did not want to pay much rent for a permanent address in London: Walham Green would do. It would do for me too; in fact, at first I quite enjoyed living there. I do not know what it is like now, but in 1922 Walham Green still seemed to belong to the London of Phil May. It was crowded and noisy with street stalls and barrows, fat women drinking stout at pub doors, young mothers shouting at wizened babies, chaps waiting to learn what won the two-thirty, greasy little eating-places; with the Granville Music-hall and Stamford Bridge (where Davison and I cheered for Chelsea) representing the arts and athletics. We were not long in Walham Green, leaving it for the Chilterns the following spring, and I will not pretend I was sorry to go; but for the first two or three months I certainly relished what seemed to me its thick Cockney atmosphere, very different from anything I had known in the North. To this day there is a certain kind of smoky autumn morning, coolish but with the sun somewhere not far away, with a railway station smell about it, that brings back to mind those first days in London, when I would hurry out of King Edward's Mansions to catch an 11 bus to Fleet Street, hoping to find some books to review.

I was already writing critical articles and miscellaneous essays, but I had to depend largely on reviewing, for which then there was ample space. Most daily papers carried at least one book page a week; there were far more bookish weeklies than there are now; and various monthly reviews and magazines were open to young writers. The pay was low, especially for unsigned short notices, but often these bulky volumes of travel and memoirs were fairly expensive, and we could sell our review copies at half the published price. The old fellow who bought them had one touch of genius: he always paid us in new pound notes, deliciously clean and crisp, and to be handed seven or eight of these was always an exhilarating experience, like being in a fairy tale for a few minutes. We used to hurry out of that shop, all Fleet Street ours, like Ali Baba out of the robbers' cave. It is, I think, the only money I have ever had that brought with it every possible good sensation of wealth. Even the faint feeling of guilt – for the publishers' and booksellers' associations were for ever denouncing this outrageous practice – only added its final flicker of zest, a garlic touch of the disreputable.

All this reviewing, however, was fairly hard work, even if, as I was, you were a fast skimmer and gutter of books that did not pretend to be literature. To go through a pile of them, for the purpose of sending in a half-column of *Shorter Notices*, could be sheer drudgery, especially if you were tackling the job at the end of a day spent on your own writing. But I was more fortunate than most new arrivals – or indeed many of the old hands, for in those days there was in every Fleet Street pub at least one man who earned a living of sorts out of minor reviewing. During this first year I did regular reviewing, mostly signed, for the *London Mercury*, the *Outlook*, the *Bookman*, the *Daily News*, the *Daily Chronicle*. And a little later I wrote long signed reviews too for the *Spectator* and the

Saturday Review. I had little difficulty with literary editors, although there were plenty of us asking for books. This was not because I was particularly wise or witty but because, unlike many of my rivals, I took my reviewing seriously, bringing to it a solid North-country conscientiousness; I never left my review copies unread at studios where too much cheap Chianti had been gulped down; I was always reasonably on time; and I never delivered two hundred or two thousand words when I had been asked for five hundred. Again, even in those early days I never asked for a book because I disliked its author and so wanted to attack him; and I have kept to this rule. Anonymous reviewing, a bad practice, has always particularly encouraged the 'stealthy assassins', and at no time have I ever been one of them.

While I was still in Walham Green I became a publisher's reader, thanks to J. C. (now Sir John) Squire, who had been asked by John Lane to recommend somebody for the job. I was paid about six pounds a week, though I seem to remember this covered a certain amount of editorial work, of which *The Bodley Head Book of Verse* was one of the fruits. I spent only one morning a week, generally Tuesday, in the offices in Vigo Street, where I went through the manuscripts that had arrived during the previous week, threw out the obviously unacceptable, and put aside, to be sent home, anything that looked at all promising. John Lane, who died in 1925 at the age of 71, seemed to me much older than he actually was; he had almost lost his sight and appeared to move like a very old man; also, he was one of the representative figures of a vanished era, at his best as a publisher about the time I was born. As soon as he was successful he must always have spent more time lunching and dining out than he did in reading manuscripts and books; nevertheless, he had a remarkable 'nose' for books and authors, not because he himself represented a new and growing public – he was not like Dent or C. S. Evans of Heinemann (who almost did more for Galsworthy than Galsworthy did) – but because he had a flair for knowing what book would get itself talked about where he lunched and dined. He moved easily and surely in the region, far more important in the 'nineties than it has ever been since, somewhere between literature and fashion. He was the dandy among publishers – just the man to bring out Max Beerbohm – though, oddly enough, he was the son of a North Devon miller and spent his first eighteen years in London as a clerk in the Railway Clearing House. (A good-looking alert youth I used to run into at Vigo Street had a better start. His name was Allen Lane.) Like many old-fashioned publishers, John Lane would spend money lavishly *on* an author, offering him some of the best wines and brandies from the Café Royal cellars, but disliked handing over money *to* the author; so that his usual terms were shocking, with royalty scales cut to the bone, thirteen copies counting as twelve, and much jiggery-pokery with subsidiary rights. This combination of parsimony with flair meant that the Bodley Head had probably the best list of good *first* books in town. The tradition still existed in my time.

If as a reader I missed anything first-class, successfully published elsewhere, I am unable to recall a single example. What I do know for certain is that I recommended – and without difficulty, because there was much new talent about in those years – an impressive list of first books and new authors, headed by Graham Greene and C. S. Forester. Perhaps my oddest find was a huge Amazonian jungle of a manuscript, which after a great deal of cutting and rearranging appeared as *Cubwood*, with an introduction, at my request, from Walter de la Mare. It was an involved and highly introverted account of the adventures of some children in a wood, and was the work, over years, of a fantastic old gentleman who looked and was ready to behave like one of Emmet's creations. Unless my memory is tricking me, he would suddenly appear and disappear in Vigo Street, depositing with wool-mittened hands further and more involved instalments of his book, as if we were all in *Through the Looking Glass*. The story reads like an actual remembrance of childhood, recalled in great detail, yet in fact, he assured us, it was all an invention, the record of a dream life he had enjoyed for many years. In spite of Walter de la Mare's Introduction – 'It is a visit,' he said, 'into a country of uncontaminated delight and loveliness and freedom, not unknown, but more or less forgotten. And fresh and sweet are its airs and scenes, its dreams and solemn absurdities, its perennial nonsense and enthusiasms ...' – *Cubwood* never received the attention it deserved, and must now be long out of print. And as the world of childhood never dates itself out of all meaning and force, somebody, perhaps Sir Allen Lane, ought to re-issue *Cubwood*.

It must have been later in the autumn of 1922, for the weather had broken, that Davison and I set out one Sunday for a long walk, somewhere Richmond way. We returned to eat dinner in one of our greasy and smelly little restaurants, and then remembered we had been invited to a party that night at Queen's Gate given by Robert and Sylvia Lynd, soon to be among my closest friends. We were wearing tweeds and muddy walking shoes, but as it was Sunday night, we imagined, not unreasonably, that we were being asked to join a few of our literary elders for an informal drink. So off we went to Queen's Gate, to discover, when it was too late to retire, that in the Lynds' large drawing-room was most of literary London in full evening dress. Among the guests, seeming in our fancy to pull themselves away from us a little, were fabulous beings like Shaw and Wells and Bennett, no longer caricatures but living breathing men, chattering away in easily recognizable accents. This must have been the beginning, a sadly oafish entry, of much party-going that ran right through the 'twenties and 'thirties. As I have pointed out elsewhere, these large evening parties, superior in every way to the cocktail parties that gradually superseded them, had more than a social value. They made something like a literary society possible. They enabled young writers to meet, on easy convivial terms, their distinguished elders, who became men and women instead of being mere names, reputations, outlooks and styles. This encouraged a healthy feeling of continuity in letters. It helped to banish those peculiar and often morbid notions that young writers cherish in loneliness. The elderly and famous, now fellow guests in search of a drink and a sandwich, ceased to be legendary figures or monstrous ruins barring the way for the young. I count it another piece of luck that I came to London when such parties were still given, and youthful writers, however oafish and bumptious, were invited to them. Literary London would be better off, far more soundly based, if we returned to the habit of giving such parties, open to writers of all ages. If our grim economics prevent private persons from giving them, then publishers and editors, with solid expense accounts behind them, should fulfil the need. For if I do not know, as I should like to know, more than ten writers under 40, the fault is not mine: I am never invited where I might find more of them. But in 1922 you could begin taking a good look at your colleagues. There may have been feuds among the shindies, but the atmosphere of authorship was neither sour nor desolate.

We youngsters, having neither the money nor the space, were of course always guests and never hosts at those large full-dress affairs. But we gave and received a lot of hospitality of our own modest kind. Food, drink and service were still comparatively cheap. In Soho, for which I soon left the Fulham and King's Roads, you could buy a dinner for two shillings, and for ten shillings you could add a bottle of wine, a brandy or two, a cigar with your coffee. My own favourite place, discovered a little later, was the one-roomed *Escargot* in Greek Street, not to be confused with the more ambitious restaurant, run by the same family, on the opposite side of the street. There were only about four tables in the original restaurant, which might have been transported, proprietor and all, from any French small town. It was no use hurrying in there for a theatre dinner, for they did not keep a number of cooked dishes ready to be warmed up for the table; your order was shouted by the proprietor, usually with a word of commendation for your choice, down the shaft into the kitchen below; and it was usually about two hours or so before you were asking for their black and bitter coffee. The son opened a good place across the way, but my heart remained with the father, who looked like a French general of the old school.

I rarely patronized the better-known restaurants, such as the *Eiffel Tower*, which served as meeting places for painters and writers. Our haunt was the pub, just one longish bar, in Poppins Court, underneath the *London Mercury* offices. There, every week-day between twelve-thirty and two, was a gathering of wits who produced the liveliest talk I ever remember hearing. Squire and Shanks and many of the regular contributors to the *London Mercury* would often be joined by Lynd, James Bone, George Mair, Belloc, J. B. Morton, Bohun Lynch and many another good talker. Other places where we sometimes met were the *Rainbow* and the wine vaults under Ludgate Circus. I have sometimes thought that this overfondness for drink and good talk from midday onwards was partly responsible for a marked change – not, in my view, for the better – in English literary criticism, values and fashions. Some of these convivial souls, with others I have not named, talked away the books they ought to have written, books in which they could have displayed their love, knowledge, and understanding of literature, their ability to relate it to life, books that would have been at once urbane and generous yet sharply critical of any writing that lacked either heart or mind. And it was about this time, I feel, that the reading public was fatally divided into high, low and middle brows, that writing began to be assessed not in terms of its own qualities, which are what the true critic should be concerned with, but in terms of its possible audience, that writers whose books began to sell (and I have yet to meet one who did not want his books to sell) were denounced at once as charlatans. More than thirty years have passed, the world has been turned upside down, but we are still suffering from this change of literary climate. There were too many rounds, too much talk, in those pubs. But it was fun at the time; and I suspect that our newest writers, even though not disdaining pubs, could do with a few sessions of such talk.

Good theatre seats were comparatively dear then, just as they are comparatively cheap now, so if we could not find somebody, a dramatic critic or friendly editor, to give us complimentary tickets, we went in the pit or gallery. I remember paying about ninepence or so at the old Alhambra to see the most astonishing galaxy of prima ballerinas that ever blazed on one stage. And the Lyric, Hammersmith, was cheap enough, and there Nigel Playfair's production of *The Beggar's Opera* was running. We knew every word and note of it, used to roar them out round the piano, but still returned, time after time, to the Lyric. It seemed to me then – and after a quarter of a century of work in the Theatre, I am not prepared to change my mind – an enchanting production, the best in its kind we have ever had in this country, never beaten by later attempts to get away from Playfair's style, Lovat Fraser's decor, Frederick Austin's modest but rather luscious arrangement of the music. On the other hand, although I saw the production, I was never an enthusiastic admirer of the other long run, *The Immortal Hour*, at another old theatre brought out of shabbiness and neglect, the Regent, near King's Cross. But if you wanted perfection of a very different theatrical style, extreme naturalism, there were the productions of Galsworthy's plays by Basil Dean at the St Martin's, where so many good actors learnt their trade. You might dislike this kind of play, this method of production, yet could not deny Dean the triumph of his formidable qualities, which we are beginning to miss in the Theatre. There was also some good new work being done up at the Everyman Theatre, Hampstead, by Norman Macdermott. And Gerald du Maurier, who as actor-manager had every virtue except the courage necessary for experiment, was still at Wyndham's. I was told not long ago, by way of a rebuke, that our London post-war Theatre might no longer be creative but that it has reached greatness in its interpretation; but it seems to me – and I speak of one of my own trades – that outside Shakespeare both the production and acting in the 'twenties were generally superior to ours. But then the economics of the Theatre were much sounder. It had hardly begun to have colossal rivals that drew on its talent without making any adequate return for their loans and raids.

During the last few years the intimate revue, which I have always preferred to musical comedy, has been revived with considerable success, and I fancy it offers us more genuine satire and wit than it did thirty years ago. But I do not think it is mere age that makes me believe the original *Nine O'Clock Revue* at the Little and the early Charlot revues were much better, filled with richer talent, bigger personalities, funnier sketches, more artful tunes. And what is certain is that the music-hall of today is nothing but the ghost of what it was in the early 'twenties in London. It had already passed its peak even then, but some of the ripe old turns were still with us. You could look in at the Coliseum, as I often did on a winter afternoon, and see Little Tich and Harry Tate, and there were still some glorious drolls at the Holborn Empire (a sad loss; it had a fine thick atmosphere of its own), the Victoria Palace, and the rest. There were no microphones and nobody needed them. There were no stars who had arrived by way of amusing farmers' wives and invalids on the radio. There were no reputations that had been created by American gramophone records for teenagers. The men and women who topped the bills had spent years getting there, learning how to perfect their acts and to handle their audiences. Of course there was plenty of vulgar rubbish, but all but the very worst of it had at least some zest and vitality. And the audiences, which laughed at jokes and did not solemnly applaud them as BBC audiences do now, were an essential part of the show; they too had vitality, and were still close to the Cockneys who helped to create, a generation earlier, the English music-hall of the great period, the folk art out of which, among other things, came the slapstick of the silent films, especially those of Chaplin.

I was never out of London very long throughout the 'twenties, and probably would never have left it at all if I had not had a young family, for I soon came to feel an affection for the sprawling monster. Even its shocking extremes of wealth and poverty I disliked more in theory than in actuality. I was fond of wandering about in it and taking buses and trams to its remote suburbs, and must have written scores of essays – I wrote at least one essay a week for many years – that had a

London background, as well as one long novel, *Angel Pavement*. Its life then had many blots that have now been sponged out. There is now far less truly appalling misery. But most other changes have been for the worse. There is now far more cheap spivvery, even in the West End. The kind of sub-human faces you see in the neon lighting of Coventry Street any night now, passing like an unending parade of the seven deadly sins, I do not remember seeing when I was first in London. Many of the best little old shops, eating houses, pubs, seem to have vanished, and in their places are shoddy establishments that look like Broadway rejects. London in fact has been Americanized, and not by what is best but by what is worst in America, by over-advertised soft drinks and not by unadvertised old bourbon, by snack bars and cafeterias and not by sea-food restaurants and steak houses, by boogie-woogies and not by the Boston Symphony. And because of the intolerable strain of contemporary metropolitan living, the growing defeat of human zest and sympathy by the mere mechanics of existence, London, like New York and Paris, is rapidly becoming a bad-tempered city, filled with the sour smell of that defeat.

No doubt if I were arriving again as a young man, scurrying round not only to make a living, to establish myself, but also to explore and to savour this vast oyster-bed of a capital, I would see a different London, one perhaps far closer to the city I began to discover in the autumn of 1922. I believe, as I never for an hour ceased to believe then, that I could make my way in it. But I am not sorry that I am not having my try now. I had a harder time, for private and tragic reasons, than I have suggested here, worked all day and half the night for a long unhappy period, with one burden piled on another; but even so, given my profession, I fancy I chose the right time both to be born and to arrive in London. Yes, I had the luck.

JEAN RHYS

TIGERS ARE
BETTER-LOOKING
(1964)

'MEIN LIEB, Mon Cher, My Dear, Amigo,' the letter began:

I'm off. I've been wanting to go for some time, as I'm sure you know, but was waiting for the moment when I had the courage to step out into the cold world again. Didn't feel like a farewell scene.

Apart from much that it is *better* not to go into, you haven't any idea how sick I am of all the phoney talk about Communism – and the phoney talk of the other lot too, if it comes to that. You people are exactly alike, whatever you call yourselves – Untouchable. Indispensable is the motto, and you'd pine to death if you hadn't someone to look down on and insult. I got the feeling that I was surrounded by a pack of timid tigers waiting to spring the moment anybody is in trouble or hasn't any money. *But tigers are better-looking, aren't they?*

I'm taking the coach to Plymouth. I have my plans.

I came to London with high hopes, but all I got out of it was a broken leg and enough sneers to last me for the next thirty years if I live so long, which may God forbid.

Don't think I'll forget how kind you were after my accident – having me to stay with you and all that. But assez means enough.

I've drunk the milk in the refrigerator. I was thirsty after that party last night, though if you call that a party

I call it a wake. Besides, I know how you dislike the stuff (Freud! Bow-wow-wow!!) So you'll have to have your tea straight, my dear.

Goodbye. I'll write you again when times are better.

HANS

There was a postscript:

Mind you write a swell article today, you tame grey mare.

Mr Severn sighed. He had always known Hans would hop it sooner or later, so why this taste in his mouth, as if he had eaten dust?

A swell article.

The band in the Embankment Gardens played. It's the same old song again. It's the same old tender refrain. *As the carriage came into sight some of the crowd cheered and a fat man said he couldn't see and he was going to climb a lamp post. The figures in the carriages bowed from right to left – victims bowed to victimized. The bloodless sacrifice was being exhibited, the reminder that somewhere the sun is shining, even if it doesn't shine on everybody.*

''E looked just like a waxwork, didn't 'e?' a woman said with satisfaction....

No, that would never do.

He looked out of the window at the Lunch Edition placards outside the newspaper shop opposite. 'JUBILEE PICTURES – PICTURES – PICTURES' *and* 'HEAT WAVE COMING'.

The flat over the shop was occupied by a raffish middle-aged woman. But today her lace-curtained windows, usually not unfriendly, added to his feeling of desolation. So did the words 'PICTURES – PICTURES – PICTURES'.

By six o'clock the floor was covered with newspapers and

crumpled, discarded starts of the article which he wrote every week for an Australian paper.

He couldn't get the swing of it. The swing's the thing, as everybody knows – otherwise the cadence of the sentence. Once into it, and he could go ahead like an old horse trotting, saying anything that anybody liked.

'The tame grey mare,' he thought. Then he took up one of the newspapers and, because he had the statistical mania, began to count the advertisements. Two remedies for constipation, three for wind and stomach pains, three face creams, one skin food, one cruise to Morocco. At the end of the personal column, in small print, 'I will slay in the day of My wrath and spare not, saith the Lord God.' Who pays to put these things in anyway, who pays?

'This perpetual covert threat,' he thought. 'Everything's based on it. Disgusting. What Will They Say? And down at the bottom of the page you see what will happen to you if you don't toe the line. You will be slain and not spared. Threats and mockery, mockery and threats . . .' And desolation, desertion and crumpled newspapers in the room.

The only comfort allowed was the money which would buy the warm glow of drink before eating, the jubilee laughter afterwards. Jubilant – Jubilee – Joy . . . Words whirled round in his head, but he could not make them take shape.

'If you won't, you bloody well won't,' he said to his typewriter before he rushed down the stairs, counting the steps as he went.

After two double whiskies at his usual pub, Time, which had dragged so drearily all day, began to move faster, began to gallop.

At half-past eleven Mr Severn was walking up and down Wardour Street between two young women. The things one does on the rebound.

He knew one of them fairly well – the fatter one. She was often at the pub and he liked talking to her, and sometimes stood her drinks because she was good-natured and never made him feel nervous. That was her secret. If fair was fair, it would be her epitaph: 'I have never made anybody feel nervous – on purpose.' Doomed, of course, for that very reason. But pleasant to talk to and, usually, to look at. Her name was Maidie – Maidie Richards.

He had never seen the other girl before. She was very young and fresh, with a really glittering smile and an accent he didn't quite recognize. She was called Heather Something-or-other. In the noisy pub he thought she said Hedda. 'What an unusual name!' he remarked. 'I said Heather, not Hedda, Hedda! I wouldn't be seen dead with a name like that.' She was sharp, bright, self-confident – nothing flabby there. It was she who had suggested this final drink.

The girls argued. They each had an arm in one of Mr Severn's, and they argued across him. They got to Shaftes-bury Avenue, turned and walked back.

'I tell you the place is in this street,' Heather said. 'The "Jim-Jam" – haven't you ever heard of it?'

'Are you sure?' Mr Severn asked.

'Of course I'm sure. It's on the left-hand side. We've missed it somehow.'

'Well, I'm sick of walking up and down looking for it,' Maidie said. 'It's a lousy hole anyway. I don't particularly want to go, do you?'

'Not particularly,' said Mr Severn.

'There it is,' Heather said. 'We've passed it twice. It's changed its name, that's what.'

They went up a narrow stone staircase and on the first landing a man with a yellow face appeared from behind drawn curtains and glared at them. Heather smiled. 'Good evening, Mr Johnson. I've brought two friends along.'

'Three of you? That'll be fifteen shillings.'

'I thought it was half a crown entrance,' Maidie said so aggrievedly that Mr Johnson looked at her with surprise and explained, 'This is a special night.'

'The orchestra's playing rotten, anyway,' Maidie remarked when they got into the room.

An elderly woman wearing steel-rimmed glasses was serving behind the bar. The mulatto who was playing the saxophone leaned forward and whooped.

'They play so rotten,' Maidie said, when the party was seated at a table against the wall, 'that you'd think they were doing it on purpose.'

'Oh stop grumbling,' Heather said. 'Other people don't agree with you. The place is packed every night. Besides, why should they play well. What's the difference?'

'Ah-ha,' Mr Severn said.

'There isn't any difference if you ask me. It's all a lot of talk.'

'Quite right. All an illusion,' Mr Severn agreed. 'A bottle of ginger ale,' he said to the waiter.

Heather said, 'We'll have to have a bottle of whisky. You don't mind, do you, dear?'

'Don't worry, child, don't worry,' Mr Severn said. 'It was only my little joke . . . a bottle of whisky,' he told the waiter.

'Will you pay now, if you please?' the waiter asked when he brought the bottle.

'What a price!' Maidie said, frowning boldly at the waiter. 'Never mind, by the time I've had a few goes at this I ought to have forgotten my troubles.'

Heather pinched up her lips. 'Very little for me.'

355

'Well, it's going to be drunk,' Mr Severn said. 'Play *Dinah*,' he shouted at the orchestra.

The saxophonist glanced at him and tittered. Nobody else took any notice.

'Sit down and have a drink, won't you?' Heather clutched at Mr Johnson's sleeve as he passed the table, but he answered loftily, 'Sorry, I'm afraid I can't just now,' and passed on.

'People are funny about drinking,' Maidie remarked. 'They get you to buy as much as they can and then afterwards they laugh at you behind your back for buying it. But on the other hand, if you try to get out of buying it, they're damned rude. Damned rude, they can be. I went into a place the other night where they have music – the International Café, they call it. I had a whisky and I drank it a bit quick, because I was thirsty and feeling down and so on. Then I thought I'd like to listen to the music – they don't play so badly there because they say they're Hungarians – and a waiter came along, yelling "Last drinks". "Can I have some water?" I said, "I'm not here to serve you with water," he said. "This isn't a place to drink water in," he said, just like that. So loud! Everybody was staring at me.'

'Well, what do you expect?' Heather said. 'Asking for water! You haven't got any sense. No more for me, thank you.' She put her hand over her glass.

'Don't you trust me?' Mr Severn asked, leering.

'I don't trust anybody. For why? Because I don't want to be let down, that's why.'

'Sophisticated, she is,' said Maidie.

'I'd rather be sophisticated than a damned pushover like you,' Heather retorted. 'You don't mind if I go and talk to some friends over there, do you, dear?'

'Admirable.' Mr Severn watched her cross the room. 'Admirable. Disdainful, debonair and with a touch of the tar-brush too, or I'm much mistaken. Just my type. One of my types. Why is it that she isn't quite – Now, why?' He took a yellow pencil out of his pocket and began to draw on the tablecloth.

Pictures, pictures, pictures. ... Face, faces, faces. ... Like hyaenas, like swine, like goats, like apes, like parrots. But not tigers, because tigers are better-looking, aren't they? as Hans says.

Maidie was saying, 'They've got an awfully nice "Ladies" here. I've been having a chat with the woman; she's a friend of mine. The window was open and the street looked so cool and peaceful. That's why I've been so long.'

'London is getting very odd, isn't it?' Mr Severn said in a thick voice. 'Do you see that tall female over there, the one in the backless evening gown? Of course, I've got my own theory about backless evening gowns, but this isn't the moment to tell you of it. Well, that sweetiepie's got to be at Brixton tomorrow morning at a quarter past nine to give a music lesson. And her greatest ambition is to get a job as stewardess on a line running to South Africa.'

'Well, what's wrong with that?' Maidie said.

'Nothing – I just thought it was a bit mixed. Never mind. And do you see that couple over there at the bar? The lovely dark brown couple. Well, I went over to have a change of drinks and got into conversation with them. I rather palled up with the man, so I asked them to come and see me one day. When I gave them my address the girl said at once, "Is that in Mayfair?" "Good Lord, no; it's in the darkest, dingiest Bloomsbury." "I didn't come to London to go to the slums," she said with the most perfect British accent, high, sharp, clear and shattering. Then she turned her back on me and hauled the man off to the other end of the bar.'

'Girls always cotton on to things quicker,' Maidie asserted.

'The social climate of a place?' said Mr Severn. 'Yes, I suppose they do. But some men aren't so slow either. Well, well, tigers are better-looking, aren't they?'

'You haven't been doing too badly with the whisky, dear, have you?' Maidie said rather uneasily. 'What's all this about tigers?'

Mr Severn again addressed the orchestra in a loud voice. 'Play *Dinah*. I hate that bloody tune you keep playing. It's always the same one too. You can't fool me. Play *Dinah, is there anyone finer?* That's a good old tune.'

'I shouldn't shout so loud,' Maidie said. 'They don't like it here if you shout. Don't you see the way Johnson's looking at you?'

'Let him look.'

'Oh, do shut up. He's sending the waiter to us now.'

'Obscene drawings on the tablecloth not allowed here,' the waiter said as he approached.

'Go to hell,' Mr Severn said. 'What obscene drawings?'

Maidie nudged him and shook her head violently.

The waiter removed the tablecloth and brought a clean one. He pursed his lips up as he spread it and looked severely at Mr Severn. 'No drawings of any description on tablecloths are allowed here,' he said.

'I'll draw as much as I like,' Mr Severn said defiantly. And the next thing he knew two men had him by the collar and were pushing him towards the door.

'You let him alone,' said Maidie. 'He hasn't done anything. You are a lot of sugars.'

'Gently, gently,' said Mr Johnson, perspiring. 'What do you want to be so rough for? I'm always telling you to do it quietly.'

As he was being hauled past the bar, Mr Severn saw Heather, her eyes beady with disapproval, her plump face lengthened into something twice the size of life. He made a hideous grimace at her.

'My Lawd,' she said, and averted her eyes. 'My Lawd!'

Only four men pushed them down the stairs, but when they were out in the street it took more like fourteen, and all howling and booing. 'Now, who are all these people?' Mr Severn thought. Then someone hit him. The man who had hit him was exactly like the waiter who had changed the tablecloth. Mr Severn hit back as hard as he could and the waiter, if he was the waiter, staggered against the wall and toppled slowly to the ground. 'I've knocked him down,' Mr Severn thought. 'Knocked him down!'

'Tally-ho!' he yelled in a high voice. 'What price the tame grey mare?'

The waiter got up, hesitated, thought better of it, turned round and hit Maidie instead.

'Shut up, you bloody basket,' somebody said when she began to swear, and kicked her. Three men seized Mr Severn, ran him off the pavement and sprawled him in the middle of Wardour Street. He lay there, feeling sick, listening to Maidie. The lid was properly off there.

'Yah!' the crowd round her jeered. 'Boo!' Then it opened up, servile and respectful, to let two policemen pass.

'You big blanks,' Maidie yelled defiantly. 'You something somethings. I wasn't doing anything. That man knocked me down. How much does Johnson pay you every week for this?'

Mr Severn got up, still feeling very sick. He heard a voice: 'That's 'im. That's the chap. That's 'im what started everything.' Two policemen took him by the arms and marched him along. Maidie, also between two policemen, walked in front, weeping. As they passed through Piccadilly Circus, empty and desolate, she wailed, 'I've lost my shoe. I must stop and pick it up. I can't walk without it.'

The older policeman seemed to want to force her on, but the younger one stopped, picked the shoe up and gave it to her with a grin.

'What's she want to cry for?' Mr Severn thought. He shouted 'Hoi, Maidie, cheer up. Cheer up, Maidie.'

'None of that,' one of his policemen said.

But when they arrived at the police station she had stopped crying, he was glad to see. She powdered her face and began to argue with the sergeant behind the desk.

'You want to see a doctor, do you?' the sergeant said.

'I certainly do. It's a disgrace, a perfect disgrace.'

'And do you also want to see a doctor?' the sergeant asked coldly polite, glancing at Mr Severn.

'Why not?' Mr Severn answered.

Maidie powdered her face again and shouted, 'God save Ireland. To hell with all dirty sneaks and Comic Cuts and what-have-yous.'

'That was my father speaking,' she said over her shoulder as she was led off.

As soon as Mr Severn was locked into a cell he lay down on the bunk and went to sleep. When they woke him to see the doctor he was cold sober.

'What time is it?' the doctor asked. With a clock over his head, the old fool!

Mr Severn answered coldly, 'A quarter past four.'

'Walk straight ahead. Shut your eyes and stand on one leg,' the doctor demanded, and the policeman watching this performance sneered vaguely, like schoolboys when the master baits an unpopular one.

When he got back to his cell Mr Severn could not sleep. He lay down, stared at the lavatory seat and thought of the black eye he would have in the morning. Words and meaningless phrases still whirled tormentingly round in his head.

He read the inscription on the grim walls. 'Be sure your sins will find you out. B. Lewis.' 'Anne is a fine girl, one of the best, and I don't care who knows it. (Signed) Charlie S.' Somebody else had written up, 'Lord save me; I perish', and underneath, 'SOS, SOS, SOS (signed) G.R.'

'Appropriate,' Mr Severn thought, took his pencil from his pocket, wrote, 'SOS, SOS, SOS (Signed) N.S.,' and dated it.

Then he lay down with his face to the wall and saw, on a level with his eyes, the words, 'I died waiting'.

Sitting in the prison van before it started, he heard somebody whistling *The Londonderry Air* and a girl talking and joking with the policemen. She had a deep, soft voice. The appropriate adjective came at once into his mind – a sexy voice.

'Sex, sexy,' he thought. 'Ridiculous word! What a give-away!'

'What is wanted,' he decided, 'is a brand-new lot of words, words that will mean something. The only word that means anything now is death – and then it has to be my death. Your death doesn't mean much.'

The girl said, 'Ah, if I was a bird and had wings, I could fly away, couldn't I?'

'Might get shot as you went,' one of the policemen answered.

'This must be a dream,' Mr Severn thought. He listened for Maidie's voice, but there was not a sound of her. Then the van started.

It seemed a long way to Bow Street. As soon as they got out of the van he saw Maidie, looking as if she had spent the whole night in tears. She put her hand up to her hair apologetically.

'They took my handbag away. It's awful.'

'I wish it had been Heather,' Mr Severn thought. He tried to smile kindly.

'It'll soon be over now, we've only got to plead guilty.'

And it was over very quickly. The magistrate hardly looked at them, but for reasons of his own he fined them each thirty shillings, which entailed telephoning to a friend, getting the money sent by special messenger and an interminable wait.

It was half-past twelve when they were outside in Bow Street. Maidie stood hesitating, looking worse than ever in the yellowish, livid light. Mr Severn hailed a taxi and offered to take her home. It was the least he could do, he told himself. Also the most.

'Oh, your poor eye!' Maidie said. 'Does it hurt?'

'Not at all now. I feel astonishingly well. It must have been good whisky.'

She stared into the cracked mirror of her handbag.

'And don't I look terrible too? But it's no use; I can't do anything with my face when it's as bad as this.'

'I'm sorry.'

'Oh, well,' she said, 'I was feeling pretty bad on account of the way that chap knocked me down and kicked me, and afterwards on account of the way the doctor asked me my age. "This woman's very drunk," he said. But I wasn't, was I? . . . Well, and when I got back into the cell, the first thing I saw was my own name written up. My Christ, it did give me a turn! Gladys Reilly – that's my real name. Maidie Richards is only what I call myself. There it was staring me in the face. "Gladys Reilly, October 15th, 1934 . . ." Besides, I hate being locked up. Whenever I think of all these people they lock up for years I shiver all over.'

362

'Yes,' Mr Severn said, 'so do I.' *I died waiting.*

'I'd rather die quick, wouldn't you?'

'Yes.'

'I couldn't sleep and I kept on remembering the way the doctor said, "How old are you?" And all the policemen round were laughing, as if it was a joke. Why should it be such a joke? But they're hard up for jokes, aren't they? So when I got back I couldn't stop crying. And when I woke up I hadn't got my bag. The wardress lent me a comb. She wasn't so bad. But I do feel fed up . . .'

'You know the room I was waiting in while you were telephoning for money?' she said. 'There was such a pretty girl there.'

'Was there?'

'Yes, a very dark girl. Rather like Dolores del Rio, only younger. But it isn't the pretty ones who get on – oh no, on the contrary. For instance, this girl. She couldn't have been prettier – lovely, she was. And she was dressed awfully nicely in a black coat and skirt and a lovely clean white blouse and a little white hat and lovely stockings and shoes. But she was frightened. She was so frightened that she was shaking all over. You saw somehow that she wasn't going to last it out. No, it isn't being pretty that does it . . . And there was another one, with great hairy legs and no stockings, only sandals. I do think that when people have hairy legs they ought to wear stockings, don't you? Or do something about it. But no, she was just laughing and joking and you saw whatever happened to her she'd come out all right. A great big, red, square face she had, and those hairy legs. But she didn't care a damn.'

'Perhaps it's being sophisticated,' Mr Severn suggested, 'like your friend Heather.'

'Oh, her – no, she won't get on either. She's too ambitious, she wants too much. She's so sharp she cuts herself as you might say . . . No, it isn't being pretty and it isn't being sophis-ticated. It's being – adapted, that's what it is. And it isn't any good wanting to be adapted, you've got to be born adapted.'

'Very clear,' Mr Severn said. Adapted to the livid sky, the ugly houses, the grinning policemen, the placards in shop windows.

'You've got to be young, too. You've got to be young to enjoy a thing like this – younger than we are,' Maidie said as the taxi drew up.

Mr Severn stared at her, too shocked to be angry.

'Well, goodbye.'

'*Good*bye,' said Mr Severn, giving her a black look and ignoring her outstretched hand. 'We' indeed!

Two hundred and ninety-six steps along Coptic Street. One hundred and twenty round the corner. Forty stairs up to his flat. A dozen inside it. He stopped counting.

His sitting-room looked well, he thought, in spite of the crumpled papers. It was one of its good times, when the light was just right, when all the incongruous colours and shapes became a whole – the yellow-white brick wall with several of the Museum pigeons perched on it, the silvered drainpipe, the chimneys of every fantastical shape, round, square, poin-ted, and the odd one with the mysterious hole in the middle through which the grey, steely sky looked at you, the solitary trees – all framed in the silver oilcloth curtains (Hans's idea), and then with a turn of his head he saw the woodcuts from Amsterdam, the chintz-covered armchairs, the fading bowl of flowers in the long mirror.

An old gentleman wearing a felt hat and carrying a walk-ing-stick passed the window. He stopped, took off his hat and coat and, balancing the stick on the end of his nose, walked backwards and forwards, looking up expectantly.

Nothing happened. Nobody thought him worth a penny. He put his hat and coat on again and, carrying the stick in a respectable manner, vanished round the corner. And, as he did so, the tormenting phrases vanished too – 'Who pays? Will you pay now, please? You don't mind if I leave you, dear? I died waiting. I died waiting. (Or was it I died hating?) That was my father speaking. Pictures, pictures, pictures. You've got to be young. But tigers are better-looking, aren't they? SOS, SOS, SOS. If I was a bird and had wings I could fly away, couldn't I? Might get shot as you went. But tigers are better-looking, aren't they? You've got to be younger than we are ...' Other phrases, suave and slick, took their place.

The swing's the thing, the cadence of the sentence. He had got it.

He looked at his eye in the mirror, then sat down at the typewriter and with great assurance tapped out 'JUBILEE ...'

MURIEL SPARK

DAISY OVEREND
(1967)

IT IS HARDLY ever that I think of her, but sometimes, if I happen to pass Clarges Street or Albemarle Street on a sunny afternoon, she comes to mind. Or if, in a little crowd waiting to cross the road, I hear behind me two women meet, and the one exclaim:

'Darling!' (or 'Bobbie!' or 'Goo!') and the other answer: 'Goo!' (or 'Billie!' or 'Bobbie!' or 'Darling!') – if I hear these words, spoken in a certain trill which betokens the period 1920–9, I know that I have by chance entered the world of Daisy Overend, Bruton Street, W.1.

Ideally, these Bobbies and Darlings are sheathed in short frocks, the hems of which dangle about their knees like sea-weed, the waistlines of which encircle their hips, loose and effortless, following the droop of shoulder and mouth. Ideally, the whole is upheld by a pair of shiny silk stockings of a bright hue known as, but not resembling a, peach.

But in reality it is only by the voice you can tell them. The voice harks back to days bright and young and unredeemable whence the involuntary echoes arise – *Billie! ... Goo! ... heavenly! ... divine!* like the motto and crest which adorn the letter-paper of a family whose silver is pawned and forgotten.

Daisy Overend, small, imperious, smart, was to my mind the flower and consummation of her kind, and this is not to discount the male of the species *Daisy Overend*, with his wee face, blue eyes, bad teeth and nerves. But if you have met Mrs Overend, you have as good as met him too, he is so unlike her, and yet so much her kind.

I met her, myself, in the prodigious and lovely summer of 1947. Very charming she was. A tubular skirt clung to her hips, a tiny cap to her hair, and her hair clung, bronzed and shingled, to her head, like the cup of a toy egg of which her face was the other half. Her face was a mere lobe. Her eyes were considered to be expressive and they expressed avarice in various forms, the pupils were round and watchful. Mrs Overend engaged me for three weeks to help her with some committee work. As you will see, we parted in three days.

I found that literature and politics took up most of Daisy's days and many of her nights. She wrote a regular column in a small political paper and she belonged to all the literary societies. Thus, it was the literature of politics and the politics of literature which occupied Daisy, and thus she bamboozled many politicians who thought she was a writer, and writers who believed her to be a political theorist. But these activities failed to satisfy, that is to say, intoxicate her.

Now, she did not drink. I saw her sipping barley water while her guests drank her gin. But Daisy had danced the Charleston in her youth with a royal prince, and of this she assured me several times, speaking with swift greed while an alcoholic look came over her.

'Those times were divine,' she boozily concluded, 'they were ripping.' And I realized she was quite drunk with the idea. Normally as precise as a bird, she reached out blunderingly for the cigarettes, knocking the whole lot over. Literature and politics failed to affect her in this way, though she sat on many committees. Therefore she had taken – it is her expression – two lovers: one an expert, as she put it, on politics, and the other a poet.

The political expert, Lotti, was a fair Central European, an exiled man. The skin of his upper lip was drawn taut across his top jaw; this gave Lotti the appearance, together with his high cheekbones, of having had his face lifted. But it was not so; it was a natural defect which made his smile look like a baring of the teeth. He was perhaps the best of the lot that I met at Daisy Overend's.

Lotti could name each member of every Western Cabinet which had sat since the Treaty of Versailles. Daisy found this invaluable for her monthly column. Never did Lotti speak of these men but with contempt. He was a member of three shadow cabinets.

On the Sunday which, as it turned out, was my last day with Daisy, she laid aside her library book and said to Lotti:

'I'm bored with Cronin.'

Lotti, to whom all statesmen were as the ash he was just then flicking to the floor, looked at her all amazed.

'Daisy, mei gurl, you crazy?' he said.

'A Cronin!' he said, handing me an armful of air to convey the full extent of his derision, 'She is bored with a Cronin.'

At that moment, Daisy's vexed misunderstood expression reminded me that her other lover, the poet Tom Pfeffer, had brought the same look to her face two days before. When, rushing into the flat as was her wont, she said, gasping, to Tom:

'Things have been happening in the House.'

Tom, who was reading the *Notebooks of Malte Laurids Brigge*, looked up.

'Nothing's been happening in the house,' he assured her.

Tom Pfeffer is dead now. Mrs Overend told me the story of how she rescued him from lunacy, and I think Tom believed this. It is true she had prevented his being taken to a mental home for treatment.

The time came when Tom wanted, on an autumn morning, a ticket to Burton-on-Trent to visit a friend, and he wanted this more than he wanted a room in Mrs Overend's flat and regular meals. In his own interests she refused, obliterating the last traces of insurrection by giving Lotti six pound notes, clean from the bank, in front of Tom.

How jealous Tom Pfeffer was of Lotti, how indifferent was Lotti to him! But on this last day that I spent with Mrs Overend, the poet was fairly calm, although there were signs of the awful neurotic dance of his facial muscles which were later to distort him utterly before he died insane.

Daisy was preparing for a party, the reason for my presence on a Sunday, and for the arrival at five o'clock of her secretary Miss Rilke, a displaced European, got cheap. When anyone said to Daisy, 'Is she related to the poet Rilke?' Daisy replied, 'Oh, I should *think* so,' indignant almost, that it should be doubted.

'Be an angel,' said Daisy to Miss Rilke when she arrived, 'run down to the café and get me two packets of twenty. Is it still raining? How priceless the weather is. Take my awning.'

'Awning?'

'*Umbrella, umbrella, umbrella*,' said Daisy, jabbing her finger at it fractiously.

Like ping-pong, Miss Rilke's glance met Lotti's, and Lotti's hers. She took the umbrella and went.

'What are you looking at?' Daisy said quickly to Lotti.

'Nothing,' said Tom Pfeffer, thinking he was being addressed and looking up from his book.

'Not you,' said Daisy.

'Do you mean me?' I said.

'No,' she said, and kept her peace.

Miss Rilke returned to say that the shop would give Mrs Overend no more credit.

'This is the end,' said Daisy as she shook out the money from her purse. 'Tell them I'm livid.'

'Yes,' said Miss Rilke, looking at Lotti.

'What are you looking at?' Daisy demanded of her.

'Looking at?'

'Have you got the right money?' Daisy said.

'Yes.'

'Well, go.'

'I think,' said Daisy when she had gone, 'she's a bit dotty owing to her awful experiences.'

Nobody replied.

'Don't you think so?' she said to Lotti.

'Could be,' said Lotti.

Tom looked up suddenly. 'She's bats,' he hastened to say, 'the silly bitch is bats.'

As soon as Miss Rilke returned Daisy started becking and calling in preparation for her party. Her papers, which lay on every plane surface in the room, were moved into her bedroom in several piles.

The drawing-room was furnished in a style which in many ways anticipated the members' room at the Institute of Contemporary Arts. Mrs Overend had recently got rid of her black-and-orange striped divans, cushions and sofas. In their place were curiously cut slabs, polygons and three-legged manifestations of Daisy Overend's personality, done in El Greco's colours. As Daisy kept on saying, no two pieces were alike, and each was a contemporary version of a traditional design.

In her attempt to create a Contemporary interior she was, I felt, successful, and I was quite dazzled by its period charm. 'A rare old Contemporary piece,' some curio dealer, not yet born, might one day aver of Daisy's citrine settle or her blue glass-topped telephone table, adding in the same breath and pointing elsewhere, 'A genuine brass-bracket gas jet, nineteenth century'.... But I was dreaming, and Daisy was working, shifting things, blowing the powdery dust off things. She trotted and tripped amid the pretty jig-saw puzzle of her furniture, making a clean sweep of letters, bills, pamphlets and all that suggested a past or a future, with one exception. This was the photograph of Daisy Overend, haughty and beplumed in presentation dress, queening it over the Contemporary prospect of the light-grey grand piano.

Sometimes, while placing glasses and plates now here, now there, Daisy stopped short to take in the effect; and at this sign we all of us did the same. I realized then how silently and well did Daisy induce people to humour her. I discovered that the place was charged on a high voltage with the constant menace of a scene.

'I've put the papers on your bed,' said Miss Rilke from the bedroom.

'Is *she* saying something?' said Daisy, as if it were the last straw.

'Yes,' said Miss Rilke in a loud voice.

'They are not to go on my bed,' replied Daisy, having heard her in the first place.

'She's off her head, my dear,' said the poet to his mistress, 'putting your papers on your bed.'

'Go and see what she's doing,' said Daisy to me.

I went, and there found Miss Rilke moving the papers off the bed on to the floor. I was impressed by the pinkness of Daisy's bedroom. Where on earth did she get her taste in pink? Now this was not in the Contemporary style, nor was it in the manner of Daisy's heyday, the nineteen-twenties. The kidney-shaped dressing table was tricked out with tulle, unhappy spoiled stuff which cold cream had long ago stained, cigarettes burned, and various jagged objects ripped. In among the folds the original colour had survived here and there, and this fervid pink reminded me of a colour I had seen before, a pink much loved and worn by the women of the Malay colony at Capetown.

No, this was not a bedroom of the 'twenties; it belonged, surely, to the first ten years of the century: an Edwardian bedroom. But then, even then, it was hardly the sort of room Daisy would have inherited, since neither her mother nor her grandmother had kicked her height at the Gaiety. No, it was Daisy's own inarticulate exacting instinct which had bestowed on this room its frilly bed, its frilly curtains, the silken and sorry roses on its mantelpiece and its all-but-perished powder-cuffs. And all in pink, and all in pink. I did not solve the mystery of Daisy's taste in bedrooms, not then nor at any time. For, whenever I provide a category of time and place for her, the evidence is in default. A plant of the 'twenties, she is also the perpetrator of that vintage bedroom. A lingering limb of the old leisured class, she is also the author of that pink room.

I devoted the rest of the evening to the destruction of Daisy's party, I regret to say, and the subversion of her purpose in giving it.

Her purpose was the usual thing. She had joined a new international guild, and wanted to sit on the committee. Several Members of Parliament, a director of a mineral-water factory, a Brigadier-General who was also an Earl, a retired Admiral, some wives, a few women journalists, were expected. In addition, she had asked some of her older friends, those who were summoned to all her parties and whom she called her 'basics'; they were the walkers-on or the chorus of Daisy's social drama. There was also a Mr Jamieson, who was not invited but who played an unseen part as the chairman of the committee. He did not want Mrs Overend to sit on his committee. We were therefore assembled, though few guessed it, to inaugurate a campaign to remove from office this Mr Jamieson, whose colleagues and acquaintances presently began to arrive.

Parted from the drawing-room by folding doors was an ante-room leading out of the flat. I was put in charge of this room where a buffet had been laid. Here Daisy had repaired, when dressing for the party, to change her stockings. It was her habit to dress in every room in the house, anxiously moving from place to place. Miss Rilke had been sent on a tour of the premises to collect the discarded clothes, the comb, the lipstick from the various stations of Daisy's journey; but the secretary had overlooked, on a table in the centre of this ante-room, a pair of black satin garters a quarter of a century old, each bearing a very large grimy pink disintegrating rosette.

Just before the first guests began to arrive, Daisy Overend saw her garters lying there.

'Put those away,' she commanded Miss Rilke.

The Admiral came first. I opened the door, while with swift and practised skill Daisy and Lotti began a lively conversation, in the midst of which the Admiral was intended to come upon them. Behind the Admiral came a Member of Parliament. They had never been to the house before, not being among Daisy's 'basics'.

'Do come in,' said Miss Rilke, holding open the folding doors.

'This way,' said Tom Pfeffer from the drawing-room.

The two guests stared at the table. Daisy's garters were still there. The Admiral, I could see, was puzzled. Not knowing Daisy very well, he thought, no doubt, she was eccentric. He tried to smile. The political man took rather longer to decide on an attitude. He must have concluded that the garters were not Daisy's, for next I saw him looking curiously at me.

'They are not mine,' I rapidly said, 'those garters.'

'Whose are they?' said the Admiral, drawing near.

'They are Mrs Overend's garters,' I said, 'she changed her stockings in here.'

Now the garters had never really been serviceable; even now, with the help of safety pins, they did not so much keep Daisy's stockings, as her spirits up, for she liked them. They were historic in the sense that they had at first, I suppose, looked merely naughty. In about five years they had entered their most interesting, their old-fashioned, their lewd period. A little while, and the rosettes had begun to fray: the decadence. And now, with the impurity of those to whom all things pertaining to themselves are pure, Daisy did not see them as junk, but as part of herself, as she had cause to tell me later.

The Admiral walked warily into the drawing-room, but the Member of Parliament lingered to examine a picture on the wall, one eye on the garters. I was, I must say, tempted to hide them somewhere out of sight. More people were arriving, and the garters were causing them to think. If only for this reason, it was perhaps inhospitable to leave them so prominently on the table.

I resisted the temptation. Miss Rilke had suddenly become very excited. She flew to open the door to each guest, and, copying my tone, exclaimed:

'Please to excuse the garters. They are the garters of Mrs Overend. She changed her stockings in here.'

Daisy, Daisy Overend! I hope you have forgotten me. The party got out of hand. Lotti was not long in leaving the relatively sedative drawing-room in favour of the little room where Daisy's old basics were foregathered. These erstwhile adherents to the Young Idea, arriving in twos and threes, were filled with a great joy on hearing Miss Rilke's speech:

'Please to excuse those garters which you see. They are the garters of Mrs Overend. . . .'

But there was none more delighted than Lotti.

It was some minutes before the commotion was heard by Daisy in the drawing-room, where she was soliciting the badwill of a journalist against Mr Jamieson. Meanwhile, the ante-room party joined hands, clinked glasses and danced round Lotti who held the garters aloft with a pair of sugar tongs. Tom Pfeffer so far forgot himself as to curl up with mirth on a sofa.

I remember Daisy as she stood between the folding doors in her black party dress, like an infolded undernourished tulip. Behind her clustered her new friends, slightly offended, though prepared to join in the spirit of the thing, whatever it should be. Before her pranced the old, led by Lotti, in a primitive mountain jig. The sugar tongs with the garters in their jaws Lotti held high in one hand, and with the other he plucked the knee of his trouser-leg as if it were a skirt.

'*Ai, Ai, Ai,*' chanted Lotti, 'Daisy's dirty old garters, *Ai!*'

'*Ai, Ai, Ai,*' responded the chorus, while Miss Rilke looked lovingly on, holding in one hand Lotti's drink, in the other her own.

I remember Daisy as she stood there, not altogether without charm, beside herself. While laughter rebounded like plunging breakers from her mouth, she guided her eyes towards myself and trained on me the missiles of her fury. For a full three minutes Daisy's mouth continued to laugh.

I am seldom in the West End of London. But sometimes I have to hurry across the Piccadilly end of Albemarle Street where the buses crash past like giant orgulous parakeets, more thunderous and more hectic than the Household Cavalry. The shops are on my left and the Green Park lies on my right under the broad countenance of drowsy summer. It is then that, in my mind's eye, Daisy Overend gads again, diminutive, charming, vicious, and tarted up to the nines.

By district messenger she sent me a note early on the morning after the party. I was to come no more. Herewith a cheque. The garters were part of herself and I would understand how she felt.

The cheque was a dud. I did not pursue the matter, and in fact I have forgotten the real name of Daisy Overend. I have forgotten her name but I shall remember it at the Bar of Judgment.

DORIS LESSING

IN DEFENCE
OF THE
UNDERGROUND
(1992)

IN A SMALL cigarette and sweet shop outside the Underground station, the Indian behind the counter is in energetic conversation with a young man. They are both so angry that customers thinking of coming in change their minds.

'They did my car in, they drove past so near they scraped all the paint off that side. I saw them do it. I was at my window – just luck, that was. They were laughing like dogs. Then they turned around and drove back and scraped the paint off the other side. They went off like bats out of hell. They saw me at the window and laughed.'

'You're going to have to take it into your own hands,' says the Indian. 'They did up my brother's shop last month. They put burning paper through the letter box. It was luck the whole shop didn't burn. The police didn't do anything. He rang them, and then he went round to the station. Nothing doing. So we found out where they lived and we went and smashed their car in.'

'Yes,' says the other, who is a white man, not an Indian. 'The police don't want to know. I told them. I saw them do it. They were drunk, I said. What do you expect us to do? the police said.'

'I'll tell you what you can do,' says the Indian.

All this time I stand there, disregarded. They are too angry to care who hears them and, it follows, might report them. Then the young white man says – he could be something in building, or a driver, 'You think I should do the same, then?'

'You take a good sized hammer or a crowbar to their car, if you know where they live.'

'I've a fair old idea, yes.'

'Then that's it.'

'Right, that's it.' And he goes out, though he has to return for the cigarettes he came to buy, for in his rage he has forgotten them.

The Indian serves me. He is on automatic, his hands at work, his mind elsewhere.

As I go out, 'Cheers,' he says, and then, continuing the other conversation, 'That's it, then.'

In our area the Indian shop-keepers defend their shops at night with close-meshed grills, like chain mail – and it is not only the Indian shops.

Now I am standing on the pavement in a garden. It is a pavement garden, for the florist puts her plants out here, disciplined ranks of them, but hopeful plants, aspiring, because it is bedding plant time, in other words, late spring. A lily flowering a good month early scents the air stronger than the stinks of the traffic that pounds up this main route north all day and half the night. It is an ugly road, one you avoid if in a car, for one may need half an hour to go a few hundred yards.

Not long ago just where I stand marked the end of London. I know this because an old woman told me she used to take a penny bus here from Marble Arch, every Sunday. That is, she did, 'If I had a penny to spare, I used to save up from my dinners, I used to look forward all week. It was all fields and little streams, and we took off our shoes and stockings and sat with our feet in the water and looked at the cows. They used to come and look at us. And the birds – there were plenty of those.' That was before the First World War, in that period described in books of memoirs as a Golden Age. Yet you can find on stationers' counters postcards made from photographs of this street a hundred years or so ago. It has never not been a poor street, and it is a poor one now, even in this particular age of Peace and Plenty. Not much has changed, though shop fronts are flashier, and full of bright cheap clothes, and there is a petrol station. The postcards show modest self-regarding buildings and the ground floor of every one is a shop of a kind long since extinct, where each customer was served individually. Outside them, invited from behind a counter to centre the picture, stand men in bowler hats or serving aprons; if it is a woman she has a hat on of the kind that insisted on obdurate respectability, for that is a necessary attribute of the poor. But only a couple of hundred yards north-west my friend sat on Sundays with her feet in the little streams, while the cows crowded close. 'Oh, it was so cold, the water'd take your breath away, but you'd soon forget that, and it was the best day of the week.' A few hundred yards north there used to be a mill. Another woman, younger than the first, told me she remembered the Mill. 'Mill Lane – the name's because there used to be a mill, you see. But they pulled the mill down.' And where it was is a building no one would notice, if you didn't know what it replaced. If they had let the mill stand we would be proud of it, and they would charge us to go in and see how things used to be.

I enter the station, buy a ticket from a machine that works most of the time, and go up long stairs. There used to be decent lavatories, but now they are locked up because they are vandalized as soon as repaired. There is a good waiting room with heating, but often a window is smashed, and there is always graffiti. What are the young people saying when they smash everything they can? – for it is young people who do it, usually men. It is not that they are depraved because they are deprived, for I have just visited a famous university up north, where they have twenty applications for every place, where ninety-nine per cent of the graduates get jobs within a year of leaving. These are the privileged young, and they make for themselves a lively and ingenious social life their teachers clearly admire, if not envy. Yet they too smash everything up, not just the usual undergraduate loutishness, boys will be boys, but what seems to be a need for systematic destruction. What need? Do we know?

At the station you stand to wait for trains on a platform high above roofs and the tree tops are level with you. You feel thrust up into the sky. The sun, the wind, the rain, arrive unmediated by buildings. Exhilarating.

I like travelling by Underground. This is a defiant admission. I am always hearing, reading, I hate the Underground. In a book I have just picked up the author says he seldom uses it, but when he did have to go a few stops, he found it disgusting. A strong word. If people have to travel in the rush hour, then all is understood, but you may hear people who know nothing about rush hours say how terrible the Underground is. This is the Jubilee Line and I use it all the time. Fifteen minutes at the most to get in to the centre. The carriages are bright and new – well, almost. There are efficient indicators, Charing Cross: five minutes, three minutes, one minute. The platforms are no more littered than the streets, often less, or not at all. 'Ah but you should have seen what they were like in the old days. The Tube was different then.'

I know an old woman, I am sure I should say lady, who says, 'People like you ...' She means aliens, foreigners, though I have lived here forty years ... 'have no idea what London was like. You could travel from one side of London to the other by taxi for half a crown.' (In Elizabeth I's time you could buy a sheep for a few pence and under the Romans doubtless you could buy a villa for a silver coin, but currencies never devaluate when Nostalgia is in this gear.) 'And everything was so nice and clean and people were polite. Buses were always on time and the Tube was cheap.'

This woman was one of London's Bright Young Things, her young time was the twenties. As she speaks her face is tenderly reminiscent, but lonely, and she does not expect to persuade me or anyone else. What is the point of having lived in that Paradise Isle if no one believes you? As she sings her praise-songs for the past one sees hosts of pretty girls with pastel mouths and rouged cheeks wearing waistless petal-hemmed dresses, their hair marcelled in finger-waves, and as they flit from party to party they step in and out of obedient taxis driven by men only too happy to accept a penny tip. It was unlikely those women ever came as far north as West Hampstead or Kilburn, and I think Hampstead wasn't fashionable then, though in D. H. Lawrence's stories artists and writers live there. What is astonishing about reminiscences of those times is not only that there were different Londons for the poor and the middle class, let alone the rich, but the pedlars of memories never seem to be aware of this: 'In those days, when I was a little girl, I used to scrub steps. I did even when it was snowing, and I had bare feet, they were blue with cold sometimes, and I went to the baker's for yesterday's bread, cheap, and my poor little mother slaved sixteen hours a day, six days a week, oh those were wicked times, cruel times they were.' 'In those days we were proud to live in London. Now it's just horrid, full of horrid people.'

In my half of the carriage are three white people and the rest are black and brown and yellowish. Or, by another division, five females and six males. Or, four young people and seven middle-aged or elderly. Two Japanese girls, as glossy and self-sufficient as young cats, sit smiling. Surely the mourners for old London must applaud the Japanese, who are never, ever, scruffy or careless? Probably not: in that other London there were no foreigners, only English, pinko-grey as Shaw said, always *chez nous*, for the Empire had not imploded, the world had not invaded, and while every family had at least one relative abroad administering colonies or dominions, or being soldiers, that was abroad, it was there, not here, the colonies had not come home to roost.

These Japanese girls are inside an invisible bubble, they look out from a safe world. When I was in Japan I met many Japanese young ladies, who all seemed concerned to be Yum Yum. They giggled and went oooh – oooh – oooh as they jumped up and down, goody goody, and gently squealed with pleasure or with shock. But if you got them by themselves they were tough young women with a sharp view of life. Not that it was easy, for there always hovered some professor or mentor concerned to return them to their group, keep them safe and corporate.

A young black man sits dreaming, his ears wired to his Walkman, and his feet jig gently to some private rhythm. He wears clothes more expensive, more stylish, than anyone else in this travelling room. Next to him is an Indian woman with a girl of ten or so. They wear saris that show brown midriffs as glossy as toffee, but they have cardigans over them. Butterfly saris, workaday cardigans that make the statement, if you choose to live in a cold northern country, then this is the penalty. Never has there been a sadder sartorial marriage than saris with cardigans. They sit quietly conversing, in a way that makes the little girl seem a woman. These three get out at Finchley Road. In get four Americans, two boys, two girls, in their uniform of jeans and T-shirts and sports shoes. They talk loudly and do not see anyone else. Two sprawl opposite, and two loll on either side of, a tall old woman, possibly Scottish, who sits with her burnished shoes side by side, her fine bony hands on the handle of a wheeled shopping basket. She gazes ahead of her, as if the loud youngsters do not exist, and she is possibly remembering – but what London? The war? (Second World War, this time.) Not a poor London, that is certain. She is elegant, in tweeds and a silk shirt and her rings are fine. She and the four Americans get out at St John's Wood, the youngsters off to the American School, but she probably lives here. St John's Wood, so we are told by Galsworthy, for one, was where kept women were put in discreetly pretty villas by rich or at least respectable lovers. Now these villas can be afforded only by the rich, often Arabs.

As people get into the waiting train, I sit remembering how not long ago I visited a French friend in a St John's Wood hotel. While I stood at the reception desk three Arabs in white robes went through from a back part of the hotel to the lift, carrying at shoulder level a tray heaped with rice, and on that a whole roasted sheep. The lobby swooned with the smell of spices and roast meat. The receptionist said, to my enquiring look, 'Oh, it's for Sheikh So-and-So, he has a feast every night.' And she continued to chat on the telephone to a boyfriend. 'Oh, you only say that, oh I know all about men, you can't tell me anything' – using these words, as far as she was concerned, for the first time in history. And she caressed the hair above her left ear with a complacent white hand that had on it a lump of synthetic amber the size of a hen's egg. Her shining hair was amber, cut in a 1920s shingle. Four more Arabs flowed past, their long brown fingers playing with their prayer beads, like nuns who repel the world with their rosaries. 'Hail Mary Full of Grace . . .' their lips moving as they smile and nod, taking part in worldly conversation: but their fingers holding tight to righteousness. The Arabs disappeared into the lift, presumably on their way to the feast, while the revolving doors admitted four more, a congregation of sheikhs.

Not far from here, in Abbey Road, are the studios where the Beatles recorded. At the pedestrian crossing made famous by the Four are always platoons of tourists, of all ages and races, standing to stare with their souls in their eyes, while their fingers go click-click on their cameras. All over the world, in thousands of albums, are cherished photographs of this dingy place.

This part of London is not old. When the villas were full of mistresses and ladies of pleasure it was a newish suburb. Travelling from NW6 or NW2 into the centre is to leave recently settled suburbs for the London that has risen and fallen in successive incarnations since before the Romans. Not long ago I was at lunch in the house that was Gladstone's, now a Press Club. For most of us it is hard to imagine a family actually living in a house that seems built only to present people for public occasions, but above all, no one could stand on Carlton House Terrace and think: Not long ago there was a wood here, running water, grazing beasts. No, Nature is away down a flight of grandiose steps, across the Mall, and kept well in its place in St James's Park. The weight of those buildings, pavements, roads, forbids thoughts of the kind still so natural in St John's Wood, where you think: there must have been a wood here, and who was St John? – almost certainly a church. Easy to see the many trees as survivors of that wood: unlikely, but not impossible.

Today I am glad I am not getting off here. The escalator often doesn't work. Only a month ago, on one of the blackboards the staff use to communicate their thoughts to passengers was written in jaunty white chalk: 'You are probably wondering why the escalators so often aren't working? We shall tell you! It is because they are old and often go out of order. Sorry! Have a good day!' Which message, absolutely in the style of London humour, sardonic and with its edge of brutality, was enough to cheer one up, and ready to make the long descent on foot.

In jump three youngsters. Yobbos. Louts. Hooligans. They are sixteen or so, in other words adolescents, male, with their loud raucous unhappy braying laughter, their raging sex, their savagery. Two white and a black. Their cries, their jeers, command everyone's attention – which is after all the point. One white youth and the black are jostling and the third, who puts up with it in a manner of stylized resignation, smiling like a sophisticated Christian martyr: probably some film or television hero. Impossible to understand what they are saying, for their speech is as unformed as if they had speech defects – probably intentionally, for who wants to be understood too well by adults at sixteen? All this aggro is only horseplay, on the edge of harm, no more. At Baker Street the two tormentors push out the third, try to prevent him from re-entering. Not so easy, this, for trains take their time at Baker Street, the all-purpose junction for many-suburbed London. The three tire of the scuffle and step inside to stand near the door, preventing others from entering, but only by their passivity. Excuse me, excuse me, travellers say, confronted by these three large youths who neither resist nor attack, but only take up a lot of room, knowing that they do, knowing they are a damned nuisance, but preserving innocent faces that ignore mutters and angry stares. As the doors begin to close, the two aggressors push out the victim, and stand making all kinds of abusive gestures at him, and mouthing silent insults as the train starts to move. The lad on the platform shouts insults back but points in the direction the train is going, presumably to some agreed destination. As we

gather speed he is half-strolling, half-dancing, along the platform, and he sends a forked-fingered gesture after us. The
two seem to miss him, and they sit loosely, gathering energy
for the next explosion, which occurs at Bond Street, where
they are off the train in dangerous kangaroo leaps, shouting
abuse. At whom? Does it matter? Where they sat roll two soft-
drink cans, as bright and seductive as advertisements. Now
in the coach are people who have not seen the whole
sequence, and they are probably thinking, Thank God I shall
never have to be that age again! Or are they? Is it possible that
when people sigh, Oh if only I was young again, they are
regretting what we have just seen, but remembered as an
interior landscape of limitless possibilities?

At Bond Street a lot of people get out, and the train stays
still long enough to read comfortably the poem provided by
the Keepers of the Underground, inserted into a row of
advertisements.

THE EAGLE

He clasps the crag with crooked hands:
Close to the sun in lonely lands.
Ring'd with the azure world he stands.

The wrinkled sea beneath him crawls:
He watches from his mountain walls.
And like a thunderbolt he falls.

ALFRED LORD TENNYSON

In get a crowd of Danish school-children, perhaps on a day
trip. They are well-behaved, and watched over by a smiling
girl, who does not seem much older than they are. Tidily
they descend at Green Park, and the carriage fills up again.
All tourists. Is that what people mean when they complain
the Underground is so untidy? It is the xenophobia of the

British again? Rather, the older generations of the British. Is what I enjoy about London, its variety, its populations from everywhere in the world, its transitoriness – for sometimes London can give you the same feeling as when you stand to watch cloud shadows chase across a plain – exactly what they so hate?

Yet for people so threatened they are doing, I think, rather well. Not long ago I saw this incident. It was a large London hospital, in a geriatric ward. 'I'm just on my way to Geriatrics' you may hear one sprightly young nurse tell another, as she darts her finger to the lift button. An old white woman, brought in because she had fallen, was being offered a bedpan. She was not only old, in fact ancient, and therefore by rights an inhabitant of that lost Eden of decently uniform pinko-grey people, but working class and a spinster. (One may still see women described on old documents, Status: Spinster.) For such a woman to be invited to use a bedpan in a public place before the curtains had even been drawn about her was bad enough. To be nursed by a man, a male nurse, something she had never imagined possible. Worst of all, he was black, a young calm black man, in a nurse's uniform. ('No, I'm not a doctor, I'm a nurse – yes, that's right, a nurse.') He turned back the bed covers, assisted the old woman on to the bedpan, nicely pulling down her nightgown over her old thighs, and drew the curtains. 'I'll be back in just a minute, love.' And off he went. Behind that curtain went on an internal drama hard to imagine by people used to polyglot and casually mannered London, whether they enjoy it or not. When he returned to pull back the curtains, ask if she was all right – did she want him to clean her up a little? – and then remove the pan, her eyes were bright with dignified defiance. She had come to terms with the impossible. 'No, dear, it's all right, I can still do that for myself.'

In a school in South London where a friend is governor, twenty-five languages are spoken.

Now we are tunnelling under old London, though not the oldest, for that is a mile, or two or three, further East. On the other side of thick shelves of earth as full of pipes and cables, wires, sewers, the detritus of former buildings and towns as garden soil is of worms and roots, is St James's Park – Downing Street – Whitehall. If someone travelled these under-earth galleries and never came up into the air it would be easy to believe this was all there could be to life, to living. There is a sci-fi story about a planet where suns and moons appear only every so many years, and the citizens wait for the miracle, the revelation of their situation in the universe, which of course the priests have taken possession of, claiming the splendour of stars as proof of their right to rule. There are already cities where an under-earth town repeats the one above it, built in air – for instance, Houston, Texas. You enter an unremarkable door, just as in a dream, and you are in an underground city, miles of it, with shops, restaurants, offices. You need never come up. There are people who actually like basement flats, choose them, draw curtains, turn on lights, create for themselves an underground, and to them above-ground living seems as dangerous as ordinary life does to an ex-prisoner or someone too long in hospital. They institutionalize themselves, create a place where everything is controlled by them, a calm concealed place, away from critical eyes, and the hazards of weather and the changes of light are shut out. Unless the machinery fails: a gas leak, the telephone goes wrong.

In the fifties I knew a man who spent all day going around the Circle Line. It was like a job, a discipline, from nine till six. *They* couldn't get at him, he claimed. He was having a breakdown. Did people go in for more imaginative breakdowns, then? It sometimes seems a certain flair has gone out of the business. And yet, a few days ago, on the Heath, there approached a Saxon – well, a young man wearing clothes it would be possible to agree Saxons might have worn. A brown woollen shirt. Over it a belted jerkin contrived from thick brown paper. Breeches were made with elastic bands up the calves. A draped brown scarf made a monkish hood. He held a spear from a toy shop. 'Prithee, kind sir,' said my companion, somewhat out of period, 'whither goest thou?' The young Saxon stopped, delighted and smiling, while his companion, a young woman full of concern, looked on. 'Out,' said the young man. 'Away.'

'What is your name? Beowulf? Olaf the Red? Eric the Brave?'

'Eric the Black.'

'It isn't your name *really*,' said his minder, claiming him for fact.

'Yes it is,' we heard as they wandered off into the russets, the yellows, the scorched greens of the unforgettable autumn of 1990. 'My name is Eric, isn't it? Well then, it *is* Eric.'

Charing Cross and everyone gets out. At the exit machine a girl appears running up from the deeper levels, and she is chirping like an alarm. Now she has drawn our attention to it, in fact a steady bleeping is going on, and for all we know, it is a fire alarm. These days there are so many electronic bleeps, cheeps, buzzes, blurps, that we don't hear them. The girl is a fey creature, blonde locks flying around a flushed face. She is laughing dizzily, and racing a flight or flock of young things coming into the West End for an evening's adventure, all of them already crazed with pleasure, and in another dimension of speed and lightness, like sparks speeding up and out. She and two girls push in their tickets and flee along a tunnel to the upper world, but three youths vault over, with cries of triumph, and their state of being young is such a claim on us all that the attendant decides not to notice, for it would be as mad as swatting butterflies.

Now I am going out to Trafalgar Square, along a tunnel, and there, against a wall, is a site where groups of youngsters are always bending, crouching, squatting, to examine goods laid on boxes, and bits of cloth. Rings and earrings, bracelets, brooches, all kinds of glitter and glitz, brass and glass, white metal and cheap silver, cheap things but full of promise and possibility.

I follow this tunnel and that, go up some steps, and I am in Trafalgar Square. Ahead of me across the great grey space with its low pale fountains is the National Gallery, and near it the National Portrait Gallery. The sky is a light blue, sparkling, and fragile clouds are being blown about by winds at work far above our level of living, for down here it is quiet. Now I may enjoyably let time slide away in one Gallery or both, and not decide till the last possible moment, shall I turn left to the National, or walk another fifty paces and look at the faces of our history? When I come out, the sky, though it will not have lost light, will have acquired an intense late-afternoon look, time to find a café, to meet friends and then ... in an hour or so the curtain will go up in a theatre, or the English National Opera. Still, after all these years, these decades, there is no moment like that when the curtain goes up, the house lights dim ... Or, having dawdled about, one can after all simply go home, taking care to miss the rush hour.

Not long ago, at the height of the rush hour, I was strap-hanging, and in that half of the carriage, that is, among fourteen people, three people read books among all the newspapers. In the morning, off to work, people betray their allegiances: *The Times*, the *Independent*, the *Guardian*, the

Telegraph, the *Mail*. The bad papers some of us are ashamed of don't seem much in evidence, but then this is a classy line, at least at some hours and in some stretches of it. At night the *Evening Standard* adds itself to the display. Three people. At my right elbow a man was reading the *Iliad*. Across the aisle a woman read *Moby Dick*. As I pushed out, a girl held up *Wuthering Heights* over the head of a new baby asleep on her chest. When people talk glumly about our state of illiteracy I tell them I saw this, and they are pleased, but sceptical.

The poem holding its own among the advertisements was:

INFANT JOY

'I have no name:
I am but two days old.'
What shall I call thee?
'I happy am.
Joy is my name.'
Sweet joy befall thee!

Pretty joy!
Sweet joy but two days old.
Sweet joy I call thee:
Thou dost smile.
I sing the while
Sweet joy befall thee.

WILLIAM BLAKE

Walking back from the Underground I pass three churches. Two of them are no longer conduits for celestial currents: one is a theatre, one derelict. In such a small bit of London, three churches ... that other-worldly visitor so useful for enlivening our organs of comparison might, seventy years ago, have wondered, 'What are they for, these buildings, so like each other, so unlike all the others, several to a district?

Administrative buildings? A network of governmental offices? Newly built, too!' But these days this person, she, he or it, would note the buildings are often unused. 'A change of government perhaps?' Yet certain types of buildings repeat themselves from one end of the city to the other. 'Just as I saw on my last visit, there are "pubs" for dispensing intoxicants, and centres for fast movement by means of rail. Others are for the maintenance of machines like metal bugs or beetles – a new thing this, nothing like that last time I was here. And there is another new thing. Every few yards is a centre for the sale of drugs, chemical substances.' A funny business – he, she or it might muse, mentally arranging the items of the report that will be faxed back to Canopus. 'If I put them in order of frequency of occurrence, then chemists' shops must come first. This is a species dependent on chemical additions to what they eat and drink.' Within a mile of where I live there are at least fifteen chemists' shops, and every grocery has shelves of medicines.

As I turn the corner past where the old mill stood I leave behind the stink and roar of vehicles pushing their way north-wards and I realize that for some minutes it has been un-pleasant to breathe. Now Mill Lane, where shops are always starting up, going bankrupt, changing hands, particularly now with the trebling and quadrupling of rents and rates. Soon, I am in the little roads full of houses, and the traffic has become a steady but minor din. The streets here are classically inclined. Agamemnon, Achilles, Ulysses, and there is an Orestes Mews. Add to these names Gondar, and one may postulate an army man, classically educated, who was given the job of naming these streets. In fact, this was not so far wrong. The story was this. (True or false? Who cares? Every story of the past, recent or old, is bound to be tidied up, rounded off, made consequential.) An ex-army man, minor gentry, had a wife in the country with many children, and a mistress in town, with many more. To educate all these he went in for property, bought farmland that spread attractively over a hill with views of London, and built what must have been one of the first northern commuter suburbs ... for remember, in the valley just down from this hill, towards London, were the streams, the cows and the green fields my old friend took a penny bus ride to visit every Sunday. The commuters went in by horse-bus or by train to the City.

Some of the buildings are Mansions, built from the start as flats, but most were houses, since converted into three flats. Hard to work out how these houses functioned. The cellars are all wet. In mine labels come off bottles in three months. Yet there was a lavatory down here. Used by whom? Surely nobody could have lived in this earthy cave? Perhaps it wasn't wet then. Now a circular hole or mini shaft has been dug into the soil, for the damp has long ago heaved off the cement floor, and in it one may watch the water level rise and fall. Not according to the rainfall: all of us in this area know the tides have something to do with the leaking pipes of the reservoir, which from my top window looks like an enormous green field, or village green, for there are great trees all around it: the Victorians put their reservoirs underground. (They say that if you know the man who has the task of guarding the precious waters, one may be taken through a small door and find oneself on the edge of a reach of still black water, under a low ceiling where lights gleam down. One may add to this attractively theatrical picture the faint plop of a rat swimming away from sudden light, and a single slow-spreading ripple.) The top of my house is a converted attic. But the attics were not converted then. There are three bedrooms on the second floor, one too small to share. Two rooms on the first floor, now one room, but then probably dining room and sitting room. A kitchen is pleasantly but inconveniently off a veranda or 'patio' – a recent addition. It was not a kitchen then. On the ground floor is one room, once two, and 'conveniences' also added recently. A garden room, most likely a nursery. In those days they had so many children, they often had relatives living with them, and every middle-class household had at least one servant, usually more. How were they all fitted in? Where did they cook, where was the larder, how did they get the washing done? And how did they keep warm? There are minuscule fire baskets in small fireplaces in every room.

A hundred years ago this suburb, these houses, were built, and they are solid and thick-walled and all the builders who come to mend roofs or fix plumbing tell you how well they were put up, how good the materials were. 'We don't build like that now.' Nor are these experts dismayed by the wet cellar. 'You keep that clay good and wet around your foundations, and it won't shrink in these summers we are having now, and you won't be sorry.'

As I turn the corner into the street I live in the light is arranging the clouds into tinted masses. The sunsets up here are, to say the least, satisfactory.

Ivy loads the corner house, and starlings are crowding themselves in there, swooping out, swirling back, to become invisible and silent until the morning.

IRMA KURTZ

ISLINGTON
(1997)

ONE EVENING AT a posh house in Islington, a borough which in the 1970s had started to overtake Hampstead as the venue for London's bloodiest ritual dinner-parties, I found myself at table next to a grizzled American academic of some renown. Only a few years older than I, he had stormed out of our homeland during the McCarthy era and was often quoted as saying he had no intention of ever going back. He saw himself as European by affinity, British by preference, a Londoner by adoption: much as I see myself, except my choices were not made in anger. It was well known he was an angry American who wanted nothing to do with his country-men unless they were of Nobel stature, and even then he kept his gloves on. During the long dinner he ignored me until I said thoughtlessly, more to myself than to him, as I passed the cream for his gooseberry fool: 'Double your pleasure...'

He looked directly at me then, and his blue eyes gleamed through their old cobwebs.

'Double your fun...?' he said tentatively.

'Doublemint, Doublemint, Doublemint gum!' we sang in unison.

'Would you walk a mile for a Camel?' he asked. 'Do you wonder where the yellow went?'

'What do you think has happened to "Mr Keene, Tracer of Lost Persons"?'

'I don't suppose you remember "pickle in the middle..."?'

'Jack Benny. "Allen's Alley"? "Kimo Sabe"?'

' "Hi-ho, Silver!" "Shazam"?'

'Captain Marvel. Do they still have O'Henry bars, I wonder?'

'God, they were tasty,' he said with a downward glance at his gooseberry fool.

'Blueberry bunkers. MacIntosh apples in bushel baskets. Poison ivy. Poison sumac . . .'

'Oh God! Yes. Yes. Can you ever forget humming-birds? Fireflies? Frost that turned your bedroom window into a valentine. Remember? And October. Will you ever forget our eastern October? Armies of pumpkins springing out of the fields . . .'

The Londoners had stopped talking. They had drawn back in their chairs, and they were watching us. We two Yanks smiled at each other; his smile creaked a little, but there was hope for it. Then he sighed, and looking around he addressed the table at large: 'Who knows what evil lurks in the hearts of men?' he asked, shaking his big egghead sadly.

'The Shadow knows,' I whispered to him.

And we nearly fell in love.

Expatriation, as the Americanized execs at JWT would have said, is 'an ongoing process'. Probably a sex change is similarly subject to fits and starts. Even now after more than three decades of living in London there are days when I'm waiting in a queue for a bus in Upper Street, Islington, let's say, and it's inevitably raining; and what do you want to bet I've just crossed half the city to a shop that no longer stocks whatever item I used to buy there: 'Oh no, there's no call for those,' the salesman said, probably adding a cluck of disapproval that I should dare to ask, and naturally, for this *is* London, the bus is twenty minutes overdue. And I look around at the other wretches in the queue because I'm longing for a little commiserating kibbutz. But they turn away from my wild eye. And that's when suddenly I wonder: 'Who are these people? What sunless place is this that they call Lun-dun? How the hell did I wash up in Lun-dun? I am undone in Lun-dun. A stranger and a sojourner here. This city is so far gone in restraint and attic codification it's more like Tokyo at heart than any other western city I know.'

Even the street-crazed don't wave their arms around and call loudly on God the way they do in New York; instead, they shuffle along mumbling, and it is they, the London lunatics, who give us sane ones a wide berth on the pavement. Then just in time, before I start to babble or cry, not one, not two, but three number 28 buses loom on the horizon. The bald girl in front of me in black fake leather pants, high-heeled boots and a ring through her nose turns to me, or maybe it's the old man using his pensioner's pass for free off-peak travel (I keep meaning to go to the post office and apply for mine) who turns and asks: 'Do you know why they always come three at a time?'

I shake my head, no, as if I've not heard the punch-line countless times before.

'Because,' she, or he, or whoever, says loud enough for everyone to hear, and it's all in the delivery: 'they're bloody terrified to travel alone, aren't they? The timorous buggers.'

People laugh and my heart lifts, and then we disperse, far away from one another on the bus, opening our newspapers: true Londoners, too respectful of each other's space to push an old joke beyond its range.

Back in the 1960s, there I was, a foolhardy, moody, unfinished expatriate, full of curiosity, self-doubt and hope, not much changed in fact from long gone days in Jersey City where Donald and I had both been born and disdainfully grew up. Except of course that I was no longer in love with

Donald by the time we met again in London. Falling in love with a nervy, literate homosexual was easily done back in the mid-twentieth century by a romantic young virgin who found herself in a town overstocked with louts and budding hooligans. I was never again driven to repeat the phenomenon of falling for a gay man, mind you; only very dissatisfied women are. A woman in love with a homosexual man is being constantly rejected, or always seducing him in spite of himself, and either way reeks of self-loathing. Not that I was alone in fancying Don-Don: back in the 1950s at Columbia, such a number of undergraduates of both sexes were joined in love with him, all we needed were the Greek letters – a psi, a psi again, and how many more psis? – to qualify as a fraternity on campus. People who knew Don-Don only in his querulous middle years would hardly believe how startling and distracting and priapic was his very presence alone or in a crowd when he was young. Cheekbones like little suspension bridges and narrow cunning eyes set slightly askew, his face belonged on a runaway Russian ballet dancer, while his spare, knobbly body had the slightly spastic coordination of a dedicated intellectual, or a sailor on shore leave. Of us all, he was the best read and for a while the best writer, too. Only Don-Don in that place and time possessed a crooked, playful wit that was English in style, though back then we doe-eyed American kids didn't appreciate irony, and we complained to each other that he was cruel.

In the 1950s Donald was working as a fellow at Cambridge University. Between terms at Barnard, on my maiden trip to Britain, I slipped away from my student tour group in damp, grey old London – 'I could never live in this weary burg', I find written in my journal of the time – to visit him in Cambridge. An endless party was going on, well, that was the impression given by the stale air and young men slumped in corners. It was late afternoon and outside the windows of Donald's rooms the River Cam was orange and gold, running along the edge of centuries and through the bones of science, rinsing the soft tissue of how many sainted poets?

'La, la, la!' came Donald's most sardonic voice suddenly. 'I see we are yet again to be subjected to the sunset.'

I turned: it was not Donald after all who had sliced through my reverie – it was a tall Englishman I later came to know well, called Simon Hodgson. Simon died not long ago, too soon, and forever missed. Talking to naughty, darling Simon for the first time, I began to realize that Donald's pawky irreverence, rare though it was among Americans of the day, blended into the ordinary mass at Cambridge. Evidently his ability with hard drink was nothing special there either. And perceptible tremors in the room hinted how thirstily his sexuality was being absorbed too, and probably going for a lot less in such an overheated atmosphere than it was worth at home.

Abroad is death for some very bright people. They are fixed stars, distance dims them and in a little while they burn out, then disappear. Though Don-Don was daring of brain and groin, he turned out to be a stay-at-home at heart, and Cambridge, UK was the beginning of the end of him. At Cambridge Donald's sense of being special, always more fragile than his admirers at home realized, was converted into camp extravagance. When he found it not so easy to impress in this old country as he had back home, he started to imagine that the hyphenated bastards had it in for him, and were joining forces to keep him out of their inner circle and out of print. With every lost engagement of wit, he became increasingly convinced the cold-blooded, lily-livered, English intellectual establishment was out to get him because his alien gifts threatened their pre-eminence. It's a common enough brand of paranoia among American scribblers in London, and believe me, it is not unjustifiable. Nevertheless, in the end, it's our own vanity that drives us crazy. As soon as Donald convinced himself that they wouldn't let him win any glittering prizes, he stopped trying. Eventually, when he was around 50, still writing copy for agencies in London, he chucked it all in to return to America once and for all, to his mother's retirement home in the Florida boondocks. But it was too late. He was a half-baked expatriate: too soft to stick it out abroad, too bitter and crusty to go back to being American.

Islington was a north London slum in the early stages of gentrification in the 1960s, and my new boss, Robert Carrier, the celebrated gourmet and cook, owned a big house in one of its prettiest squares: Gibson Square – 'the Gibson girls', Don-Don used to call Bob's ménage. His own basement flat in Bob's house was bright and airy and not at all what the word 'basement' brings to mind. Were there three of us or four employed by Bob? For the life of me I can't remember. I remember the small office we shared, jerry-built shelves running the length of it, I think it was near the top of the house; I'm sure it faced the garden. Details of this period are hazy not because of drink or drugs; luxury is an opiate too, and five-star memories have the sameness of blood heat. Bob's sensuous gift for luxury is rare enough among men, and it was at a premium in London. To have good taste or a good time among the English has always been a test of stamina. Things have improved slowly over the years, but there are still plenty of freezing corridors in art galleries, crush bars at the opera, queues for loos at theatres, warm beer, spot heaters, and too often even now standard lumpy gravy that belies good cuts of meat.

Paris is a city famed for charm yet practically uncharmable

by anything outside its own invention. New York is dazzled by novelty, but competitive and frenetically on the hop, with too much to do to hang around for as long as it takes to be spellbound. London, on the other hand, though it has been battered past being easily impressed, is nevertheless very easily, almost childishly, charmed. It will stop in its tracks for a Canadian circus, say, or an Australian stand-up comic, or an enthusiastic American evangelist, or any other import with the power to beguile. Generally, London behaves very like a man, and, as any woman who has been around will agree, this means that like a man London prefers being seduced to being seductive. Bob was a handsome, charming flirt from the USA who soon had *le tout Londres* eating *brandade de morue* out of his hand. He'd learned to cook when he was young and lovely, while being wined and dined in St Tropez; his style was adapted from the French and jazzed up with merciless lashings of champagne, cognac and cream. When his recipes began appearing all over the place in London, everyone was captivated by their sheer sybaritic chutzpah. Bob was essentially a merry man, and the business of publicizing apples and pears, for which he'd set up our small PR office in his house, would have to depress anyone with a heart bigger than a Bramley, so he left that boring stuff pretty much to the three or four of us on his staff. All Bob needed to do was breeze in one door of the office and out the other once a day or so, talking fast and musically in his operatic tenor voice, and we were inspired to work our tails off for British fruits. Meanwhile, he and a few other emergent cooks of the period were having a great time charming England out of its penitential eating habits. Thanks to them, English cuisine, which had for a long time with perfect justification been a worldwide joke, slowly began to shake itself free of clinging limp greens and gravy. Bob's energy and charisma galvanized the domestic staff too, though they were mostly francophone North Africans who didn't always grasp what he was getting at. Ahmed the houseboy, fresh from the Casbah, was often to be seen clutching his forehead and frowning over an order Bob had let fly while he was rushing by. One morning there was Ahmed in the garden under our window, humming to himself and sticking cut long-stemmed red roses in even rows into the turned earth of a border.

'Ahmed,' I called down, 'just what are you doing?'

When Ahmed smiled, his teeth had the tinged whiteness of a bitten Russet apple.

'Mister Carrier, he say to me, "Ahmed," he say, "for summer, I wish you plant roses in the garden." So I am planting roses . . .'

One advantage attaching to a woman, at least while she is young and reasonably attractive, is the chance to lead a high life even while she's worrying sick about the rent money. Every so often Bob used to invite me to a dinner at home with A-list guests, or to a restaurant opening or a private view, and as these occasions always came up at short notice I kept my only party garment on a hook behind the office door. It was a black silk jumpsuit which five years later was going to be instrumental in the seduction of my child's father. Wherever in London Bob and I happened to be, on the stroke of midnight he saw me into a taxi home, and it wasn't my glass slipper in his pocket, or on his mind, as he sauntered off towards the late-night pleasures of London's West End.

Christopher Kinimonth was a published author, temporarily on his uppers, who worked alongside me in the apple and pear division which Bob ran as a sort of orphanage for neglected writers. On cold wet nights in the winter, Christopher and I used to go to a local pub where we sat as near as we could to the window so we could spot the oncoming lights of our separate buses home in good time to run for them. More than once we'd let a bus or two go by in favour of another round of Whisky Macs. The pub we used was on the verge of schizophrenia as it affects long-standing local businesses in parts of London where gentrification sets in. The plebeian dart-board remained as tradition would have it, right next to the Ladies' Room door – they put them there, you know, to make women think twice about popping into the local for a drink with the boys – but it had already taken on the dusted look of an artefact, and no serious game was ever in progress. Like most London pubs in those days, there was still a lounge bar where nice folks paid a few pence more per pint for a genteel atmosphere, and there was the public bar with its own entrance, where men on their own could get roaring drunk and use bad language. These old distinctions went by the board as soon as interlopers like Christopher and me chose to drink in the public bar, not the lounge, on egalitarian principles, and because it was more fun. Gradually the public bar filled up with art editors and their wives who had just moved into the neighbourhood, and the old regulars began to huddle in a shrinking group; a few of them suddenly died, others fell to the staggering prices outsiders were starting to offer for their rundown homes. With their windfalls they bought bungalows in suburban green belts where their grown-up children were already installed, having been unable to afford houses in the upwardly mobile neighbourhoods where they and their ancestors had grown up.

In Paris, unless something is added to the central nervous system of the city, such as the new opera house near the Bastille, or subtracted from it, the way the inner-city market of Les Halles was not long ago, the use and personality of neighbourhoods are set in stone. A girl from the sixteenth arrondissement now is still the Parisian princess she was

30 years ago; the Left Bank retains bohemian credentials; anyone who lives on the Île Saint-Louis is going to be interesting, anyone who lives in the fifteenth probably isn't. Parisians are scared of their suburbs, for it is there in high-rise buildings that grip the city like a claw they stow their Arab and African immigrants. As for New York, the outer boroughs are a mystery to me: I've only ever been to the Bronx for the zoo. The permutations of where is 'in' and where is 'out' are bound to be limited on a small electrically-charged island like Manhattan. A residential see-saw seems to be at work there: west side, up; east side, down; uptown, oops! downtown, whee! Then practically overnight all change sides. In central London gentrification sprinkles itself around here and there and wherever it sets in, it's there for keeps. Terraces, crescents and squares compose most of the sprawl-ing residential areas of London, and their design succumbs to pockets of infection faster than you can say 'carriage-lamp'.

I recall another Islington dinner-party in the late '60s, when our rich socialist oxymoron of a hostess boasted of how much good she and her husband, a famous journalist, were doing the north London backwater to which they had recently moved.

'We're the thin end of a caring wedge . . .' she said.

These days Islington's Upper Street has gone posh enough so that a hostess in a hurry could shop locally for her dreaded dinner-parties. Back then, the roast on her table certainly did not come from the corner butcher. But who am I to blame early affluent settlers for choosing Harrod's Food Hall over local butcher shops that still smelled in those days of cheap cuts and suet? The local school was a disaster area too; it probably still is. Why shouldn't they have put their infant son down for Eton? There is no logic in my dislike of gentri-fication. After all, nice people have to live somewhere too, right? They restore dilapidated properties of real architectural merit. Their advent doesn't necessarily create such an uneasy 'them' and 'us' condition as I feel even now in Islington. All I know for sure is that when Christopher and I went for a drink one night, having not been to the pub for a while, and found the original dusty lighting replaced by lamps set in mock wagon-wheels, new ashtrays stamped 'Martini', and an eager young company man from a big brewery behind the bar instead of the cynical old publican, I knew then that I didn't like Islington.

Fruit pretty much takes care of itself in the publicity department. Apart from digging up a few odd recipes and circulating them around the cooking press, there wasn't a whole lot to do. Once in a while we'd arrange a competition for new uses of apples and pears: they had to be culinary, of course. There were photo sessions to attend for the illustrations of Bob's books, where I picked up a few useful hints: the best way to put a high gloss on a turkey, for instance, is with hairspray, and ice-cream won't melt under hot lights if it's sculpted out of play-dough. For hours on end in the office I tapped happily at letters to Rhoda [a college friend], and I wrote pieces mostly for my own amusement. Christopher must have been doing the same thing: his machine was going steadily too, and he had no more than I or any other normal person has to say about apples and pears. Finally, on a whim I sent a piece called 'Love in Capital Cities' to a London women's magazine, *Queen*, that years later merged with *Harper's Bazaar*. They returned it with a letter saying it was too 'idiosyncratic' for their readership.

'What the hell,' I thought.

I helped myself to another couple of big envelopes from the supply cupboard, wrote another covering letter on office stationery, and sent the piece out again, this time to a brand new publication I'd read for the first time that very morning on the bus into work. It was a large-format glossy called *Nova*. The piece was sent on Monday and I put it out of my mind. On Friday morning my phone rang. Maybe I'm romancing but it seems to me in retrospect that the moment Dennis Hackett introduced himself in a north country accent buoyant with energy, I knew he was the man I'd been waiting for. Indeed, Dennis turned out to be one of the three or four most important men in my life. To hear an editor, or *anyone*, say he liked my work made me tongue-tied with embarrassment; it's a miracle that he didn't write me off as a drivelling idiot before the end of our conversation when he said he not only wanted the piece, he wanted me on *Nova's* staff. Bob never quite forgave me for the speed and excitement with which I left his employ.

On the Sunday before my first day at *Nova* Lillian [a friend and fellow journalist] called me. On principle, Lil preferred to use her phone at work for all private calls, and she so rarely rang at weekends from home that I asked immediately if everything was all right? She told me she had just returned a few hours earlier from a short trip to Ireland with Angelica. They'd shared a cabin on the overnight boat from Cork, and in the small hours of the morning, Lil had been awakened when Angelica jumped on her pounding with her fists and screaming.

'She was yelling that we had to run away. There was a fire in the house. Water from the firemen's hoses had filled the streets, and was streaming down the window.'

All Lil could do was hold her struggling mother and immobilize her until a stewardess, alarmed by all the racket, summoned a doctor who fed Angelica sedatives until she finally stopped screaming and fell asleep.

'She must have been having a bad dream, Lil. That's all it was . . .'

'Do you think so, Kurtz?'

'Sure. Of course. Sure. How is she now?'

'She doesn't remember what happened.'

'See? She woke from a bad dream, saw the sea against the porthole and it scared her. That's all it was.'

Something genuinely promising was starting for me at last. Good times made me too selfish to imagine that something horrible could be about to begin for someone close to me. In any case what could I have done for Lillian? Sometimes the only way to help a friend in trouble is to lie to her.

HANIF KUREISHI

THE UMBRELLA
(1999)

THE MINUTE THEY arrived at the adventure playground, Roger's two sons charged up a long ramp and soon were clinging to the steel netting that hung from a high beam. Satisfied that it would take them some time to extract themselves, Roger sat on a bench and turned to the sports section of his newspaper. He had always found it relaxing to read reports of football matches he had not seen. Then it started to rain.

His sons, aged four and five and a half, had refused to put on their coats when he picked them up from the au pair half an hour before. Coats made them look 'fat', they claimed, and Roger had had to carry the coats under his arm. The older boy was dressed in a thin tight-fitting green outfit and a cardboard cap with a feather in it: he was either Robin Hood or Peter Pan. The younger wore a plastic belt with holsters containing two silver guns, a plastic dagger and a sword, blue wellington boots, jeans with the fly open, and a chequered neckerchief which he pulled over his mouth. 'Cowboys don't wear raincoats,' he said through a mouthful of cloth. The boys frequently refused Roger's commands, though he could not say that their stubbornness and pluck annoyed him. It did, however, cause him trouble with his wife, from whom he had separated a year previously. Only that morning she had said on the phone, 'You are a weak and inadequate disciplinarian. You only want their favour.'

For as long as he could, Roger pretended it was not raining, but when his newspaper began to go soggy and everyone else left the playground, he called the boys over.

'Damn this rain,' he said as he hustled them into their yellow hooded raincoats.

'Don't swear,' said the younger. 'Women think it's naughty.'

'Sorry.' Roger laughed. 'I was thinking I should have got a raincoat as well as the suit.'

'You do need a lovely raincoat, Daddy,' said Oliver, the eldest.

'My friend would have given me a raincoat, but I liked the suit more.'

He had picked up the chocolate-coloured suit from the shop that morning. Since that most extravagant of periods, the early Seventies, Roger had fancied himself as a restrained but amateur dandy. One of his best friends was a clothes designer with shops in Europe and Japan. A few years ago this friend, amused by Roger's interest in his business, had invited Roger, during a fashion show in the British Embassy in Paris, to parade on the catwalk in front of the fashion press, alongside men taller and younger than him. Roger's friend had given him the chocolate suit for his fortieth birthday, and had insisted he wear it with a blue silk shirt. Roger's sons liked to sleep in their newly acquired clothes, and he understood their enthusiasm. He would not normally wear a suit for the park, but that evening he was going to a publishing party, and on to his third date with a woman he had been introduced to at a friend's house, a woman he liked.

Roger took the boys' hands and pulled them along.

'We'd better go to the tea house,' he said. 'I hope I don't ruin my shoes.'

'They're beautiful,' said Oliver.

Eddie stopped to bend down and rub his father's loafers. 'I'll put my hands over your shoes while you walk,' he said.

'That might slow us down a little,' Roger said. 'Run for it, mates!'

He picked Eddie up, holding him flat in his arms like a baby, with his muddy boots pointing away from him. The three of them hurried across the darkening park.

The tea house was a wide, low-ceilinged shed, warm, brightly lit and decorated in the black-and-white colours and flags of Newcastle United. The coffee was good and they had all the newspapers. The place was crowded but Roger spotted a table and sent Oliver over to sit at it.

Roger recognized the mother of a boy in Eddie's nursery, as well as several nannies and au pairs, who seemed to congregate in some part of this park on most days. Three or four of them had come often to his house with their charges when he lived with his wife. If they seemed reticent with him, he doubted whether this was because they were young and simple, but rather that they saw him as an employer, as the boss. He was aware that he was the only man in the tea house. The men he ran into with children were either younger than him, or older, on their second families. He wished his children were older, and understood more; he should have had them earlier. He'd both enjoyed and wasted the years before they were born; it had been a long dissatisfied ease.

A girl in the queue turned to him.

'Thinking again?' she said.

He recognized her voice but had not brought his glasses. 'Hello,' he said at last. He called to Eddie, 'Hey, it's Lindy.' Eddie covered his face with both hands. 'You remember her giving you a bath and washing your hair.'

'Hey cowboy,' she said.

Lindy had looked after both children when Eddie was born, and lived in the house until precipitately deciding to leave. She had told them she wanted to do something else but, instead, had gone to work for a couple nearby. She bent over and kissed Oliver, as she used to, and he put his arms around her. The last time Roger had run into Lindy, he had overheard her imitating his sons' accents and laughing. They were 'posh'. He had been shocked by how early these notions of 'class' started.

'Haven't seen you for a while,' she said.

'I've been travelling.'

'Where to?'

'Belfast, Cape Town, Sarajevo.'

'Lovely,' she said.

'I'm off to the States next week,' he said.

'Doing what?'

'Lecturing on human rights. On the development of the notion of the individual ... of the idea of the separate self.' He wanted to say something about Shakespeare and Montaigne here, as he had been thinking about them, but realized she would refuse to be curious about the subject. 'And on the idea of human rights in the post-war period. All of that kind of thing. I hope there's going to be a TV series.'

She said, 'I came back from the pub and turned on the TV last week, and there you were, criticizing some clever book or other. I didn't understand it.'

'Right.'

He had always been polite to her, even when he had been unable to wake her up because she had been drinking the previous night. She had seen him unshaven, and in his pyjamas at four in the morning; she had opened doors and found him and his wife abusing one another behind them; she had been at their rented villa in Assisi when his wife tore the cloth from the table with four bowls of pasta on it. She must have heard energetic reconciliations.

'I hope it goes well,' she said.

'Thank you.'

The boys ordered big doughnuts and juice. The juice spilled over the table and the doughnuts were smeared round their mouths. Roger had to hold his cappuccino out in front of him to stop the boys sticking their grimy fingers in the froth and sucking the chocolate from them. To his relief they joined Lindy's child.

Roger began a conversation with a woman at the next table who had complimented him on his sons. She told him she wanted to write a newspaper article on how difficult some people found it to say 'no' to children. You could not charm them, she maintained, as you could people at a cocktail party; they had to know what the limits were. He did not like the idea that she shouted at her child, but he decided to ask for her phone number before he left. For more than a year he had not gone out socially, fearing that people would see his anguish.

He was extracting his notebook and pen when Lindy called him. He turned round. His sons were at the far end of the tea house, rolling on top of another, larger, boy, who was wailing, 'He's biting me!'

Eddie did bite; he kicked too.

'Boys!' Roger called.

He hurried them into their coats again, whispering furiously at them to shut up. He said goodbye to the woman without getting her phone number. He did not want to appear lecherous. He had always been timid, and proud of the idea that he was a good man who treated people fairly. He did not want to impose himself. The world would be a better place if people considered their actions. Perhaps he had put himself on a pedestal. 'You have a high reputation – with yourself!' a friend had said. Everyone was entitled to some pride and vanity. However, this whole business with his wife had stripped him of his moral certainties. There was no just or objective way to resolve competing claims: those of freedom – his freedom – to live and develop as he liked, against the right of his family to have his dependable presence. But no amount of conscience or morality would make him go back. He had not missed his wife for a moment.

As they were leaving the park, Eddie tore some daffodils from a flower bed and stuffed them in his pocket. 'For Mummy,' he explained.

The house was a ten-minute walk away. Holding hands, they ran home through the rain. His wife would be back soon, and he would be off.

It was not until he had taken out his key that he remembered his wife had changed the lock last week. What she had done was illegal; he owned the house, but he had laughed at the idea that she thought he would intrude, when he wanted to be as far away as possible.

He told the boys they would have to wait. They sheltered in the little porch where water dripped on their heads. The boys soon tired of standing with him and refused to sing the songs he started. They pulled their hoods down and chased one another up and down the path.

It was dark. People were coming home from work.

The next-door neighbour passed by. 'Locked out?' he said.

''Fraid so.'

Oliver said, 'Daddy, why can't we go in and watch the cartoons?'

'It's only me she's locked out,' he said. 'Not you. But you are, of course, with me.'

'Why has she locked us out?'

'Why don't you ask her?' he said.

His wife confused and frightened him. But he would greet her civilly, send the children into the house and say goodbye.

It was, however, difficult to get cabs in the area; impossible at this time and in this weather. It was a twenty-minute walk to the tube station, across a dripping park where alcoholics and junkies gathered under the trees. His shoes, already wet, would be filthy. At the party he would have to try and remove the worst of the mud in the toilet.

After the violence of separation he had expected a diminishment of interest and of loathing, on her part. He himself had survived the worst of it and anticipated a quietness. Kind indifference had come to seem an important blessing. But as well as refusing to divorce him, she sent him lawyer's letters about the most trivial matters. One letter, he recalled, was entirely about a cheese sandwich he had made for himself when visiting the children. He was ordered to bring his own food in future. He thought of his wife years ago, laughing and putting out her tongue with his semen on it.

'Hey there,' she said, coming up the path.

'Mummy!' they called.

'Look at them,' he said. 'They're soaked through.'

'Oh dear.'

She unlocked the door and the children ran into the hall. She nodded at him. 'You're going out.'

'Sorry?'

'You've got a suit on.'

He stepped into the hall. 'Yes. A little party.'

He glanced into his former study where his books were packed in boxes on the floor. He had, as yet, nowhere to take them. Beside them were a pair of men's black shoes he had not seen before.

She said to the children, 'I'll get your tea.' To him she said, 'You haven't given them anything to eat, have you?'

'Doughnuts,' said Eddie. 'I had chocolate.'

'I had jam,' said Oliver.

She said, 'You let them eat that rubbish?'

Eddie pushed the crushed flowers at her. 'There you are, Mummy.'

'You must not take flowers from the park,' she said. 'They are for everyone.'

'Fuck, fuck, fuck,' said Eddie suddenly, with his hand over his mouth.

'Shut up! People don't like it!' said Oliver, and hit Eddie, who started to cry.

'Listen to him,' she said to Roger. 'You've taught them to use filthy language. You are really hopeless.'

'So are you,' he said.

In the past few months, preparing his lectures, he had visited some disorderly and murderous places. The hatred he witnessed puzzled him still. It was atavistic but abstract; mostly the people did not know one another. It had made him aware of how people clung to their antipathies, and used them to maintain an important distance, but in the end he failed to understand why this was. After all the political analysis and talk of rights, he had concluded that people had to grasp the necessity of loving one another; and if that was too much, they had to let one another alone. When this still seemed inadequate and banal, he suspected he was on the wrong path, that he was trying to say something about his own difficulties in the guise of intellectual discourse. Why could he not find a more direct method? He had, in fact, considered writing a novel. He had plenty to say, but could not afford the time, unpaid.

He looked out at the street. 'It's raining quite hard.'

'It's not too bad now.'

He said, 'You haven't got an umbrella, have you?'

'An umbrella?'

He was becoming impatient. 'Yes. An umbrella. You know, you hold it over your head.'

She sighed and went back into the house. He presumed she was opening the door to the airing cupboard in the bathroom.

He was standing in the porch, ready to go. After a while she returned empty-handed.

'No. No umbrella,' she said.

He said, 'There were three there last week.'

'Maybe there were.'

'Are there not still three umbrellas there?'

'Maybe there are,' she said.

'Give me one.'

'No.'

'Sorry?'

'I'm not giving you one,' she said. 'If there were a thousand umbrellas there I would not give you one.'

He had noticed how persistent his children were; they asked, pleaded, threatened and screamed, until he yielded.

He said, 'They are my umbrellas.'

'No,' she repeated.

'How petty you've become.'

'Didn't I give you everything?'

He cleared his throat. 'Everything but love.'

'I did give you that, actually.' She said, 'I've rung my friend. He's on his way.'

He said, 'I don't care. Just give me an umbrella.'

She shook her head. She went to shut the door. He put his foot out and she banged the door against his leg. He wanted to rub his shin but could not give her the pleasure.

He said, 'Let's try and be rational.'

He had hated before, his parents and brother, at certain

times. But it was a fury, not a deep intellectual and emotional hatred like this. He had had psychotherapy; he took tranquillizers, but still he wanted to pulverize his wife. None of the ideas he had about life would make this feeling go away. A friend had suggested it would be no bad thing if he lost the 'good' idea of himself, seeing himself as more complicated and passionate. But he could not understand the advantage of seeing himself as unhinged.

'You used to find the rain "refreshing",' she said with a sneer.

'It has come to this,' he said.

'Here we are then,' she said. 'Don't start crying about it.'

He pushed the door. 'I'll get the umbrella.'

She pushed the door back at him. 'You cannot come in.'

'It is my house.'

'Not without prior arrangement.'

'We arranged it,' he said.

'The arrangement's off.'

He pushed her.

'Are you assaulting me?' she said.

He looked outside. An alcoholic woman he had had to remove from the front step on several occasions was standing at the end of the path holding a can of lager.

'I'm watching you,' she shouted. 'If you touch her you are reported!'

'Watch on!' he shouted back.

He pushed into the house. He placed his hand on his wife's chest and forced her against the wall. She cried out. She did bang her head, but it was, in football jargon, a 'dive'. The children ran at his legs. He pushed them away. He went to the airing cupboard, seized an umbrella and made his way to the front door.

As he passed her she snatched it. Her strength surprised

him, but he yanked the umbrella back and went to move away. She raised her hand. He thought she would slap him. It would be the first time.

But she made a fist. As she punched him in the face she continued to look at him. He had not been hit since he left school. He had forgotten the physical shock and then the disbelief, the shattering of the belief that the world was a safe place.

The boys had started to scream. He had dropped the umbrella. His mouth throbbed; his lip was bleeding. He must have staggered and lost his balance for she was able to push him outside.

He heard the door slam behind him. He could hear the children crying. He walked away, past the alcoholic woman still standing at the end of the path. He turned to look at the lighted house. When they had calmed down, the children would have their bath and get ready for bed. They liked being read to. It was a part of the day he had always enjoyed.

He turned his collar up but knew he would get soaked. He wiped his mouth with his hand. She had landed him quite a hit. He would not be able to find out until later whether it would show.

ACKNOWLEDGMENTS
AND SOURCES

R. ANDOM (Alfred Walter Barrett): 'The Fetching of Susan' from *Neighbours of Mine*, 1912.

ELIZABETH BOWEN: 'Mysterious Kôr' (1945) from *A Day in the Dark and Other Stories*, 1965. Reproduced with permission of Curtis Brown Group Limited, London, on behalf of The Estate of Elizabeth Bowen. Copyright © Elizabeth Bowen, 1965.

C. MAURICE DAVIES: 'The Walworth Jumpers' from *Unorthodox London* (Series 1), 1876.

DANIEL DEFOE: 'A Ragged Boyhood' from *The History and Remarkable Life of the Truly Honourable Colonel Jack*, 1722.

THOMAS DEKKER: 'London, lying sicke of the Plague' from *The Wonderfull Yeare, 1603* in F. P. Wilson (Ed.), *The Plague Pamphlets of Thomas Dekker*, 1925.

THOMAS DE QUINCEY: 'Ann of Oxford Street' from *Confessions of an English Opium Eater*, 1822 (separately published as *Ann of Oxford Street*, 1948).

CHARLES DICKENS: 'Down with the Tide' (*Household Words*, February 1853) from Michael Slater (Ed.), *The Dent Uniform Edition of Dickens' Journalism*, Vol. 3, 1998.

ARTHUR CONAN DOYLE: 'The Adventure of the Blue Carbuncle' from *The Adventures of Sherlock Holmes*, 1891–2.

JOHN EVELYN: 'The Great Fire of London, 1666', from H. B. Wheatley (Ed.), *The Diary of John Evelyn, Esq. F.R.S.*, vol. 2, 1906.